Leather Wishes
The Adventures of
the Fancy Man

Julian Keys

ForbiddenFiction
www.forbiddenfiction.com

an imprint of

Fantastic Fiction Publishing
www.fantasticfictionpub.com

LEATHER WISHES
A Forbidden Fiction book

Fantastic Fiction Publishing
Hayward, California

© Julian Keys, 2012-2015

CREDITS
Editor: D.M. Atkins, Rylan Hunter
Cover Design: Siolnatine
Cover Art: Photos by Karyna Che and Felix Miznoznikov at Shutterstock, and MattesonScott0 at Pixabay
Production Editor: Erika L Firanc
Proofreading: Aislinn

SKU: T13-100023-02 FFP
ISBN: 978-1-62234-266-2

Published in the United States of America

"Sir," he whispered, "Give me the rest."

"Not until I know the extent of this. Are you hearing voices? Are you on medications? Do you know your diagnosis?"

"I'm not schizophrenic or bi-polar," he assured me. "I'm not on meds."

"This isn't therapy and I'm not a doctor," I curtly reminded him.

"I know that, sir. I really do. But please, don't say no. I don't expect you to cure me, but I think you can make things better."

I chewed on my lip. This was one crazy white man. Did I really want to do this? That, by the way, was a rhetorical question. A man with a body to die for was begging me to make him my slave and use him as sadistically as I wished. And the cherry topping this temptation was that no one and nothing else had helped him with his problem. Could I?

He might as well have waved a red flag before my eyes. I charge at challenges. No. The question wasn't whether I wanted to do this. It was whether I *should* do it.

Also recommended...

You may also enjoy these other ForbiddenFiction works:

Inherent Risk by Alicia Cameron
Jere never wanted to be a slave owner, but despite that, he and his slave, Wren, are building a life together. However, a new addition to their household challenges their relationship. Jealousy, anger, and broken slaves dominate Jere's world as he continues to navigate a slave state that seems intent on forcing Jere to be a master in more than just name. With all of Hojer watching, Jere fights to save a young life and his fragile relationship. If he fails at either, he could lose everything. (M/M)
http://forbiddenfiction.com/story/AC2-1.000096

Bound by Lies by Lynn Kelling
Brayden Clare never wanted to return to small town life. Blond, athletic, and struggling with his sexual identity, a beach in Florida suits him much better. When a family emergency calls him home, he is forced to trade his personal freedom for a job as a bartender in a town where everybody thinks they know who he is. Jenner Parrish, the owner of Parrish Pub, is charming, dominant, and popular since they were both in high school together. Brayden finds his new boss intimidating, and is daunted to find that turns him on. Jenner finds his new recruit intriguing but mustn't dare to ask an employee to submit to him. The two men find what they're seeking at a masked BDSM ball in the next town over, and are startled to discover their desires rest much, much closer to home. (M/M)
http://forbiddenfiction.com/story/LK1-1.000109

DISCLAIMER

This book is a work of fiction which contains explicit erotic content; it is intended for mature readers. Do not read this if it's not legal for you.

All the characters, locations and events herein are fictional. While elements of existing locations or historical characters or events may be used fictitiously, any resemblance to actual people, places or events is coincidental.

This story is not intended to be used as an instruction manual. It may contain descriptions of erotic acts that are immoral, illegal, or unsafe. Do not take the events in this story as proof of the plausibility or safety of any particular practice.

This story depicts fictional BDSM; it is not intended to be used as an instruction manual. It contains descriptions of erotic acts that may be immoral, illegal, or unsafe. The characters are not models for the Safe, Sane and Consensual forms embraced by most current practitioners of BDSM. The author takes license with the use of BDSM for dramatic effect. Do not take the events in this story as proof of the plausibility or safety of any particular practice."

To each and every editor, artist, and staff member at ForbiddenFiction, most especially the mad genius behind FFP, D.M. Atkins.

The Fancy Man stories were brought to life by your efforts, and this anthology, a wish come true, exists only because of your determination to make it real.

Thank you.

Contents

The Fancy Man and
the Black Lion's Mark

Just hand me a good idea, and I'll set the stage and create the costumes. I'll make it real. Such is the motto of Mason, a big black leatherman with a reputation for intense role-playing. Unfortunately, most of the bottoms in Mason's local leather bar have cliché fantasies. They want him to play the stereotypical role of bad-ass cellmate or gangbanger. Then enters Leo—an older gent who had nothing at all to offer—not youth or good looks, or even stamina. Leo, however, has something Mason hasn't had before—a pulpy fetish decades old and far from the usual. The Fancy Man cannot refuse such a challenge! (M/M)

Chapter 1
Shark-Infested Waters

We had a few new faces in the bar that night. Every other week or so, they turn up for a peek, creeping in meekly, on rare occasions with a bravado swagger. My friend Robbie, the bartender, would call them desperate. I think they're pretty courageous.

There they are, often dressed uncomfortably in tight jeans and a tee shirt they hope displays their muscles to their best advantage. Once inside, they look like they're holding their breath, as if they've just dived into shark infested waters. It's their first time in a leather bar and they're scared shitless.

Hey, they've a lot to fear. Most of them haven't left the closet, and even if they have, they don't want their kinky secret getting out. We may live in a city, but it's a small and fairly conservative city. Word does get around. You can imagine the nightmares these guys have: they'll live out their darkest fantasy only to go to work the next day and find a picture of themselves, on all fours and wearing a studded leather harness, as the new office screensaver. One asshole with a camera phone is all it takes.

And yet, they still step through those doors.

They're scared as well that someone like big, black me is going to take advantage of them. Rob or abuse them. I'm a stranger and they're going to be putting themselves, bound and gagged in some cases, into my massive hands.

And they still step through those doors.

Robbie would say it's the need, and he's right. You see it in their eyes. They've thought about it, jerked off about it, searched the internet for help and answers. They've wept in despair over it. They need to play that role, to satisfy that pornographic dream. So they step through those doors, risking everything to have it, to have it just once and know if it really is what they want. It's desperation. But it's also very brave of them.

Among the new faces that night was an older guy. He couldn't have been more than 5'6" in height, silver mane of hair and one of those hound-dog faces older men get, bags under lost hazel eyes. He wore a gray suit that wasn't cheap, but it wasn't tailored either. It hung on his thin frame as if he were a hanger. Stepping in he didn't quite hold his breath, but his eyes flicked side to side and he made for a shadowed booth, like a fish darting into a coral reef.

Now maybe in your leather bar there's a wide range of ages, but in our modest dive we just don't get that many grandfathers. We've a few middle-aged gents and sometimes a daddy from some great metropolis will arrive to regale us, his country cousins, with stories of real leather bars and what it was like back when tops were tops and bottoms were on the bottom. But for the most part, men over fifty are a rarity.

Not that any of us regulars made a big deal of it. We all noticed, of course, but we pretended not to. Robbie went over to put down a napkin and ask the old guy what he was having. I finished off my beer and watched in the bar mirror, a little curious. The man kept his hands laced together, his body huddled as far back in the booth as he could get. Robbie fetched him a scotch on the rocks.

I lost interest and went back to scoping the room. The Cockpit, or just The Pit, actually got its name honestly. A grounded airline pilot opened it back in the mid-70's. Two-and-a-half decades later, he died, and his widow carried on until this part of town became trendy and gay. Then she sold it to Nash, a crusty top who smokes with a cigarette holder and has his nails manicured every Thursday. Serendipity, Nash likes to call it. He wanted to open a leather bar, and there the Cockpit was, up for sale. With a name like that it had to be right.

The décor of the Pit is pretty much as it was the day it opened: light oak wood paneling, western style bar stools and an island bar. Nash removed a lot of the tables, but not the orange vinyl booths that stud the far wall. Above these booths are photos of forgotten airline crews, pilots in starched, gold buttoned uniforms or bomber jackets, stewardesses wearing brightly colored mini-skirts, little caps on their hair-sprayed dos. They smile earnestly from the glossy snapshots, young and living out their dreams.

Those who aren't prowling restlessly round the watering hole or offering themselves up as prey by hugging the walls, feed the juke-box, play pool or talk earnestly in booths. We haven't any back room or dungeon. The point of coming here is to either hang or take some-one home. This means everyone is scoping and being scoped. On the being-scoped end, me especially. There are other tops at The Pit, but not one of them can match me in size or color. I'm 6'4" of pure sculpt-ed muscle and teakwood brown from shaved head to big toe. Add to that my typically Afrocentric features: wide mouth, arrowhead nose, almond eyes, and you've got the guy from every downtown-blue cop show you've ever watched. There's me as "scary guy in the holding cell," and there I am playing, "rapper with gun." Oh, and there's my Shakespearian performance as a defiant gangbanger ("I ain't tellin' you nothin'!").

A white boy comes into the bar, takes one look at me (and believe me, I'm the first thing he locks eyes on, always), and gets what I like to call "Tyrone Syndrome." That means he doesn't see *me*, nor does he see another gay man, or even a man at all. He sees a big black cell-mate. A big black cellmate who's going to make his life exquisite hell. I swear guys have creamed their nice new jeans just looking at me. Such is the power of the imagination.

In leather terms, I am the belle of the ball. All night, every night. The decision of who gets to be on my dance card, who "Tyrone" is going to fuck up the ass, is all up to me. There's only one problem. I don't much like playing Tyrone, the big black cellmate. Which means that sometimes, when there's no other choice, I do go home alone.

"Trying to decide whose heart you're going to break?" asked Rob-bie that night.

"I don't break hearts," I said. "I break cocks."

"And sometime I'm going to ask you to let me watch." Robbie, the Cockpit's primary bartender, looks like a leprechaun on steroids. A cute leprechaun. He's short with red hair, a boyish face and freckles galore. But he's a powerhouse from the neck down. When he's not tending bar he works as a personal trainer at a downtown gym.

Non-regulars find Robbie confusing. They hit on him with all their might, but he just remains friendly and disinterested. What they don't know is that Robbie's in the wrong bar. He's got no interest in beating anyone's ass or having a collar around his neck. What Robbie wants is a bed scattered with rose petals, a candle-lit dinner and a warm oil massage.

"Why aren't you tending bar down at The Stardust?" I once asked him. That's the bar where guys slow-dance to love songs and order up champagne for their one-month anniversaries.

"Are you fucking kidding me?" he laughed. "I tried that. It was a disaster. I fell in love every other night and got fired for mooning over customers instead of pouring drinks. Here's a null temptation. I can do my job. Chat folks up, keep the beer glasses full. Besides, you sad fuckers need me."

I liked Robbie. And someday, maybe for his birthday, and if I'm absolutely certain it won't hurt his romantic soul, I'll put on a tux and give him his fantasy for a night.

That's what I do. What I get off on. Giving men their fantasies. It's why I'm called the Fancy Man. Not like in natty dresser, but rather, flights of fancy. The name use to be Fantasy Man, but that didn't scan. I'll explain later.

I'm an actor. I love acting. I was the kid who drove my parents nuts by always being in the land of pretend, every minute, every hour of the day. I never wanted to be in the real world. When I hit my teens, rather than giving up pretend, I went into drama. My one wish is to be given great parts. Unfortunately, most directors aren't interested in casting me as Uncle Vanya.

Othello, maybe, but they just don't want me for Ibsen or Chekhov or Shaw.

And we know how I'll end up if I ever try to get into television or movies: "I ain't tellin' you nothing!"

Which is why most of the acting I do is voice. Commercials, animation, documentary voice-overs. I can pitch my voice down to a deep bass or up to a whispering lisp, and with voice acting I can play roles no one would give me in a million years: a kindly old doctor, a woodland elf, a British butler, an eager young sidekick.

It's a little harder to get the same kind of range in my sex life. I don't think the guys who take me home understand just how desperately willing I'd be to play other roles. Just hand me a good idea, and I'll set the stage and create the costumes. I'll make it real.

But all I ever get from most of them is the plea to play Tyrone the cellmate. It can make me pretty depressed if I think on it too long and hard.

"Terry's been edging his way towards you," Robbie said now. "Did you notice? I guess it didn't work out between him and that other guy."

"God, not Terry." Not tonight. Terry was into fraternity hazings. He liked to cast me as the black, bullying frat brother, which involved me paddling his ass and then ordering him to jerk off. Only he took forever to come when he did that. He made me want to read the newspaper. Unprofessional as it was, I sometimes did.

"Carl then? Al?" Robbie was ragging on me. Carl's role for me was that of motorcycle pack leader, and with him as the wannabe who'd just fucked up my bike. The fantasy was for me to make him pay for that mistake till he cried. Blubbered, actually. Al's fantasy is that of lowly private with me as the brutal drill sergeant. Unfortunately, he has this squeak to his voice which, when he barks, "Yes, sir!" can be like nails on a chalkboard. Then again, he did have a good ass and I could always gag him.

I don't mean to make these boys sound like losers. They're hard-working, stand-up guys, and darn good-looking come to that. And while they may have started out, as all my fuck-buddies do, scared and awed of me, we're friends now. We watch football games together, celebrate each other's birthdays.... That, in fact, is how I got my name, if a brother may digress....

It was some eight months ago, my birthday, and Robbie had just brought out this cake alight with candles when suddenly, those very three guys stepped forward, put their arms around each other and started singing, to the "Candy Man" tune:

> *"Who can take a wet dream,*
> *Sprinkle it with piss...*
> *Whip and beat and burn us,*
> *And then make it better with a kiss?*
> *The Fancy Man can! Oh the Fancy Man can!"*

Brought tears to my eyes. Not one of them white boys can carry a tune in a bucket.

Anyway, that's how I got my name, and that's my reputation. When a man takes me home, he doesn't just get the big black man, he gets the fantasy, in living color and with special effects. I deliver.

"You are one mopey fuck tonight," Robbie said as he pulled beers on tap. "You could stand up right now, say, 'Who will suck my cock?' and everyone in this room would take a number. And those at the end of the line would cry. Yet you're sitting here in a funk?"

How to explain? It sounded so drama queen to say that I was tired of playing the same old roles, that I was an artist and wanted... needed a chance to put on a real play. Something that excited me. Something, for Christ's sake, that wasn't just going to get a man's rocks off. If I have to be the fantasy, then just once I wanted to be one that transformed, that inspired.

"I mean, my God," Robbie was still going on, "Grandpa over there would probably hock his bifocals for a glimpse of your dick. You want to be gloomy, just imagine yourself in his place. He's never going to get what he wants."

"Hm? Who?" I wasn't quite paying attention.

"The scotch drinker. He's hasn't taken his eyes off you."

I peered into the curving mirror behind the bar. The silver-haired gent was fixated on me. In fact, he was gazing at me with a kind of hopeless hope that was positively heart rending.

"I think he's in love," Robbie shook his head at the sad, sad thought of a doomed romance. "Too bad his fantasy won't ever get fulfilled."

"Who says it won't?"

Robbie's ginger-colored brows shot up. "You're joking."

I shrugged. I was strangely intrigued, and that embarrassed me. "You're the one said I should imagine myself in his place. Well, I am. One day, I could be like him. Can't stay young and beautiful forever."

"I can," Robbie grinned. "I have faith in the future of plastic surgery."

"Still. I'd like to think what goes around comes around. Maybe when I get to be his age, some young stud will grant me a wish or two."

I stood up. Robbie's mouth fell open. "You're serious?"

I winked at him. I wasn't really sure I was going to go through with it, but a fey mood had come over me. It was long past time I shook things up.

Cocks quivered and came to attention as I stepped away from the bar. Would they be the one to get me tonight? It only took a few steps to reach the booth. I heard gasps of disbelief, whispers as I slid in beside the old man. Very satisfying.

The silver-haired gent jerked his head up, eyes widening, as if a killer whale had just found his hiding place. For one moment I thought he was going to have a heart attack. Most men don't realize what a hulk I am till I'm in their space, gazing down at them. My massive shoulders, nicely displayed by a gray, ribbed tank, took up half of the booth. His sharp Adam's apple bobbed.

"You were looking my way," I observed.

"Yes, sir," he murmured.

Three guesses which one of us was going to be the top. For one quick moment I amused myself by envisioning the old man standing over me, barking orders. Ha. Fat chance.

He didn't apologize or demur. He just waited, as if he'd already given up on escaping whatever punishment I was going to mete out.

"So, you're interested in me?"

"I... beg your pardon?"

"Mason," I touched on my chest. "And you are?"

"L-Leo."

"Well, Leo, I'm about to grant your wish. Whatever that wish may be."

His hazel eyes blinked, and he took a sip of his scotch. The ice rattled in his glass and the liquor spilled over the napkin as he brought it down. "Young man," he said faintly, "I know... I know how very out of place I am here. Please don't make fun of me."

"What if I'm serious?"

He shook his head as if that wasn't possible and started to scoot out of the booth. I set my hand down on his wrist, not hard, but he froze. There was regret on his face now, and misery. He thought I was going to keep him here until I, and probably a few of my friends, finished humiliating him.

"I only torture people in the bedroom," I told him. "Are you really going to pass this up, Leo? You came in here looking for someone to fulfill a fantasy, didn't you? Or did you think this was just a regular bar?"

"No. I-I knew what this place was... is." His eyes slid away. "I've been hoping... thinking about coming into a bar like this for decades. Decades," he confessed with sad wonder.

"What made you finally do it?" I asked.

"My sister passed away. She was the only family I had left."

"I'm sorry."

"S'kay." He took in a breath. "You see, when I was your age, we kept everything secret, in the dark. I was convinced that I had to wait till... till no one but me would be shamed by my conduct; by my coming to a place like this. Now it's too late. Everything I wanted is outdated. Old-fashioned."

Damn. How that must have been, I thought, to drift like a phantom through the world, feeling alive only in flashes, when sucking off anonymous men in movie theatres and alleys. A life like that, holding to your fantasies like childhood toys, waiting for the day when you might come out and play in the open. And then, finally, decades later, that day comes. Only, when you look around, and see all the youngsters there, you realize that you're obsolete, archaic. No one's going to want to play with you and your outmoded toys. The best you figure you can hope for is to gaze at bodies still fresh and firm and *imagine* what it would be like to play with them... and have them play with you.

Well, fuck that. Fuck if I was going to let Leo be satisfied with that.

"Come on," I urged him, getting out of the booth and pulling gently at his arm. "You're taking me home."

Leo looked ready to balk, but you don't argue with "Tyrone." He had enough presence of mind to fumble money for the scotch out of his billfold, and then he let me lead him. I don't think he'd have known how to resist even if that were possible.

Behind us I heard nothing but the music from the jukebox. Glancing back I saw mouths agape. I saw Carl and Al looking to Robbie for help, wondering if they should tackle me because, clearly, I'd lost my mind.

"*Mason,*" they screamed with their eyes, "*are you really going home with that?*"

I touched my middle finger to my brow, a salute of sorts, and laughed. Whatever else happened, it had been worth it just to see their faces.

We came out into the glare of streetlamps, the flow of pedestrians on their way to restaurants and movie theatres. I stopped us at my car so I could get my kit, a leather satchel filled with accoutrements in case Leo didn't have any toys at home.

I think he was mollified by the fact that I drove a Scion.

Chapter 2
Welcome to the Jungle

Leo drove a hybrid. It was cramped. Most cars are for me, and I always have to watch my head. But I liked how quiet it was. Leo didn't say anything, he just drove, white-knuckled, and sometimes glanced over at me.

I'm not sure if he was afraid I'd disappear, or if he was hoping I'd disappear. Likely both. Finally, we got to his house, a small, bungalow affair with a carport.

He kept looking back at me as he led the way up to the front door. He couldn't reconcile the incongruity of a muscled, black giant being on his street, let alone being with *him*. He fumbled and dropped the keys. It took three tries for him to get the door open. He let me in, then rushed around turning on lights.

"Excuse me," he muttered, "I h-have t-to —" He gestured and I nodded. Of course he had to use the bathroom. It's a wonder the man hadn't peed in his pants. I saw him dart in and shut the door.

While Leo eased his bladder and splashed water on his face, I took a gander. I like to get to know my environment, see what I have to work with. It was one of those modest homes once describe as belonging to "confirmed bachelors." Low, cottage-cheese ceilings, a galley kitchen and breakfast nook, a square den with a sliding door that opened up onto a tiny back porch. The place was neat as a pin, the furnishings, in browns and golds, a little worn but not without a certain deco style. There were potted palms in the corners and watercolors on the walls, all by the same artist. Imaginary, Shangri-La scenes of tropical gardens and lost ruins. Some featured fantastic jungle cats.

The place smelled of paint and cleaning products.

"C-can I get you anything?" Leo asked, reappearing from the bathroom.

"Water," I said, checking out the rest of the place. There were two bedrooms; the smaller one was filled with art books, a great many of them on male models. There were also books on Africa and tribal masks. There were canvasses, folded easels, a drafting table, colored pencils, ink, pens and coffee cans stuffed with paintbrushes.

I came back into the living room as Leo deferentially handed me my water. "Did you paint all these?" I asked, motioning to the water-colors.

"Yes. That's... what I do. Not paintings. I'm a commercial artist. Cereal boxes, magazine covers. These I do for myself."

"They're good." They had a vintage poster style that I liked very much.

He blushed. "Thank you."

I settled onto the couch, and waved for him to do the same. It's an odd thing, this relationship I end up having with those I pick. It's their house, but they act as if it were mine; they start to look to me for every little direction. Leo obediently settled as far from me as he could get, but kept leaning forward, as if I were a magnet. I noticed that he was wearing some lilac scented aftershave. His shoes were polished, his nails were clean. It occurred to me that he might have gotten spruced and dressed up for tonight's visit to the Cockpit. That the reason the house was so spic-n'-span was because he'd held some forlorn hope of bringing someone home.

I wondered what he thought he'd net. Certainly not me.

"You doing okay?" I asked.

That got a faint laugh. "I'm a wreck. I can't believe this."

"And you can't stop wondering why I'm here. Look, you're scared of me. And you should be. I'm young, and I'm huge, and you don't know me. But I promise, I'm not here to steal anything or hurt you. You couldn't keep your eyes off me because you've got a fantasy, one that involves a big black man. One you've been jerking off to since...?" I left off, waiting for him to fill in the blank.

"Since I was fourteen," he admitted.

Shit. I hope I didn't have to wait that long to have *my* most desperately held fantasy fulfilled. "Sounds like you're way overdue then."

He licked dry lips. "If you... if you mean what you say... if you do this for me... you can have what you like. Rob me blind. I'll give you my credit card and ATM number —"

"Shut that down right now," I snapped. "I am *not* a thug."

"Sorry! I'm sorry!" he back-pedaled, "I didn't mean — I'm just... nervous. Very nervous."

My temper doesn't surface often. I can do real damage if I strike out, so I've learned to maintain a sense of humor. But I was irked. "Haven't you been listening to anything I've been saying?"

"I didn't mean to offend you! Please don't be mad." Leo was visibly panicked. His cultural stereotyping had finally pissed me off and that put him into a terrible quandary. His fantasy contained just such typecasting. Hell, I knew it had to. You don't pick out the big black man to play Maria von Trapp in *The Sound of Music*. Given what Leo had said in the bar, we were probably looking at some very dated and offensive caricatures, nothing PC about them. To risk being mocked for his fantasy was hard enough for Leo. He didn't want me angry as well.

The pain in his eyes brought my temper back down. Had to remember that the poor man was a virgin at this.

"Listen," I said, quietly, "I've got this friend. A lawyer. Specializes in sexual discrimination cases. Instances where women have been paid less than men for doing the same job or haven't gotten an equal chance at management positions. There is nothing, and I mean nothing he is more sincerely passionate about than equal rights for women. He will rage for hours on the injustices done to women and how much better the world would be if they were running it. His wife's a chemistry professor and he's proud as can be that she's smarter than he is. But —"

I paused dramatically. Leo was leaning in. All ears.

"But," I said again, "every now and then he calls the wife and asks for a special evening. When he gets home, she greets him at the door in a fifties' style, Father-Knows-Best gown. Stockings, garter belt, no underwear — and don't ask me how I know that. Let's just say people tell me things they'd never tell their mothers."

Leo nodded his understanding.

"She welcomes him home, takes his coat, helps him on with slippers and smoking jacket, dusts the furniture and serves him dinner. One of the dishes is always burned. Deliberately. The potatoes or the macaroni. He expresses his disappointment in her failure of wifely duties and spanks her for it. Which leads to great sex under the table or in the bedroom."

I took in a breath. Leo was wide-eyed. He wasn't naïve, at least I didn't think he was, but perhaps he'd only read about such things, never suspected that respectable lawyers, his neighbors even, might be doing it.

"The moral of the story is this," I said. "Stereotypes are bad. They imprison people in boxes and lead to terrible injustices. But when it comes to erotic role-playing they can be very useful. Maybe even essential. I understand that. I won't be insulted by the part you want me to play. But you're going to do me a favor right here and now. You're going to look at me, and you're not going to see a big black man. You're going to see a gay man, just like you."

"Yes, sir," he said. His gaze fastened on me and he tried to do as I asked. But I could tell that he still wasn't seeing me. He was not, however, seeing a big black man, in that I was wrong. He was, he would later tell me, seeing me as I'd been in the bar: the crown prince, the star quarterback. With a snap of my fingers I could have him banished forever or welcomed in. I could change his life.

I'm sure, at that moment, that he'd have rather seen me as a thug. Far less frightening.

"All right," I said. It was time to set up the rules. "Here's how this is going to work. We do your fantasy, and afterwards, nothing gets said about it, not by me. Not unless you give me permission. So you don't have to worry about anyone ever hearing of this."

His face relaxed. So, he'd been worried about that.

"If, at any time," I went on, "things feel like they're going very wrong, you get really scared or unhappy, then we stop it. But understand this is my show. I'm the director. No argument. You go with it, or you stop it, but you don't tell me how to do it. Are we agreed?"

"Yes, sir."

"Good. Then let's hear this fantasy that's been enthralling you since puberty."

He licked his lips again, and rubbed sweaty palms down his pants' legs. Here it was, the moment of truth. He could ask me to leave or he could trust me. Trust me with his deepest, darkest secret.

Desperation? I don't think so. Maybe that's why I like to fulfill such fantasies, because that kind of courage deserves a reward.

He got up and made for his office. I heard a lot of shuffling and searching. He finally returned with a book-sized magazine in a protective plastic bag. He stopped in front of me, like a schoolboy before a teacher, and held it out. I've never seen anyone's hands shake that badly.

I took it, blinked at it. Then blinked again. "Leo," I said, "I don't want to hurt your feelings by laughing, but do you mind if I smile?"

He blew out a chuckle and I took that as permission. I grinned, bigger and wider than I had in a long, long time.

It was a pulp magazine. Likely Leo had read the original as a boy, over and over until it had fallen to pieces. In adulthood, unable to forget it, he had searched used bookstores and garage sales for a fresh copy. I could imagine how his heart had thumped with joy when he'd found it again, his holy grail. I was guessing that he now had several copies. This one was probably bought from a collector. It was in pristine condition.

The cover featured a rugged, blond hero, shirtless, of course, trousers ripped to pieces so he was hardly clothed at all. His bare back was crisscrossed with whip marks. He was in a jungle setting, hemmed in on all sides by black natives wearing animal skins and holding spears.

Foremost among these, the jewel in the crown as it were, was their king, a mighty giant of a black gent in a leopard skin breechclout and cape. His majesty was gazing down at our kneeling hero like a god on high.

It was a stunningly wrought cover. How sad that the artist who had worked so hard, who had put so much personal effort into this painting, was now long forgotten. Or not. Leo had never forgotten his work. But then, the cover was so transparently homoerotic. This was probably the closest that young Leo had gotten to gay porn. The white guy's gaze was, I suppose, meant to be proud and defiant, but it looked awed and worshipful instead. He was kneeling with his head at exactly the right level, as if waiting for that great jungle king to lift his breechclout and honor the beaten white man with his (of course) big, black cock.

Had the artist, like Leo, only had this as a way to fulfill his sexual fantasies, a bit of paint and canvas?

I gave the picture a closer examination, checking out the details, getting ideas. The blond, bedraggled white man had red tribal lines painted on his face similar to the white ones marking the natives. He also had a black symbol on his bare shoulder, a claw/paw print.

The title of the story represented by the picture: "The Mark of the Black Lion."

"May I read it?" I asked Leo. He'd been standing by patiently this whole time. He nodded his head eagerly.

I'm a fast reader and even if I weren't, I only needed to flip through the pulpy story to get the idea. The tall tale concerned a white man's trials and tribulations in the secret, mysterious Valley of the Black Lion. It was bigoted as hell, but highly entertaining.

This could be fun, I thought. And there were at least two parts for me to play, which I liked.

"I hope you don't expect me to follow this script word-for-word," I murmured, scanning the cheesy dialogue.

"Oh, no," Leo breathed. "Do anything... anything you want."

Which was exactly the right thing to say. The man was learning. I absorbed the style and cadence of the archaic, B-movie speeches, thought about ways to translate events, memorized a few important lines. Then I closed the mag and slipped it back into its protective plastic. My creative juices were flowing. "I'm going to need twenty minutes or so to set up," I told him.

"You... you'll do it?"

"Leo, you could not tear me away from this. You go into your bedroom. Find a shirt that you were thinking of throwing out, one that you're never going to wear again. Also a pair of pants that are as close as you have to something safari like. No underwear. No socks. No shoes."

"Yes, sir."

"You don't come out till I say so."

"No, sir." Poor Leo was in that dazed, it's-really-going-to-happen-to-me state. Well, so long as he did what I told him. He left for the bedroom and I got to work.

I kicked off my shoes and socks then searched through my kit for rope and a riding crop. Also a bottle of lube and a small knife. For the rest I used what was around the house. I found a dozen, unused kitchen tiles and put them on a cookie sheet. I put the oven on low. The cookie sheet and tiles went in.

I found jars of red, white and black watercolor paint and set them up in the bathroom along with some tea candles, matches, a throw pillow and the lube. I stoppered the basin and filled it with water. While I was in there I filched tweezers from the cabinet. These, along with some paint brushes and a shoebox that I cut in half and poked with holes, went into the den.

There was a coat rack on one of the walls. I removed umbrellas, sweaters, coats, a hat, measured the height of the hooks. They looked to be about right and fairly sturdy.

By now, my energy was up and I was feeling more excited than I'd been in, well, a year at least. I moved potted palms into the tub to complete my jungle scenery and then, done, came close to clapping my hands and bouncing on my toes.

Dishtowels. I thought suddenly. Dishtowels. I found a pile, knotted together four of them and folded the last for a blindfold.

Was that everything? Yes. I adjusted the lights, cutting them down till the room was mostly in shadow. This was more for me than Leo, to maintain the mood. My heart was pounding and I actually had butterflies in my stomach. Here we go, I thought, striding up to Leo's bedroom door. I knocked politely.

He threw open the door. He was dressed in an old, paint-splattered undershirt that exposed his wiry arms and equally paint-splattered, safari-green trousers. His bare feet were long and boney, the toes curling into the carpet. He tried to peer past me into the living room, but I knew it was too dark for him to see anything. I wondered what he'd thought of all the sounds I'd been making. He was pale and there was sweat on his upper lip. His hands twisted as he gazed up at me. I was almost a foot taller than him, and without his suit, he looked pretty small.

"Put out your hands," I told him, holding up the rope. It was a soft, white cord that wouldn't leave marks. I didn't mean to tie it that tightly anyway.

His throat bobbed, and he obediently stretched forth his arms. I wrapped the rope about his wrists and knotted it. Then I brought out the blindfold.

"Once I put this on, we start," I let him know. "Have you heard of safe words?"

He nodded. I honestly don't think he was capable of speaking at that moment.

"Okay. Anytime you feel things have gone too far and you want it all to stop, you yell out '*Tarzan.*' That good for you?"

He laughed. It was a nervous laugh but I was very glad of it. I didn't want him to take this too seriously. Not that it wasn't important. It was very important. Maybe the most important thing that had ever happened to him. But it's always good to keep a healthy perspective on role-playing. And honestly, this was a pretty ridiculous story we were about to enact.

"You ready?" It was my final and last time asking him. After this, I'd be in control. And he... he'd be at my mercy.

"Y-yes, sir," he managed, as if he realized, as well, that he needed to make his consent clear.

I came around and knotted the folded dishtowel about his eyes, making sure it was comfortable and that he couldn't see. He touched at it, tentatively. I took hold of the rope about his wrists and pulled him forward.

"Come, white man," I dropped my voice to a growl. He jumped. I guess nothing could have really prepared him for my sudden switch into character. "There is no escape," I added mockingly, "from the Valley of the Black Lion!"

The cover featured a rugged, blond hero, shirtless, of course, trousers ripped to pieces so he was hardly clothed at all.

Chapter 3
Trials

I dragged him over to the wall hooks. I hoped they were well secured. I grabbed his arms, put them over his head and hauled him up on tip-toe to get the rope over the hook. As I'd hoped, he was able to come down on his heels once it slipped over, but his arms were stretched high above his head.

"You wanted to meet our king, you said. Well, you will have your chance. Here he comes." I stepped back to quickly slip off my jeans and gray tank. I wanted to make sure that if Leo happened to touch me, he'd feel near-naked jungle native, not twenty-first century tex-tiles.

I left on my briefs for now. I didn't want him accidentally touch-ing my cock. Not yet.

Cupping a hand about my mouth, I called out, "The King comes! All bow to King Otawa, ruler of the Black Lion tribe!"

Leo twitched as I stomped forward. He didn't smile or laugh as others might have, but it was clear that he wasn't into the fantasy yet. He was still on that edge of disbelief, of wondering what the fuck he was doing. Grown men don't play pretend.

Not true, actually. We do it all the time. Just not so deliberately and, usually, with less pulpy material. I still thought this could work and I hoped he'd go with it. I knew, I knew in my gut and as I am the Fancy Man, that if he did, he would have the time of his life.

I came close to him, close enough that he could smell me, feel my heat.

"So. This is the white man," I said in my kingly voice, and though he was blindfolded, Leo's head went back as if to gaze up at me. I'd used my deepest intonation, the one that could rattle glass. His face expressed amazement. The story described Otawa as: "A giant of a man. Skin black and gleaming like ebony. Muscles hard as rocks. A gaze that pierced like a spear. His enemies feared him as a demon, his people worshiped him as a god!" Nice press release, that. The king was also supposed to have a voice like the "darkest, most velvet night." (The writer must have been gay, too.)

Leo surely had his own idea of what King Otawa sounded like, and from his astonished expression, I guessed I'd captured it.

"This," I went on, "is the stranger who found the secret gateway into our forbidden kingdom. Now he wants to learn all about us. Let us see what kind of man he *really* is."

I snapped my fingers as if commanding one of my men. A step to the side, so I could play the role of obedient native. I grabbed Leo's undershirt. He gasped, as he hadn't felt me move and my hand was coming from a different direction than my voice. And then he cried out as I sliced the material to ribbons with my knife. Likely he'd expected scissors.

His exposed chest was thin and boney with a scattering of gray hair. I let the knife brush past his nipples as I cut away the short sleeves. He yelped in surprise and shivered. But the nipples went hard.

Setting aside the rags and knife, I grabbed at the waistband of his trousers.

"No—" he breathed.

I smiled. Now we were getting into it. The pants had buttons. Good choice, Leo. I popped the top button. The next. He twitched with each one. Last one. I spread open the crotch, exposing his naked cock.

Leo was panting for breath now, struggling even. I let myself imagine for a moment what it was like for him behind the blindfold. He was in the fantasy now, I was sure of it. And he was no longer Leo, but that young, brawny hero of the story. Bound, blinded, surrounded by a tribe of hostile natives as they tore away his clothes and examined his white "manhood."

How humiliating, how exciting, how true in a way, as I was giving his cock the once over. His pubic hair was as silver as that on his head, his uncut member... impressive. It wasn't erect, but it had come out to see what was going on. The balls were large and weighty.

I jerked the pants down and off him. There was nothing muscular or firm on his body, but he didn't look bad all in all. A little sad, being naked, and with that blindfold, rather like a prisoner about to face a firing squad.

"So this is a white man's cock," I said in my kingly voice, and took it in hand.

Leo sucked in his breath so fast I thought he was going into convulsions. His head banged against the wall. I guess I'd surprised him. It must have been a singular moment for him, who'd had pubescent wet dreams of Otawa, to feel, not merely imagine that great jungle king holding his dick.

His cock jumped and started to rise up out of its sheath. I rubbed my thumb over his tip, over the slit there, liking the reaction. He uttered a helpless moan and shivered.

I released him and stepped back.

"Mabawa!" I said to the man who, according to the story, was the king's faithful but implacable bodyguard. "I wonder. What does a white man's cock taste like?"

What little blood was left in Leo's face drained right out. "No, I—"

I switched voices, going for the less deep but harder bodyguard voice. "What the king wishes to know, he will know!" I slipped my hand under Leo's balls and gripped them not hard, but threatening. "Do you object to a black man's tongue, white man? Well, there's no escape. We'll do with you what we like!" And then, bending, I gave his cock a nice, slow lick.

His whole body went taut and he gave this strangled cry. Leo had never, ever expected anything like this. As he'd tell me later, he'd thought, at best, that he was going to get rubbed a little through his pants. It was hardly to be believed that he'd feel a soft, hot tongue on his sensitive head. That it was my tongue was so impossible as to be miraculous.

A part of him knew what was really happening and was stunned; the other half of him, sinking ever deeper into the fantasy, was fixed on my deliberate mention of a black man's tongue. It put into his head the image of Mabawa, fierce and dark, licking his captured penis. His cock hardened up the rest of the way. It was thick and had beautiful blue veins; drops of precum dewed its slit. I flicked at that helmet twice more, liking the tangy flavor, then released him.

Leo was gasping by now, trembling. "Oh, God," he gibbered, "Oh, God—"

Tempting as it was, I didn't dare do more. I wanted his cock buzzing, aching, not coming. And he'd come in a red hot second if I kept toying with him.

"Majesty," I said in bodyguard voice, "the white man's cock tastes less salty, less dark than ours."

Leo had been hanging there, gaping like a fish. Now he closed his mouth and swallowed hard. Let's not fool ourselves. The one thing Leo wanted more than anything was a chance at my dick. I'd just placed in his mind the erotic image of all those tribesmen sucking each other off—how else would Mabawa know their flavor? —and suggested that Leo might get his own taste later on. He was salivating so hard he looked likely to drool all over himself.

"Mabawa," I said in my kingly voice, "instruct the white man, then prepare him for the first test." I stomped away, grabbed up the riding crop, then slipped back to play bodyguard.

I set a hand about Leo's scrawny neck. His chin came up, his breath went shallow with anticipation. "Listen to me, white man," I hissed. "I do not like you, but my king thinks you may be worthy. He is willing to let you attempt our trials. No white man has ever been allowed to do such a thing. Know that there is no going back. Fail or refuse a trial and you will be taken from our hidden kingdom and left to live or die out in the red desert. Do you understand?"

"Y-yes."

"*Master*. When you address me, you will call me master. When you address my king, you will call him sire or majesty. As you value your life, do not forget this."

"Yes, master."

"Very good. In a moment, I will go prepare the first trial, then I will be back to get you. One caution. When your hands are brought down, you will be tempted to touch your cock. That is not allowed, by order of the king." I pressed the whip across his chest, rubbed it down to his pelvis and back up again, lightly tapping it over his pebbly nipples. "This is a crop made from the toughest elephant hide. Touch your cock, brush it even accidentally, and I shall hold you down and whip you in punishment. No one is allowed to disobey the king. Do you understand?"

He shivered. "Yes, master." His cock, I was pleased to see, was still half erect and throbbing with excitement.

I crossed into the kitchen. As fast and quietly as I could, I removed the cookie sheet of tiles and shut off the oven. They were quite toasty and I had to use a mitt to lay them out on the floor.

Kids, don't try this at home! I'm a trained professional.

Back to Leo. "Your first trial awaits!" I said in bodyguard voice. Hauling him on tiptoe, I got him off the hook, so to speak. I dragged him into the kitchen, stopping him just short of the tiles.

"Before you is a bed of hot coals," I said. I myself could feel their warmth near my bare feet. Leo, blinded, head tilting, had to be trying to figure out what I'd done. Kneeling, I lifted one of his feet and brought it down for a quick touch on one of the tiles.

"Ouch!" he flinched back, "What the...what is that?" I could see the pulse in his throat racing with fear. The tiles, hot as sand on a summer beach, were going to make for a damned uncomfortable walk. Using the kitchen counters as parallel bars, I silently hopped over the mini-bed of "coals."

"White man!" I bellowed from the opposite side in my kingly

voice.

Leo's head came up. "Sire?"

Excellent. Back in the game. "You will walk over these coals to me. Or do you want this to end now?"

There it was. Double challenge. One for the fantasy hero, one for Leo. He drew in a breath, put a foot out and stepped onto the tiles.

"Ouch! Ah! Ouch! For heaven's sake!" He hissed even as he danced the few steps required to reach the other side. I kept my hands near him the entire time, but he didn't slip or bang into the counters.

He made it and I took hold of his shoulder as he rocked from foot to heated foot. I gave his thin bicep a squeeze.

"I am pleased and amazed, white man. None of our tribe has ever endured coals so hot."

"Thank you, sire," he ventured.

"Come, I will lead you myself to the next trial."

I brought him back into the living room.

"For this trial, you must stand and not move, no matter what pain you feel. This is my command. Can you obey it, white man? Can you obey me as king?"

"Y-yes, sire." There was a surprising amount of passion in his answer. "I can and I will obey you."

"Bring the box," I ordered regally, even as I gathered up the perforated shoebox. I slipped paintbrushes and the tweezers under the elastic waistband of my briefs, hoping none of them would slip. I adjusted the open part of the box at Leo's groin, making sure it covered his cock and balls.

"W-what's that?"

Switch of voice back to the menacing bodyguard. "That, white man, is the box of horrors. It is filled with spiders, scorpions and other vile creatures. None is poisonous, but they will sting. The king is watching to see whether you can endure. Whether you can obey him as we, his tribe, would obey. I do not think you will last."

Leo gulped, but he also took a firmer stance and held his hands up against his chest. I took the tweezers and poked them into a hole. Pinched quickly. Leo yelped and almost leaped back. Then he seemed to remember and clenched his teeth. I poked into another hole, pinching, another. He twitched and cried out, but he didn't grab at the box, and he didn't call for Tarzan.

I knew I had to be tweezing thighs, scrotum, penis. Truth was, I wasn't altogether sure what I was doing to him. I poked in through the holes and whatever I got, I got. Only Leo knew what that was for sure.

I switched to a hard bristled paintbrush, poking in the brush end. He flinched and shuddered when those bristles touched him. To be expecting the painful pinch of those tweezers and then to suddenly feel those harsh bristles must have been very frightening.

I turned the brush around and poked with the blunt end. Out and into another hole. Again with the tweezers. A bit of a juggling act as I was also holding steady the box, but I got into a rhythm and tried to be random. Leo cried out each time I poked into his balls or brushed his cock with those rough bristles, or pinched him with the tweezers. His body broke out in a sweat. But he did not move.

Once more I sunk into his mind; one of the pleasures of topping is being able to imagine what the other person is feeling. Leo was imagining this box filled with nasty creatures, scuttling over his sensitive scrotum, nipping at the tip of his penis. Tugging, maybe nesting in his pubic hair. And he dare do nothing as they tormented him, because he knew the king was watching, approving. Knew that the king's spiteful bodyguard was also watching and beginning to marvel at the white man's fortitude.

Leo was gasping and whimpering by the time I finished. I removed the box and he almost sobbed with relief.

And then, just as I'd anticipated, his bound and trembling hands went right to his groin.

Chapter 4
The Lion's Den

Too late, he remembered. His face went gray and the hands came back up.

"I told you, white man!" I said in the bodyguard's voice and grabbed him by his skinny arm. I snatched up the crop and I shoved him over to the back of the couch, bending him till his scrawny ass was high in the air. I've been told that my enormous, heavy hand, hot on a man's bare back, feels very powerful. I've been told that it's even more exciting when that hand is holding a man down for a whipping.

"No, I'm sorry!" he gasped for air.

"You've earned my admiration and that of the king," I added, angling myself and the crop for just the right slap. "But you've also earned this punishment."

The crop cut with a whistle through the air and he screamed as it stung his ass. Again, and again. Guessing that his poor behind hadn't felt anything like this since childhood, I went easy, but he cried out quite piteously each time it landed.

"No, no, please—"

I hit a little harder, a little sharper. His ass reddened and I knew he was feeling the burn. He screamed and struggled quite futilely against my hand. The huge native guard was holding him helpless. There would be no evading this punishment.

Nine... ten.... I counted in my head. Imagining the stings, as the whip struck and Leo squirmed.

"I won't do it again! I'll obey the king!" he wept.

Twelve... thirteen....

"I want to obey the king!"

Fifteen. I stopped, but I kept my hand on his back, feeling his sobbing breaths. I let him wonder for a moment if I was done, allowed myself the sadistic pleasure of feeling how he was shaking. To be suffused with that much sensation, to be that much out of control; it had to be both exhausting and exhilarating.

Fifteen light strokes were nothing for me, but I exaggerated my breathing to give him the illusion of a bodyguard who'd given his all into the whipping and was amazed that the penitent had not fainted from the pain.

"By the Lion!" I put astonishment into Mabawa's voice. "I did not think any man could survive such a beating. Your ass," I added in a husky whisper, "is crossed with welts." I brushed a hand over them.

He twitched in pain and caught a breath. A shiver went through him as it came to him. He had criss-crossing whip marks, just like the man on the cover of the magazine.

"Come," I said, easing him up onto his feet. He wobbled and had to steady himself on the back of the couch. I held him there for a moment, suddenly worried. Had I asked too much of him? He wasn't decrepit, but he was no spring chicken.

"Do you wish to stop, white man?"

A beat. Another. He straightened up. I didn't know it at the time, but his perception of himself had just shifted. He'd gone through three very scary situations; he hadn't really been hurt, but hadn't known how difficult or damaging each trial would be or how long it would last. He'd survived the pain and the fear, even the humiliation. He hadn't spoken the safe word.

Leo had always assumed that he had no moral fiber. Now he began to wonder if he did. Maybe his vision of himself, as that blond, pulp hero, wasn't so far-fetched after all.

"Do you wish to stop?" I asked again, "Or will you see the king?"

"W-what..." A pause. And then he said, quite calmly, "What is the will of the king?"

Oh. Oh, my. Leo, you brave, beautiful man. You are on the inside, aren't you?

"The king would see you, white man."

"He honors me. Let's go, then."

"I have underestimated you, white man," I said as I led him to the bathroom. We'd reached that point in the story where the bodyguard finally concedes that the hero is a hero. Oddly, however, I really did feel that I'd underestimated Leo. "His majesty was right. You are worthy."

I stopped him a few steps from the bathroom door. "Wait here."

I slipped in, got off my briefs and made my quick change, dabbed my face with white paint. All the while, Leo stood there out in the hall, drifting on all that he'd experienced and endured. It really hadn't been that much or that long, but I'm sure it seemed like a lifetime.

I lit the candles.

"White man," I said in my deep kingly voice, and stepped up to draw him inside. I shut the door and carefully directed him to the pillow I'd placed on the floor.

"Kneel."

He sunk down and was a little surprised and pleased to find the pillow.

"You have suffered much to learn the secret ways of our tribe," I said kindly. "More than any other tribesman in the history of our kingdom. You have been true and brave."

"But-but not obedient, sire," he whispered, bowing his head. "Forgive me."

"There is nothing to forgive. Even your punishment was a test of your character. Hold up your hands." He did so, and I pulled at the knot. "You have earned the right to take the last and most secret trial," I said, unwrapping the rope and freeing his wrists. Then I pulled off the blindfold. Some of his silver hair was caught in it, but he kept his eyes shut till it was free and gone. When he did open those clear, hazel eyes, his pupils widened, and glowed with awe.

Which surprised me. Deep as I can get into these fantasies, and I'd gone farther into this one than most, there are times when I can't help but step aside and shake my head at what I'm doing.

I'd rolled up two dishtowels and knotted them to the corners of the other two so as to form a breechclout. The back dishtowel flap was ridiculous as it barely covered my ass crack. As for the front dishtowel, it might as well have been a dinner napkin. So there I was standing in front of a pair of potted palms, lit by tea candles, wearing dishtowels.

I absolutely would not have blamed Leo for busting out laughing, but I must have done something right because he looked at me as if I were a god. He was so deep into the fantasy that, to his eyes, those potted plants were the fronds of jungle palms, their shadows against the wall a great, dark, primal forest. The sink and bath were the ancient stones of a forgotten kingdom and my dishtowels were the pelts of predatory cats.

And I, looming there above him, I was Otawa, ruler of the Black Lion tribe.

I suppose my near nakedness helped, and I suppose, having spent his entire sexual life dreaming of black men like me, that Leo was going to savor the moment no matter what I was wearing. Still, I couldn't help but feel smug. Almost gleeful. I'd forgotten what it was like to stir a man's imagination, to transport him to another world. It made me remember why I loved bringing fantasies to life.

His eyes slowly scanned me. Up my washboard stomach, my pecs, my huge shoulders. All the way to my face, which I'd painted with white, "tribal" lines. Then his hazel eyes started back down, visually caressing every muscle as if I'd been sculpted by Michelangelo. He lingered on my crotch.

"Don't you want to know what the third trial is?" I finally asked, amused.

"Yes, sire," he whispered.

I pulled my regal persona back around me and stepped forward, right into his space. He didn't shrink back. I was not, as when we'd started this, a potentially dangerous stranger; I was his fantasy come to life, every experience he'd ever wanted, and many he'd never imagined. I was King Otawa, and Leo was the white man who'd braved all to be right where he was at this moment, kneeling at my feet.

"The third thing you must do," I told him, "is pleasure your king and drink of his essence."

He released a faint breath and touched his hand to his mouth, as if to hold back the saliva. Then he came forward on those boney knees and reached, very tentatively, for one of the knotted corners of my makeshift breechclout. His hands were shaking again, but it didn't take him long. This wasn't just what he'd been hoping for all night, it was what he'd been after since puberty. To see what was underneath that painted leopard skin. The dishcloths fell away.

Leo gasped. It wasn't my size. I wasn't that much larger than him. What startled him was that I was shaved clean, something he'd probably never seen up close and personal.

He put a hand onto my pelvis, disbelieving. Frosting on the cake was an understatement. He was enraptured. Reverently, lovingly, his fingers explored the smooth skin around my shaft, sending flutters of pleasure through my groin. My cock slid out of its foreskin. Emboldened, Leo added his other hand, and together they stroked me from naked groin area back along my flanks to my ass. His hands stopped there, and I saw him blinking, breathing faintly.

I think he was having one of those horrible moments, so overwhelmed by his good fortune that he was suddenly sure it must all be a dream.

He waited to wake up. And when he didn't, he licked his lips and leaned in. He rubbed his face against my uncut cock. I felt the softness of his shaven cheeks, the brush of his silver hair. His breath on my scrotum was very warm and soft. He inhaled my aroma, his hands remaining on my ass as if they didn't dare let go.

Lips kissed my shaven balls, and then his tongue licked out. I felt my nuts moving and shifting in their sacs. My balls tightened up at the attention, and sizzled as he sucked on one, then the other. Blood raced through my cock and it rose.

Leo's mouth left my balls, tracing my thickening stem up to the slit. He lapped at it, making me sweat precome, and then he sighed, as if he'd just tasted nectar. His tongue begged for more. My cock answered, and he sucked the tip like a kitten nursing. Waves of heat and pleasure pulsed through my shaft.

I was very hard now, empowered, and I had to resist the urge to grab Leo by the hair and start thrusting my cock down his gullet. For decades, Leo had dreamed of everything he'd do if he could just have one chance at King Otawa's cock. So. Let him relish it. I could hold back till he'd done everything he wanted to do. Or so I thought.

And then Leo took me in his mouth.

He started by opening his lips and sliding down. His tongue

swirled over my tip and then stroked down my sensitive ridge, which just about drove me nuts. The mouth began to move up and down, and Leo sucked on me like a kid with a candy cane. The veins in my shaft came alert. A moan escaped me. That sound must have excited him. The king lost in the pleasure that he, Leo, was giving him.

My hands touched down on his silver hair. I couldn't stop my pelvis from rocking, fucking that mouth.

And then, quite unexpectedly, that shy, reclusive man who'd spent the entire night trembling or in awe of me, deep throated my cock. I mean, my erect cock just slid into his warm, open throat, not a pause, not a gag.

This time, I was the one who gasped.

Suddenly my balls were slapping Leo's chin, and my cock was captured by this pulsing suction. I started to thrust, quite helplessly.

"Oh, God," *Character. Keep in character.* "W-white man... no one... in my tribe has — has ever given me such pleasure. Oh, FUCK!"

My entire crotch felt like it was on fire, and all that existed were the sensations, lips gliding up and down at the root, a tongue still rubbing sparks underneath, a pulse at my swollen, sensitive tip as the throat swallowed. All of it causing a lava-like roil of delicious heat to rise and rise up my shaft.

I don't know if it was my ass that gave it away by clenching in, or the way I was face-fucking him. But Leo held on as my muscles contracted, my balls went hard, and my penis, filled with come, shot out its load.

I roared like a lion.

Chapter 5
Tribal Markings

Sweat dripped down from my bald head and I gasped for air as I came down from that soaring high. I was a little surprised to find my hands locked in Leo's hair, his face still in my crotch. For a moment I worried that I might have hurt him. But for once this night there was no shaking on his part, just on mine. He had, it seemed, swallowed every drop and was busy cleaning my softening cock.

I flinched as my penis became hyper-sensitive. Gasping, trembling, I gently withdrew from him. Damn.

This is my show, I'd told him, *I'm the director*. Boy, did I feel like an ass. Leo had certainly been in charge of that part of this fantasy and if it wouldn't have ruined the mood, I'd have applauded and handed him an Oscar.

Who would have imagined it? Not me. I'd come here on a lark, because I was bored and wanted to shake things up. I'd figured that all I was going to get out of this was some fun. I mean, come on. You thought it too! What could this old fuck possibly do for *me*, Mason, the crown prince of the Cockpit? A lot as it turned out, and it had taken that orgasmic wake-up call to make me see it.

Leo had given me his fantasy. Sure, it wasn't Shakespeare, but look at the roles I'd been playing up till now: drill sergeant, gangbanger... Tyrone. This was like doing comedy after a year of tragedy; like being cast as the wise hero after months of playing dumb villains. Otawa was this cool, warrior king. Even his fucking bodyguard had layers. This Black Lion fantasy had let me stretch my improvisational talents and ham it up.

Leo had also handed me his trust. Of everyone in that bar, he'd had the most to fear from me. Yet he hadn't tried to escape out the bathroom window, or called the police. He'd let me tie his hands, strip him naked, take charge of his darkest secret. Me. The big black man you'd cross the street to avoid, who would make you flip the locks on your car doors at a stoplight.

That kind of trust was beyond price. It touched and humbled me.

And last, last we have what he'd just done to my cock. I'd never once imagined that Leo would be able to get me off. I'd thought, truth to tell, that I'd have to help him along. But you know what? I've been sucked by some of the best-looking motherfuckers in this city and Leo... I would place Leo in the top five.

I am so not shitting you.

Sometimes, I step back from myself and I see a real asshole. Arrogant and full of himself. This was one of those times. I'd typecast Leo as badly as he had me. This all might have been a game of pretend, but Leo had proven himself a real hero. Given half-a-chance, he could do a man a world of good. Even the Fancy Man.

So. Time for Fancy Man to return the favor. I caught my breath and composed myself.

"White man," I said, and had to clear my throat because I'd completely lost the regal voice. Leo rested there on his knees, his eyes dreamy. There was great pride and satisfaction on his face. He knew he'd gotten this part right in every particular.

"You've passed every test, done all that we asked," I said, reaching for the open jar of red paint. I dipped my finger into it.

"This is the blood of the black lion," I said, following the script directly this time, "our god and sacred animal. With this I make you one of us. The blood of our tribe now flows in you."

I marked his face to look just like that of the blond guy on the cover. Leo's eyes glistened, and I heard him gulp, as if swallowing down tears. I pulled up his right arm and dipped another finger into the black paint. I'm no artist and I knew it wouldn't look like the cover art, but I made a circle on his shoulder and added four strokes over it, the best imitation of the claw symbol I could manage.

"This is so that all will know you belong to the Black Lion and his tribe. From now on you will be known as White Leopard, kin and tribesman. You are brother to any who bear this mark and may call on them in need, as they may call on you. Serve your people well, White Leopard."

"I-I will, sire," he whispered, powerfully moved.

I cleaned my fingers in the water-filled basin then I grabbed the lube and slipped around behind him. I lubed up my palms and crouched down. Reaching about, I took hold of his cock with one hand. It rose out of its sheath immediately, as if summoned by its master.

He drew in a breath as I began to stroke him.

"I am your king," I whispered in his ear, inhaling that lilac after-shave of his. I slipped my other hand down between his ass cheeks, found his sphincter, and let my lubed finger circle it. He groaned and shifted into a kneeling crouch that was, unconsciously or no, identical to the posture of the white hero on the cover.

He was held between the Otawa's two great hands, a willing captive, the black king's white subject and servant.

"This is your rite of initiation," I said, speeding up my strokes on his hardening cock. "Only the king of the tribe can do this."

"Sire—" he moaned. He was holding with his thin hands to my muscled arm. His cock was engorged and pulsing. I let the finger rimming his hole slip in. He made that strangled cry again, as if he couldn't believe what was happening to him, what he was feeling.

I'd kept him on the edge all night, I expected him to come fast and he did. I'd barely started moving my finger in and out of his anus when he went stiff. His cock twitched and spasmed and suddenly he was shouting and shooting his cream all over the bathroom tiles.

He gasped and shivered and gasped again, sinking into my arms as I released him. *Initiation's over*, I thought.

I let him rest against me, there in my lap, till his breathing quieted and he stopped trembling. Then I kissed him on the cheek. "Tarzan, Leo. How was that?"

He blinked at me in blind wonder, his dear, old, hound-dog face still marked with red lines. A breath. Two. Then tears welled up in his eyes, and he began to cry. He bawled like a baby for nearly half an hour while I sat and rocked him in my lap.

We got the paint cleaned off our faces. I dressed, and Leo put his trousers back on. He offered to drive me but I told him I'd catch a bus on back to the Cockpit's parking lot. I wanted to leave him to his bed and contemplations.

"Is there... anything I can give you?" he finally asked as I finished packing up my kit.

"I do this because I like doing it, Leo. And hard as it may be for you to believe, I got as much enjoyment out of it as you did." It was true. Leo would probably never know how much I owed *him* for the evening.

"I don't think that's possible," he murmured. He was still floating, probably would be for days.

"Would you," he added, walking me to the door, "happen to know of a good tattoo artist?"

My brows went up. "There's a place on 4th and Main. Ask for Mike. From what I hear, he's the best."

"Thanks." Leo touched on the faux black lion mark still on his shoulder. He'd refused to wash that off.

"Oh," I said with a grin. "Good idea." I opened the door. Then I thought about it.

"*...it's too late. Everything I wanted is outdated*," Leo had said at the beginning of our evening. To my shame, I'd thought the same thing. I'd assumed I'd show him a little charity, give him his obsolete fantasy. Then we'd both go back to our places, me to the spotlight, he to the shadows.

I'd assumed wrong.

There was no way I was going back to playing the same old roles, not after what I'd had tonight. And fuck if I was going to let Leo gutter out like a candle. A real king, I thought fiercely, wouldn't let that happen to one of his subjects.

I turned to face him. "Actually, there is something you can do for me."

"Anything," he said, and I knew he was finally speaking to me. Mason.

I put a hand on his shoulder. "You went through the trials, and I initiated you with my own hands. The blood of the Black Lion flows through your veins, now and forever. So there's no going back to being who you were. Do you understand me?"

He blinked his red eyes and swallowed several times. He was still very fragile. "Yes, sire."

"You're a member of the tribe now. If one of your brothers is in need, you have to help. Don't shirk your duty just because you're afraid they won't accept what you have to offer."

He mused on that, translating it. "Knowing that the king, himself, has faith in me," he said at last, "makes all the difference." The hazel eyes met mine. "I won't fail you."

"I know you won't." I bent to give him a kiss on the lips. Then I stepped out and shut the door behind me.

Leo came by the Cockpit a few weeks later. He was too shy to step in, but when I heard that an older gent was asking for me, I stepped right out.

We hugged and he showed me his new tat. It looked just like the beautifully stylized mark on the magazine cover. He grinned like a little boy as he proudly displayed his shoulder.

He didn't return to the Pit; I think he'd gotten all he'd needed from it. Instead, he hung out at other bars, went to lectures and plays, exploring the secret kingdom he'd found. One day, I saw him seated at an outdoor table at a popular café. He was in the company of a balding black gentleman with a bit of paunch. Leo was leaning in to fondly wipe crumbs from the fellow's beard. He looked happy.

I wondered if his companion was willing to wear a dishtowel breechclout. *He'd better be,* I thought. *Or I'll kick his ass.*

The regulars at the Pit wanted to know what had happened between me and the silver-haired gent, of course, but they're aware of my policy. I never kiss and tell. So they stayed in the dark, mostly, until one day...

"Hey, Fancy Man," Robbie greeted me as I came in. It was a Saturday afternoon. Carl and Al and Terry were there watching baseball on one of the bar's two televisions.

"This came for you," Robbie said, and he brought out a large, cardboard delivery tube.

"For me?" I echoed, checking it out. It was addressed only to *Mason, c/o the Cockpit,* etc.

"That's one hell of a dildo, Mason," Al laughed, as the guys wandered up to the bar to refresh their beers.

"Will you use it on me, pretty please, Fancy Man?" Terry asked.

"Only if you really beg for it," I smiled, and popped open one end of the tube. I peered in. No dildo. Something was rolled up in there. I shook it out. Then brought it over to one of the tables.

I let it unfurl. It was a poster-sized canvas painting.

"Whoa," Robbie breathed. "They don't do art like that anymore."

No. They certainly did not. It looked to be the cover of an old pulp magazine, stunningly, beautifully rendered. There was an exotic Shangri-La landscape all in vivid greens and golds, including a misty kingdom in the background. In the foreground was a young, white man, slender with longish blond hair and hazel eyes. He was wearing a white, leopard skin breechclout and cape. A black, stylized claw symbol marked his right shoulder.

He was kneeling in the grass. The homoeroticism of his appearance and poise was unmistakable.

"Wonder what he's got under that leopard skin," Carl murmured, and the guys chuckled.

Something impressive and tasty, I thought.

Behind and above the man, posed on a rock, was a magnificent black lion with a heavy, windswept mane. The fine musculature of the beast had been delineated in blues, and its white fangs were bared in a defiant growl. The cat spoke of courage and heart, emblematic, it seemed, of the young man's spirit and sexuality.

"So who is he?" Robbie asked me.

"He's a pulp hero. A white guy who finds this secret jungle kingdom and becomes part of a mysterious tribe. This," I smiled, "this is from the sequel, where he travels around the kingdom having all sorts of adventures."

"Bet you hate that cliché," Robbie said to me. "White man as hero of the jungle. With the black man just there to help."

37

"It's a very outdated stereotype," I agreed.

"So, why would someone send you this?"

"Because I fancied him."

Robbie frowned. "The artist? Or," he nodded at the white youth in the picture, "him."

"Both," I said, gazing at the painted young man, kneeling in the grass. Kneeling in homage to his king.

I'm the Fancy Man. If you see me and you're worried that I'm not going to notice you because of your age or looks, think again. If you've got a fantasy that interests me, I might just grant it. I might just bring it to life.

And I might just bring you to life, too.

If you enjoyed this story, you can sign up for a free membership at ForbiddenFiction and discuss it with other readers and the author at the *Fancy Man and the Black Lion's Mark* story page at http://forbiddenfiction.com/story/T13-1.000040.

The Fancy Man and
the Southern Gentleman

The Fancy Man is used to strange requests, but the one from Charles Beaumont, a masochist from the Deep South, is the strangest yet. Long troubled by the fact that his ancestors were slave owners, Charles wants Mason punish him for his family's sins. Despite his misgivings, Mason is drawn to this young white Southern gentleman. Mason agrees to take on the challenge of exorcizing Charles' ghosts, but he soon learns that freeing a modern slave from the chains of the past isn't so easy—nor will it leave the modern man playing his Master unchanged. (M/M)

Dear Readers: **WARNING**. This is a much darker story than the first. This writer begs you to remember that this is *fiction*. Trained professionals and therapists are best suited to handle mental and emotional disorders. Please do not try any of the acts portrayed in this story unless both you and your partner are knowledgeable and/or trained, consenting, and properly protected against injury and accident.

Chapter 1
Orothodox Traditions

The Cockpit was the sort of leather bar that kept to those traditions that worked, and made the rest up on the fly. Which is to say, we had our own particular way of doing things. Some of it fell into long accepted leather norms, other bits were highly idiosyncratic.

There were orthodox daddies who, like Marine drill sergeants grousing about the half-assed methods of other military branches, insisted that we were not a *real* leather bar. Which meant fuck all to Master Nash, the Cockpit's owner. Come to that, some of these self-righteous tops had informed *me* that I wasn't a real leatherman. But then, I've never been a slave to labels or tradition. Not that I don't respect the rules. And we do have rules at the Cockpit.

One such rule is that Happy Hour is the demarcation point. Before that, everyone in the place is just folk; they drink, shoot pool, watch the televisions. Chatter is casual and friendly. For the most part, tops and bottoms mingle.

After Happy Hour, however, things change. Jeans and shirts come off to reveal leather jockstraps and harnesses. Tattoos are displayed. Men in chaps and Brando biker caps begin to circle the bar. Uncollared boys stand against the walls. When they get nodded over by a Sir, they either follow him to someplace private or take orders.

The pool table, post happy hour, is for tops; that's where they talk shop and display themselves. Booths are for heavy discussions. Doesn't mean a man can't take one for himself if he likes. It just means that they're usually reserved for negotiations or that first rough kiss, or even unzipping a pair of jeans to surreptitiously feel what a guy's really got.

The island bar itself is neutral territory. Can't make up your mind if you want to top or bottom? Have a drink, scope out the room and see which way your cock shifts. See who chats you up. Maybe you'll want to wander over to a booth with him, or better yet, take him home. Not that anyone ever chats *me* up. I always sit at the bar, but I've got looks and a reputation that keeps all but my fellow tops at a respectful distance.

I'm a 6'4", bald, black hulk of a man with a face that would land me in any number of prison movies if that was the sort of acting I wanted to do. Boys wait like prom girls with fluttering hearts to be invited to join me in a booth. For me to say to them, with a glint in my eye, "Tell me your fantasy."

Actually, there's nothing to fear. I'm a pretty regular guy. I keep up with current affairs, vote, help old ladies (and men) across the street. I'm an environmentalist. I also have this soft spot for animal films. If you ever want to see me cry, show me a movie where the dog dies. And if you ever want to make me really angry — and I assure you, you don't — beat or kick a loving pet. I *will* put you in the hospital.

Some of the regulars at the Cockpit know all this, but the boys against the wall have their own myths about "The Fancy Man," and I don't disabuse them. Especially when it comes to the really scary stories. That would ruin their fun and mine as part of the thrill a master gets comes from eliciting some healthy fear. Hearing a wobble in the voice or smelling a man break out in a cold sweat can be as erotic as a strip-tease.

It was thanks to these rumors and tall tales, however, that the southern gentleman decided to violate his own deeply held sense of decorum and talk to me that particular Saturday night. Jordan was working the bar at the time. He's a jet-haired, bi-bottom with a roguish smile and an ass to die for. Advice to tops, don't ever try to humiliate Jordan. The man has no personal sense of shame. You could strip him naked in a public park, tie him to a tree and he'd just smile and wish everyone passing by a nice day.

"Come on, Fancy Man," Jordan was saying as he set before me the local, pale ale that the bar had on tap. Jordan was always after me to grant him a fantasy, any fantasy. I kept refusing. Edible as he was, Jordan didn't need my help getting what he wanted.

"You *and* a dominatrix. In matching leather outfits." Jordan shut his eyes in rapture. "You could stretch me out between the two of you."

"And you'd get fucked by us both," I smirked. "Poor you."

I drew on my beer, listened to the murmured conversations, the clack-clack of pool balls. Someone had fed the digital jukebox and it was making its way through Nine Inch Nails. "Happiness in Slavery," was currently playing. I took a gander in the bar mirror at the gaggle of awkward boys, some nearly naked, lining the open walls. I rely on instinct and sometimes my penis to find the right pup, the one who needs my training. Tonight, both instincts and penis lay dormant.

"Hi."

The chair next to me was empty and he sat right down, not even a by-your-leave. He had a nice enough face with a pert chin and a strong nose. His best features, however, were his wistful gray eyes, his head of thick black curls... and his body. My God, that body. It was muscled in a way that spoke of long hours bench-pressing weights and was accentuated by a traditional white tee-shirt, Levi's jeans and black engineer boots. Keys hung at his right side declaring him a bottom. He smelled of beer and sweat.

"Charles." He offered me a broad hand and spoke with a distinct Southern drawl. "Charles Beaumont, sir, the sixth of that name."

Sixth?

Jordan, wide-eyed at the man's chutzpah, shifted nervously to another customer. He need not have worried. I was actually more confused than offended. I had seen this guy a few times before. He was new to our bar and, so far as I knew, had come in alone and left alone each time. Curious.

"You know who I am," I said, crossing my arms rather than taking the offered hand. I was half-convinced that this was some sort of joke.

"God, yes." He smiled and jerked his thumb back at the guys standing against the wall. At least five of them dropped their eyes and tried to turn invisible. *"Not me, sir!"* their attitude clearly said. *"I didn't have anything to do with that fool approaching you. No, sir!"*

I don't know if they were horrified by Charles' bold move or envious that they'd never tried it.

"They told me all about you," he explained. "Hardly wanted to discuss anyone else. They said I shouldn't go near you. That it just wasn't done. But where I'm from, sir, a gent introduces himself. So here I am."

"Here you are," I agreed coolly. I wasn't going to do anything until I figured out what Charles was about. Nothing that is, except let him sweat and wonder what I was going to do. "And you're from?"

"Atlanta, originally. Well, just outside of Atlanta; a suburb I'm sure you've never heard of."

"Is that a fact? Are you scared of me, Charles?"

"Terrified."

I was getting a sense of him now. Take, for example, his ordinary tee and jeans. That suggested modesty, a willingness to learn the Cockpit's customs before flaunting himself. Which meant that line about introducing himself was a crock. Charles was a gentleman to the hilt, and it disturbed him on a gut level to do what he was doing right now: pushing himself on me. So what had made him go against his own sense of propriety?

"What are you after?" I asked him point blank.

A beat. I saw his lips part, the tip of his tongue rubbing between his teeth. His eyes met mine. "How about you throw me over that pool table and beat my ass with a cue, sir?"

He did not, I thought, *just say that.* This boy had not just topped from the bottom. My cock, however, liked the suggestion and swelled at the image Charles had just planted in my mind. That's when it occurred to me that he wasn't being a brat. He was flirting. Trying to tempt me into going for him. He was also evading my question.

"Like an audience, do you?" I played along.

"I like what you like," he said. I saw the pulse in his throat beating and wanted to run my fingers over it. I guessed that he was having trouble reading me, telling if his ploy was working, and that was undermining his confidence. "You can do what you want. Anything you want."

"Anything, huh?" I murmured skeptically. He was lying, of course. A bottom who says you can do "anything" to them is either desperate or doesn't think much of a top's intelligence. "You're not interested in *my* fantasies, Charlie boy, and we both know it. Stop

43

fucking around or I will get angry. What are you really after?"

For a moment he looked trapped, like he couldn't decide if it was better to risk losing his one chance with me by telling the truth or by bailing. That pretty much confirmed what I'd guessed. He *did* have a fantasy, one requiring someone like me to fulfill it. It was so dark and shameful, however, that he was sure I'd reject it outright if he told it to me straight.

I waited patiently. He warred with himself for another minute, licking his lips, breathing in shallow breaths. Finally he looked at me, a silent plea in his eyes, and spit it out.

"My family owned a plantation back in the day," he said, voice pitched under the music and chatter. "And slaves. Generations of slaves from 1750 to 1865."

Oh. Joy. I thought. Let me guess. The mystery fantasy is: white man is owner by day, but big, black slave owns him at night? Or maybe a Nat Turner scenario? Slaves revolt and master has to beg for his life? Sorry, not interested. There are lines I won't cross and this was one of them. I don't do plantation slave.

Charles wasn't finished, however. He leaned forward and whispered the punch line in my ear. "I want you to avenge them."

"The slaves?"

"Yes, sir. Avenge them. On me."

Okay. Didn't see that coming.

He had one hand on his knee, rubbing it as if to wipe away a stain. "Ever since I was taught about slavery in elementary school... and learned from my parents about my family history, I've been haunted by these ghosts. The slaves my family owned and wronged. I'm obsessed with slave accounts even though they turn my stomach. I see a black person looking at me and I think — I'm sure they hate me. I've asked other men... to punish me for it. White men. It works for a while. But then the ghosts come back."

"Therapy?" I had to ask.

He shook his head. "Therapy, pills, religion. I've tried them all. Only this —" he waved at the bar and I understood that he meant being a leatherman. "Only this has ever helped."

"Pumping iron as well," I ventured, eying his musculature, "You work out till you drop, don't you?"

"How did you...?" He shook his head. "I do, yes. It drives the ghosts back, but never away. They're always there, in my peripheral vision. I think, however... I hope that *you* can satisfy them."

Because I was black, he meant. Because, like the vast majority of African-Americans, I was descended from slaves. And probably because he believed those stories he'd been hearing from the boys against the wall.

"You're asking me to channel these ghosts?"

"Yes, sir. If it... if it would please you to do so." Very formal now, his Southern dialect thickening.

I leaned back. Charles had his head bowed, his hand still rubbing over his jeans, like Lady MacBeth trying to rid herself of bloody spots. "I know how crazy this sounds," he added, "but I'm serious."

Fuck. This man wasn't asking for a fantasy. He wanted an exorcism. I wasn't unfamiliar with such things, but I usually steered clear of them. Punishing a man, really punishing him so that he could exonerate himself, was draining and exhausting. On both of us. And there was no guarantee that Charles would be free of his ghosts when it was over. Or that I'd still have my soul. Viscerally seductive things, exorcisms.

Charles was waiting for my answer, head still down. His face looked very white. Which told me in no uncertain terms why he'd gone against all his decorous and genteel instincts and propositioned me with this nightmare instead of waiting for me to proposition him. He was at the end of his tether and saw me as the last and final answer to his prayers.

If I said no, what might he do to himself in those deep, dark, lonely hours of the night? I could guess. I could guess all too well.

I thought long and hard before I finally asked him, "Did you drive here?"

"Walked."

"Where do you live?"

He gave me an address, an apartment in a nearby neighborhood.

"Stay," I told him, pushing off the barstool. Something in my attitude must have cued the regular boys; they came to attention, as if a ship's Captain had just stepped out on deck.

"Jordan," I said, and the bartender, excusing himself, came out and around. I handed him my car keys and gave him instructions. He was off and out the front doors at a run.

My eyes went to the wall. Al, a dark-haired stork of a man, was there. I'd no doubt that he'd been watching me since Charles had stepped my way. I lifted my chin. Al was into military fantasies, and I'd played the strict drill sergeant to his new recruit more than once. He fell into that role now, marching swiftly across the room. My posture responded as if I'd just put on a uniform. Al was a friend. We watched sports together on Sunday afternoons. But at this moment he was a slave and I was a master.

"With my compliments to the gentlemen at the pool table," I said as he stood at parade rest before me. I detailed what I wanted done. Al repeated the instructions back to me word perfect, then was away. He cut by patrons with all politeness till he got to the three billiard players.

One of them was Nash, owner of the Cockpit. Nash's graying-brown hair was combed back in waves from his forehead, his still trim and powerful body clothed in desert fatigues and Third Watch paratrooper boots. He and the other two stopped playing their game as Al arrived and explained what I wanted. Their eyes came up to meet mine. Nods were exchanged and Nash put down his cue.

Jordan came panting back inside. He had a pair of cuffs, a chain and a leash. He presented them to me along with my keys. Nash arrived as I returned to Charles.

The gentleman from the south was watching, apprehension in his eyes. I snagged his tee and hauled him off his perch, getting a feel for his weight, which I guessed was almost equal to mine though he was a head shorter. Then I spun and slammed him face down into the bar.

The guys to either side jumped and Charles' hands went to his head in submission.

"Behind your back," I snapped, and down they came. I fitted the cuffs on his wrists, snapping them shut. The chain went about his throat, the clip of the leash locking the ends together. I handed him over to Nash.

"Gentlemen, I have here an unclaimed slave!" Nash shouted, jerking the leash and leading dazed Charles into the center of the bar. The bulge in Charles' pants visibly swelled at the attention and his jeans began to look very tight. "Anyone interested in making him your property?"

"I'll have me a look." Burke was a wiry top, tough as nails with mousy hair, a Fu Manchu mustache and the soul of a poet. Nash motioned to Al who obediently broke open Charles' jeans for the buyers. A quick pull and there Charles stood with pants about his ankles. His thin cotton briefs did little to hide his erection. Damp spots appeared on the crotch.

For a moment I mistook those signs as meaning that he did like an audience. Then I caught his quick glance my way, saw him blush and understood. He was aroused because *I* was watching him being humiliated.

The music of the jukebox pounded, but most of the bar had gone quiet; some of the newer bottoms were aghast. They were still in the shallow end of the leather lake, and this was way outside their comfort zone. Most, however, were watching with interest. Meanwhile, the star of the show gulped and lifted his chin, braving it out. Hard thing to do in a room filled with lustful strangers.

"Not too bad," Burke judged and I had to agree.

"How 'bout the other end?" Owen, his fellow top, demanded. Owen was a brick: linebacker shaped. He had straight, brown hair and the mind of a mischievous elf.

"Give the man a look at that ass." Nash shoved Charles over the table. The entire bar took in a collective breath as the briefs rode up to display muscled thighs and buttocks.

Owen tsked. "Not rosy enough for me."

"Here, let me remedy that," Burke politely offered, and before anyone could move he swung the pool cue. It made a crack that could be heard over the music, and Charles let out a yelp. Some patrons shot to their feet, others just leaned forward. I mentioned how our bar is small and fairly casual. This sort of thing wasn't outrageous, but it wasn't common either. I could almost sense cocks vibrating with excitement. This was *real* leather-bar entertainment!

Again the pool cue caned that fine ass and then the thighs, leaving red streaks. Burke is an expert; he's given classes in the fine art of wielding whips and canes. It was always a treat to watch him at work.

Another sharp strike. Charles' cuffed hands jerked up. Burke whacked twice more, his aim impeccable. I'd asked him to keep it short and sweet. I didn't want Charles' ass too bruised, not before I got to it.

"How's that?" Burke waved at the thighs and buttocks, the exposed flesh now a hot red.

"Much better." Owen had a hand at his crotch and I'm sure everyone, Charles included, thought he was about to pull out his cock and have his way with the slaveboy. "But he looks to be too much trouble. I'll pass."

"Anyone?" Nash shouted, yanking Charles back up. The Southerner had tears in his eyes and his knees were shaking. He swallowed and kept his head up.

Oh, you so know this is a test, I thought. *Either that or you've been reading too much John Preston.*

"Anyone want to claim this slave?" Nash repeated.

"He's *my* property," I said, pitching my voice at its most menacing. It was the tone I used when I was really angry and meant business. Even Burke and Owen grew wary.

Nash nodded and tossed me the leash. "Fancy Man claims ownership. No dispute."

I signaled Al. He got Charles' jeans back up in a hurry, though his hands were trembling too much to zip the poor guy up. Al was thinking that here was a part of me he didn't know, a part far scarier than the drill sergeant I sometimes played with him. He was right.

The rules of civilization are like bars on a cage. You can look through them to see the animal urges in all of us: competition, sexual drive, dominance and submission, brutality even, but most times those urges are at least mitigated by the bars; sometimes, however, they reach through the bars, or escape entirely. When they do, the world seems to change wave-lengths. In fact, I often think there must be a state higher than Alpha male. Xi, maybe, the Greek letter used in mathematics to signify random variables. This was one such moment. Everything felt pitched and tilted sideways toward me.

I was at the top of the food chain in that room, the leader of leaders. If I'd wanted to, I could have led the other tops like a pack of wolves to the pups against the wall. And every one of those boys would have dropped their pants, gone to their knees and offered me and my brothers their asses to plunder.

But Nash would have probably lost his liquor license. So I took Charles' leash instead. My fellow tops nodded respect, and everyone kept quiet as I made for the exit. Jordan leapt forward to play door-man for us. We left the musk-heated bar for a soft summer evening.

"In front," I snapped, angling myself so that the pedestrians we passed wouldn't notice that Charles was handcuffed.

And so I escorted my prize back to his home. My burden, as it were. All mine.

Chapter 2

Classical Training

Charles' apartment was one of those 40's-style places, several apartments ringed together about a common walkway. The whole complex had been given a facelift about a decade ago. The one in the far back was a small, single dwelling surrounded by trees and brush. I stopped us under the porch light, got the cuffs, leash and chain off Charles, then spun him to face me.

"We're going to step out," I said, "Take a moment to get things clear."

I always do this. Standard operating procedure. No one walks out on stage until everyone's got the same script. I wanted no misunderstandings.

"Yes sir," he said, gaze lowered.

"Look at me," I ordered, and the gray eyes came up, worried but determined. He thought I was going to try to talk him out of this, and I was, just not like he imagined. "Were you surprised when you ended up across the pool table?"

"No, sir. I deserved it. I-I just didn't expect the added twist."

"Auctioning you off as a slave? You wanted me channeling those ghosts and that's what I did. So now you've had a taste of what they went through up there on the auction block. That, however, was just the appetizer."

"Sir," he whispered, "Give me the rest."

"Not until I know the extent of this. Are you hearing voices? Are you on medications? Do you know your diagnosis?"

"I'm not schizophrenic or bi-polar," he assured me. "I'm not on meds."

"This isn't therapy and I'm not a doctor," I curtly reminded him.

"I know that, sir. I really do. But please, don't say no. I don't expect you to cure me, but I think you can make things better."

I chewed on my lip. This was one crazy white man. Did I really want to do this? That, by the way, was a rhetorical question. A man with a body to die for was begging me to make him my slave and use him as sadistically as I wished. And the cherry topping this temptation was that no one and nothing else had helped him with his problem. Could I?

He might as well have waved a red flag before my eyes. I charge at challenges. No. The question wasn't whether I wanted to do this. It was whether I *should* do it. Probably not... but I was going to anyway, and I'd better make sure Charles knew what he was in for.

"If we go through with this, then things are going to get a lot worse," I warned him. "You will come out of this with scars. Physical scars. No shit."

"I believe you. I've gotten scars before. Go ahead."

"There's more. Those slaves, my ancestors if you'd like to think of them that way, didn't get a safe word. So you don't either. I punish you for as long as the ghosts want me to. Hours, days even. You'll get no say in what happens. And you won't be able to stop anything."

There. Now the eyes were locked on me. He shivered, telling me that he knew just how salient that point was. I don't know what other tops had done to him, but if *I* was going to do this, then I was going to do it my way. Meaning no micromanagement from Charles, no changing his mind later. He was going to have to give me the freedom and control to do as I saw fit.

"You will know we're finished when I say the words, 'Abraham Lincoln.'" It was my own idiosyncrasy. Bottoms have safe words to stop a session, I have one to bring it to a conclusion. The role-playing can get so intense that it's almost like hypnosis; this was my snap of the fingers. "When I say that, we're done. It's over, no argument, no appeal. Clear?"

"Yes, sir."

"And just so you know, whatever happens is between us, I won't say anything about it afterwards."

"That's very considerate of you. Is that all?"

51

"This doesn't come free."

He flushed. "I don't have much—"

I leaned in on him; his situation at the bar had made him sweat and he had a sharp aroma. I loved the way his cheeks got those bright spots of red. "I don't take money."

"The favor," he nodded. So those busy bottoms along the wall *had* been gossiping. There's another unwritten law, one I didn't start but is now part of my mystique: if Fancy Man grants you your wish, you owe him a favor. Now, I assure you I do what I do because it turns me on, but bottoms make up their own rules, and a top needs to respect them. When I thought it was needed, I took advantage of this mythical rule. In Charles' case, I figured it might be needed.

"Don't imagine you'll know what I'm going to ask you to do or when," I went on, "or that you'll want to do it. I'm not going to ask for sex or the keys to your car. I might, however, tell you to spend another year in therapy."

That froze him. This is why I never believe bottoms who tell me they'll do "anything." He thought about it, and I was glad he did. I wanted him to know that I wasn't going to use and desert him. I would do whatever it took to help him, however long it took. And I would make sure he did whatever it took as well.

"I agree to all of it," he said in that soft, gentleman's drawl. "You don't know what it's like here in my head, the self-loathing. I feel like I'm pounding at my skull to get out. I've been wanting—looking for someone like you for... a while. I want... need to give this a try. So I guess I'm all yours, sir."

I bent then, and kissed him, which I'd wanted to do from the moment I'd come face to face with those gray eyes. He was surprised enough to suck in a breath through his nostrils, and then his lips parted and his tongue welcomed mine. I dueled with him, tasting his clean saliva. Then I pulled back and brushed the back of my hand down his cheek. He'd shaven before coming to the Cockpit, and his skin was butter smooth.

"That you are," I agreed. "Open the door. Once we step in, you will call me 'Master,' and I will call you any damn thing I please."

He blushed fiercely, then brought forward his keys and unlocked the door. We took a step in. Time to start my exorcism.

"Get your clothes off," I told him. "Clean up. When next I see you, I want you naked and kneeling."

"Yes, Master," he acknowledged and was gone.

I scanned the place, which had one large room containing a den and dining area. It had the bungalow charm of hardwood floors, a small fireplace and craftsman style furniture. On the dining table was a computer and printer.

A quick glimpse round showed me the bedroom and the door to the bathroom. Charles was in there now. I heard him moving around, water running. I turned back to the bed. It had old-fashioned posts and eyebolts screwed in at strategic places. Lube and condoms were on the nightstand. I set down the cuffs and leash there, just in case I might need them later, but a glance in one dresser drawer showed me I probably wouldn't.

Charles had a neatly arranged collection of padded cuffs, butt plugs, etc. The usual paraphernalia. Not very interesting but I did appreciate how he'd laid it all out. Nothing sours the mood quicker for a master then having that bound-and-gagged slave-for-the-night watching as he searches through clutter for nipple clips.

That wasn't all, however. Another door in the bedroom led out into an old garage. It looked to be soundproofed. I'd find out later that it had belonged to a musician. Of course Charles had wanted this apartment. Less chance of the neighbors hearing screams and calling the cops. It was there that I found the really interesting things.

There was a whipping post, and rings bolted to the floor, one for hands, two triangulated below for feet. On shelves and hooks, almost reverently arranged like icons were rawhide whips, ropes, leather straps and birch switches. Even a small bullwhip. It was clear that Charles had done his antebellum homework. There was nothing modern here.

Just how far had he gone with this stuff?

I went back through bedroom and den to the kitchen. A quick scour though pantry and refrigerator showed me that Charles liked to cook. I found one very valuable item, and several bottles of water. I also searched out and found a small paring knife, metal waste can, a broom handle and some matches. Everything went into the garage.

By the time Charles came out I was at the computer, printing up some things I'd downloaded off the internet. I glanced over at him. He was naked, on his knees, hands behind his head. A black, chain tattoo braceleted his right bicep and some sort of brand scarred his right hip. His body was shaved hairless and even more magnificent unclothed, as sculpted as a Greek statue.

Even his posture was elegant, his thighs spread just so — it was perfect. If I wasn't mistaken — and I don't think I was — Charles had been classically trained, his movements and attitude pre-80's. Very old school leatherman. That was a rarity, one that suited him and really impressed me. Here I was studying and admiring him and he'd yet to move a muscle or lift his eyes from the floor.

The tell-tale flush in his cheeks and the way his cock was extended, however, told me he knew he was on display.

"What are you thinking?" I demanded.

"I'm hoping that I please you," he said without hesitation or evasion. "I hope you like how I look. I'm scared of what you're going to do to me, but I'm more scared that you'll change your mind. I'm also worried that you hate me. For what I am."

The white oppressor, he meant. I picked up the stack of papers I'd printed and stepped up to him.

"Hands down," I told him, running my fingers through his hair. I took hold of the curls and yanked his head back. Charles flinched and shut his eyes, as if he expected me to bite him. I set my mouth to his, brushing his lips with mine before giving him another kiss, this one long and gentle.

He moaned and tried to kiss me back.

I broke off. "You said you'd had other masters. How many?"

He caught his breath, blinked open his eyes and licked his lips as if trying to hold onto my flavor. "Excluding one-nighters, three. I met my first when I was going to college in Atlanta. Older gent. He was my mentor and I was with him for just over a year. Then I moved to Salt Lake City and had a guy there. We met on the internet. He wasn't very experienced and our relationship didn't last long. The last one was in Boise, Idaho. I was a few months with him."

I released his hair. "What's the brand?" It was a white, puckered mark that looked like a calligraphic letter "B."

"It's the brand my family used on their slaves," he said. "My first master honored my request for it."

I winced. Good... *God!*

"Come on," I ordered, heading through the bedroom. He scrambled to follow. "What did these other masters do to you? One-nighters included."

That confused him. "I guess... the usual."

Meaning paddles, whips, suspension, watersports, yadda, yadda, yadda. I was guessing that only his first master had had any real imagination.

"What about sex? Was there any, or was it just punishment?"

"Sometimes." Read that as he gave blowjobs and got taken up the ass. I doubted he'd ever been blown or done the fucking.

We were in the garage now. I put down my papers and picked up several cords of rope. "And these tops were all white?"

He looked like he didn't want to answer that. Those spots of color reappeared. I loved the fact that he couldn't hide his emotions from me; they displayed themselves like fireworks in shades of white and pink.

"The places where I've lived... there haven't been a lot of black leathermen. I asked other black men for help, when I could get up the courage, but none of them were ever able to give me what I... needed."

Meaning concentrated attention. I was willing to bet he'd found men of all races happy to humiliate or hurt him before taking his ass. Whatever our color, we of the y-chromosome do think with our dicks, and a gay man would have to be stone blind not to want to fuck Charles. To want to save his soul, however, took a bit more of a commitment.

"You mean," I said, "they weren't willing to play the part of vengeful plantation slave. Gosh. Go figure."

His face went a deeper shade of red. Poor son-of-a-bitch. What a pathetic story. I'm always faced with pathetic stories. Then again, happy and content folk don't need me, so there's no asking the gift horse for dental records.

I tossed rope down on the ground, then stepped around him. For my size, I can move pretty quickly. I cut a forearm about his throat. He was on his knees in an instant, surrendering, but I pretended that he was fighting me. I squeezed till his neck was corded and he reacted, struggling against me, hands prying at my arm. Which was my aim. I wanted him to realize that unlike with other tops who, likely, hadn't been as big or as strong, he could fight me. Lose control even. He didn't have to restrain or watch himself with me. I could handle him.

Or at least I had a chance of handling him. He almost broke my hold. Almost.

I let him experience a heartbeat more of my muscle, then released his throat and shoved him to the floor. He whimpered as I pinned him with my weight and got his hands bound over his head to the iron ring bolted into the floor. Kicking his feet apart, I got them tied as well. The floor was bare concrete and cold. Uncomfortable and rough on that naked cock now trapped under his belly. I gazed down at his helpless ass, spread open almost wide enough to display his little, pink asshole. His balls were also exposed, pooled there on the floor.

I went to the front, crouched and grabbed him by the hair. "Your forefathers whipped the flesh off the backs of slaves with cowhide whips."

"Yes, Master, they did." He looked guilty, sick to his stomach as if he'd just raped a child. I was summoning the ghosts, making him hear their accusations. Good. If I just gave him pain, as I assumed his previous tops had done, nothing would change. The ghosts needed to be invited to the table before Charles was fed the punishment he craved. He needed to know they were there.

"So that's where we start," I said, snatching a whip off the shelves and stepping back to the other end of him. I swung the braided leather, making it whistle and snap at Charles' bare ass. A tricky operation, striking down from above, but it was one of those authentic methods mentioned in slave narratives. I'd manage it.

His body arched against his bonds as the whip licked his skin. I had the second stroke down before he could even breathe in. It must have felt like an electric shock because his whole body jumped and twitched. I got up a rhythm and whaled on him. He jolted helplessly against the pain, and I felt my blood pump as he began to yell. I was careful as I could be to raise only welts. Drawing blood was for later.

A slice under the cheeks, between them, across the thighs, until he was sobbing. When I snapped the tip at his exposed scrotum, he squealed in agony. My cock fought to get out of my pants. His sculpted body was, to my eyes, the more helpless for its muscles, suggesting power under my control, submitting to me. Merge this rush with my imaginings of what he was feeling: lines of stinging fire on an ass already tenderized by the pool cue, utter vulnerability and powerlessness. The fear response cascaded until he fought to escape. He couldn't. Freedom and surrender crashed like waves under the storm of endorphins. All thoughts vanished from his head and there was only sensation.

I stopped. His formerly lily-white ass and thighs were now almost purple with welts and pain. He was gasping and choking, his great body shaking, groveling before me.

I dabbed at the sweat trickling down from my bald head. I felt good. Excellent. I had an erection and it was difficult to keep myself from unzipping and getting between those splayed legs. I wanted to rip right into that tender asshole and make him acknowledge, again and again, my power.

This is why exorcisms are dangerous. That Xi power there. More high-octane than Alpha Male dominance. A top gets the almost uncontrollable urge to rut.

Charles was trying to catch his breath, fighting for control. Setting aside the whip, I brought over the trashcan, matches and printed sheets of paper as well as the paring knife and my prize from the refrigerator: a ginger root.

Settling onto the floor, I grabbed Charles by the hair. His tear-streaked face was beautiful. I showed him two of the printed sheets. "Slave accounts of being on the auction block," I explained. "How men and women were exposed, examined, treated like property."

I released his hair. Those strong neck muscles managed to keep his head up, watching me as if I held his life in his hands, or, in this case, his sanity.

"We've done that," I said, ripping up the sheets and tossing them into the trashcan. I swept another two sheets under his nose. "Accounts of whippings. There's a lot of these. I'm afraid we haven't finished with the subject."

"No, Master."

"But we got past some of it." I ripped up the sheets and tossed them in the trashcan. Then I lit a match and dropped it in. The flames leapt up and flickered. A few bits of burning paper floated on the hot air and curled to ash.

I put a gentle hand under Charles' jaw. *Hang in there,* I thought, *I'll get you through this.* Then I leaned in and kissed him.

"Your forefathers whipped the flesh off the backs of slaves with cowhide whips."

Chapter 3

Heresies

Over. Well done, I tried to communicate to him, as I tasted the salt of his tears. I ran my tongue over his. He answered with his own desperate kiss. I don't imagine he'd gotten many such rewards in the past.

Cutting off the kiss, I opened up the bottled water and gave Charles a drink. He sucked it down thirstily. I took my own swallow when he was finished, then I leaned back against the whipping post and started peeling the ginger. Rest periods are important in BDSM, and in this instance in particular, they were going to be essential. Besides, it gave me a chance to admire Charles' humiliating position: hands bound and muscled legs stretched wide, his powerful back shimmering with sweat. He knew I was looking at his exposed and beaten body, and he felt debased, shamed. I could see it in his blush, in the squirm of that whipped ass.

This boy is not into pain, I thought. Humiliation and bondage.

Those were Charles' stimulants. Two of my favorites as well, though from the other side.

Tempting. So tempting. I wanted to lick the tender welts on that still stinging buttocks, dip into the crack until Charles writhed in pain and arousal and begged me to fuck him. I wanted to bite and leave my mark on him, make him suck my cock. But this was not playtime, I reminded myself, not yet.

His head came up, eyes wary and curious. So. He didn't know what I was about with the paring knife and the ginger. This was one of the reasons I like to fraternize with different types of SM folk; you learn new tricks.

"That plantation of your ancestors' still standing?" I asked him.

"No." He rested his head back down on his stretched arms. "God bless General Sherman. His soldiers burned the fucking thing to the ground."

I smiled. "Why don't you tell me how you really feel about it."

He snorted. "If I'd ever had to see my ancestral home, as some sort of museum with the slave shacks and the big house, I think I would have slit my wrists."

"Remnants of an empire," I reflected, peeling and carving my root.

"Built on the back-breaking labor of enslaved human beings, on exploitation and torture—"

"Aren't all empires? Are you up on William Faulkner's writings? The book *Absalom, Absalom!*? The character of Tom Stupen builds up this personal empire, a plantation, slaves, wife and children. It's all a metaphor for the Satanic power mongering of the old South. He also has black mistresses and breeds children with them. This implies that racial relationships under the imperial tree of the old South were so incestuous, they not only brought down the empire, but left the roots hopelessly entangled for generations."

Charles blinked up at me, stunned. I put down the knife and grabbed his hair. I liked grabbing him by the hair, pulling his head back. His throat bobbed with sudden fear.

"You didn't think you were talking to some dumb nigger, now did you?" I asked softly.

His whole body quivered at the tone, and I wondered what his penis was doing there, trapped under his belly. Getting hard, maybe? "No, Master. Never. I would never, ever think that. I just didn't imagine that... this would involve a discussion of literature."

"Great American literature," I corrected him. Charles was being a gentleman again. What he was really trying to point out was that intellectual conversation didn't usually enter into sadomasochistic sessions. You certainly weren't going to find any mention of such things in *The Leatherman's Handbook*. And those traditionalist assholes I mentioned would likely have had me publicly burned at the Inferno (just google it, okay?) for just such heresy.

Which made me, maverick that I am, want to put on my chaps and start talking about ballet and opera. I do so like to fuck around. Maybe I ought to start a new club?... the Literary Leatherman's Book Club? Truth was, I didn't usually pause the action for cerebral chit-chat. This, however, was an exorcism. It required unorthodox methods.

"Don't you think some of those ghosts might want to discuss the subject?" I asked Charles. "Or do you imagine *them* to have all been dumb, vengeful niggers?" I released his hair and went back to trimming my ginger. "Literate or not, some of them had to have been smart. Brilliant, even. Perhaps they'd rather talk it out."

He thought about that. I don't suppose such an idea had ever entered his head.

"Yes, Master," he said at last, "And you're right about *Absalom, Absalom!* It focuses on the sins of the father being passed down to the sons, both white and black."

Bastard. I smirked. He'd just stolen my ball and taken it in his own direction.

I finished with the ginger and set it down to undo his bonds. "The past haunts the present and there's no escaping the sins of pre-Civil War America. Or so say a good many black writers."

"They're right," he insisted, sighing and rubbing at his wrists. He bent and shifted as I freed his legs. "It's like radioactive material. It poisons the ground and anything that grows or tries to live on it."

"I dunno. I'm a modern black man and I'd like to think that any problems in my life, any racism I'm facing, is in the here and now, not just a long-lasting tradition."

"There's no hiding from the past," he murmured.

"Not in this room," I agreed, re-tying his hands and then his ankles together. "Knees up. You'll like this pose. It's traditional. Written up in the slave narratives, drawn in pictures...."

He flinched as he settled on his whipped butt, knees under his chin. I brought his bound arms down till they were almost to his bound ankles. Then I slipped the broom handle through the bend in his knees. It was quite a nifty little trick. I sat back to admire it. The broom handle, resting on his powerful biceps, kept the bound arms down and locked about his knees. This forced the knees to stay bent. Meanwhile, the bent knees kept the broom handle in place. Trussed like a turkey.

His eyes were apprehensive now, his body trembling. My whipping had made an impression on him. I pushed him forward so that he was squatting on hands and toes.

"Don't move." He hissed as I spread his tender ass cheeks and shoved the ginger into his anus, a long, thick, carved plug of it.

He gasped at the slippery coldness of the peeled root. "W-what—?"

"Never heard of figging?" I smiled. It was going to be a delight to introduce him to it. I held him by the back of the neck. "Feels nice and cool, doesn't it?"

"Y-yes, Master."

"This is relevant to what we were discussing. Miscegenation. Rape of black women by white men, as in Faulkner. And though I didn't find any accounts of it, I'm sure there were plenty of rapes, as well, of black men and boys by white men. By your horny ancestors."

His breath was getting faster, his skin had gone chill. "It's burning."

"Like ice," I agreed. Like menthol right up that rectum. And it had only just started. I shifted Charles onto his knees, head to the ground. The position had to be brutally uncomfortable with his bound hands trapped between shins and floor. It gave me a good view of his whipped ass and the ginger root plugging it. He started squirming.

"Oh, Jesus! Jesus Christ!" he choked. The ginger was starting to sear him, and he was fighting his bonds. *"Take it out! Take it out!"*

"I'm sure that's what those virgin slaves begged of their kind masters," I said.

"Fuck! Oh, fuck!" His entire universe was locked on his rectum, now, and the scorching icicle knife buried there. Now for the crescendo. I pressed one hand down on his back, pinning him in place. Then took hold of the plug and eased it out. There was no way for Charles to relax, he was feeling the burn too badly, but somewhere in his mind there must have been a profound relief. I was going to show mercy.

I pulled it almost out, and then I pushed it back in. Slowly. He shrieked and tried to fall onto his side, to buck me off, impossible given how he was bound. I kept him where he was. The jerk of his muscles, the screams from his lungs echoed up through my hand and arm.

I pumped the ginger in and out quite mercilessly, fucking him with it. Now and then I gave it twist. Charles started to curse me out.

"You fucking son-of-a-bitch—!"

Good for you, Charlie boy! Knock me back anyway you can.

He endured a full fifteen minutes of this torture, though it must have seemed an eternity. By the time I removed the root, Charles was drenched in sweat and hoarse from screaming. He was still writhing in his bonds as I stepped out to wash my hands. (You don't want to accidentally rub your eyes after handling peeled ginger.) I removed the broom handle when I got back, eased his strained arms from around his knees and got him onto his belly, hands before him.

He lay there, ribs heaving, perspiration dripping off him. His hips kept thrusting, fighting the horniness that the ginger had induced. I crouched down and ran my fingers through his sweat-soaked curls before clenching them and yanking his head back.

"Slave narratives of masters having their way with women," I said, holding up the pages. He kept his teary gaze on me as I ripped up the sheets and set them on fire. The man was really scared now. If he'd had a safe word, he might have used it.

For a moment, I just watched the flames consume the paper, smelled the burn in the air. I waited for Charles' breaths to quiet. "How are you doing?" I asked.

"I'm not hearing the ghosts, that's for sure," he huffed.

"The sting should be gone soon." I gave him a light kiss. "And I think I'd like a bath," I added, freeing his wrists and ankles.

He had to scrabble a little to get up on hands and knees, but up he came, shaking badly. Classical training, all right. I was his master for the night and my wish was his command, no putting it off, even if he was about to collapse from exhaustion. "T-the tub's going to be too s-small for you."

"They always are. A sponge bath, then. Fill the tub with hot water."

"Y-yes. Do you... want bath oil, Master?"

How thoughtful. "I do."

Somehow he got to his feet and wobbled out. I don't know how he did it; the man was utterly wrung out.

I gave him ten minutes, then headed to the bathroom. It was an old pink-and-maroon tile affair with a square-shaped shower-tub. Charles already had it filled with steaming hot water. Golden droplets of what smelled like almond oil floated atop and the counters were alight with candles.

"Is this all right?" he asked. He still smelled powerfully of sweat and fear.

"Splendid."

Charles knelt. His trembling hands unlaced my boots

"You know," I added as he did so, "I've been meaning to tell you, I'm very impressed with your training. It's as old school as I've ever seen. Your teacher really knew what he was about."

He paused with one of my boots off to look up at me. His flush this time was one of pleasure. "You're the only one who's ever noticed," he said and the smile he gave me — shit. So that's what he looked like when his mind took a moment off and allowed itself to be happy.

"Or, at least," he added ruefully, "the only one to ever remark on it. Next time I e-mail my old master, I'll let him know. It'll be nice to tell him that all the hours he spent on me finally paid off. Thank you."

That made me blush, though I didn't know why. I covered it by slipping off my tank while Charles got off my other shoe and socks. He picked up my boots meaning to move them, then hesitated.

"Would you let...." He started, then licked his lips and changed direction. "Do you wish your boots blackened, Master?"

Ah. Add something else to Charles' turn-ons: humiliation, bondage... and boot worship. I could see it in the hungry way he eyed that black leather. He wanted to carefully shine up my boots, finish 'em off with a meticulously licking then go to sleep beside them. I wasn't surprised. Bootblacking is one of the most time-honored of leatherman traditions, either giving or receiving it. It can be a form of foreplay, but it can also be deeply meditative.

It can also be, quite literally, a type of worship. I suspected that's how it was for Charles. Bedeviled by accusing voices, the southern boy relied on his chosen masters to stand between him and damnation. Polishing and licking their boots would be a form of prayer, of homage. He was waiting for an answer, eyes lowered.

"My boots are yours for the night," I said.

I suppose it was an odd way to put it. Untraditional. It certainly startled Charles. He looked taken aback, as if I'd just given him the keys to my house. Then he reverently put the boots outside the steamy bathroom and returned to kneel and open my jeans. I don't know if he was surprised or not to find that I wasn't wearing anything underneath. He stripped off the jeans and folded them. I stepped into the water and faced him, giving him a good look. There are moments in what I do that reoccur; one of them is when I present myself naked, on center stage as it were, to the awe and wonder of my audience.

I'm not a narcissist, but fuck modesty. I am one hell of a good-looking brother, at least from the neck down. Whether you think wide lips, an arrowhead nose and almond eyes are handsome is up to you. But I was gifted with nice proportions, wide shoulders, a slim waist, good ass and long legs. Gay photographers go ape shit over my body.

What struck me about Charles was that he didn't gape or gawk or even sigh with wonder. So many men do. Charles just lifted his brows and nodded approval, as if he thought I would do. Fucker.

"The result of that breeding program in the old South," I remarked wryly, and offered up a few poses.

A breath of a laugh from Charles. "Some say that's why African-Americans dominate sports."

Candlelight glowed in his eyes. He stood with a dripping sponge in hand and started at my shoulders, bathing my arms.

"It seems likely, doesn't it?" I asked him as steam drifted up off my skin. "Darwinism decided who survived the slave ships, and slave owners decided who would breed with whom. They bought and bred slaves for their strength. So maybe that is why we're good at sports."

He shrugged and sponged my underarms. "I think the reason you see so many African-Americans in sports is due to the limited choices of institutionalized racism."

Oh, my! There was a brain under those pretty dark curls. I ran my hand through them as Charles bathed my chest, then clutched at them. He stilled, head coming up. I hardly had to pull for his chin to lift; he was learning. I expected to see apprehension in his eyes, but there was only attention. Setting my hand at his throat so I could feel his pulse, I bent and ran my tongue over his lips. The beat of his pulse intensified as I went in for an exchange of saliva. He gave back, his tongue very enthusiastic.

He liked the kisses. Good. I wondered if he understood yet what I was doing. Exposing his throat, pressing my mouth to his. I wondered, come to that, if *I* knew what I was doing. Near as I was to him, I felt his cock twitching erect. My own came up to meet it, to cross with it as our tongues were crossing.

"Institutionalized racism?" I echoed, releasing him.

He swallowed, and looked anxious. He was wondering why I'd stopped, if he'd done something wrong. After a moment, he went back to sponging hot water over my washboard stomach. His cock remained half-erect, uncertain which way to go.

He cleared his throat. "If you're only allowed to excel in certain areas or only see desirable ends achieved in those areas, then that's where you go. You don't get a Tiger Woods if the golf course refuses to allow blacks to play. And you don't get young black men wanting to become golfers until one of them is a household name, successful and respected."

Excellent point, that. I turned around so he could wash my back. "So you're saying that we got a Louis Armstrong because musical entertainment is where blacks were allowed to succeed back then. Similarly, we got a Tupac because years of black men succeeding in music induced them to become musicians. It's the only role model for success that they had."

"Vicious circle, yes. Careers that have real influence, like politics or big business, are still dominated by white men. And white boys are still the ones urged to be doctors or lawyers. Schools with a lot of minority students don't offer college prep, just vocational classes."

"Sounds like a conspiracy to me," I agreed easily. Actually, the man from the South was quite convincing. "I'm reminded of that line in Ralph Ellison's *Invisible Man*. 'Keep this nigger running'?"

"Love that book."

The warm water was feeling very good across my back. I wondered if Charles was enjoying the way the oil made my skin glisten like polished teakwood. I could feel water trickling down over my spine to my ass crack.

I heard him gulp. "May I," he said, "May I bathe you down... here, Master?"

A touch of the sponge to my ass. I smirked and spread my legs.

Chapter 4

Conversions

I wasn't at all surprised when instead of the sponge a tongue licked at my thighs. I felt Charles prying apart my cheeks and then a little shock as his hot tongue hit the spot. His nose, his breath were there at my crack and I knew he was breathing in my smell. He rimmed my sphincter, tickling the sensitive nerve endings, making love to every fold. Then he pushed in far as he could with his tongue. He probed and sucked and nipped. I released a groan, and my cock hardened.

Charles was going quite crazy now, licking almost desperately at my ass, trying to delve deeper. "Enough," I told him, reaching back to gently push him away. Then I turned around to display my cock. It was out of its sheath, coffee black with a dark pink tip. Drops of precome glistened there.

Charles was standing before me, breathing heavily. His own cock was thick and pressed up tight against his belly. The helmet had gone from pale pink to a dark, throbbing red. He squeezed the sponge between his hands, waiting for orders.

I gazed down over his defined musculature. "Where are your sensitive spots?" I wondered aloud.

I didn't expect an answer, but he swallowed and responded, "Inner thighs. Back of my ball sack." He hesitated then added. "Right where you struck with the whip."

"There." I slipped a hand under his balls to give it a touch. His face flushed and he shivered. I reached round and brushed my hand over his whipped ass, watching him flinch.

"Please—" he murmured.

"I bet you like your ears and neck nibbled, too," I rumbled. "Do you want to suck my cock?"

"In the worst way." There was desolation in the soft, Southern drawl, as if he was wishing for the moon. He apparently thought I was going to deny him.

I stepped out of the tub. Toweled off quickly and led him to the bed. Propping myself up with pillows, I let him crawl between my long legs until his head was at my crotch. He leaned on my thighs, and I felt, for the first time, the warmth of his skin, the hardness of his muscles. His mouth came down over my erect cock, tongue whirling over my tip. My shaft swelled and pulsed as much from watching his head bob, his welted ass writhe, as from what he was doing. I felt again that thrill of utter domination seeing this strong man worshipping me. Precome spilled out of my slit and I felt him sucking at that juice as if were his salvation.

His mouth left my straining tip at last to slip under my foreskin, swabbing intimately. My hips rocked and I ran my hands over his curly head. Finished with the stem, he dropped down to reverently suck at my smooth, brown nuts. They rolled in their tightening sacks, growing hard and hot in response to his tonguing. Charles nuzzled in even closer then, adoring all his wet lips and tongue could reach. It was as if my cock were his god, as if pleasing me were the greatest honor in the world.

My dick was now throbbing with fierce energy; the Xi power again. This whole night had left me feeling like a lord, a master. I got my hands in Charles' hair. If he wanted my cock he was going to have it. With a buck of my hips, I forced my cockhead down his gullet and, ignoring his gags, began to fuck his mouth. My tip struck and struck again the back of his throat. Like a match, that strike made my cock catch fire and energy violent as quicksilver rushed through my body.

I came quite suddenly, my come shooting into Charles' throat as I pumped and pounded that mouth. Once, twice, three times until my balls were drained dry. Charles dutifully swallowed it all, and then, like a true gentleman, he licked me clean.

Some minutes later—my warm and happy cock softening across my thigh, sweat cooling on my shaven head—I lay with Charles. His cheek was pillowed on my stomach and I toyed with his curls.

"You don't like pain, do you?" I ventured. "Sexually, I mean."

He half-laughed. "No. I don't find pain arousing. But there are times when I really need it, when I can't escape the hell inside my head any other way. I used to hurt myself." A shrug. "Then I met my first master and learned about... this sort of thing. Having others hurt me is better for all concerned."

"Is being a slaveboy better for you, too?"

"Jesus, yes. I can still remember when my first master explained the whole Master-slave arrangement to me, what a revelation it was. So much about myself that had confused me suddenly made sense, and the symmetry of that kind of relationship sounded so right, exactly what I'd been after my whole life. I'm a slave, all right." He paused. "But that's not quite what you're asking, is it?"

"Not quite, no."

He whispered out a tired laugh. "The answer is yes, sir, I'm glad of it. Slaveboy is as far from my ancestors as I can get. I'd have fucking jumped at it if I hadn't been naturally inclined towards it."

Which made total sense given his crazy obsession. There was no chance of him even thinking of doing the brutal things his forefathers had done to others if he was the slave.

He glanced up at me, thoughtful now.

"You're not... punishing me the way others have," he ventured. "You haven't shouted obscenities at me, or told me how much I disgust you." His voice went softer. "Or that I'm not fit to lick your boots."

Ah-ha! That's what I'd sensed when he asked about blackening my boots. Boot worship was a reward to Charles, a way of showing his devotion to his top. His other masters had cut him off from it as part of the punishment. Which... when I thought about it, was incredibly stupid! They'd just reinforced his conviction that he was irredeemable. I, on the other hand, had as good as told him he could sleep with my boots if he liked. That I thought him worthy. He had to be thoroughly confounded.

"And you're not doing the usual... stuff," he went on, "You really are giving me a taste of what the ghosts went through. Right out of the slave accounts."

I'm trying to do more than that, Charlie boy. And if you're not seeing it then maybe I'm failing.

"I knew you'd be different, at least, I hoped you'd be," he added with a faint chuckle. "Though I'd no idea you'd be *this* different."

What did that mean?

"They said you were good," he finished. "The boys along the wall."

I shrugged. "The boys think I'm a fucking miracle worker. Don't buy into the hype."

"Too late," he murmured. His breathing quieted and he drifted off into exhaused sleep.

A Southern gentleman, I thought fondly. And then I went cold inside. Oh, man. I wasn't... I couldn't be *in love* with him, could I? I fell in lust, well, daily. I am a y-chromosome. I also fell in "like" with most of the guys I helped. I was not, however, the type to fall in love, at least, not on a first whipping. I, a modern, urban black man, could not be in love with traditional Charles Beaumont, the sixth of that name.

Xi energy. It was making me crazy.

When I woke up the next morning, Charles had moved. He was now kneeling by the bed, forehead pressed to my hand. It looked as if he'd been praying. He was breathing hard and I felt him quake.

"What's wrong?" I rubbed my eyes.

"Oh, God," he moaned, pressing his head down harder on the back of my hand. "Make them stop, *please*. Tell them I'm sorry. *I'm sorry!*"

I snatched my hand from him and got my legs over the side of the bed. "Look at me!"

He did. His eyes were crazed with fear, locked on whatever he was seeing inside that damn head of his.

"Are they trying to hurt you?" I asked sternly. "The ghosts?"

"Yes, they're—" I slapped his face, hard. His head went about so fast I thought I'd snapped his neck. His cheek went bright red.

"Fuck—" he breathed, touching his face and gawking at me.

"Who owns you?" I demanded. "Who laid claim to you last night?"

"You did, Master."

"Which makes you *my property* until this is over. Are the ghosts tops or bottoms, slaveboy?"

His mouth opened, shut and opened again. I don't imagine he'd ever been asked that question, or thought about it come to that. "Tops," he said automatically.

Of course they were. "So if they want to do anything to you, what must they do first?"

"They...." He paused. Blinked. "...have to go through you," he said this wonderingly.

Exactly what I'd hoped he'd say. Anyone who wanted to use my slave, my property needed my permission. That was the rule.

"Until we are done, *I* am the only one who can touch you. *No one else* is allowed," I informed him sternly.

He relaxed. It was quite remarkable. Call it sexual chemistry or the endorphins from that slap. Call it an epiphany. But you could see it. The voices of blame and accusation went silent in his head. His eyes cleared, his face grew calm. Someone had finally gagged the damned ghosts.

"Jesus, Mary and Joseph," he said, marveling like a kid at a science fair. "I can't believe you just did that. Is this your way of discrediting the hype? It didn't work. I'm converted."

"I do have my moments," I demurred.

"You sure do." Charles drew in and released a breath. He was still rubbing his cheek, staring at me as if I'd performed a miracle. "I... May I... make you breakfast, Master?"

My stomach growled. "Yes, you can. A big breakfast. No coffee."

"Have that ready for you in a jiffy."

I watched his tight, bruised ass leave, then stood up and stretched. I caught sight of my boots. Sometime in dawn hours before he'd had that panic attack, Charles had blackened my old combats. He'd done an award-winning job. The worn leather had a soft gleam and the laces had been re-done so that the left ones crossed precisely over the right ones. Nice touch.

He'd probably sat himself down on the floor here, I mused, and leaned up against the bed. Listening to my snores, he'd worked on the boots, likely shifting this way and that because his whipped ass had hurt like hell. Still, he'd probably been at peace, treating himself to one of his favorite fetishes while remembering how he'd pleased me.

Is that when the ghosts had come back down on him? As he'd finished up my boots with indulgent licks of spit, had he suddenly thought that a man carrying his inherited crimes didn't deserve such a reward? Had they maybe pointed out that I, his master, couldn't possibly feel anything but loathing for someone like him?

Shit.

It made me wonder if I could really make a difference. I knew that I could banish Charles' ghosts from moment to moment. Brutalize, scare, sexually arouse, even converse them out of his head for a night. But could I really exorcise them?

The smells of maple syrup and butter browning in a pan drew me into the living room. Charles had set out a huge stack of pancakes, scrambled eggs came out next, and turkey sausages fried up with apples. There was milk and orange juice. I sat down and snapped a napkin out across my naked lap.

"Have you eaten?" I asked, cutting into the sausage.

"No, Master." He was staring at my crotch, expecting, I suppose, that I'd feed him something special.

"Down here," I pointed and he went to his knees beside my chair. "Hold onto one of the legs and don't let go."

I cut through the pancakes and forked up a sliver dripping with syrup. I fed it to him. The syrup glistened on his mouth and he almost let go of the chair leg to wipe at it. Then he remembered and held on. I waited till he'd finished chewing and swallowing before leaning down and licking off the maple sugar glossing his lips. The second time I fed him the pancakes, I sucked the syrup off his lips, the third time I pushed my tongue into his mouth and tasted that liquid sweetness on the roof of his mouth. I continued this, alternating bites between us until the stack was gone and Charles' cock was twitching.

Finishing off eggs and sausages, I inhaled the orange juice and drank half the milk. The rest I gave to Charles, letting him gulp it down, patting his lips dry with the napkin. He was going to need his strength, I thought, with sudden regret. What I had in mind was going to test both our limits. Had this been anything other than an exorcism, I might have regretted as well that it would soon be over.

All this had better have some positive effect, I found myself brooding.

The idea of putting Charles through all this for nothing was intolerable. And it would be my fault if it ended up that way. I was the one who was so all-fire-sure I knew what I was doing. I really needed to tone down this god complex of mine.

"What are you thinking?" I abruptly asked Charles. I knew by now that he would answer. I hadn't yet figured out if his candor came from his old fashioned training, where a slave always answered his master, or because he viewed my questions as coming from the ghosts and he dared not lie or withhold.

Either way, I knew he was, at heart an honest man. Brutally honest. I admired him for that. I hadn't the courage to be that candid, not even with myself.

He gazed up at me quite guilelessly, still holding faithfully to the chair leg. "I'm thinking about how much my ass hurts this morning and how damn good you were with that whip. I'm regretting that I didn't make more pancakes." He added with a lick of his lips. "And I'm thinking about what you said, about being a modern black man."

My brows went up. That wasn't at all what I'd expected to hear. "What about it?"

He glanced away. "Don't you ever think about your ancestors? Think about all those years of slavery and racism and get angry?"

Get angry at white men like me? is what he really meant.

"Sure. I think about it. And I get angry. But if I think enough about it, go back far enough, then I have to acknowledge that some of my ancestors were probably slave owners. And I don't just mean whatever white blood runs through my veins. The slave trade flourished in Africa because tribes were willing to enslave each other, sell their enemies and rivals to white folks. If we're innocent or guilty by way of some spiritual DNA passed along father to son, then none of us is getting off scot-free."

I sighed. "Thing is, there are enough injustices happening in the here and now that I can be mad about, and maybe do something about. I'm not saying forget and forgive the past, but that forty-acres-and-a-mule reparation that great-great-grandad was promised just ain't going to materialize. Time to let it go."

Charles laughed. "I suppose."

I hesitated. "The ghosts are almost satisfied," I told him, stroking his hair. "But do you remember what I said yesterday?"

Several heartbeats passed as he cast his mind back. "Whippings."

"This one's going to be bad. Authentic."

A long silence. It felt like the ghosts really were there, standing between us, pushing us each to do and be what they wanted, not what we were. I was almost willing to end the whole thing in sheer defiance. But this wasn't about me.

"You're the master," he said, gray eyes meeting mine. "I belong to you. You said so yourself. Do what you like with me."

I recognized that expression. Trust. A desire to prove himself. To please me. Fuck.

"Crawl to the whipping post."

Chapter 5
Radical Ideologies

I watched as, scrotum swinging, he made his way to the bedroom. Then I got up and went through the pantry, getting down the item I needed, along with another bottled water. I also fetched a small bit of ginger out of the refrigerator. I prepared it and set it on a plate, which I left on a nightstand as I crossed through the bedroom.

Bad, I'd warned Charles. Bad for both of us. We were talking you-are-there shit and the problem wouldn't be doing this to him, it would be restraining my Xi energy which *wanted* to do it to him.

Charles was kneeling before the post. I bound his wrists to the ring on the opposite side. I was close, and I was naked this time around, deliberately so. What I was about to do was as intimate as any sex act. He could smell me. He could almost taste my bare skin as it brushed his.

I wrapped another rope right under his thighs, so that his legs were also tied to the post and he had to stay on his knees. His cock was pressed up against the wood. His heavy balls hung there, vulnerable yet again.

This time, however, I would have to be careful. This whip could do real damage. Was going to do damage. It was the 4' bullwhip. I gave it a few swings, a couple of cracks. I'm not a master with whips like Burke, but I have practiced, practiced, practiced. I've snapped splinters off planks of wood and gone for accuracy by putting out candles and popping balloons. I knew how to get the whip to draw blood. My heart was pounding in my chest all the same, a mix of nervous fear and vicious desire. Time to get to work.

Charles was now shaking. I didn't bother to warn him. I aimed, and sent the whip cracking. It whooshed through the air. The trick with a bullwhip is not to pull back. You toss it out, putting your whole body into the swing. The leather lashed down like fire across Charles' upper back. He yelled and arched even as that gunfire snap rang out over us.

A diagonal streak marked his broad, white shoulders. I swung out again, and this time the whip snaked about his ribs, kissing his side. He fought against his bonds. Ruby droplets appeared on the welts.

Third crack of the whip, and I felt that energy stirring in my loins as another line of blood appeared. Charles tried but couldn't hold back a howl of pain. I was feeling the heat of the exercise. A fourth slice down the back, a fifth, careful to avoid spine and kidneys. Charles was clinging to the post, trying to cower from the poisonous sting of the whip. The leather had to feel like a knife cutting through, leaving a burning throb behind. And whenever the whip cut across an existing slice, it doubled the agony.

And there were his balls, hanging defenseless. He had to be weak with terror just feeling them there. Feeling the breeze of the whip on them every time it struck his back.

I whipped him again, and again. Fifteen was the traditional number of punishment lashes back in pre-Civil War slave days, but I stopped at nine, grateful that I hadn't made any stupid mistakes. Burke would have had my hide if he'd been there, seeing us both in the nude, nothing to protect eyes or private parts. The blood trickled down from Charles' wounds across his white back creating a glistening canvass of bejeweled streaks. I dropped the whip. Time to bring this home.

I fetched up the item I'd gotten from the pantry and stepped over to where Charles hugged the post, legs spread as if trying to fuck it. His tear streaked face came up as I approached. I made sure he could see what I had in hand. Salt.

"No!" He began to struggle in genuine panic. I reached back between his legs and grabbed his balls. He stilled, and he sucked in a breath as I squeezed. Message received. I let go and poured salt into my hand. Charles started to cry. Pinning him at the back of the neck, I rubbed my handful into his shoulder wounds.

He let out an ear-splitting shriek, bucking and squirming against the ropes. I calmly poured more salt into my hand.

"Mason," he said in a strangled voice, and I grew very still. "Mason, please don't."

I'd given him no safe word, but my name was very close to one. It surprised me that he even knew it. That he used it at all, however, was even more telling. It said he knew who I was outside of the role he'd asked me to play, that he recognized me as a man, not just the ghosts' avenger. The energy pulsing through me quieted for a moment and I found myself wondering what the fuck I was doing. I didn't want to make him suffer like this, not like this, as my ancestors had.

So why was I doing it? Hadn't I done enough?

I gazed at the whip marks, the lower ones still seeping blood. No. There could be no ambiguity in Charles' mind, no hint that he hadn't suffered exactly what those black slaves had suffered. For this to have meaning, to change things, he would have to be taken beyond his own limits. In every and any direction possible.

"The ghosts demand it, Charles," I said. "Hold on."

He screamed and screamed as I rubbed salt into the lower cuts. The pulsing, searing pain of it must have been excruciating. He writhed in his agony.

I held off for as long as I could, a part of me indulging in the song and dance of pain. Then I opened the water bottle and upended it over his back. The cries quieted down to exhausted sobs.

"Thank you." Gratitude for putting an end to his misery. "Is there more? God. Tell me if there's more."

That wasn't part of the deal. I brought over the trashcan, matches, and printed sheets.

"The rest of the whipping notes." I showed him the pages. "Rubbing salt or vinegar in the wounds was a common practice. It wasn't enough to rip the flesh from their bones."

I tore up the sheets, quite vehemently, and dropped them into the trash along with a lit match. This time I watched them burn with satisfaction. I was suddenly feeling angry, though I wasn't quite sure at what or who. I guess I was angry at those outdated tree roots, the ones still entangling men like Charles, fucking them up.

When I yanked Charles' hair back this time, I not only kissed him fierce and hard, but caressed his throat. That white throat with its Adam's apple, bared to me. I bit at it, licked it. Invaded his mouth again, kissing him till I could feel the pounding of his throat pulse under my fingers.

"Who do you belong to?" I suddenly demanded. It wasn't anything I'd planned on saying; it came right from my gut. No ghosts involved, no role-playing. This was Mason talking. And I was going to have this man's soul if it was the last thing I did.

"You, Master," Charles whispered.

"Who do you submit to?"

"You, Master."

I stroked the throat again. "Who will you abase yourself for?"

"You, Master."

"You hold to that post." I untied his hands and legs. He stayed where he was, shaking with emotion and pain. I brought his hands round behind his back, tying them there. Which must have hurt like fuck, but all Charles did was suck in a breath and swallow hard.

I had one last thing to do and it was going to be as much for me as for the damn ghosts. I hauled him up by one arm and dragged him into bedroom. He was weak in the knees and quaking so badly that he could barely walk. I spun him around and shoved him onto the bed. He cried out as his whipped back landed. I'd have to get ointment on those wounds and soon. But not right now. I ran my fingers over him, muscled shoulders, chest, that shaved pelvis. Then I spread his legs, my hands pressing down on the soft flesh of his inner thighs.

I bent to suck his cock. It was flaccid but sprung up almost instantly as my lips went over the tip. I caressed the rim with my tongue, licked down the ridge and lapped at the velvet of his shaved balls. I tasted his sweat, inhaled his musk. He gasped and writhed. I held him harder. This time it wouldn't be just ropes restraining him. In my power, at my mercy. His cock was going to dance to my tune, and his body was going to do as I commanded.

I set my knees where my hands had been, pinning wide his thighs and took hold of his stiff cock, stroking it to get it harder. He was watching me, his breath coming in great gasps, both terrified and aroused; I didn't have to ask him what he was thinking, I could see it on his face. *Does my cock please you? Does my desire?*

They did. God, did they ever.

His eyes widened as I lifted into his sight what he'd missed, sitting on a plate on the nightstand: an inch-long, matchstick sliver of peeled ginger.

Sweat sprung out across his brow and upper lip, and he shook his head in a mute plea as I slipped it past the lips of his cock, just half-an-inch of it. He clenched his teeth at the cold, uncomfortable feel. It must have been almost pleasant, for a moment.

The moment ended. His pelvis began to thrust, fighting against my weight on his thighs, his arms strained against the ropes holding his hands behind his back. His body squirmed against the icy burn searing down his shaft. I held tight to his cock, rubbing the underside to keep it hard. His head snapped side to side, hissing cries coming out.

"Stop, stop—!"

He tried to throw himself off the bed. I grabbed hold of his shoulders. I've never, in my many relationships, had to use all my strength. I'm big and powerful and a little of what I've got goes a long way. But then, I'd never been with any man as beefy as Charles. It was a surprise to have to really put myself into holding him down. I broke into a sweat. It was exhilarating.

"You Motherfucker!" he screamed at me.

We were both slippery with perspiration by now, drops trickling down our sides and off our faces. Charles was fighting with all his might and if his hands hadn't been bound behind his back he might have beaten me.

I finally got fingers locked about his throat. "Some slaves fought back," I hissed into his ear. "Just like you're doing now. They used their strength to resist, to kill owners and overseers. The ones they hated, like you hate me at this moment. They ran away. Sometimes they got away. Sometimes they decided to die rather than be taken."

With that last word I removed the ginger from his cock. His breath came in great, heaving breaths and his pelvis still worked to thrust even as the burn started to fade.

"They weren't all helpless victims," I emphasized. "They did escape. They got revenge and justice, sometimes."

"Mason, please." I felt him swallow, the fury draining out of him. "Mercy. A rest. Just a rest."

Not yet. I set my hands back on his thighs and returned my mouth to the head of his twitching cock. He gasped as I tongued his slit, tasting the peppery remains of the ginger root. Against his will, Charles' cock stiffened and swelled. I lapped on down his ridge to his scrotum. I lifted his balls and paid particular attention the underside of his sack. He whimpered and moaned; on down I went to his taint and lapped at that area. He released a high cry of sudden pleasure, arching his back.

Pausing to rim his pink hole, I started a warm, wet trail back up to the tightening balls, and then back down again.

"Oh, fuck, fuck!" he hissed, as I returned to his cock, this time with tongue and lips and teeth. I licked and lipped at it very slowly, very deliberately, until he was fiercely erect and slick with saliva and tangy precome.

He was writhing under me now. I grabbed the lube at the side of the bed and slathered it between his spread cheeks, toying with his hole. His breath came sharp as I slid in a finger. I found the prostate almost immediately and rubbed at it even as I slid my other hand down his cock and squeezed, there above the balls.

"Do you want to come?" I demanded.

"W-what you want," he panted. "What you want, Master."

Standard answer. His first teacher had really done an excellent job. I pulled out from his ass and took him by the hair. I clenched, but didn't jerk. His response was instant. The head went back, offering me his throat, surrendering his mouth. Just as I'd taught him.

Fuck if he wasn't the bottom I've been looking for all my life. My cock was hard and erect as I leaned in and kissed him.

"I told you not to fuck with me," I whispered and I saw his belly ripple with fear. "You haven't tried to do that since the bar. Don't start doing it now."

He had his eyes shut. Tears leaked out from under the lids.

"I want to come," he whispered. "I want you to make me come. But I think that you'll stop. I don't think the ghosts will let you give me that reward."

I released his hair and slipped my finger back into his anus, stroking it in and out. I licked the tip of his cock, savoring the hiss of his breath in agonized pleasure.

"The ghosts have no power over *me*," I told him, "As for you... you're mine, and what happens here and now is between you and me."

The tears rolled down his cheeks and his pelvis rocked helplessly. "Then let me come."

I had a condom ready. I released him and got it on my cock quick as I could, then angled the tip at his hole. My shaft entered his hot rectum, the firm walls giving way to me. I let the Xi energy flow, pounding in, making him cry out. As I pumped, hard as I could, I sensed the sparks he was feeling, the same as I was feeling. His body tensed and spasmed. He jetted his come up across his belly almost at the same time that I shot mine within him.

In that pulse, as we let our bodies shout, there was no time, only the now. There was no one else, only us. There were no traditions, no restrictions. For that heartbeat of ecstasy and elation, we were free.

Completely free.

Chapter 6

A New Creed

Neither of us could move afterwards. We rested on the bed for I don't know how long, and then I got up the strength to untie Charles' hands and haul us both to the bath. I used the handspray to get us cleaned up. Then I dried off, and got myself completely dressed before fetching the first-aid kit.

Like all good slaves, Charles had a kit that was top notch. I had him lie face down on the couch while I tended to his back.

"I don't think there'll be much scarring," I assured him, rubbing ointment over the whip marks. I'd done a good job; the cuts were thin and light. I'd have to let Burke know how much I'd learned from his lessons.

"No matter," Charles sighed. He was spent and I felt equally exhausted. I couldn't remember the last time I'd worn myself out like this.

"Have you something to cover these?" I asked with concern as I went to work on the rope burns on his wrists and ankles. I didn't want him getting asked embarrassing questions by concerned co-workers.

"Wide band watch and a big link bracelet," he murmured. Good training again. The man knew how to keep his wounds discreetly hidden.

I wrapped Charles in blankets and settled him in one pillowed corner of the couch with bottled water. Then I fetched the final printouts from beside the computer.

"Accounts of slaves fighting back. Rebellions and such," I explained, shredding them. Into the little fireplace they went. I set them alight and sat back down on the couch. We both watched the flames, the floating bits of charred paper, until there was nothing but ash.

"Abraham Lincoln, Charles," I said then.

"It's over?"

"Yeah."

He blinked at me and shook his head in shock. "I thought... I thought there was going to be more. Worse. The two tops I had before—"

Were lazy fucks who didn't know what they were doing, I thought. "I could have done a lot of ugly things," I interrupted aloud. "But that wasn't the point of this, was it? For me to do as many horrible things to you as I could?"

"No," he conceded, "It wasn't. It was about turning me into a slave."

He met my eyes. "I figured that out this morning, while I was making you breakfast. If you made me suffer what they suffered than you made me one of them. A slave. Not a slave owner like my ancestors. That's why you tried to make my punishments correspond with what happened in the accounts. Why you didn't hold back when it came to rubbing salt in the wounds. Why you made me angry enough to fight back. Am I right? Is that what you were trying to do?"

"Did it work?" I had to ask. *Or did I completely fuck things up?*

"I don't know." He blinked. "I do know that every time you burned some of those papers I felt a difference, deep inside, as if chains were being removed from my bones."

Not all for nothing then. I sighed with relief.

He shook his head. "I still can't believe it's over. I thought we were going to go on for... a while longer," he finished lamely, and I didn't think that was quite what he'd meant to say. "It's like... waking from a dream."

"A lot of guys tell me that."

He looked suddenly lost, forlorn even. "You'll be leaving."

"Time to return to the twenty-first century," I agreed. "You know," I felt compelled to add, "Whatever lingering effects slavery has had on this country, most Southerners, black and white, do live in the present rather than in the past."

"I do know that, Mason. First-hand." He sounded a little irked; I guess I'd been patronizing. "My neighborhood was multicultural.

There was a mosque and Buddhist temple, and I went to school with kids of all kinds." He shrugged. "It made no difference when it came to this obsession. It's not rational."

"I understand, really I do. But sometimes the obsessed can be made to see reason." I leaned in. "Even a bleeding heart liberal like yourself has to believe that we have some choices. That we're responsible for what we do. So let your ancestors take their own damn blame for the decisions they made. We moderns have enough on our own plates with our own lives; we don't need to pile on every misdeed of our forefathers."

"Point," he conceded.

"And Charles, as a modern man, I have to tell you, I can't get behind the vengeful spirit thing. I mean, you die, and then, with the secrets of the universe open to your ethereal form, all you can think to do is haunt the living? What a colossal waste of time."

A smile touched his lips. "Damn, you fight dirty."

"In love and war," I agreed, standing up. "I have to go."

"Right now? I mean... what about the favor?"

"The favor." What about it indeed? "What do you do?" I realized I'd never asked him. "For a living?"

"Me? I... I'm a vet." The eyes dropped, as if he feared I'd laugh at him. "Well, still doing my residency. I work for an animal rescue center treating abused pets."

I stared at him. Someone in the universe was surely fucking with me. Classically trained, gorgeous body, smart, masochistic... *and* he was an animal lover?

"Okay." I took in a breath. "I haven't got a pet, not yet, but I've been thinking of getting a cat. When I do, I'll bring kitty into you for a free check-up and we'll call it even."

"What? That's nonsense," I heard him say as I made for the door, and, "Mason, wait—" but I was already out and closing off his words behind me.

I walked away very fast, breathing hard as if I, also, had just been freed from some very strange chains. It was a bit of a shock to see the sun up in that bright blue sky and realize it was past noon. To see cars, neighbors walking their dogs, kids on skateboards, all normal, all as if it were just another day. The way I felt at that moment, completely out of sync with the world... it was as if Charles and I had been in a time bubble.

Which wasn't how I typically came out of such sessions. Usually... usually I felt on top of the world, like I'd just stepped off a stage with wild applause for my performance still ringing in my ears. Usually I felt ready to return to normal life, confident and satisfied that I'd gotten what I wanted, and my playmate had gotten all he'd wanted and more.

This time had been different, however. There'd been nothing of "pretend" in what I'd done or in what Charles had experienced, no parts played, no stage to strut my stuff. It had all been very real, up close and personal. And I was left with... I don't know what. Something I'd never experienced before. I ought to have been relieved to have finally escaped Charles and his strange obsessions, to be finished with that damnable exorcism. But I wasn't. For some reason, leaving Charles hurt. It hurt like hell.

Two weeks later I arrived at the Cockpit to hang with Robbie the bartender and watch a little Saturday sports before the regular crowd arrived. The bar opens at noon on weekends, but it usually stays pretty empty until around three when folk start to arrive in anticipation of Happy Hour.

Such was the case when I stepped in at around two that afternoon. The Pit was empty and hollow but for red-haired Robbie setting up glasses and pulling bottles out of boxes. I nodded to him as I came in.

"Thank God," he breathed to my surprise and pointed. "He's been here since noon waiting for you."

It was Charles. I hadn't even noticed him because he was standing up against the wall, as if the night had already begun and he was hoping to be picked.

"Charles?" I said, crossing his way. He'd been staring at his perfectly polished boots. His head came up at the sound of my voice and he hurried forward to meet me. He went right to his knees.

"Hey, no," I said. "Not before Happy Hour."

"What? Really?" He frowned, but obediently got up. "Now, that's a curious rule."

The warm inflection of that southern drawl fairly melted me. Damn, he looked good, relaxed and easy, shoulders accented by that tight, white tee. My cock, recognizing his fragrance, came alert. It was remembering how it had felt to dominate that body. I wanted to do it again. Right that very moment. It was fucking hard to keep my hands out of his hair, to keep from pressing my lips to his and sticking my tongue down his throat.

Shit. In training him to like the kisses, I'd trained myself!

I got us over to a booth where I relaxed back against the vinyl orange cushions as casually as I could. "You doing all right?" I asked. "Ghosts not bothering you?"

"Not since you kicked them out." He was gazing at me as avidly as I had him, as if he was re-acquainting himself with how I looked. "You sure did something, Mason. My head's never been quieter."

"Lonely?" I wondered aloud. Sometimes it wasn't all that good a thing when you turned a man's world upside down.

He shrugged. "It's different. I'm not saying my issues are gone. A man builds up something like that over a number of years... it takes that much to tear it down. The ghosts'll probably be back. But I'm hoping that maybe I can shield myself better next time. I think a lot on how you burned the slave accounts, as if you were telling the universe that I'd paid my dues."

"Rituals do work."

"Yeah." A wry twitch of the lips. "You weren't at all worried that you might burn down my place?"

I grinned. "I had plenty of water bottles nearby."

He smiled back. "So, I remind myself that there's been some sort of reckoning. I also keep in mind what you said about spirits having better things to do than haunt the living. That's become a mantra of sorts."

"Glad to hear it."

A moment of silence. There was a reason he was here to see me, and we hadn't gotten to it yet. He cleared his throat. Those delightful, pink spots of color were on his cheeks. "Most of all, I think about the kisses."

So do I.

"Out of everything you did," he went on, "and I do mean everything, the way you kept kissing me surprised me the most."

"You didn't think the big black man was gonna be a good kisser?"

He shook his head. "It surprised me that you kissed me at all. The first few times, I thought you were getting in my face so you could spit on me. That's what other tops did. They spit in my face and yelled about how much I deserved what I was getting."

I rolled my eyes. "How unimaginative."

"When you kissed me instead... I won't say it was like a Christian kiss of forgiveness. That's blasphemous and dead wrong." His gaze was steady. "Because you never thought there was anything to forgive."

"No," I agreed.

"What it was," he hurried on, "was reconditioning. I work with animals, I know all about conditioning. I'd accustomed myself to taking on the family blame, as if I'd done those evil things myself. As if I were a bad person. But you kissed me after each punishment as if I'd taken on *the punishment*, not the crime. You made me feel that I was making reparations, not just suffering retribution. You rewarded me for being a good person."

I shrugged in acknowledgement. He was right, but there'd been more to it than that. There'd been the selfish half. I hoped like hell he wouldn't see that half. I wasn't ashamed of it—but I wasn't proud of it either.

"You went for the roots not just the tree," he said earnestly. "I understand that. What I came here to know was... were the kisses just part of the plan? Like burning those papers?"

I shifted. "They were deliberate and intentional, yes."

"So there was nothing more to them?"

"I'm not sure what you're asking."

He sucked in a breath. "I'm saying that you gave me the most frightening time of my life. You also gave me the most amazing time. And if the kisses and the sex and the talks we had weren't just a way of curing my obsession, if they were more than that, then... I'd like to be your slave, for real."

I couldn't remember how to breathe. His eyes were on me. When I didn't answer, they slid away.

"You must get this a lot," he said, and I could almost feel his heart sinking. "You give a guy something that intense, and he falls in love with you."

In love?

My heartbeat notched up. I found my breath. "You'd be surprised, actually. Most guys just want the one-time thrill. Like bungee jumping or white water rafting. They don't want a steady diet of me any more than they want spicy food night after night. And those that do — well, I'm not intense 24/7. So if that's what you're thinking —"

"No!" he said quickly. "That's just it. I mean, I admit that when I approached you that night, I was only after you because — um — well, because you were an African-American sadist and I thought you could channel the ghosts —" he blushed, "That sounds really crazy stupid said aloud, doesn't it?"

"I've heard worst," I chuckled, then added slyly, "And are you saying that's all you were after?"

"Fuck no, but I figure the other thing I was after goes without saying."

I laughed.

"Here's the thing, that's what I was after when I sat next to you, but not by the time you walked out my door," he said, waving his hands helplessly. "I look at you now and I want to make you pancakes so you can lick maple syrup off my lips. I want to read great works of literature with you —"

"Great American literature," I corrected.

" — Great American literature and discuss it at two in the morning. I want to take sponge baths with you. I want more than just the intense part."

"You sound like you're auditioning for a part," I couldn't help murmuring. Usually I'm the one who overwhelms; it was disconcerting to be on the other side.

"I've been thinking about it for two weeks," he admitted, blushing furiously. "Look. I've got problems. We know that. And if you don't want to deal with them, just say so. But I think you like me, and I get a hard on just looking at you — or just hearing your voice. Jesus, Mary and Joseph, when you called my name just now —" He shivered.

"I'm not asking for a collar," he finished up, his gray eyes meeting mine. "Only that you give me a try. That we give each other a try. Rent with the option to buy."

It was the damn ghosts, I thought. This was their last punishment. They'd made Charles fall in love with a big black top. How ironic was that? The problem was, neither he nor the ghosts were seeing me for me. I don't mind the role-playing, not for a night or even a weekend. But I wasn't going to be a fantasy in any long-term relationship. And I wasn't going to lie to Charles about who I really was. He didn't deserve that.

"Charles," I said regretfully, "this isn't real. I put myself between you and those ghosts and made you think of me as your master and savior. But I didn't have your best interests at heart. I liked whipping and kissing you. I liked trying to recondition you. You've got to see me for what I really am: an asshole. I'm vain and I've got control issues that are off the scale—"

"And you're full of yourself," he put in, his unimpressed tone stopping me dead as a punch in the gut. "Yes, I know. I saw how you were here in the bar. I'm not blind. You love being the man of mystery, the prom queen who's got everyone wrapped around her little finger. You're a regular Scarlett O'Hara."

I gawked at him. "You did *not* just say that."

"I surely did say it," his drawl was thick now, his grin turned positively roguish. He leaned across the table. "Do you want to punish me for it?"

Damn flirt. How dare he dare *me*. I leaned in as well, putting us almost nose to nose. "Rules," I said.

"Go on."

"If I punish you it will be because *I* think you deserve it. And it will be for something you've done in the here and now. I'm not for hire. Not by your ghosts or your conscience." Meaning I wasn't going to scourge Charles of inherited or imagined sins. If all he wanted from me was someone to stand between him and his problems, he'd have to find someone else.

He blinked. "Agreed, Master."

"No." Fuck if I was going to let a man with a plantation obsession use that word. "*Sir*. You call me Sir."

"I could call you Miss Scarlett. Or Mr. Tibbs maybe?"

"You're pushing it."

"So you'll call me 'boy'?"

Shit. "I'll call you what I goddamn please."

"I know what you're doing," he said, steady on. "You can pup-pet me all you like, but don't think I don't know exactly what strings you're pulling."

"Good, because I expect my partner to be smart and have an imagination."

"Oh, I've got a very vivid imagination, *Sir*. Speaking of which, if I'm your partner, does that mean I get to help with the fantasies? I would love to be Robin to your Batman, Lois Lane to your Superman, Tonto to your—"

"I get the idea." Could I do that? Let him in on my exclusive game? I would have to surrender some control, some ego. "If I can use you," I hedged. "Anything else?"

"If it would please you, Sir," he said with only a hint of irony, "I sure would appreciate it if you gave me some protocols to follow. Walk behind you, fetch your drinks, open your doors? Whatever I need to do to satisfy you and make it clear to all those other boys that I'm your slave."

I eyed him sidewise. "You son-of-a-bitch. You want to rub our relationship in their faces, don't you?"

He smirked. The new boy had bagged the prom queen and he was damn proud of it. "I figure I've earned the right."

I guess he had at that. I sucked in a breath. A part of me said it was too good and it was never going to last. The other part of me said I was an idiot if I didn't grab it with both hands. Just thinking of the yin and yang push of strength to strength in our lovemaking had me buzzing with that Xi energy. I wanted to get us back to his place and punish him right now, till he writhed and moaned under my hands. Till he was my slave.

"Safe word?" I heard myself asking him roughly.

His eyes met mine. "Your name. Or shall I just bare my throat to you?"

So. He hadn't missed that part of the conditioning. I saw it in his face. He may not have completely understood at the time, but he did now: each time I'd made Charles offer me his throat, each time

I'd kissed him, I'd been asserting my claim on him. Growling to the vengeful spirits that he was mine. Not theirs. Not anymore.

"I think that's the real reason my head's been so quiet," Charles mused. "Because I know that I belong to you. You took ownership of me away from the ghosts with that slave auction. You maintained that ownership when you insisted they ask permission to even speak to me. And with every punishment, every paper burned, you cleared the ledger. I no longer owe the ghosts anything. It's all been transferred to you." He shook his head with wonder and disbelief. "*You stole away all their power!*"

"And conditioned you to think of yourself as mine," I admitted with rueful embarrassment.

"I've thought of myself as yours from that first kiss on the porch," he confided. "You know," he added, "You may be a modern man, but you go for the throat when you fight for possession. It's very primal. Very... seductive. Your own idiosyncrasy?"

"I have a lot of them." I reached out and ran my fingers through his curls. "A big black master with a white Southern slave," I murmured. "The guys along the wall are going to go ape shit."

I clenched my hand in his hair and he surrendered to me his throat, his lips, his tongue. Such a gentleman, I thought, claiming him as my own. Such a gentleman.

If you enjoyed this story, you can sign up for a free membership at
ForbiddenFiction and discuss it with other readers and the author
at the *Fancy Man and the Southern Gentleman* story page at
http://forbiddenfiction.com/story/T13-1.000081.

The Fancy Man and the Lipstick Lesbian

When the Fancy Man discovered lipstick lesbian Katie out in the Cockpit Bar's parking lot, weeping for her lost lover, he was all sympathy. Given how perfumed and delicate she was, however, he wasn't at all sure how to get the bar's tough leatherdykes to take her seriously. Then it came to him: he'd star her in a whipping scene at the bar. The problem? The best with a whip was leatherman Burke, and Burke was not only aggressively gay, but adverse to anything remotely feminine. Could Mason and his submissive, Charles, get these two to work together? More, could he get them to connect? This one looked to be beyond even the Fancy Man's magic. (M/M)

Chapter 1
The Yin Side

Connections between people aren't always direct. Like magnets with polar charges, they may repel when face-to-face rather than attract. Bring in another magnet, however, and the two can be linked. Putting it another way, sometimes lightning won't strike without a lightning rod.

One of the strangest such connections that I ever witnessed was put into motion late one Saturday night through a very stupid mistake. The lady involved thought it was Friday night and therein lies the mistake, especially when we're talking about the Cockpit bar.

The Cockpit is my hangout, a leather bar located at the untrendy edge of the trendy and very gay part of town. Once upon a time the bar was a regular dive owned by a retired airline pilot. He died and his wife sold the place to Master Nash.

Now, Nash is first and foremost an entrepreneur; he wants as many paying customers as he can get, so he's put as few restrictions on the Cockpit as possible. What does that mean? Well, let's just say this isn't your granddaddy's leather bar. Sunday through Thursday anyone of legal drinking age can come into the bar. Anyone, that is, who isn't drenched in aftershave or perfume. That old fashioned rule still remains in effect. The smell of the bar must be that of sweat, leather and beer. If the bartender thinks your artificial fragrance is too potent, he'll ask you to leave.

Other than that, the door is open and the welcome mat is out. Nash's reasoning is that there's no need to filter out anyone but troublemakers, and he has a point. Most heteros on the prowl won't be that interested in a gay bar, and gays who aren't into leather aren't going to bother with our little corner. The inquisitive will come to satisfy their curiosity and be gone or join the tribe. The bar will, in other words, weed out undesirables all on its own. Besides, who needs a doorman when you've got bears in chaps and chains smoking in the parking lot?

So even though anyone of drinking age can walk into the Cockpit, it's rare, very rare, that outsiders drop by. But what, you might be wondering, about Friday and Saturday nights? Well, those are the nights when the Cockpit caters to the community. Friday is ladies only (read: Leatherdykes). Saturday is gents only (read: leathermen and gays into SM). Those days are gender specific, and the bartender or doorman will have you prove your sex, by taking you aside and having you drop your pants if need be. Don't even bother asking about pre-ops and male identifying dykes. We've had those arguments with Nash and he doesn't want to listen — he's greedy, not open-minded.

There was no doorman that Saturday evening. It was one of those holiday weekends when most folk go out of town, and the bar scene gets quiet. By closing time, the Pit was nearly empty. I was still there with my new boy, Charles, shooting the shit with Nash and Burke, another top. Robbie and Jordan, the bartenders, were cleaning up.

One of the front doors was propped open to let in the night air. From the sound of it, the world outside was also drawing to a close. The rush of cars, the steps and chatter of pedestrians had been replaced by the sound of tree branches groaning in the wind. All was pretty much quiet and solitary. That's how we heard her.

"Trish! Trish, I know you're in there!" The voice was sweetly female and sobbing. It echoed through the empty streets. We exchanged looks. What the fuck was this?

"I've g-g-got a razor!" That got us on our feet. "Come out of the bar. Just come out and talk to me, please! I just want to know what I did wrong...."

I was out the door first, in time to see her kneeling there in the parking lot. She was wearing a shimmery, silky dress of pastel colors. A cascade of beautiful, satin brown hair curtained her face. One bare arm with twin slices dripped blood onto the pavement. She had the razor lifted for another cut.

"Hey, now," I said, reaching her and grabbing hold of that raised wrist. I'm a hulking black man and at that moment I was terrified. Not that the girl was going to do anything to me, but that I was going to accidentally damage her. There are times when I know exactly how Superman must feel living in a world where everything is fragile. I had such a moment then, touching her. She was as delicate as fine china and it wouldn't take much at all for me to bruise or break her.

I could just see myself in court trying to explain away assault charges. The judge would take one look at massive me, one glance at delicate she, and I'd be learning firsthand how to play the part of big black cellmate.

Oddly enough, the lady didn't shrink from me nor even fight my hold. "Tell her I just want to talk," she asked me, as if I knew what was going on and could help her. "I just want to understand...."

"She's not worth it, sweetheart," I said, toning my voice at a higher, gentler register. As a voice actor, I knew how to make my pipes work for me. "Put down the razor, huh?"

I was prepared for her to finally *see* me as a threat and start screaming. It's what most ladies in designer dresses would do if someone like me had a grip on them. But she just dropped the razor. It fell with a tink onto the pavement, and the girl bowed over her knees and sobbed her heart out.

"I don't understand," she said. "I'm pretty. I dress like they want me to and do what they want me to do. But it's never enough. I'm just... decoration."

"I know how that feels," I whispered, and gathered her close. She might as well have been a soap bubble for all that she weighed anything. Her silk dress felt very nice against the bare skin of my arms. I saw a glittering, matching purse and nabbed that with two fingers.

The girl made no protest as I lifted her up into my arms. She just rested her face against my shoulder, tears wetting my tank. She didn't reek of perfume, but she did smell sweet and flowery. Bath spray, perhaps? She instinctively held her bleeding arm away from her body so as not to ruin her frock. Blood trickled off it to drip onto the asphalt.

"I thought it was real this time," she hiccuped for breath. "But it wasn't. It never is. Not with me."

"There, there," I said, taking her back to the Cockpit. The other guys were waiting at the door. "Robbie, medical kit," I said as I swung the girl in sideways. I brought her over to a booth and settled her in. Charles slid next to her with a handful of napkins to blot at her cuts. My partner is a muscular, Southern white boy with beautiful black curls and gray eyes to die for. He's a veterinarian in training so I figured he could handle this. He put pressure on the arm to slow the bleeding.

I reached across the table and brushed back the lady's long hair. The face beneath was pixyish, the skin unblemished and almost golden in hue. The weepy eyes were large with just a hint of an almond tilt to them, the irises a soft, tea brown color. The sniffling nose was small, the lips full. All in all, she resembled nothing so much as a tortoise-shell kitten, all honey and amber.

Her make-up was partially ruined from crying, but it was clear that she was... well, a girly girl. The kind who takes hours to put on her face. Her cheeks were rosy with blush, the eyelids expertly shadowed with contrasting pastels to match the dress. Her lips were swelled with gloss to a kissable allure. I don't think the Cockpit had welcomed in anyone so feminine since, well, since it was owned by the retired airline pilot.

You might be wondering how I felt about her, being that I am a leatherman. Which means I'm part and parcel of a subculture created, to some extent, as an argument against post-war America's stereotype of gay men as effeminate. Gathering as motorcycle clubs, the original leathermen proved to each other (if not to anyone else) that there was nothing "un-masculine" in men fucking men. Since being macho was one of their primary aims, it's not surprising that it's a leatherman requirement to this day, no matter what other changes new guards and post-modern guards have brought in.

Some rough and tumble daddies take this to mean that we have to sneer and shit on anything yin. I disagree. I may find black boots and beard stubble more alluring than spiked heels and lip gloss, but I've a mother and a sister who I love dearly; I've "womanish" female friends who are as close to me as the guys I hang with at the bar. And I know that should I ever donate sperm, a girl like this could be my daughter.

It seemed counterproductive to me to hold femininity in contempt—but I must admit, it was odd to have something so... soft and painted in the Cockpit. Even the leatherdykes who frequent our bar don't bring such ladies with them.

"What's your name, sweetheart?" Nash asked as Robbie handed the medical kit to Charles. I could see the bar owner wasn't too happy. Nash is something of a sexist pig. Not that he'd ever be impolite.

Burke, a wiry top with a mousy, Fu Manchu mustache, was also looking unhappy, as if his clubhouse had been invaded. *Girls, ick! Cooties!* his expression seemed to say, though I noted that he'd taken off his hat in her presence. Strange. I'd never have pegged Whip-Master Burke as having such quaint manners.

"K-Katie," she sniffled and one-handedly got a tissue out of her purse to dab at eyes and runny nose. Her fingernails were lacquered with an opal-esque polish that went perfectly with the ensemble.

"Well, Katie, Trish is not here tonight. It's Saturday night. Men only."

She flushed very sweetly and her shadowed eyelids dropped over those kittenish eyes. "Oh." Tears were still welling and falling down her cheeks. "I thought it was Friday for some reason. I... haven't been keeping track of time very well. I'm so sorry." She glanced from one of us to the other. "I'm so embarrassed."

"You should be," scolded red-haired Robbie, his freckled face all scrunched up in anger. He looked a little like a bulked up leprechaun about to throw a tantrum. "What kind of a thing was that to do? Hurting yourself like that?"

"I didn't know how else to show her how much she meant to me," Katie whispered. "I wouldn't have done it here, but she moved out of her apartment and I don't know where she's staying. She comes here on Fridays and stays till closing." She shrugged a little. "We had these three, wonderful weeks together and I really thought she was sincere. Then she went back to Dora."

"Dora?" Charles echoed, gently applying antibiotic ointment to her cuts.

"This blonde leatherdyke." Katie bit her quivering lip. "Trish was just trying to make her jealous by dating me, and it worked and now they-they're... Trish won't return my calls. Or my e-mails. She says it was never serious and I need to move on. I had to do *something*."

"But you don't really want Trish back, do you?" Jordan, the Cockpit's jet-haired, bi-bartender was unsettled. He was the only one of us males eyeing Katie with anything like desire. If she'd had a riding crop in hand he'd probably have been on his knees and calling her "Mistress."

"N-no," she admitted, trying not to break down yet again. "But this k-keeps hap-happening to m-m-me. I fall for these dykes on bikes, and I think one really likes me. *Me*. Then I find out she was just using me to get to someone else, some other dyke on a bike. It-it's like they know if they date me, the girl they really want will notice them. I'm just... some accessory that makes them desirable."

I shifted uneasily. Katie was cutting too close to the bone. Most men want me for the same reason. Not because they really want me — at least, not as anything more than a fuck buddy — but because I make them look good. On more than a few occasions, the only thing a guy has asked of me was to be seen in my presence. I give them street cred, and other men who weren't looking their way before, suddenly become interested.

If the Fancy Man wants you, the logic is, you must be special.

I felt especially uncomfortable being reminded of this right now. Charles and I were still new as a couple, and I had my doubts that he wanted me for me. He had some strange obsessions concerning black men. But that's another story.

"Am I hurting you, Miss?" Charles asked Katie in that Southern drawl of his. He was bandaging the cuts.

She shook her head. She was the type who ached so deeply inside that nothing done to her flesh could hurt worse. The tears just wouldn't stop falling from her eyes.

Nash sighed with resigned disgust. "I'm heading home. Lock up, Robbie," he said, making his way out the door.

"I'm very sorry I troubled you all," Katie said to the rest of us. She stared forlornly at her bandaged arm. "I guess I... I guess we can see now why no one really wants me."

The girl was breaking my heart, and you can imagine what that meant she was doing to a romantic like Robbie. I saw him swallow, saw a troubled look on his freckled face. He grabbed my arm and pulled me aside.

"We've got to help her."

I stared at him. "We? What's this 'we,' white man?"

"Mason, come on, I'm serious."

"So am I. What the fuck do you mean, help her? Help her do what?"

"I dunno." He waved a disgusted hand. "Gain some respect from those leatherdykes instead of just being used."

"Jesus, Robbie, what do you think this is? A romantic comedy? Let's give her a make-over, turn her into the boi of every leatherdyke's dream and help her gain the perfect Syr?"

"You're the Fancy Man," he insisted, "If anyone can do something for her, you can."

Fancy Man is my nickname. It refers to flights of fancy, not fancy dresser, and I got it because my turn-on is giving men their sexual fantasies. Emphasis on the *men* there. I've never in my life done such a thing for a woman.

"I'm an actor, not a fairy god... daddy," I told Robbie now. "If you want me to dress up in drag and perform cunnilingus on her, maybe I can grant your wish, but I don't even know if she's being honest, or how many problems she's really got, let alone how to solve them."

Robbie frowned. He wasn't happy with me. "You'd do it if she was one of the regulars in this bar."

"Yeah, well, she's not. I can't save the world."

"Do it for me, then."

"Rob—"

"Have I ever asked you for a favor?" he suddenly demanded. "Any kind of favor? Ever?"

Shit. You have to understand. In my world, men fall into top or bottom categories. You get used to receiving deference or giving it, striding forward with an aggressive look, or retreating from another man's more powerful gaze. But Robbie was not a leatherman, he was a romantic. In his world, men were equal. Give and take. When he looked you in the eyes, he wasn't trying to intimidate you, and he wasn't going to be intimidated. He was expecting equilibrium, to be met halfway.

"No, you've never asked me for a favor," I admitted.

"So I'm asking for one now. Grant this girl her fantasy."

Never argue with an over-muscled leprechaun.

"Why don't we introduce ourselves," I said reasonably, "and find out if she even wants us involved. Okay?"

"Fine," he grudged and walked us back to the booth.

Chapter 2
The Yang Side

"Katie?" Rob smiled at her like he was her new best friend. "I'd like to introduce you to Mason. We call him the Fancy Man."

"Hey," I flagged up a hand as her red eyes blinked up and up at all 6'4" of me.

Her lips parted. "Oh, gosh, I've heard of you!"

Charles, who now had a comforting, brotherly arm around Katie, smirked. "Whaddaya know? You're even famous among the dykes."

"Well," Robbie said expansively, "then you've heard, he grants fantasies if he can. He wants to grant yours."

Burke and Jordan had been hovering near by, listening if not contributing. They went stiff now. Burke with dismay, Jordan with envy.

"That's... that's very nice of you," Katie said blushing with consternation. Her kitten eyes blinked back more tears, as if the thought of anyone being nice to her was overwhelming. "And you're really sexy and handsome, but I only like girls."

It was my turn to blush furiously and damn was I glad that my brown skin doesn't make it obvious. Charles threw back his head and laughed out loud. Robbie, the fucker, chuckled. Jordan and Burke hid smirks.

"Oh." Katie blushed again. "I misunderstood didn't I? I'm not stupid, not usually. I'm just... out of my league." She offered me an apologetic smile, and the difference it made was devastating. She was charming as hell when she smiled.

"You're in a foreign land," I agreed, warming to her. "Why don't you tell me what your fantasy is? Let me worry about whether it can be made real."

"My fantasy? I don't think I've ever really had one. I've just... tried to live out what I wanted."

Oh, she was getting to me now. If my cock had been at all interested in her, I would have claimed her myself.

"I suppose..." she went on, thoughtfully, "I suppose, at the moment, my one fantasy is for those leatherdykes to really desire me. I'm sick of being treated like a toy, like something to amuse them while their motorcycles are in the shop. I mean, I know clothes and shoe shopping and make-up seem frivolous. Are frivolous. But are they that much more frivolous than detailing a car or getting a tattoo?"

She glanced earnestly at us. I thought she had a valid point, but Burke's face had gone white with outrage. Before he'd started selling handmade whips over the internet Burke *had* detailed cars and motorcycles for a living. He certainly didn't want to hear his previous livelihood called frivolous, let alone mentioned in the same breath as shoe shopping.

"I don't expect to be taken seriously," Katie went on, tears falling again. "I just want those bitches, for once, to want me as much as they want those girls they do take seriously. I want them to fight over *me*, the real Katie, not over what they think I am or what they think I can do for them."

Now there, I thought with a stirring in my blood, was a challenge. The problem, as Katie had pointed out, was that the silk dresses, the long shiny hair and perfume, would always make her seem more plaything than playmate. Leatherdykes, like leathermen, liked to play rough, and Katie was just too breakable. She wasn't for everyday use. On the other hand, trying to change her, make her more butch, would turn her into someone she wasn't and defeat the purpose.

"Give me a moment to think on this," I said, stepping away. Robbie came with me.

"So?" he said.

"Well, I can think of one easy answer. Jordan." I motioned over the other bartender.

He joined us. "What's up?"

"If Katie is seen making out with a handsome man, it will certainly draw the competitive attention of the other ladies," I pointed out to Robbie while eying Jordan.

The jet-haired bartender got the hint. His face paled. "Oh, no," he gulped. "Mason, no. I can't."

I frowned. "Why not? You're already drooling over her."

Jordan has these dark blue, guileless eyes. Just about anything he's feeling can be read in them, and at that moment he was miserable. "That's just it. I *like* women. I like her. But she doesn't like men. I haven't a hope in hell with her. You might as well drag my heart through the dirt, not to mention my cock. Don't make me do it."

Jordan's not a leatherman. He's a bisexual who's into SM. Which is why he says things like *"Don't make me do it."* He's a boy at heart. Charles has a manly strength I can push against. Jordan has none. I could rip the bartender apart like tissue paper and he knew it. A part of me wanted to, and a part of him wanted me to as well. We both knew we had to show restraint, or, after an orgy of self-indulgence, we'd both be ruined. So I cut off that sadistic streak in me, the one urging me to loom over him and say, very soft and cold, *"You will do it."*

The image gave me a thrill all the same. Someday... someday in some judicious manner, Jordan and I were going to have to have it out. But that wasn't for tonight.

"All right," I said instead. "We'll think of something else." Jordan released a breath of relief.

"What about you as the lover?" Robbie suggested.

"Don't be daft. Everyone in the bar knows Jordan's bi, so it makes sense for him to go for Katie. They're not going to believe I would. They know me too well."

"Charles?" he suggested. My boy was still a new face in town, his sexual orientation not yet firmly established.

I rolled my eyes. "I'll ask, but I don't think he can pull it off." Back to the booth.

"...for all their toughness, they just couldn't bring themselves to really flog someone," I heard Burke saying to Katie as I came up. It surprised me. The last expression on Burke's face had been one of revulsion, as if Katie were some soft worm leaving a trail of tears and perfume all over his manly bar. Yet now he was conversing with her quite earnestly.

"I don't think that was it. I think they just held back with *me*," Katie said, her sweet, demure manner contrasting with the topic. "Their beatings weren't genuine, if you know what I mean, they never gave me that rush, that drifting off on a cloud of sensations. But then," she added sadly, "I wasn't the one those dykes really wanted to flog."

How the *hell* had they gotten onto this subject? Charles glanced over at me, eyebrows lifting to tell me he'd had nothing to do with it and was just as confounded.

"More likely they just didn't know how to do it properly," Burke said. "Most folk don't take lessons like they should. They just go at it. And they don't realize how much practice it takes to really get that swing. To build up the arm."

"True. But you can't instruct them when you're tied up and they're in the heat of the moment," Katie pointed out quite seriously. "I tried to advise one of my daddies to use both hands with a belt but she just wouldn't listen."

"Got a sore wrist, did she?" Burke tsked.

"Well, she already had a bad elbow. She really shouldn't have been doing it at all." Katie shook her head. "But you know leather-dykes. They never can admit a weakness."

"I just wish they'd admit they don't know what the fuck they're doing!" Burke groused. It was one of his pet peeves.

"I wish they'd use something other than floggers," Katie had her own bone to pick. "I mean, I've nothing against floggers. Some of them sting just fine. But you don't get that pop that comes with a single tail."

There was a glint in Burke's eyes now. Katie had pushed the magic button. "Most powerful sound in the world," he agreed fervently. "Better than gunfire. You've seen demonstrations?"

"Oh, yes. Several. I was even part of one back in college. The brother of the girl I was dating at the time had a black snake—"

"Excuse me," I ventured to interrupt. An idea had sparked in my head, and I could feel it beginning to smolder. "I think... I think I may have a way of giving you your fantasy, Katie. Burke, if I can talk to you for a moment."

Burke is half a foot shorter than me and sinewy rather than strapping. The arm I put around his shoulders must have felt like a boa constrictor. He frowned suspiciously as I led him toward the island bar.

"Top to top, brother," I said, leaning on one of western style bar-stools. "Would you help me help her?"

He blinked. I might as well have asked him to go dress shopping with the girl. He tensed like a roadrunner readying for a dash.

"A whipping scene," I said quickly. "Here at the Cockpit."

The tension in his body eased. But he was still blinking. He glanced back, regarding Katie as he might a damp pile of used silk handker-chiefs. His expression said, *what the fuck am I suppose to do with these?*

"She's a girl," he said at last.

I raised my brows. "Really. Hadn't noticed."

"I don't *do* girls, Mason." He meant that in every sense of the word. Burke was a leatherman's leatherman. He whipped other leathermen. Had whipped them with everything from bamboo sticks to heavy chains one memorable year on the Delta run. Men three times Burke's bulk and muscle broke down sobbing for mercy under his kind min-istrations. And then he took them to bed and fucked them.

"So you can't do it?" I asked mildly.

That got me a hard look. Burke was no fool.

"'Course I can. I just won't. It doesn't interest me, and if it doesn't interest me I won't do it."

"Okay. That was wrong of me. I apologize for trying to play you like that."

"Accepted," he muttered.

"But come on, it's just a scene. And I can't do it like you. No one can. Think of it as a creative challenge. Hey," I added as the spice, "you heard her. She loves the sound of a cracking whip as much as you do. She'll appreciate what you're doing on an artistic level, not just for the pain you're inflicting."

That tempted him. Burke had always felt that his true efforts and abilities weren't appreciated. That the men he whipped were taking him and his genius for granted. He chewed on one corner of his mus-tache.

"I'll have to research," he ventured, sounding nervous. "Females, I mean."

Now it was my turn to be uncertain. "Research? You *do* know female anatomy, don't you?"

Another glare, this one daring me to crack a smile. "Not up close and personal," he said defensively. "No."

"You're kidding, right?"

He glanced away, arms crossed. "I ran away from home when I was twelve, Mason. I didn't go through high school and dating and being all confused about my sexuality like the rest of you. I knew what I wanted, and by the time I was legal, I'd done a lot of it. I never bothered with anything else. Why should I? I like what I like."

I was surprised. Burke had never mentioned his family or personal history. I suppose, like everyone else, I'd just assumed he'd appeared full-grown at the Cockpit, pool cue in hand.

"I didn't know —"

"S'kay," he flagged me off. His expression was strangely vulnerable, but the last thing Burke was going to do was discuss his feelings or deprived childhood. *Fuck therapy*, he'd say. In Burke's universe, men just didn't do that. All the same, I felt I'd gotten a glimpse, as if by lightning flash, of a very bleak landscape.

"I'd appreciate it if you do this for me," I said, notching my voice down to a solid masculine register. Man to man. "I'll help you with the research, set-up, everything. I'll answer any questions."

He was chewing on the other half of his mustache now. I could tell that my offer to help him fill in those holes in his education helped. They had to be something of a sore spot to him because they could make him look stupid. Burke hated being taken for a fool.

"All right. One rule," he added. "You defer to my judgment. I know how you like to run a show, Mason, but it's gonna be *my* skills on display. My reputation. I'm not going to allow anyone to fuck that up. It's that or nothing."

"Deal." It was the quality I most appreciated in Burke. The man was an impresario, a perfectionist. When it came to his chosen art form, nothing less than the very best would do. And I could certainly appreciate his desire for complete control. "Let's see if all this sits well with the lady."

I explained to her and the others what I had in mind. Robbie lifted a skeptical, ginger brow; he still didn't get the whole leather scene. Jordan, well, he sat down to hide his erection. Charles looked thoughtful and Katie... Katie was doubtful.

"This is going to make them want me?" she asked. "I mean, no disrespect, Mr. Fancy Man —" Charles smiled at her courtesy. " — but," she went on, "I've let them whip me any way they liked and I still got dumped."

"This will be different," I assured her. "Those dykes on bikes think you're just a pretty lipstick who can only take a good spanking. Burke's going to show them how far you can really go. Who you really are. They'll be falling all over themselves to get to you when he's done. Especially if they know every other sister wants you, too."

"That sounds... exciting," her tone was only half convinced. "But, are you sure?" This to Burke. She was looking very dubiously at him, as if someone had handed her a studded leather belt and told her to make it go with her prettiest dress.

Burke shrugged. *Thanks for the vote of confidence, Brother Burke.*

Katie bit her pouty lower lip. "It's going to take a lot of practice, isn't it?"

The whip-master shrugged again. He looked uneasy, but he'd agreed and Burke never went back on his word. "Yeah. I can manage if you can. Have you got protective clothing? Thick leather pants? Goggles?"

"You give me a list and I'll get it all." She pulled out a smart phone in a glittering gold and pink rhinestone holder and set to typing in what was needed. Burke told her what she had to have, and the two of them, leatherman and lipstick lesbian, worked out a schedule while the rest of us watched with bemusement.

I had no idea where this was going or how it was going to work out, but it was certainly going to be...different.

"Those dykes on bikes think you're just a pretty lipstick who can only take a good spanking. Burke's going to show them how far you can really go."

Chapter 3
Polarization

There'd been some discussion and debate with Nash over the right night for our "scene." The Cockpit is a small bar, but Burke insisted on plenty of room and a cording off of the area. When it came right down to it, the pool table would have to be moved. Nash didn't like that, not until I suggested charging a modest admission price. I even floated the idea of a percentage of the take going to the local leatherdykes' motorcycle club. If there was a charitable allure, then we'd get even more people and more money. Nash liked that.

Friday night was the most logical night, but Nash pointed out that Burke had his own fans, men who admired his whipping skills, and they would miss out. Besides, Nash didn't want the leatherdyke dating scene disrupted. So we agreed on a Sunday evening. I had Nash hand out flyers on the two prior Friday nights and got the event listed on the bar's website and on that of the leatherdykes' club.

Over those next two weeks I rushed about, arranging for the staging and clothes, publicizing the event. I even made sure to get a permit for the event. I wrote it up in the paperwork as "performance art." We'd be fine so long as Katie's private parts were covered.

I did manage to stop by in between all this to watch a few practice sessions in Burke's backyard. These, however, left me biting my nails. It wasn't that Burke was having any problems with accuracy. With Katie laid out on the picnic table in his backyard, he was quickly getting down the points, and, being a master, hitting them precisely. Leather pants and jacket notwithstanding, Katie let out some satisfying yelps when the whip struck tender areas.

The problem was that Burke was showing very little interest or passion for whipping Katie. The form was there, but the artistry was lacking. I mean, I knew he would rather be marking up firm, masculine flesh, but if he didn't put his heart into this we were screwed.

And Katie... Katie wasn't much better. She tried, and granted she wasn't feeling the full effect of the whip garbed as she was. But there was no enthusiasm. I think that was due less from wanting Burke to be a woman than from the fact that her whip-master wasn't into whipping *her*. No electricity was being transmitted.

And then there were the inevitable arguments.

"No high heels!" Burke had snapped that first time Katie arrived in a pair of designer boots. "I said no high heels!"

"They're only two inches," she protested.

"They're making divots in my lawn!"

"Well, isn't that a good thing?"

It was like Abbot and Costello.

Katie had her own complaints, of course. "Don't you ever bathe?" she'd asked, wrinkling her nose at Burke's ripe fragrance. "Or shave? Or wash your clothes?"

"Why bother?" Burke quipped back. "Men like how I stink. An' if we're going to go on about that, do you have to use all those perfumed products? Bath foams and creams and shit? You smell like a whorehouse."

"How would you know?"

Not surprisingly, the arguments had spilled over into the look of the performance as well.

"Cut out the make-up," Burke insisted. "People want to see a face, not paint. You look like you're in a kabuki play."

"Well, that mustache makes you look like one of the Village People," Katie threw back. "Talk about ridiculous. The 70's revival is over."

They didn't hate each other, but they certainly had some issues. Including Burke's house. Seeking a glass of water, Katie had taken one look at Burke's kitchen and started bringing her own bottled refreshment. But kudos to her courage, she'd only begged for my intercession with the whip-master once.

"Can't you please ask him to clean the bathroom?" she'd nearly wept. "I don't mind the dirty pictures, but the toilet and the floor... it's disgusting!"

Knowing Burke wouldn't clean up his act for Katie, I'd dragged Charles and a box of cleaning products over to the whip-master's place one afternoon.

"My bathroom's clean. Mind if I put my slave to work on yours?" I asked Burke. "I owe you for what you're doing anyway."

Being a polite top, Burke had obliged me, or at least pretended that he was helping me to work my boy. If he knew what I was really about he didn't let on. We drank beers and watched Charles, dressed only in a jock strap, scrub and de-rust the toilet, scrape and polish the floors and pipes and sink till they... well, they didn't sparkle, that would be too much to ask of any slave; but they weren't so repellent.

Which all led up to a telling moment between Charles and me. If a brother may digress...

I said that Charles and I still have new couple smell. It was more than that. He was, you see, my first real slave. My usual modus operandi is to go home with a guy and play master/slave for an evening. Sometimes, if I like the boy, I'll do it again, maybe even on a regular basis. But I'd never wanted anything lasting, not until I met Charles.

I'd barely known Charles Beaumont five minutes before I'd started thinking of him as mine. Mine as in territory. As in property. As in partner. He was the first man I'd ever met that I wanted to mark, tattoo my name on his ass and piss on him just to be sure everyone knew he belonged to me. So I'd stupidly said yes when he'd suggested that we take our relationship for a long drive.

Now I had a responsibility, and it made me nervous. With guys like us it's not just about merging personalities, it's making sure the top cares and is inventive, is masterful, not just brutal. Likewise, the bottom has to be honest and open to new experiences, submissive but not passive. It's a very delicate balancing act, especially when it involves love and sex — and making sure we both got it right was all on me. Honestly, I was as worried about failing Charles as he was about failing me.

So while Charles scrubbed the bathroom floors, I eyed the graphic images Burke had torn out of gay porno mags and plastered on the bathroom walls, seeking out ideas. Charles and I were certainly strong enough to pull off some of those positions, but were we flexible enough? Maybe yoga classes were in order. I was about to say as much to Burke when the phone rang and the whip-master went off to answer it. Charles took the opportunity to pause in his scouring.

"Sir," he said to me. "After this... is there any other way I can serve Master Burke?"

This cleaning project had been a surprise to Charles. I hadn't warned him, I'd just told him to put on a jock strap under his trousers and had taken him to the store to pick out the products. Like I said, a master's job is to be inventive, to give a slave new challenges and experiences. When Charles' had seen the bathroom, his face had gone blank for a moment with horror. Then, like a good boy, he'd said, "Yes, Sir," stripped down, and gone to work.

Now, Charles took *me* by surprise, as he sometimes did. I hadn't even considered gifting him to Burke afterwards. Thinking on it, however, it was clear that I'd been remiss in not considering this. Was Charles pointing that out to me? I took one giant step through the bathroom door and went down into a crouch, putting us face to face.

"Hands to head," I said and as he dropped the scrub brush to put his palms up, I reached for the elastic band of his strap. I pulled and jerked it down, exposing his cock, then slipped the band under his balls. He gulped, and his gray eyes flickered with apprehension. Charles gets aroused by humiliation. Exposing him even in this mild way made him blush furiously. His cock naturally began to swell, which made him blush even more. That made my cock respond in turn.

"Are *you* offering, Cadet?" I had nixed the use of words like "master," "slave" and "boy," between us for obvious reasons if you know anything about how and why we met. I was rather pleased with "Cadet" as a substitute. "Or do you think *I've* made the offer?" I added, stroking behind his balls. It was a sensitive spot for him, and his breath came short, even as his eyes grew angry. He couldn't offer himself—he belonged to me, only I could offer him to another—and he had no idea if I'd done the offering. That's what he wanted to know. I was fucking with him.

"Sir," he said, in that gentleman's drawl of his. "I assumed my ass was part of the favor owed to Master Burke, Sir."

A nicely ambiguous answer. On the one hand, it allowed Charles to obliquely present me with an idea on the oft chance I might need one. On the other hand—in case I had already thought of it—it let me know that Charles was game. A good master finds out how well his slave can swim before throwing him into dangerous waters—and whip-master Burke could certainly be more than some slaves could take. Charles was telling me he was up to it, both up to being shared, and up to whatever Master Burke demanded.

Or, more succinctly: if I was planning on springing any more unpleasant surprises on him... well, bring 'em on. The fucker. Made me love him.

I brought his jock strap back up into place. "You assumed wrong, but only because I forgot my manners. Thank you for reminding me of the courtesies, Cadet. I'll see if Master Burke's interested."

Burke came back from his phone call. I took him aside and made overtures. Charles' sweaty labor had aroused him, so he accepted my offer.

Charles' expression when we *both* went into Burke's bedroom was priceless. Even more so when Burke, kneeling on the bed, got Charles out of his jock strap, handed him a condom and, once it was on, started to suck the Southern boy's cock. Ha. That'll teach Charlie to assume. It was one of the interesting ironies of the leather world. A leather top can be, in vanilla terms, a bottom sexually. Burke liked receiving far more than giving.

I gloved and lubed up and gave Burke a very good ass fucking while he blew Charles. The real moment came when Charles and I gazed at each other over Burke's prone form. Our thrusts were so in time, back and forth, they were almost coordinated. A connection flashed between us, and we both started to come. We finished almost simultaneously, leaving the whip-master a happy man. Great sex, and his restroom was cleaner than it had been in years.

As for Charles... I took him back to his house and gave him a long, warm bath. Then I let him have what he really wanted as a reward for being such a good lad. Do you know, he even moans with a Southern accent?

Getting back to Burke and Katie: they didn't hate each other. They just had no reason, as Robbie would have put it, to meet each other halfway. If she'd been interested in Burke's dick, then Katie might have made an effort, as girls do, to buy him a six-pack of his favorite beer and learn a little about the sports he enjoyed watching. If he'd been at all interested in Katie's pussy, Burke might have bothered to wear clean underwear or get a shave. There was no such interest. As Burke had put it, he liked what he liked, and the same went for Katie. Why should either of them surrender an inch? Especially given that their hook up was temporary and for this one event only?

That said, they did respect the whip. For all his complaints about Katie's girliness, Burke could not fault her when it came to practice. She gave her all, working as long as Burke demanded, and then suggested they try one more time. And though Katie may have thought Burke vulgar, he never dressed her down or lost patience with her when that whip was in his hand.

They didn't even take their frustrations out on me, though, Lord knows, I deserved it. Now and then I had to let Katie weep on my shoulder and Burke vent, but they never berated me for my stupid idea. It gave me new respect for Burke, a man as solid as concrete, and for Katie, who managed to stay aloft like a bird on the wind.

I started to lose sleep, worrying that the whole thing would belly flop. If it did, Burke and Katie would be left with egg on their faces, all thanks to me.

That Sunday night finally came around, and we got quite a crowd of dykes mingling with the leathermen. They milled about, their buzz-cut heads moving in and out of view round the screened-off area.

"How're you doing?" I asked Burke and Katie, stepping behind those folding partitions.

"All right, I think," Katie said, wiping sweaty palms down the belted coat she wore over her costume.

Burke was far less nervous. He focused down before demonstrations. He gave me his "don't-bother-me-with-stupid-questions" look. On the other side of the screens, the crowd was getting restless.

"Up you go, Katie!" I said as she slipped off the coat. Burke came over and we got her arranged and comfortable.

"Ready?"

Burke picked up his whip, and licked his lips. He gave me the nod. I waved a hand outside the partitions and Robbie helped me to fold and carry them away. The crowd's chatter went down to a murmur as the two of them appeared.

Chapter 4
Voltage

Behind velvet ropes was a wide, clear area where the pool table had been. Burke, in black leather pants, vest, gloves and biker's cap, stood there with his whip. His corded muscles, the brush of fur on his chest, his tattoos made him into an iconic figure.

Suspended before him was Katie. I'd gone for simple ropes hanging from the ceiling to cradle her thighs; the thick, soft loops kept her braced and spread. For the wrists, chains and padded cuffs. She was mostly horizontal but the ropes were positioned so that she could sink into them a little and be less so if need be. She appeared to be floating.

Wearing thigh-high boots and a leather thong that barely hid anything, she appeared both delicate yet lushly feminine, her nearly bare ass very round and soft. Unscented glitter lotion added a sparkle to her skin, and a pair of leather falsies, chains between them, hid her nipples in a way that complimented Burke's leather look, as did the biker's cap atop her lose, satin brown hair.

"It's striking," Charles breathed as I stepped over to a spot reserved for me at the bar, and put a supportive hand on my shoulder.

It was. A larger man than Burke would have made it disturbing; a picture of heavy male dominance over helpless femininity. But Burke's leanness, his symbolic look, allowed the audience to see him as purely leather, the rough, earthiness of it, neither male nor female. Likewise the emblematic leather and chains accenting Katie allowed her to be seen as Burke's androgynous, airy counterpoint. Yin to Yang. Yang to Yin.

Burke seemed as stunned as the audience by the scenario; he remained frozen for a minute, and I thought he was going to choke. I'd had Katie model her costume for him and he'd just shrugged and stepped around her to professionally mark with his eyes where to strike with his whip. Now, however, he was faced with her there, a near naked woman, up-close and personal. He could make out the rose of her labia to either side of that leather butt floss. He could probably smell her sex.

He looked ready to throw up. Or perhaps he was just frightened of this new canvas hanging before him, demanding he use it.

He gulped, and let the whip drop down to his side. A flick of the handle caused the leather to slither like a snake. A gunfire crack rang out. The crowd twitched and caught their collective breath. Katie's head came up, as if she'd just heard her lover's voice.

And that's when Burke and Katie connected. The panic left Burke's eyes, and he got that look we all knew, one that said he was "on." Katie's body shifted, as if easing into a yoga position, indicating her readiness. The whip went up over Burke's head, right into a swirl. This was why he'd wanted plenty of room. So he could circle that leather. Off it went. Sailing toward Kate's vulnerable ass.

Crack!

Katie's head went up, her long hair swung and she released a cry that was more like a song. It mingled with the echo of the whip's snap, there in the air. Across her left ass cheek was a fine, horizontal welt. It blushed pink, then reddened almost to purple. Burke was swinging again, his body moving like a dancer. The whip looped and snapped out.

"Ah!" Katie sang, and a matching welt rose on her right cheek.

Burke picked up speed now. The whip flourished and snapped, one-two, so fast the audience gasped. Twin marks reddened the insides of Katie's thighs, right between boot tops and ass cheeks. Her gasp became a delicious moan.

The leatherdykes were breathless. They were in awe of Burke's skill, envisioning themselves in his place, creating those welts, eliciting that moaning music from beautiful Katie. Come to that, *my* cock was twitching. There was no stopping it, any more than I could stop my imagination from feeling Burke's energy and control or the sting of Katie's welts.

Male crotches all around joined me, swelling with captured erections. Hands went southward.

A snap like a gunshot as Burke sent the whip under Katie's suspended form. The leather tip flicked up before retreating, caressing her right between her breasts. The touch was so light, the chains there barely swayed. Burke's control of the whip was that masterful. Katie's breath sucked in, and in the dim light we all saw a glimmer as a slick wetness spread down from her crotch to dampen her inner thighs.

"Jesus," Charles breathed.

"What she's got that we poor males don't, Charlie boy," I murmured. "Her whole body's a sex organ."

"I have got to get me a girl."

I elbowed him.

Crack! Crack!

Another pair of welts and Katie's reddening ass squirmed; her wrists twisted in their padded cuffs.

"Oooooh," she moaned.

Members of the audience were jockeying for position now. Some wanted to watch Katie's lovely face, tears trailing down from her shut eyes. Others wanted to gaze up at the responsive ripple of her belly and pelvis. The rest were fixated on the welting of ass and thighs, the juices dripping from the barely hidden cleft between.

Crack!

Back again to the right ass cheek, and — *Snap!* — to the left. Katie's ass now had a trio of welts. Her breath caught, and caught again. Her tender backside had to be burning, the welts searing like white-hot metal.

Suddenly, she started to struggle against the ropes and the cuffs, as if she knew what was coming and had lost her nerve.

Burke said not a word, instead he threw out the whip, snapping it at her ass yet again. The crack of it called her name, commanded her attention even as vertical wheals appeared right through the horizontal welts on both cheeks. Katie's hands fisted as those acid lines seared her and all of us watching gasped in astonishment at Burke's incredible artistry.

And then, as if those final marks had been kisses from Burke rather than bites , Katie stopped struggling. She relaxed into the ropes, her moment of doubt gone, answered by Burke in those last, perfect strokes. Her thighs spread even wider, a gesture of absolute trust and surrender. *Yours, Master,* her posture seemed to say, with conviction and faith. *All yours.*

I heard Charles choke. His hand was at his crotch. I sympathized; sparks were going off in my tight, high balls, and my erection was throbbing against the denim of my jeans. Everyone's eyes were locked on Burke and Katie.

Burke spun the whip, up, over his head like a whirlwind. The audience went tense. What now?

Crack! Crack!

Up strokes, masterfully aimed at the most tender spots, just next to the red lips peering round the thong. A fine spray from her liberal juices went up into the air, shimmering in the faint light. Her cries were more like mews, plaintive, yearning.

The leatherdykes went weak in the knees, overcome with a desire to lick those tender welts. To explore those soft, wet folds. The air had gotten very thick and warm in the Pit, the breathing audible. The perfume of sex wafted up. Katie's most pungently, along with the smell of Burke's sweat. His ropey shoulders were glistening with perspiration, and there was a pool of it at the base of his throat. When he raised his arm, sweat dewed the hair underneath.

He moved as if in a trance, every muscle as sinuous. I don't think he knew anyone else was there. It was just him and her.

Another gunshot below her suspended body. This time the whip, amazingly, flicked up to brush her navel. Katie released a high note, her body jerking and rocking. Her red ass bore beautifully symmetrical welts, like a musical score, and her equally welted thighs were soaked in her slippery juices. Her head rolled, the light shimmering over her hair as her golden face appeared and vanished.

She was so lost in those jolts of pain and pleasure, in the rush of endorphins that her body was reacting to the breezing by, the crack and vibrations of the whip.

Her whip-master was panting now. I'd seen Burke swing heavy chains at a man's back and seem less exhausted. This was *art*, as much style and control as muscle, and he was putting every bit of himself into it. With great effort, he made the whip swirl and dance at his command once again, sending out some cracks, this time along the floor, under Katie. She writhed and moaned with each snap, as if it had scored her flesh. Beautifully responsive.

God. If those leatherdykes couldn't see what Katie was by now, all she was, they were fools. And if they didn't want her and all she could give them, they were idiots.

We were coming to the end, everyone, myself included, could feel it and we were all holding our breaths. Burke sent back the whip, then hurled it out before him so gracefully it seemed to sail. It didn't touch Katie, but the crack, the gunshot snap of it occurred right between her legs, and the sound of it, if not the delicate tip, must have hit her clit.

She jerked and jerked and cried out again and again. Her hair fell back, her face glowed with elation. She fucking orgasmed.

Burke took one step back, as if her response had sent a lightning strike right back at him, right through his heart. His tight leather pants showed a visible erection. As Katie sunk exhausted in her bonds, he snapped the whip, lightly at her ass twice more. Katie twitched as the tip stuck her on either ass cheek, like kisses. The finale.

And then the whip went still, lying there on the floor, depleted. Burke's lungs were heaving, Katie was sighing. And the audience... we were stone still. For a moment, no one was sure how to respond. This is the Cockpit and we're a small, backwater bar. We'd never had anything like this. But Burke's mastery of the whip, at least, deserved applause, and finally, someone started clapping. A cascade of cheers and whistles and whoops followed, a roar of enthusiasm.

I, myself, couldn't manage to join in. I was still blinking at Burke, head bowed, catching his breath and dripping perspiration, and Katie, basking in the afterglow. Charles' hand came under my chin, shutting my mouth. I hadn't even known that my jaw had come unhinged.

"You are so going to fuck me tonight," he murmured into my ear.

"In every orifice you own," I agreed, "and many that you don't."

As the applause died down, Burke finally blinked out of his trance and hurried to get Katie down. I nabbed some bar towels from Robbie, who was shaking his head in lingering shock, and got over there to help. Burke had her out of the ropes and was unlatching the cuffs when I tossed down the towels. And then the whip-master was sinking to the floor, cradling Katie in his sweaty arms.

I saw she was completely lost in what some call "subspace," her eyes dreamy and blinking without seeing, her breath coming faintly. So I set myself up to guard them, urging those pressing at the ropes to give the two room and time.

When next I glanced back at them, Burke, to my amazement, was kissing Katie. Kissing her on the mouth, beautifully and simply. It was the most chaste kiss I'd ever seen in my life, as if he was touching his lips to those of a saint.

What the fuck? I took a step near. Burke's head shot up, and I immediately stepped back. I was twice Burke's size and muscle but I would not have gone near Katie at that moment if a gun had been pressed against my head, not with Burke glaring at me like that. If I'd even tried to touch her I think he would have torn out my throat with his teeth, he was that protective of her right then.

"Oh, Daddy," Katie whispered. "You were magnificent!"

"So were you, Angel."

God, help us. They had pet names for each other! I hadn't intended this, and I could not fucking believe it, but there it was. No denying it. Burke had found his muse, and he was laying claim to her. If he'd snapped a collar on Katie's neck and branded his name on her ass he could not have made it more clear. And I would have sooner faced a rabid badger then argue the point with him.

"You carried me through it," Katie went on. "I could hear every word you said to me, in every sting and pop."

"I was just responding to you," Burke answered, stroking her hair, "Every move, every cry, I knew exactly what you wanted."

Right. This was getting way too intimate for me. Understand, they didn't want to fuck each other. In fact they likely would have made faces of disgust at the very idea. It wasn't even like with Charles and me, a Master/slave relationship. This was pure sadomasochism, the purest possible, as it involved just one instrument. Burke didn't want to dominate Katie, he just wanted to whip her. And Katie didn't want to submit to Burke, she just wanted to be whipped by him.

They'd finally found a reason to meet halfway. Or, to put it simply: love is a many splendored thing and these two... had fallen in love.

"I don't know how to thank you," Katie breathed to Burke, tears of joy in her eyes. "That was the most amazing experience of my life."

"I was about to say the same thing," Burke said wonderingly.

"Uh," Charles was at my shoulder, speaking in hushed tones as if in a library. "Master Nash wants to know if they're going to sit there all day. He wants to get the pool table back in."

"If Nash wants to try and move them," I whispered back, "he can try. I ain't gonna touch no one."

"Am I seeing what I think I'm seeing?" Charles asked.

"You're seeing it. And it's going to strike us all blind."

"Fuck me sideways."

"What a good idea," I murmured.

Chapter 5
Lightning Rods

We convinced Burke that Katie needed to go home. He agreed, wrapping the coat about her shoulders and keeping his arm around her the whole time. He opened the car door for her, buckled her in, and seated himself beside her. When we got to her apartment building, he got her out and escorted her up the stairs, refusing our help and telling us to vamoose.

So far as I know, he tucked her into bed and stayed the night with her. I'm guessing he cooked her breakfast and doted on her all throughout the next day.

Me, I took Charles back to his house and barely got him through the door before I had my hands in his hair and my tongue down his throat. Next thing I knew, we were kicking off shoes and tearing off each other's clothes. I got his tee half over his head, trapping his arms for a moment and biting at his nipples, then he was clear and yanking off my trousers. Practically ripping off the buttons, I got his fly open and clear. Naked at last, I tackled him and for a moment we were two hot, muscled bodies wrestling on the floor, biting and groping.

At last, I got Charles on his back, my knees on his shoulders, my hands on his wrists. Angling my ass up, I got my erect cock pointed down at his mouth. He fought to bring himself up, struggling and fighting my hold. His lips and tongue reached for my dick. It was already slick with precome and nearly dripping over his mouth, but just out of range.

"Motherfucker," he snarled, trying to throw me off. "Give it to me."

"Slowly," I commanded him. "Like it's the handle of a whip that's going to mark your ass."

I lowered it till the tip was within reach. He was sweating now, drooling, but he did as he was told and licked out his tongue to give my mushroom head a slow, loving lick. Fuck! The electricity of that sizzled across my groin and my balls went tight. I gripped his wrists the harder to keep control.

"That's right," I whispered. "Worship it."

"Fucker," he growled, even as he licked out again, this time trying to curl his tongue around, to rub at the sensitive seam at the back. His tongue caressed that pleasure point and sweet delight popped like little bubbles up my rod into my groin, making it jerk. Sweat sprung out over my forehead and my arms shook with the effort to keep from fucking his mouth.

Dipping down, I let my slippery crown play over his lips. He kissed the almost purple colored tip reverently, lips parting and breath soft, inviting me in. I had intended to hold out longer, but surrendered to that wooing. With a moan of delight, Charles latched on, and sucked my cock, pulling, drinking, asking for more.

Gently, I pumped, in and out, letting the sparks build and spread to my fingers and toes. I listened with pleasure to his groans and gags, to the feel of his desperation on my dick as he worked to please me.

"Time to whip your ass," I murmured. It took all my concentration, but I pulled out, loving how he whimpered and tried to chase after my saliva slicked dick. Rolling him over, I jerked his hips into place and struck.

In that moment I could swear I heard that amazing sound of the cracking whip, and from the jerk and cry Charles gave as I entered into his hot ass, I could swear he did, too. Clamping my hands down over his arms again, I remembered the cuffs on Katie's delicate wrists, how she'd floated vulnerable and yielding before Burke's whip. Charles was that way now as I roughly took him, fucking him hard and steady, making him shout.

I felt the connection then. Fiery as the strikes of a whip on flesh. Intensifying, burning through me, through Charles.

"Come now," I managed to order even as his ass went tight and, like a static charge, my power shot out of me and into him. He yelled as if I'd electrified him, and creamed over the floor.

It was a great fuck, one that left us soaked in sweat and gasping for breath...and ready to do it all over again an hour later. I can't speak for anyone else, but Burke and Katie's performance had certainly served as a lightning rod for us.

The patrons of the Cockpit talked of it all week long and, as hoped, offers of courtship came in for Katie from many an enamored leather-dyke. Lustful inquires came in as well from more than a few boys wanting Burke. Both sexes left gifts with Robbie: leather bracelets, boxes of candy, corn whiskey, riding crops. Neither Katie nor Burke, however, resurfaced. For the entirety of that week, they were MIA.

I called and sent e-mails, but got no answer. Finally, eight days after the performance, at the start of Happy Hour, the two of them stepped into the Cockpit.

Burke looked clean, as if he'd showered, and laundered his clothes. He still had his mustache, but he'd had a professional shave; the scruffiness was gone and the facial hair was neatly trimmed. Katie looked fresh and happy, a smile beaming from her face. It was a far cry from the weepy girl we'd found that Saturday night. She had on chic jeans, a leather bustier and low-heeled boots. Her make-up was subdued and she had not used any perfumed products.

Both of them wore biker hats, and around Katie's neck was a delicate, heart-shaped lock on a gold and diamond chain. It looked like an expensive fashion accessory but we all knew it was more than that. Burke had asked, really asked with Katie's pleasure and tastes in mind. And Katie had accepted. Katie was collared, and the two of them now belonged to one another.

"I guess congratulations are in order," I said scooping her feather-weight up and hugging her.

"In more ways than one," Katie said, kissing me full on the lips. For a girl, she was a damn good kisser.

"We've been busy," Burke explained as I put Katie down. "All kinds of requests are coming in for demonstrations. Some of them want to pay for travel and rooms and everything."

"Which he deserves," Katie said, taking Burke by the hand.

"Now, Angel—"

"Daddy," she stopped him, "you are the best in the whole wide world, and it's time everyone knew it."

A few minutes later as Burke got himself a beer, she confided to me: "He told me all about that Delta Run thingy. They had him whipping men with *chains*! Can you believe that?" She was aghast.

"It's not as bad as it sounds —" I tried.

"Chains!" she interrupted, angrily. "That's like handing a concert violinist an accordion! How could anyone have been that *insensitive*?"

"Um, well...."

"His whole life men have been taking advantage of him. Using him, never giving him a chance to really display his art." Tears glimmered in her kittenish eyes. "Well, no more. Not while I'm with him. From now on, he gets treated right."

I would never have imagined delicate Katie could be so passionate. So fierce.

"Isn't she amazing?" Burke said, when I stepped up to join him at the bar. "Do you know," he added confidentially, "Women are more empathetic than men? They feel *everything*, and they're not afraid to show it!"

"I had heard something about that," I responded, bemused.

"It makes such a difference. I never realized how all that take-it-like-a-man attitude was interfering with the feedback I was getting. With Katie I can use finesse, technique. I don't have to whale on her like I do with guys."

See what happens when you finally leave your comfort zone? A world of possibilities opens up to you.

"You're going to get razzed about having a girly boy," I warned him.

He shrugged. "I can take any grief any guy wants to dish out, so long as he remembers to show Katie respect. Anyone who doesn't is going to find out what I can really do with a whip."

The newlyweds (sic) chatted with us a little longer and then it was time for them to go. They were, they informed us, on their way to a Des Moines leather fair.

Robbie came up to me as they left. "You out did yourself, Fancy Man."

"Nope." I shook my head. "I didn't do a thing this time. It was all them."

In spite of my protests, however, the story spread, and I was held responsible for the miracle love affair. Robbie warned me that Fancy Man's reputation as a fantasy granting genie was spreading beyond our little leather bar, and inquiries were coming in from an odd assortment of folk. But those are other stories.

As for Burke and Katie, they went on tour. Katie garnered a lot of admirers, of course, but she made it clear to her suitors that if they wanted to spend even one night with her, they needed to win over her very protective Daddy. Burke, likewise, let anyone who asked for a whipping know that they had to get approval from his Guardian Angel and manager. Neither one of them might have known how to defend themselves, but they knew how to shield each other.

And Charles and I? We're still seeing which way the relationship takes us. It's not often you get that lightning strike of true partnership, and while there have been moments when I've felt such currents, as I did following Burke and Katie's show, I'm still waiting for that one, particular surge. The one that, like the whip crack that brought together the leatherman and the lipstick lesbian, will convince me that we were meant to be.

If you enjoyed this story, you can sign up for a free membership at ForbiddenFiction and discuss it with other readers and the author at the *Fancy Man and the Lipstick Lesbian* story page at http://forbiddenfiction.com/story/T13-1.000082.

The Fancy Man and
the Three Princes

When Mason's best friend Robbie is dumped by his boyfriend a week before his birthday, it's up the "Fancy Man" to try and repair the bartender's broken heart with a natal day fantasy. He comes up with the idea of offering Robbie three "princes," each with a special gift—and sexual expertise. Even as these princes woo Robbie "on-stage," however, backstage has its problems. The reality as much as the fantasy will determine not only Robbie's future happiness, but that of Charles and Mason. (M/M)

Chapter 1

Fancy Man and the British Cowboy

Relationships launch like ships, with cheers and champagne, with high spirits and excitement. Everything the other person does is fascinating, wonderful. And you want it to stay that way. You don't want to have that first bitter argument, you don't want to feel that first stab of disappointment. As with a new car, you don't want to be the one to put that first scratch on the romance.

Sometimes though, you manage to avoid the scratch only to end up in a car wreck. I was heading for just such a wreck and didn't know it. In fact, it took another's heartache and a mission to save him to make me aware of my own peril.

It started on a Wednesday afternoon at the Cockpit Bar, a little before happy hour. Humpday, relaxed though it may be, is the second most popular day for cruising at the Pit. Perhaps it's because those who patronize the bar don't mind staying up late Wednesday night and being tardy for work on Thursday. Or perhaps they just need a little tease and spank to get them through the rest of the week.

A Wednesday night fuck expects less and is easier to satisfy. Which is why I'd picked it over bump-and-grind Saturday for the experiment I had in mind. I'm a big, black, role-playing top known as the Fancy Man. Bringing fantasies to life is my specialty. I'm talking private, shameful, S&M dramas that most men wouldn't confess to their priests. The ones that have them furiously blushing even as they spit them out and beg me to make them real.

I love being privy to such secrets. And I love bringing them to life. Being a vain and arrogant asshole, I also get off on being the object of fear, awe and desire in these fantasies. It's a dirty job, but someone's dick has to get sucked.

Two-and-a-half months back, however, I'd seriously fallen for one of these desperate men: a sexy, southern bottom named Charles Beaumont. Charles had some very strange issues and problems, but that's another story. In a nutshell: I hadn't given him a collar, but we were in a master-slave relationship, arguably the most serious relationship of my life. Yet every Saturday night, I went to the Cockpit and picked out a new toy. Charles understood and accepted this; it was part and parcel of being with the Fancy Man.

Recently, however, I'd gotten the feeling that something was gnawing at him. I ought to have asked what it was, but I arrogantly assumed it had to do with being left out of my Saturday night adventures. So, I'd decided it was time to take my boy-wonder to work with me, give him a chance to help.

The Cockpit is my bar, the place where everyone knows my name and, hopefully, shivers with fearful pleasure when they hear it. I know its smell, its flavor. Walking through the door that evening, I also knew that something was very wrong.

Only a few of the regulars were there, which wasn't unusual prior to happy hour. But they were all huddled at one spot of the island bar. Charles, catching sight of me, hurried over. He was wearing jeans and a white tee as always, his muscular shoulders straining against the cotton fabric in a way that always warmed my blood. His pale gray eyes were anxious.

"Sir." Whatever was bothering him, he didn't let it interfere with the protocols I'd set up between us. He came to attention, hands clasped behind the small of his back. Charles is broad, but not that tall. At 6'4", I'm at least a head taller than him. Which I liked. It allowed me to lean in and, grabbing him by his curly, black hair, kiss him rough and hard.

It doesn't matter how many times I've done this, Charles always catches his breath as if surprised. He may well be. He has this odd idea that he's unworthy of my kisses.

Our tongues dueled for a moment, and I could almost hear his Adam's apple bob with desire. I ran a hand down his throat and over his shoulder and felt a quiver. It was very flattering. Nearly three months together and Charlie was still hopelessly in lust with me. Every kiss I gave him promised sex and torment and left him weak in the knees.

And every kiss I got from him had me wanting to rip off his jeans and pin him to the wall.

"What's up?" I breathed.

"Up?" he was gratifyingly glassy-eyed. "Oh." He glanced over his shoulder and dropped his voice. "Robbie got dumped."

"Shit." Robbie was senior bartender at the Pit and one of my closest friends. He wasn't into the leather scene at all, in fact, the man is a dyed-in-the-wool romantic of the most peaceable and tasteful kind. The past six weeks he'd been deeply into a new boyfriend and it had seemed serious. Love-letters, phone calls, walks in the park. There'd been candlelit dinners, and, on Sunday mornings, breakfast in bed, including mimosas and a red rose. Even the sex, from what Robbie had breathlessly described, had been romantic and tender. Little wonder that Robbie had been sure, oh-so-sure, that this guy was "the one."

I'd been more skeptical, but then I know something about Robbie and the kinds of guys he picks. Let's just say this has happened before.

"He didn't see it coming at all," Charles whispered on. "They were going to go to some bed-and-breakfast for his birthday. Then he got the e-mail. Son-of-bitch didn't even have the courage to break with him in person."

Robbie's birthday was some eight days away, toward the end of October. Libra.

Double shit. I'd strangle the asshole.

"We're trying to cheer him up," Charles said as I made for the bar. We included the Pit's other bartender, Jordon, jet-haired and bisexual, and two of our regulars, Terry, an old fuck buddy of mine, and Katie, the Cockpit's only leatherfemme.

Robbie was behind the bar. He works as a personal trainer when he isn't at the Pit and from the neck down he's a powerhouse. Above he's freckle-faced and red-haired, a true carrot-top. He's also short, which is why I jokingly refer to him as an over-muscled leprechaun. He looked as if he'd just lost his pot of gold. His blue eyes were bloodshot, the lids all red and puffy from crying.

Katie was holding his hand. It rested limp and huge in her delicate fingers.

"Hey Mason," he rubbed at his damp lashes with his free hand. "Get ya something?"

"I'll get it," Jordon said, snagging down a beer glass.

"You're just in time," Terry said with false cheer, "We were talking cartoons. Classic, animated films with singing animals and shit."

"Cartoons?" I matched his tone, playing along. No, of course Robbie's fine. He hasn't just had the stuffing ripped out of him. Let's all pretend everything's peachy. "Please!"

"What's wrong with liking cartoons?" Katie asked, which was a little strange as with her kittenish face and satin brown hair, she might have stepped out of a cartoon herself.

"It's *queer*." I pitched my voice just so to get a laugh. *It's queer* was a favorite put-down of Master Nash, the bar's owner.

A smile twitched at Robbie's lips. Good enough.

"Come on, Mason," Terry urged, right on cue. "You were a little kid once. Your mommy must have taken you to one of those films. Or shown you one at home. What was your favorite? Who did you want to be?"

"Snow White," Jordan sighed as he set a beer before me.

"You liked *Snow White*?" Charles quipped. "Did you want to be one of the dwarves or the prince?"

"I wanted to be Snow White," Jordan grinned. "Hauling water and scrubbing floors for that wicked stepmother. Is she a dream dominatrix or what?"

"Hadn't viewed it in that way," Charles admitted.

"Mason?" Terry urged.

"I hate to burst your bubble, but while you all were watching girly fairytales, I was watching sci-fi. *Star Wars* n' shit. Guy stuff."

"I'm betting his favorite was *Tarzan*," Jordon said.

"You call me King of the Jungle and I will beat your ass like a drum, white man."

Jordan perked. "Promise?"

"Doesn't count," Terry objected. "The characters have to sing."

"Okay, wiseass, then what's your favorite?"

Terry had curly brown hair and a boyish face. He was deeply into fraternity hazing fantasies. I mean deeply. New pledge at the brutal frat house was the only game he ever wanted to play. So I wasn't at all surprised when he said, ruefully, "That one where the girl dresses as a boy and joins the army. I wanted to join up, too."

"And get fucked in the ass by every cartoon recruit," I mocked. That got another laugh.

"While they're singing!" Jordan added, which prompted more laughter.

"Charles?" Robbie asked. He seemed to be getting into it, or at least he was letting us think we were helping him.

My partner blushed, as he has a tendency to do. "*Aladdin*. I know," he added quickly, "that it's got some terrible stereotypes —"

"*Aladdin*?" I cut him off. Like I said, Charles has issues and if he gets on one of those tracks he'll speed off like a run-away train. Most times I let him as I enjoy arguing with him, but we were trying to make Robbie feel better. "You wanted to be Aladdin?"

"Um, no, I wanted to be the genie."

Stupid me. Of course, Charles wanted to be the slave of the lamp, forced to grant wishes and call the owner "Master." What else was new?

"Katie?" Jordon nodded to her.

She smiled sweetly while stroking the coppery hair on the back of Robbie's wrist. "Cinderella. I wanted her dress and her carriage and those beautiful glass slippers."

I snorted. "I can see you talking to your fairy godmother now," I notched my voice falsetto, "'Fuck the prince, just let me go shopping!'"

The laughter was louder this time, more genuine. So I took a chance. "What about you, Rob?"

"Ah." He smirked and rubbed at his eyes again. "*Beauty and the Beast*. I like that the guy and the girl spend the whole movie getting to know each other. Dining, dancing. Winning each other's hearts." He sighed wistfully.

"You're sure you don't have a favorite, Mason?" Terry asked. "*Lady and the Tramp*? *Princess and the Frog* —"

"Oh, please!" Charles winced. "Don't even get me started on the racial stereotypes in the *Princess and the Frog*!"

"...*Bambi*?"

I flipped him off. Fucker knew I had a soft spot for animal movies.

"'Fess up, Fancy Man!" Jordon urged.

"Only if we're counting Pixar buddy films." I took a draft of beer. "They're for *guys*."

I got booed and raspberried. Customers were drifting in and Robbie and Jordon had to break away to fill orders.

"You holding up?" I managed to ask Rob at one point.

"As best I can," he said getting down a bottle of gin. "But I think I'm going to be more like Cinderella from now on. All she wanted was that one night at the ball, a chance to be the center of attention and dance with the prince. Happily-ever-after was an unforeseen bonus. I think it'll be easier on my poor heart if I lower my expectations to that. One happy night and nothing more."

"Good thinking."

He had something of a smile on his face, but he wiped at his eyes for the rest of the night.

"The older guy," Charles said, sipping at his beer. Happy Hour was at an end and you could smell the mood shifting. Electronica was pounding out of Nash's digital jukebox, bottles and glasses were clanking, and the murmur in the air had turned to a kind of sexual purr. A chill, October wind had driven in the bears and biker gals who usually smoked out in the parking lot. They were huddled about the pool table, smacking around the balls, amping up the hormone level.

Around the island bar hung men and women in leather vests and chaps, demanding drinks. A few were restlessly circling round, uncertain if they wanted to top or bottom. They were searching for that one sexy ass or pair of demanding eyes to knock them into position. Meanwhile, against the walls, unclaimed bottoms waited for the summons of a hungry top. This included a couple of leather dykes who'd placed themselves right under the club flags that bore names like "Crusaders" and "Vikings." They had on cropped tees to display the colorful, Japanese dragons tattooing their skin. The rest of the bottoms were crew-cut boys in harnesses and jeans, one was wearing only a white jock strap and boots.

I liked the way his wiry pubic hair flared out around that pouch.

The older guy Charles was referring to was off to the side, standing apart from the rest. He looked to be in his forties, rangy in build and long in the face. He had flaxen hair and pale eyes.

"Interesting choice." I swigged down my third beer of the night. Charles and I were in one of the orange booths that studded the opposite wall. The ones that still had framed pictures of 70's airline crews above them, a remnant from when the Cockpit had been a regular bar owned by a retired pilot.

"Why that one?" I asked.

Charles, who had once been against that wall, shifted uncomfortably. He didn't like making decisions, slave-types never do. For Charles, however, it went deeper than that. He had some strange notions, ones usually held by Afrocentric types who think that Caucasians can't be trusted. Which meant he held my dark-skinned judgments as naturally more valid than his white-skinned own. He was worried that he'd picked wrong.

"He's been in here a few times," my boy nervously explained, "and he's always looking our way. So, he might be interested in the two of us. Mostly, though, he just...seems different."

"You're right." Usually there's some clue about a guy, what he's into, a colored handkerchief or the way he wears his belt. This guy had on jeans, cowboy boots and shirt and bolo tie. He was leaning back against the wall relaxed. Almost as if he were watching a TV show.

"Go over and see if he wants to join us," I told Charles.

The boys against the wall, even the dykes, straightened up as Charles approached. When he went to the flaxen-haired fellow, shoulders slumped in disappointment. Why did the Fancy Man want *him*? A valid question as our choice was the frog among princes, the oldest and plainest of the lot.

His blond brows furrowed as Charles spoke, uncertain. Then a look of pure delight came across his long face. He pushed away from the wall to follow Charles back to our booth.

"Sir." My boy brought him up to the table. "This is Nigel."

The man smiled brightly. "A pleasure." Was that a British accent?

"Been hearing all about you."

He held out a hand. I gamely shook it, and invited him to sit. He slid in and Charles followed. For a moment the music pulsed around us, mingling with the chatter and clink of beer bottles. Most gents, lean and boney and middle aged, would've been intimidated trapped as he was between two brawny leathermen. Nigel, far from apprehensive, kept glancing from one to the other of us like a boy in candyland. It was decidedly un-bottom-like.

"So, tell us about yourself," I ventured.

"Oh, well, I've moved here from Brighton...England that is. Got transferred." His dialect had a hint of Michael Cane to it, making him sound even more jocular. "This is my new home, also my first time in the States. And I am loving it!"

He certainly seemed to be. Whoever said the British were reserved hadn't met Nigel. The man gushed.

"Welcome to the colonies. So what's your fantasy, Nigel?"

"Oh, yes, that's right, that's right. Um, well." He chewed on his lower lip, "Well, I don't expect very much, really. I mean, two lads like yourselves...I know you aren't interested in banging an old geezer like me. But I'm fine just watching. Anything you'd like to do, if I could just watch."

Charles and I exchanged startled looks.

"That's pretty tame," I said.

"Well, actually..." He glanced down at his laced hands. "I'm vanilla."

"Pardon?"

"As vanilla as an old poof can be," he confessed. "Little kissing and stroking, cocksucking. Up one arse or the other and that's it for me."

I leaned my chin on my fist. Like most leatherbars the Pit catered to the top/bottom and S&M scene. But it did have patrons with other tastes, including those who just had a fetish for leather or big guys in leather. Which was all well and good, but....

"If you aren't into anything else, why were you standing against the wall?"

"Because I wanted to meet him," he said, smiling at Charles.

My partner blinked as if he'd just been targeted.

I leaned back and grinned. "Seems you have a secret admirer, Charlie Boy."

My slave flushed in that charming way of his, pink spots appearing on his alabaster cheeks.

"I noticed him at the bank a few days ago, followed him here hoping to introduce myself, then learned that I couldn't have him without your permission. And," Nigel added, "that I could only get that by standing against the wall. That wasn't wrong, was it?"

This time I laughed out loud. I could see exactly how the foul up must have happened. A polite foreigner inquires after Charles. The bears out front inform him that he'll have to get my permission. True, as Charles is my property and no one can use him without my say so. Nigel steps inside and chats with the boys, asking them about speaking to me. They mistake him for a bottom and tell him he'll have to stand and wait his turn if he wants the Fancy Man.

Thus, Nigel ends up against the wall. Talk about crossed wiring.

"I know you two are into far more interesting scenes than anything my addled imagination can provide," Nigel went on with resigned humor. "But if I could just watch...just watch once?"

"That would be up to Charles," I said, still enjoying myself. My poor slave was blushing up to the roots of his hair now. "So what was it attracted you to him?"

"Besides the muscles you mean?" Nigel sighed. "The accent. Texas isn't it? I love American accents."

"I'm from Georgia," Charles corrected him. He was looking a little panicked now.

"Even better!" Nigel enthused. "*Jezebel*, *Gone with the Wind*, *The Little Foxes*...."

I was laughing my ass off. Charles kicked me under the table.

"Doc Holliday was from Georgia," Nigel added happily.

"Like stories of the American West, do you?" I managed to catch my breath.

"Westerns," Nigel amended. "The myth, not the truth. The truth is too gritty, too messy. I like my cowboy movies pure and fictional."

"Well," I said, with a Texas twang. "Why didn't you say so, buckaroo?"

Chapter 2
Dodge City

I gazed over my cards and downed my second shot of whiskey. The Southern Gent across from me, I figured, had a pair. I had three ladies.

"Raise ya," I tossed in a coin.

The Southern gent pushed up his Stetson and eyed me suspiciously. Not a bad bit of acting for a veterinarian. Especially given how nervous Charles had been.

Once the creative light had flicked on in my head, I'd sent Charles up to Jordon for a roll of quarters, a bottle of whiskey, and a deck of cards. Then I'd laid out the rules to Nigel, which were fairly simple: One, it was his fantasy, but I'd be directing. Two, once the scene was underway, it was underway until either he stopped it with a safeword, or I said we were finished.

End of rules.

Nigel, interested and apparently so enthralled by Charles' accent that he was willing to take a risk, had readily agreed.

With Charles following in my Scion, I'd gone with Nigel in his car. Actually, I'd driven as the Brit was still learning how to navigate the city and the right hand side of the road. I'd stopped us at the playhouse where I sometimes work and borrowed cowboy hats and fake guns with holsters from the costume department.

Off again, we'd arrived at Nigel's rather nice townhouse.

Sending Nigel to the bedroom, I'd gotten to work with Charles moving a round dining table. Nigel's place was still half in boxes with overseas labels, but I'd found and dug out a trio of cordial glasses.

"This," I'd informed Charles getting some rope out of my handy-dandy traveling kit and tying it to the rod-iron staircase rails, "is going to be our hitching post." I had a hat on my shaved crown and tin sheriff's badge pinned to my teeshirt.

"Mason," Charles rubbed his hands down his jeans, "I wanted to be part of this, and I'm not trying to back out, but I really don't know —"

I put a Stetson on his head and tilted back his chin. His words stopped as his eyes met mine. He looked cute, adorable even in that hat.

I stroked my fingers from chin on down his throat. He shivered and swallowed, but his hungry eyes never left me. "Three things I want you to do," I told him. "First, follow my lead. Second, remember that this is *Nigel's* fantasy. Think about what he likes, what you feel will please him. Not me. Can you do that? You do like Nigel, don't you?"

"Well, yeah. He's a great guy —"

"Good," I cut him off. Letting Charles think too much would make him anxious. "Then we should all have a nice time."

His eyes flickered over to the ropes, then to the riding crop that waited on a telephone table along with a bottle of lube. His cheeks flushed. Pain, real pain, doesn't turn Charles on. But he loves to be bound and helpless. And stinging slaps or whips to his ass can bring him almost to orgasm. I knew that handsome, white cock of his was already stiff and wetting his button-down jeans.

I touched him on his cheek, regaining his eyes. In them I saw a mix of lust and fear that made me tingle with anticipation. Leaning in and knocking back the Stetson, I kissed him. He pushed forward, crushing his lips to mine, asking for more even as I broke it off and backed away.

"Remember to cheat."

"Cheat?" he echoed, his breath coming short.

"That's the third thing I want you to do." I snatched the deck of cards off the table and handed it to him. "You've got three minutes." I said stepping up to Nigel's bedroom.

I knocked. "Ready?" I asked as the Brit opened the door. He had on his hat and fake gun like the rest of us.

The man from Brighton grinned at me. "Feel a right bit odd.

Haven't played cowboys since I was a tyke."

"Just go with it. You'll have fun."

"I'm with two gorgeous men. I'm already having fun. In fact, I don't think I've had this much fun since I was a worthless lad sucking off sailors. And you," he grinned up at me, "are a right good bloke. Ain't many strapping fellows willing to waste their valuable evening with a potty old fruit like me."

I smiled back. Nigel was one of the few men I'd ever granted a fantasy to who saw me exactly as I was, no mystique, no stereotype. It was refreshing.

I put a hand on his shoulder.

"Doc," I said with a Texas drawl and directed him into the living room. "Glad you could make it. Got this new fella, he heard about your reputation as the best poker player in town. He'd been itchin' to play against ya. Claims to have been a riverboat gambler. Ain't that right, Mister Beau."

Charles, put on the spot, looked taken aback. For a heartbeat, I thought he'd panic. Then he managed, "Yes, sir. That's right. River-boats."

So here we were, playing poker and drinking shots of whiskey. A nice way to ease into the fantasy.

"So whadda ya think of Dodge, Mr. Beau?" I asked casually.

"Exciting place," Charles answered, tossing in two quarters, meeting and raising the bet.

"But don't you miss traveling up and down the Mississippi?" Nigel added his own pair of quarters. The Brit was getting into the game in more ways than one. Good for you, Nigel.

"No sir, I most certainly do not," Charles said, exaggerating his southern drawl. I almost laughed. There was my boy! He'd figured it out. Nigel loved the accent, so give him the accent. "It's a slow and muddy river. But I sure do miss the food. I could do with a mint julep, a little fried catfish...."

He winked my way, and I smirked. It was an inside joke. If a brother might digress....Not long after we became a couple, Charles asked if he could cook me dinner. What immediately popped to mind was a hearty southern meal, and so I'd requested catfish. You can imagine my surprise when, seated at the dining table that fateful night, I was ceremoniously presented with a whole fried catfish, sizzling on an iron serving platter and dressed with ponzu sauce.

Charles, it turned out, was deeply into Asian fusion. After putting down the catfish, he'd leaned in and given me a crushing hug.

"Thank you," he'd said, and I swear there were tears of culinary joy in his eyes. "Most tops only want meat and potatoes." Then he handed me a pair of chopsticks.

Luckily for both of us, I like a wide range of cuisines. So I dove in with gusto. The catfish was delicious, fantastic. I just about ate it all and I didn't confess the truth till later, after I'd rewarded Charles properly and we were lying sated in bed.

He was mortified. "Oh, no! Oh, Jesus!" He'd blushed and covered his eyes, "I'm so stupid! I swear, it never even occurred to me! You said catfish and I just thought of that dish—"

"Hey, hey," I'd laughed. "It's no problem. You can fry it up southern style next time."

"No, I can't. I mean, I can find a recipe—"

"Can't?"

Turned out, Charles didn't know dick about southern cooking. His parents, cosmopolitan and health conscious, had rarely served him the comfort food of their youth. In fact, they hadn't even taught him how to cook. He'd learned that from a neighboring Vietnamese family.

"I can't wait to make you my Banh Xeo," Charles had said after informing me of this. "It's my signature dish."

Sometimes I hate multiculturalism.

"Three ladies, gentlemen." I set down my cards proudly.

"Damn," Nigel laid out his hand. "Pair of nines."

"No luck for you tonight, Doc," I said. We'd played four hands and Nigel had lost every one.

"Read 'em and weep." Charles displayed his cards. A trio of aces.

"You're having the devil's own luck, Mr. Beau," I murmured.

Charles reached for the quarters. I slapped my hand down on his wrist. He jumped and so did Nigel.

"The devil's own luck," I repeated, "playing the devil's own game. Doc, could you check Mr. Beau's left boot."

Blinking, Nigel did as I asked. He came back up with a two and four. I'd seen Charles rather clumsily scratching at his ankle and switching out those cards for the aces. If Nigel had been paying any attention he would have noticed, too. He hadn't, and now the fantasy was really underway.

I brought up my toy gun and pointed it at Charles. "We take cheating very seriously in this town, Mr. Beau."

Charles slowly raised his hands, almost clasping them behind his head before he remembered and kept them apart. "No harm intended, sheriff—"

"Stand up! Up!"

The chair fell to the floor as Charles did so.

"Get those boots and socks off. Now!" Off came the boots, a card fluttering out of the right one. I tsked and Charles blushed as if he really had done something wrong.

I removed his hat and shook it. Another card fell out.

"Shameful!" I shook my head. "Off with your shirt."

The tee was pulled off and I heard Nigel suck in a breath as he got his first unhampered look at Charles' washboard stomach and bulging biceps. A blue chain tattoo circled the right one.

"Now the trousers," I commanded, unable to keep back a growl of passion.

Charles hands went to the fly, then I saw a flicker. He seemed to remember he was playing a part. "Now just a minute, sheriff—" he protested.

Bravo! I cocked the gun and put it right into his face. It was a toy gun but he actually paled. My pulse amped up. Fear excites me. "You're gonna prove to the whole saloon that you don't have any more hidden cards."

Charles hastily unbuttoned his jeans, and the tremor in his fingers made my cock stiffen. He wore nothing underneath. That's the wardrobe rules I've created for him. When he's not at work he has to wear button-down jeans and go commando.

Nigel's intake of breath wheezed as Charles' circumcised cock came flopping out. The B-shaped branding scar near his right hipbone blazed stark and pale on his shaved pelvis. His balls swung as he kicked aside the pants. Then he stood there, naked as a Greek statue.

Beautiful.

"Doc, come straighten up this chair and have a seat," I invited. Nigel, eyes wide, did as he was told. He looked like a man in a dream, wondering what was going to happen next.

"Now," I said to Charles, "I believe you owe the Doc a public apology." I stepped around behind him, set his hat back on his head. "On your knees."

Charles dropped.

"Suck his cock."

"Sheriff—" Charles objected.

"It's a dick in your mouth or lead in your teeth." I pressed the gun against his head. Charles shivered and reached for Nigel's belt. Nigel was breathing softly now, as if afraid of interrupting. The only move he made was to spread his thighs a bit after Charles unzipped him.

Charles barely had to draw down Nigel's underwear before the Brit's excited cock sprung out, thin and rosy from a wild patch of straw colored hair. Its flared head was already gleaming with anticipatory precome. Charles' forced striptease had certainly aroused Nigel.

A fiery tingle was sparkling down my own rod. I could well imagine the sexual hum that was going through Nigel as this muscled, American cowboy, kneeling at his feet, bent forward, breathed on his cock...

The Brit's hips bucked as Charles' lips enfolded him. He moaned and his hands gripped the chair.

I shifted to the side to get a better view. Charles bobbed and slurped then came off to lick and caress those pulsing veins before returning to the head. Charles was a damn good cocksucker and he was doing his award-winning best. But then he knew I was watching his performance, rating it.

Nigel, who I'm guessing hadn't had it this good in a while, was completely lost. "Jesus, Jesus—" He gasped and groaned and his arms trembled. Having experienced Charles' talent I knew that Nigel was helplessly leaking musky juices down my boy's throat, that his balls were now high and hard and boiling. The way that warm mouth was stroking him, the way that tongue was teasing him, he'd be coming any second now.

He did, thrusting and shuddering so hard I was afraid he'd gone into convulsions. A gargled sound from Charles as he rode the wave and swallowed down Nigel's hot cream. A pause as both of them caught their breaths.

"Lick it clean, boy," I growled, redundant as Charles was already at it, but we were still in the fantasy, and he need to be reminded of that.

"Jesus fucking Christ," Nigel gasped as Charles' tongue polished his still bobbing cock.

"That apology to your satisfaction, Doc?"

"Shit, yes!"

"Good. Then there's only one more lesson to teach." I snagged Charles under the arm. I pulled him up and spun him toward the stair rails. "Hands on the hitching post!"

He obeyed, still breathing hard, lips glistening with saliva and come. I holstered my gun and got the ropes tied about his wrists.

"W-what are you going to do?" he managed to get out.

"You're going to show the whole town what happens to cheats." I snatched up the riding crop. "Meaning I'm gonna horsewhip you."

"Sheriff, please—"

I slapped the whip across his tight, muscled ass. He jerked and caught a strangled breath. I laid another whipping across his crack and followed it with one up under his buns. Charles has a great ass. Muscled and white enough to show off those red welts. Neat, clean stripes appeared on his tender skin. I whipped him again, loving the whistling swish that always warns the victim that an evil, burning sting is coming. Charles cried out and clung to the rails, legs apart and trembling.

The shaking wasn't from pain. Charles has taken worse than what I could inflict with my riding crop. It was the fantasy. He was into it now and his vivid imagination had him tied to a hitching post, naked and whipped in public.

Knowing that's what he was imagining made my cock rock hard. It throbbed with each mark I gave him, twitched with each yelp and moan.

I unbuckled and unzipped. I didn't have anything on underneath either and my cock slapped up against my stomach, ready to pummel that sore, red ass. A final few whips made Charles' breath come in hissing gasps and his hands clutch white knuckled on the bars.

Precome spilled out of my slit in such copious amounts that I almost didn't need the lube. But I exchanged the whip for the bottle and covered myself with it.

Then I spread his ass cheeks.

I paused, breathing hard. Sweat was itching down from under my hat. I glanced back at Nigel. The Brit was watching avidly. I almost wished we had some popcorn for him to munch on, he looked that enthralled.

"Let's give the whole town a look at that pucker," I said in my lowest, meanest voice and Charles shivered down from shoulders to ass. In his mind, every occupant of our mythical Dodge City was now stepping out or leaning from their windows to watch his humiliation. The very thought left him breathless with arousal. Sweat trickled down his spine and crawled into his crack. His pink hole fluttered with need and my lubed finger easily slid in.

I fucked him like that for a minute, stretching and greasing his warm, eager interior. "That's right. Everybody's watching me toy with you."

Charles gulped and pressed his burning face into the bars, even as his welted ass pushed back, begging for me. My cock responded, barely letting my fingers escape before it plunged in. Charles groaned as I entered in one smooth glide. As I passed over his prostate he uttered a cry that was almost a sob.

I fucked him slow and steady, making sure to hit that sweet spot again and again. I could see, below, drips of precome from his cock falling and puddling on the floor along with drops of sweat. But when I reached around to give his dick a stoke I found it only at half-mast. Velvety slick with juice, but still not stiff.

He must be more anxious about his performance than I thought. Well, there was an easy enough way to get him hard, one I'd never used, but I knew would work. I rested myself along his sweaty backbone and whispered into his ear, "You're mine, white boy. And I'll give you to whomever I damn please."

His cock leapt up from my hand like a jack-in-the-box. I swear I've never felt a dick go so hard so fast.

"Doc!" I called. "Would you care to milk this steer for me?"

Nigel didn't need to be asked twice. He stumbled over, holding up his still unzipped pants, and went to his knees. He latched his lips onto Charles cock.

I increased my speed, banging away at Charles, grunting and loving that slow burn making its way up and down my cock. Nigel hummed, and Charles rocked to and from our combined assault.

"Gonna learn you a lesson, cheater," I said. Below, Nigel licked and relished Charles' cock like a kid with a bright red licorice stick. "Take your medicine from both ends."

"I'm gonna... gonna come—" he panted.

"Think so?" I growled, tugging at his hair and jolting him up the ass with my thrusts.

"Please, can I come—"

"Come," I commanded, and he did, his ass bucking, his sphincter clamping hard and tight on my rod. The squeezing sent a sizzle through me, one that pulled the trigger and made me fire my load deep into his chute.

Charles shuddered to an end even as I rode him.

"Oh, fucking Christ!" I heard Nigel moaning from the floor.

I finished, sweat dripping down my face and making my shirt stick to my back. Fuck. I thought, wiping a shaking hand across my brow. I love role-playing.

Nigel was slumped against the stairs, his mouth and chin bathed in come. He shut his eyes and licked at his shiny lips. I pulled my cock free and without bothering to zip up, came around and untied Charles. Released, he collapsed, wincing as his welted behind hit the cold floor. He was gasping for breath and bathed in perspiration. I leaned against the rails myself, fighting for a second wind. There was a third act to the play involving another round of poker with some very different stakes. I was about to suggest it when Nigel interrupted.

"O.K. Corral," he wheezed.

I wiped at my face again, taken aback. "Really?" It was the safe-word. "Are you sure?"

Nigel laughed weakly. "God, yes. You two do any more and you'll give me heart failure. I'm not a horny, young lad, just a dirty, middle-aged fart. Not that I wouldn't like to keep going if I could. That was the best fuck I've had in years." There was a bittersweet glimmer to his eyes. "Too many years." He wiped at his sticky chin with his fingers and licked the tips as if finishing off the butter and salt from his popcorn.

"Glad you enjoyed it."

"Enjoyed? I fucking loved it!" The Brit glanced over at Charles. "Can I hug him?"

I might have said no. Bottoms can get ultra-sensitive after an intense session, and this had been pretty intense. I wasn't sure if anyone but me ought to touch Charles, but Nigel was a good guy. I didn't think he'd overdo it. "Go ahead."

Coming up on his knees, the Brit threw his long arms about Charles' neck, which got a blink of surprise from my boy.

"Thank you!" he said effusively, and almost knocked Charles hat off as he kissed him on the cheek. "That was wonderful! Splendid! I'm so glad I came to the States! I will love you both forever!"

I had to laugh. "Could you get us some damp towels so we can clean up?"

"Of course, of course. And I'll make us all a cuppa, shall I?"

Cup of tea, I assumed he meant. "Sure."

Nigel stumbled off to the bathroom. I settled down next to Charles and used my hat to fan myself.

"Was that okay?" Charles asked anxiously. He still looked dazed and lost. "Did I do all right?"

I put my arm across his bare shoulders and dragged him in close. "You did right well, partner."

Chapter 3
Challenges

Nash wanted to see me. He'd said as much on my voice mail.

"I want to see you. Ten-thirty, my place."

Which, as a top, made me bristle, but Nash talked to everyone like that. As if he were General Patton and we were grunts in his army. So, at ten-twenty-five, I turned my Scion into the horseshoe drive of Nash's opulent, ranch-style home.

Nash's personality is well known, his background less so. He was in the marines once upon a time, which I knew but most of his patrons did not. I also knew, from the twang in his speech that he came from the Midwest. As a voice actor, I'm pretty good with dialects.

As for the rest, he smoked either slim cigars, or cigarettes in a holder, and was fastidious especially when it came to personal hygiene. His hair was regularly trimmed and he had his nails manicured every Thursday. He liked raw oysters, golf, gambling on the horses, and slender, obedient young men. This last had made more than one self-righteous top question whether Nash was a "real" leatherman. I tended to think he was, but then I think anyone with enough rebellious, fighting spirit and a taste for fetishware qualifies as a leatherman.

Nash also had money, though where and how he'd come by it no one knew. He'd been able to buy the Cockpit Bar outright, no loans needed, and his five-room, hillside house was in the upscale part of town. It had glitter in the stuccoed walls and a backyard that included fruit trees, a badminton net and a guesthouse with a hot tub.

I had just gotten out of my car and crossed to the steps of this house when Hadji threw open one of the double doors. He was a little out of breath and I got the feeling that he'd made a dash for the entrance hall, as if letting me ring the bell would have been an insult. Hadji was nineteen going on twenty but he still looked like a boy: small and slender with smooth, dusty brown skin, silky black hair and jet eyes.

The last time I'd seen him, he'd been serving drinks in the nude. This morning he was more modestly dressed in a leather jockstrap and Nash's distinctive black dog collar complete with dog tags. He shivered as the October wind struck him. No surprise. I was wearing a fleece-lined coat and I was cold.

"Sir!" He stepped back as I entered, shutting the door behind me as quickly as decorum allowed. Nash didn't bring his boys to the Cockpit, so the only way a person was likely to encounter them was if they visited Nash's home. I'd met Hadji at the annual Fourth of July backyard barbecue, and all that I remembered about him was Nash's insistence that the boy was Pakistani even though his accent was Canadian.

As for what the kid remembered about me... I had thought that I'd melted in with the other leathermen that night, but evidently not. Hadji, going up on tiptoe to help me off with my jacket, was scanning my height, my muscles and, most especially, my crotch with lustful nostalgia. It was the sort of look I got from men who'd been fantasizing about me for a while. And masturbating in the shower while doing it.

I saw him lick his lips as he hung my coat in the hall closet. Hadji, by the way, was not his name. That's just what Nash called him, much to my annoyance. He might as well call *me* Sambo. But it was Nash's home, Nash's boy and I doubted that Hadji had any objections anyway.

"This way, sir," Hadji said, with an attitude reminiscent of a small, eager-to-please dog. He took me down an airy hallway with overhead lamps shaped like stars. The place was immaculate, the floors polished smooth as mirrors, the white rugs spotless. It was quite warm and smelled of furniture polish and cigarettes.

"Is there anything I can get you sir?" Hadji asked. "We have hot coffee and tea, soft drinks—"

"Mineral water?"

"Yes, sir. Right away, sir. Ice? Master Nash is in there, sir." He waved to the living room before hurrying off. I watched him go. I'm not into twinks, especially overly submissive ones, but Hadji did have a very tempting bubble butt. I liked the way those brown globes sifted against one another as he walked. Very spankable.

Nash's living room had 60's modern furniture, including low couches and a kidney-shaped coffee table. The color scheme was all gold and avocado green. He was standing at an easel near the picture window. Out in the backyard flame colored trees rustled and shed their leaves.

For a man nearing sixty, Nash still looked hard and strong. He was dressed in a black tee, combat trousers and boots, as confident and arrogant as an aging commander. His wavy brown hair was streaked with gray. His eyes were very light in color, close to amber and very cold. They were perusing the image on the canvas, which, to me, looked like a five-year-old's finger painting.

No, I take that back. A five-year-old would have done a better job.

"You can't paint worth shit." I flopped down on one of the low couches. My knees came up almost to my chin forcing me to push back into a corner in order to stretch my legs.

"Well, I guess I won't waste money on art classes then." Nash put down his paintbrush. He had a holder in his teeth, the cigarette at the end was almost all ash.

"Thanks for coming," he said, settling down across from me and, thankfully, tapping his cigarette into a vintage ashtray. "I'll get right to the point. I want to talk about Robbie."

Robbie? I stiffened up. Nash had never been able to sympathize with Robbie's romantic nature and I'd often feared that he might one day fire the bartender. I hoped that wasn't what this was about, because if it came to that I'd have to leave the Cockpit in protest. A lot of us would.

Hadji reappeared with my sparkling water and cup of rooibos tea for Nash. The boy set the drinks on coasters before going to stand at Nash's elbow.

"Robbie is very well liked," Nash went on. "He's the sort of bartender who turns newcomers into regulars and keeps regulars feeling special. An asset to the bar."

"No argument," I said, relieved enough by the direction this was taking to sip at my water.

"Now, I don't pretend to understand his love life," Nash went on, "and I don't want to understand it. Too queer for me. But I know some asshole broke up with him and made him unhappy. And that's not good for business."

"It's not too good for Robbie, either," I noted sarcastically.

Nash shrugged. "I suppose not. That's why I want you to give him a fantasy for his birthday. My treat."

I nearly spit up my water. "Say what?"

Nash flipped his cigarette holder. "You know. Lift his spirits. Make him feel better about himself. All that queer self-esteem shit."

"That'd be a great idea, except that I haven't any inclinations toward Rob and he hasn't any toward me."

Swirls of smoke drifted up to the ceiling. Nash's amber eyes mocked me. "What about all those times you said that one day you'd give Robbie the romantic evening of his dreams?"

"I meant that as a...as an enchanted fuck buddy night. You know. Wine, poetry and sex and then everything back to the way it was in the morning, no harm, no foul."

"Queer shit." Nash snorted and drank his tea.

"Yeah, well, none of that's gonna fly given the state he's in right now. He'd take it as pity fuck and he'd be right."

"His birthday's in a week," Nash dismissively pointed out. "He ought to be over it by then."

Sometimes, I think that Nash is just clueless. Other times I think, like all tops, he likes jerking chains, the shithead. "Look, Nash..." I started. Then stopped. Wait. Maybe this wasn't such a bad an idea.

"I'm not meaning you should do it all on your own." Nash blithely waved about his cigarette holder like a conductor leading an orchestra. "I'd be happy to provide anything you might need...within reason, of course."

"Of course." Cheapskate. "How about the guest house? Could I have that for the evening?"

He shrugged. "Why not? I'll be out of town anyway, so...*mi casa es su casa*."

"How about the black Beamer?" Nash owned one sweet, BMW sedan, a carriage for a Cinderfella if there ever was one.

He hesitated at that, flicking ash into the tray. "Well, it's insured. Okay."

"And Hadji." I glanced over at his boy who stood there absolutely still, eyes lowered and hands behind his back. "I'll need Hadji."

"Sure. Take him."

I leaned forward. "I mean, I going to *really* need him. He has to be completely at my beck and call."

Nash smirked. "Fancy Man, you can do whatever the fuck you like to him. Sodomize him with the garden hose if you want. Just make sure he can still walk when you're done." Nash was far less worried about me denting his slave than he was about me denting his car. "Hadji?"

"Master?" the boy perked, and I could swear he was trembling with excitement.

"From now till next, oh, next Friday, you will answer to Master Mason as you would answer to me. Anything he wants you to do, and I mean anything, you do. *Capisce*?"

Hadji sucked in a breath. "Yes sir!"

"Then it's settled," Nash stood up and I rose with him. "Keep the expenses minor and I'll pay those as well." He stuck out his hand.

I hesitated. Shaking hands with Nash was as good as signing a contract. It was the one other thing I knew for sure about the man, you did not screw him. If I shook, I was committed. If it had been for anyone else, I probably wouldn't have done it. But this was Robbie. I grabbed hold of Nash's hand and we sealed the deal.

"You've just hired the Fancy Man," I told him. "You'll get my best."

"That's all I'm askin'. Robbie's a wreck." It was the closest Nash was going to get to saying that he cared.

Walking out to my car afterwards I wondered what kind of headache I'd just inherited. Giving Robbie a romantic evening was easy enough, but giving him a romantic fairytale after his heart had just been badly broken?

That was going to be a challenge.

Rituals are an important part of a Master/slave relationship. Friday night was shaving night. Charles kept himself clean-shaven, but on Friday night, he let me do the honors.

With a straight razor.

Not on his testicles. Give me some credit, for those I use a very good safety razor. But for just about everywhere else, there's nothing like a straight razor to give a man a smooth and perfect shave.

I have Charles line the square tub at his house with a waterproof mat and strip. Then I bind his hands behind his back with bondage tape and settle him in with his feet up and wide apart. Wearing only my shorts, I get to work. First, I give his cock, balls and ass a good scrub with a soapy washcloth. When he starts to moan, I stop and rinse him. It's time to move onto the fun part.

Next, comes the shaving soap, which I froth up in a cup with a soft, badger-hair brush. I brush it on, stroke by stroke across his pelvis, finishing up that area with swirl about the stem of his rising cock. Then on down under his balls and between his spread cheeks. This usually leaves him groaning and gasping, especially if I a give his balls a bit of a roll in my hand while doing it.

By this time his cock is pointing at the ceiling. I strop the razor, a nice sound that sends a shiver of anticipation through my boy.

It stiffens my dick as well.

Starting down below, I lift the balls and carefully scrape the inside of his butt cheeks with short stokes. I take my time, especially near the hole. Now and then, I look up at him. I love the way his eyes watch me with a delicious mix of desire and dread. No matter how many times I've done this, how much he trusts me, he's restrained and I've a straight razor in my hand. I can't tell you what a hot sight it is to see his belly fluttering with fear.

Usually he keeps deathly quiet unless I make him talk. But this time around, he surprised me by speaking up. "S-so you're going to go to your mother's for Christmas?"

I raised my brows. The game we're playing here works like this: Charles tries to stay strong and calm as I arouse him past bearing, and I try to get him to crack and beg. Asking questions and forcing him to answer helps to shake his concentration. I was impressed that he'd pre-empted my strike, but a little mystified by the subject.

"As always," I answered, cleaning the razor on a wet towel. "My sister will probably bring that Latino boyfriend of hers..." I carefully scraped at the very tender skin right around his cute, pink pucker.

His breath went shallow. "Y-you should give him a ch-chance."

"I don't dislike him. It's just hard to stop being a big brother." I finished up with his ass and, wiping the blade again, moved to his pelvis.

"What's his name anyway?"

"My sister's boyfriend," I muttered shortly. "Have you decided if you're going back to Georgia for Thanksgiving or Christmas?"

"Thanksgiving, not Christmas. It'd be too hard to manage both trips. And more of the extended family come for turkey day."

"Hmmm." I started right below his navel. Scrape, scrape, scrape. Clearing away small stubble and soap. Charles' breathing was very measured now. His cock was nice and stiff, making it easier to manipulate and work around. I liked its patriotic coloring: white skinned and blue veined stem, blushing red tip.

Tempting to give that yummy head a lick. But that would be cheating. My unwritten rule was that I couldn't use any unusual means to break him.

I glanced up as I scraped oh-so-carefully around the root of his penis. He was biting his lip, stubbornly refusing to yield. He was also eying the bulge in my briefs like a man dying of thirst. I thought of pulling them down and flaunting my erection but that, again, would be cheating.

Scrape, scrape, scrape. I wiped the blade clean and went to work on the other side of his straining cock.

"Those Vietnamese neighbors you had back in Georgia," I said, "The ones that taught you how to cook, you said one of them was in town?"

"Uh? Ah...yes." Charles swallowed and tried to concentrate. "Drew was the gay son of the family. He was one of my f-first fuck buddies."

"Ah, yes," I was below his dick now. Just about finished. I kept my strokes tiny to draw it out. Scrape, scrape. "The kid you jerked off with and then, later, started fooling around with?"

"T-that one, yes."

"Finished," I said. Which meant I was done with the razor, not with the shave. I got up and wet a towel at the sink, using water that was almost hot. "You had lunch with him last week?"

"Yes, we caught up and all." Charles was looking very worried now. "Did you...want to meet him?"

"I might. You said he's a musician? Looking for a hot time?" I wrung out the steaming towel.

"Singer. He's in a gay chorus. That's why he's out here. They're touring." Charles's own voice notched up as I laid the hot towel on his freshly shaven flesh. His cock jumped and leaked precome. I moved the wet terry cloth down his freshly shaved crack. That was allowed. His hips bucked and his face went red. I expected him to curse me out, but, strangely, he didn't. He kept his desires stubbornly behind his teeth.

After a moment, the towel cooled and he got his breath back. "Drew can be wild, but he's not into any of this. It's not his kind of thing."

"Would his kind of thing include a one-night, romantic fantasy?" I tossed aside the towel, wet my hands with almond oil and began my massage. I'd learned this, along with how to use a straight razor, from a barber. It was a massage for head and face, but I found it worked very well down below.

It started with light strokes. Charles' freshly shaven skin was wonderful to the touch. Baby smooth and sensitive. My caresses made him pump his hips, searching for friction.

"He-he might. I-I could ask."

I let my fingers trail down between the thighs "If he seems interested, invite him to join us at the Pit on Sunday."

"Y-yes sir—Jesus, Mary and Joseph!" he gasped as my slippery fingers explored his crack and touched on his hot, pulsing sphincter.

Again, I expected him to call me dirty names for toying with him, instead he held out, even when I stroked him under his balls, one of his sensitive spots. Those rosy nuts were high and tight, just asking to be licked into submission. Cheating. But then, this was my game. I could change the rules. It was, after all, my job in this relationship to be new and inventive.

I continued my massage, up and over the thighs, around his cock. He moaned and squirmed, arm muscles flexing against his restrained wrists.

I licked at his wrinkled sacks, causing him to jump as if jolted. More licks, small and slow, like the scrapes of the razor. He writhed and whimpered, his legs spreading wider for me. Still no swearing.

Finally, I heard those sweet words, all the sweeter given how much of a fight Charles had put up, "Please, sir..."

I love to win.

Chapter 4

Discoveries

Drew was too fey for my tastes, but I figured him right for Robbie. He had almond eyes and blue-black hair, a triangular shaped face and a golden complexion. His body was on the lanky side, but that was fine. Robbie liked rangy, Viggo Mortensen types.

"Pleased to meet you," Drew said over the Cockpit's music and the clack of billiard balls. His accent was deeply southern, more so than Charles. Its inflection was also decidedly gay or "queer" as Nash would have put it. "Charles has been telling me all about ya."

"Good things, I hope." Drew's handshake was firm, a point in his favor.

"Good? I thought he was taking me to meet Jesus Christ himself." Drew settled into the booth and glanced around. He wasn't nervous, but he wasn't comfortable either. This wasn't his kind of bar, as his blue Gap sweater and brown Dockers proclaimed. That didn't stop him from being curious, especially about the guys in tight leather pants.

"Naw. I'm more of a Moses type," I grinned, "parting the seas and bringing down commandments. Charles had been telling me about you, too. Said you've been buds since you were like four years old."

"Buds?" he gave Charles a nudge. "We're like brothers. I mean, he ate and slept at my house more than he did his own. My parents forgot he wasn't their son."

Charles rolled his eyes and snorted. "Did not."

"Did so. They were always saying, 'why can't you be more like your brother, Charles?' And I'd say, 'he's not your son!' and they'd say, 'he should be!' When they found out I was gay, they were disappointed. When they found out he was gay, they blamed me! He didn't

157

make me gay, I made him gay! Can you believe that?"

"He's full of shit," Charles told me, then, back to Drew, "What are you drinking?"

Drew requested a whiskey sour. I just nodded for my usual.

As soon as Charles was out of earshot, Drew became cooler and less dramatically fey. "So," he said in a man-to-man tone. "You're the love of Charles' life."

"Is that what he called me?"

"Not in so many words. But I've known him a long time. Seen his highs and lows. Know a bit about his problems. You certainly look the part. He's always wanted a big, black stud."

That sounded... catty. I didn't think Drew was jealous of me, but I got the feeling that he was giving me a warning.

"I'm not going to hurt Charles."

"No? Isn't that what he wants?" Now the tone was barbed and impatient, but not, I surmised, with me.

"You're not happy with his lifestyle?"

"It don't seem healthy. I mean, I get the bedroom antics, spankings and all. I just don't get this." I knew exactly what "this" meant as he was looking at a collared boy setting out drinks for his master and friends. Drew didn't understand why his old buddy wanted to be a slave. Not play at it, *be* it twenty-four-seven.

"I don't always understand it myself," I confessed. "But then I'm at the other end of the spectrum. I don't want to surrender anything."

Drew snorted. "Naw, I don't suppose you do. Charles says this sort of leaning might be... I dunno. Something you're born with?"

I shrugged. "There is a case for that."

"So, it was evident from childhood? I mean, yeah, Charles never did want to be the 'leader' when we played follow the leader. And he liked getting tied up and handcuffed when we played superhero."

"Aw. That's too cute."

He laughed, looking for a moment like he'd relax. Instead he tensed. "Honestly, it's not the bondage that bothers me, or even the submissiveness. It's his obsession with slavery and I know where that started. With his fucking, fifth grade history teacher. You know about that?"

"Yeah, I know," I said, meeting his eyes. He was talking about Charles's obsession with his family history. What had set him on *that* particular road. But that's another story. "I'm doing what I can to help him."

"Good to know." There followed a pause where Drew seemed to brood and consider. "Truthfully, I haven't seen him this together in a long time," he admitted. "So you must be doing something right. I also don't suppose the pot oughta be calling the kettle black."

"What does that mean?"

He gazed at me sidewise with those mischievous almond eyes and said, "I'm a glory-hole boy."

Good...God. Pot calling the kettle black indeed. So that's what Charles meant by "wild."

"Which side of the hole?" I asked.

Drew smacked his lips in answer.

Charles reappeared with our drinks then settled in next to me. I put my arm around him, my way of staking a claim, including the right to defend him. Drew's eyes flickered, but he lifted his drink in salute to me.

"What did you tell him?" I asked Charles.

Drew answered for him, "That you're looking for someone to romance a guy for his birthday. Which sounds like fun, but none of these guys —"

"How about him?" I pointed to Robbie, moving about behind the bar.

Drew's brows shot up. "The hot redhead?" A beat. "Shoot. Okay, yeppers, I'd give him a try. Unless...." His tone went suspicious. "Just how kinky is he?"

"He's not. That's why we need outside help. He likes long walks in the moonlight, soft music, and being in the arms of one, attentive lover. Pretty kinky, huh?"

"You ain't kidding. He's tamer than I am." Drew considered. "I wouldn't say no."

"Getting onboard with us means you agree not to say no," I pointed out. "Only he gets to. And he might. You could go home alone. Can you be okay with that?"

"Interesting way of propositioning a gent. Offer him a hot fella and then warn him that he might not get any."

"I like to keep things honest. It saves time. Are you in?"

A thoughtful sigh, but I knew he was hooked. "Do I get a solo?"

"A solo? A song you mean?"

"He has a good voice," Charles said, his way of assuring me that this wasn't going to turn into karaoke night.

"If you want to serenade him, that's fine with me," I said. "It'd be great, so long as it's appropriate, romantic."

"Oh," Drew grinned, now looking very interested. "It will be."

I watched as Charles walked Drew out to his waiting cab. The singer seemed a nice guy. I wished, however, that there was some way to actually audition him for the part of romantic-lover-for-Robbie. The last thing I wanted for my fantasy evening was to stick Robbie with someone he didn't like.

"Sir?"

I blinked up. Terry was standing before my table, hands behind his back, eyes submissively down.

"Sir," he repeated over the music and chatter. Not "Mason" or "Fancy Man." Shit. "May I speak with you? Privately?"

I got up, stopped to tell Katie where I was going so she could pass it onto Charles, then headed to the only private place in the Pit outside the bathroom: the storage area. It was a cramped room filled with crates of liquor, boxes of toilet paper, bar towels and old decorations. It smelled of the chili Nash served for happy hour.

"What is it?"

"Sir," Terry said, shutting the door. The noise from without became muffled, "Word is that you're looking for guys to participate in a birthday fantasy for Robbie—"

"Oh, good God!" My stupid mistake. I'd made an inquiry or two and the news had gotten out. "This better not get back to Robbie. I'm so not shitting you, Terry, I will go on a killing spree."

Terry looked aggrieved. "No one would do that, especially not to you."

"Yeah, sure."

"The thing is, I want to volunteer."

"Oh, fuck me. No, Terry, just no."

"I'm not trying to get my fantasy," he argued, "this is all about Robbie, I know that. That's why I want to help."

"It's also about romance, which is why I'm looking for guys outside the bar. There's nothing you can do that I need."

"I can dance."

"Yeah, I'm sure you can —"

"No, I mean really dance. Waltz, Samba, Foxtrot...."

I blinked. You have to understand, Terry was standing before me in tight jeans, his bare and slightly furry chest exposed under a leather vest, a biker's cap on his short, brown curls. And he was talking about dancing.

"I used to teach dancing," he explained.

"You *taught* dancing?"

"Before I moved here."

Unbelievable. And the worst thing was, he was right. I could use him. "If you are lying or even exaggerating to me —"

"I wouldn't do that, not even if I were stupid. And I'd have to be really stupid to do that to you. You're not Robbie's only friend, Mason. Let me help."

I kept him in suspense for a moment, first so that I could think it through and make sure I wouldn't regret it, second because I'm a sadist who likes to keep guys on tender hooks.

"All right," I said at last. "You're in."

"I am? I mean, thank you, sir. You won't be sorry." I caught sight of his shining brown eyes and moaned within. I didn't doubt that he'd do his best, for me if not for Rob. I was just a worried what that might mean.

It did resolve one thing, however. I could stop looking for actors and start rehearsing this play. I kinda wanted to know if there was any chance of pulling it off.

Four days later, I arrived at the Cockpit just after sunset in Nash's Black BMW. It was D-day. I was not driving. Nigel was. This would have terrified me if I hadn't spent an entire afternoon getting him accustomed to driving around town. On the right side.

Big hairy men and butch women smoking in the parking lot paused in their conversations as Nigel pulled up. He left the motor purring as he hopped out and hurried around the car. He had on a dark suit and chauffeur's cap. The befuddled bears and dykes watched him open the back door.

I stepped out.

Jaws dropped and eyes popped. I swear I thought one or more heads were going to explode.

"Fancy Man?" someone choked.

In the flesh I almost said. I straightened my bow tie. It went with the black tux I was wearing, a stylish outfit complete with a gold, brocade waistcoat. Terry had mockingly fainted when he saw me wearing it, and Nigel had remarked that I could be the new James Bond. Charles had just crossed his arms and pointed out that I looked like I was about to comment on a boxing match. Fucker.

"Anyone going to get the door?" I asked, striding forward. Someone pulled it open and in I walked. The crisp air vanished and the familiar masculine warmth of the bar enfolded me. The jukebox was pounding away as always, but the rest of the noise suddenly vanished as everyone's eyes locked on me. I tugged at my jacket and kept my head up.

"I don't fuckin' believe it!" I think it was Jordon who broke the ice. Suddenly there was laughter and applause, wolf-whistles and whoops. Cellphones came out and, because someone had leaked word about this, digital cameras.

Hey, I'm too vain to say I wasn't pleased. Dutifully, I posed for pictures, solo and then with others. My friend Al got a group of collared bottoms to bow down before me, and then some fellow tops posed around me with fists up, as if we were about to fight. Flashes went off. Dykes pretended to swoon in my arms and Katie got me to lift her up, which wasn't hard as she's a featherweight. She curled up kittenishly in my grip, looking as if I'd just saved her from Dr. No. More flashes. When I finally put her down, she tugged on my lapel.

"You smell nice!" she whispered and gave me a kiss on the cheek. "If I was into guys I would so want you right now."

That left me blushing. A few more pictures, and then I finally raised my hand. Robbie was behind the bar, frozen in the middle of tapping out a glass of beer. I'd called him and told him that I was taking him out for his birthday and he wasn't allowed to refuse.

Now he looked as if he wished he had refused. I strode up to him and held out my hand. "Your carriage awaits."

That got more whoops and whistles and the cameras came back out. Robbie turned so red his freckles vanished.

"Mason, you asshole —" he hissed, but he allowed me to lead him to the door. I even helped him on with his jacket, which earned us several sly comments and more pictures.

"I am going to get you for this," Robbie said as we stepped out, then froze. "Is that..." he tried, licked his lips, then tried again. "That's not Nash's beamer... is it?"

"You were expecting a pumpkin?" I motioned him toward the open door. Half the bar had followed us out and there were plenty of rude comments and more camera flashes taking in the car, us and our "chauffeur."

"Good evening, sir," Nigel touched on his hat and grinned. The Brit was the only actor in my play who wasn't worried about tonight. In fact, he was positively sanguine.

"You boys planning on acting out High Noon?" he'd asked when I rung him up.

"Nope." I said, *"This time we're putting a play on in the barn. Wanna help?"*

"Can I be Mickey Rooney?"

I appreciated his willingness and spirit, but I was still anxious about his driving. If Nash found one dent on his beloved BMW I'd have to leave the country and take on a new identity. I am so not shitting you.

"You look handsome," Robbie said when we were finally settled in that plush back seat and underway. His massive arms were crossed, which meant that he was pissed at me.

"Thank you."

"I suppose this is some sort of birthday present fantasy?"

"You suppose right."

By the light of passing streetlamps, I saw his lips thin. "I appreciate it, but I really don't think I can imagine you as someone else—"

"You don't have to imagine me as anyone else, Rob. I'm not the fantasy, just your host."

"Like bleeding Rod Serling in the bloody *Twilight Zone*," Nigel helpfully put in from the front seat.

Robbie did a double take. He'd assumed that Nigel was a well-behaved bottom, but that outburst made it pretty clear he wasn't.

"Concentrate on the road," I told Nigel. We'd gotten into the up-scale part of town and were winding our way toward the top of the hill. Robbie noticed.

"Wait a minute. Are we going to Nash's place?"

"His guesthouse," I affirmed. "Don't worry, I got Nash to promise on his honor that all webcams would be off, and then I had Gina check things over to make sure he'd kept that promise." Gina was a leather-dyke with a genius for electronics. If she said all the bugs were dead, then they probably were. "Not saying I won't be peeking, but what you do in there will stay in there—not show up on Nash's blog."

"Mason—"

"You were the one who said that you were going to be like Cinderella," I pointed out, "Enjoying the ball, no more hoping for any-thing other than a dance with Prince Charming. Isn't that what you said?"

"Well, yeah."

"So? This is the ball. A small, private ball. Enjoy it. In the morning you can go back to sweeping out ashes and running chores for your wicked stepmother."

He was still frowning.

"Go for it, Gov!" Nigel urged.

"The road!" I said. "We're almost at our turn off."

"I see it," Nigel spun the wheel. We slipped around behind Nash's home along a secondary drive that went right to the guesthouse. Ni-gel didn't smash the car into anything, for which I was grateful. He got it parked beside my Scion, shut it off and came around to open our door.

I slipped out and waited. Robbie remained in the back seat. I was ready to argue him out when he finally surrendered.

"Let's get this over with," he grumbled.

Not the best attitude, but it would do for now. It was a clear, crisp night, the kind that carries the smell of magic on it. Orange and yellow leaved trees swayed overhead as we walked the cobbled path. Gazing across the darkened backyard I could see city lights twinkling in the distance.

"I'd better get a safeword," Robbie muttered as I opened the guesthouse door for him.

"Of course," I said. "It's 'glass slipper.'"

"You were the one who said that you were going to be like Cinderella," I pointed out, "Enjoying the ball."

Chapter 5
Fancy Man and the Brokenhearted Bartender

"Holy Mother Mary!" That was Robbie's opinion when I flicked on the lights to show him the transformed guesthouse. The original dé-cor, in true Nash fashion, had been that of hunting lodge including a mahogany card table and a rod-iron bed covered in furs. To make it homey, Nash had tossed about bearskins, nailed up elk heads, and even placed a large, mounted trout on the wall above the hot tub. The barbarian.

We'd moved out the dead animals, laid down Indian carpets, got-ten a burgundy cloth on the table, draped the bed in gold satin, tossed a dozen throw pillows about and put up a few landscape paintings.

A fire crackled in the wood burning stove and rose petals floated on the hot tub's steaming water. Sandalwood incense covered the usual smell of cigarettes and cigars.

"I don't believe this!" Robbie made the tour. "It's got style. And no whips!" He was referring to the fact that, being for Nash's guests, the room had also included a spanking bench and several switches shelved like pool cues.

"Yeah. Who says leathermen haven't got the decorator gene? Anyway, this is it: Cinderella's ballroom, the Beast's castle, the Sultan's palace."

"So, I'm getting a fairytale for my birthday?"

"G-rated if you'd like, but why waste the hot tub. Speaking of which, why don't you start there. Undress, sink in, unwind."

"Sure, why not?" Robbie's resistance was fading.

"I'll be back later," I told him as he shrugged off his coat and started unbuttoning his shirt. He just grunted. I stepped out and made a dash across the lawn, past the badminton net to the back door of Nash's house. I went from chill to warm again and with a few steps down the hall from the kitchen, entered Nash's dungeon.

Odd place for a base of operations, but it was quiet and central. Like most dungeons it was dark and cluttered with benches and padded tables, swings and chains, shelves of rope, butt plugs, paddles and the like. We'd set up shop on an old, oak desk. Remaining bits of costumes and props were laid out along with bottles of water and snacks.

My four actors and Charles were huddled around Charles' new laptop computer. Drew in particular was leaning in, his hands on Charles's shoulders as he ogled the screen.

"Oh, baby! That's right, show us that tight, muscled ass."

I sighed and slipped off my black jacket. "I'd tell you all to be ashamed of yourselves. But what would be the point?"

Thing was, I had kinda lied to Robbie... a little. There was one active camera... okay, two in the guesthouse. Both were mine, and I wasn't going to use them for anything so innocent as a quick peek. Nor for prurient interest, either. I was the director of this drama and I had to make sure things moved along smoothly, that no one drowned in the hot tub or set fire to the drapery.

Okay, yeah, so the cameras were being used for the prurient interest of five horny guys right now, but that wasn't the point. This was serious business. All the same...I enjoyed the view, too. Robbie, naked and displaying his white, freckled body, was stepping into the hot tub. His cock was nestled in a patch of coppery pubic hair and bobbed a little as he slipped beneath the bubbling water. Next into the water was his washboard stomach, followed by that rock-hard chest with its swirl of reddish chest hair. His nipples looked chewably small and pink on his solid pecs. When he bent his arms behind his head, the bulge of his biceps had us all sighing. He was one sexy bastard.

"Blimey," Nigel said appreciatively.

"Do I *have* to go last?" Drew asked.

"We stick to the script. Nigel, are you ready?"

"How do I look?" he asked, turning. He'd changed out of his driver's outfit into pinstriped trousers and a swallow-tailed jacket. His ascot tie was perfectly knotted, likely Charles' doing, and neatly tucked into a striped waistcoat.

"Perfect. Get your ass over there."

He was off. Charles vacated the chair for me. I settled in and divided the view on screen between the three webcams. Two in the guesthouse, the other, Nash's own, overlooking the backyard. I watched Nigel cross the lawn to knock at the guesthouse door.

"Hello?" the Brit said, cracking it open. "May I come in?"

Robbie, who'd been resting back in the hot water with eyes closed, sat up. "Um, sure."

"Good evening." Nigel said striding in. "I am your butler, Nigel."

Robbie's brows went up. "My butler. Okay. Is that accent real?"

"Yes, and I'm hoping it will get me laid. By the way, happy birthday."

"Thanks, I think." Robbie crossed his arms on the edge of the tub, resting his chin on them.

"It is my job to inform you of the details of this unique birthday gift, and then get you anything you might like from the liquor cabinet." Nigel, very un-butler-like, snatched a chair and straddled it. "You know how in some fairytales there's an enchanted lady with all these princely suitors trying to win her hand and break the spell?

Well, mate, there are three handsome gents coming to try their luck with you. One at a time, that is."

Robbie got that stubborn-sour look. "I really think I'd rather spend my birthday alone—"

"Now, now, give the lads a chance. Take it from me, you want to enjoy those erections while you've still got 'em. Anyway, after each of these princes has put on his show, you get to decide which one you want to have dinner with."

"Dinner? That's all."

"That's all the management will be providing, though there are condoms and other useful items in the loo." Nigel stood and set the chair back at the table. "Anything you care to do once you've picked your prince is entirely up to you. Now, what do you say to a drink?"

Way to go, Nigel, I thought. The man was a natural cheerleader. "Hadji, are you ready?"

"Yes, sir." He was fiddling with the clasp on his cape. I stepped up and helped to get it clipped on. I'd dressed him up in the stereotypical white turban and tunic. Blousy trousers were tucked into suede boots. A red cape and sash along with some costume jewelry made him more princely, but he still looked like a boy sultan rather than a rajah. It wasn't just the outfit or his twinkness. It was his attitude. As much as we'd worked on it, he was still too subservient.

"Remember," I said confidentially, "no calling Robbie 'sir.' You don't have to be aggressive, but you have to meet his eyes and be romantic. Can you do that?"

"Yes sir," Hadji said with puppy-like sincerity. "I know this is important to Master Nash. I won't disappoint you or him."

Oh, kid, I winced. *Nash is not a nice man.* Not an evil man come to that, but not nice. I knew sure as the sun was gonna shine that one fine day Nash would kick this bewildered boy out of his house, making room for some new lad he'd taken an interest in. He'd do it without a twinge of regret and counter any accusations of heartlessness by pointing out how well Hadji had been treated. Free room, free meals, spoilt rotten by his benevolent master. The twink could have no complaints.

I could hear it now, and I would have warned Hadji about it, but I knew he wouldn't listen. There are some things we just have to learn the hard way, especially when we're youthful and in love.

I stepped back and had him turn, displaying his finery.

"He should salaam when he enters," Terry recommended from the spanking bench where he sat munching on corn chips.

"That's Arabic," Charles objected. "He's Pakistani."

"So shouldn't he press his hands together at his forehead?" Drew said.

"Only if he's Hindu."

"Are you Hindu?" Terry asked, and I found myself rubbing at the spot of pain growing between my eyes.

"Presbyterian," Hadji said.

"How about the salute of the Mounted Police?" Terry touched three fingers to his forehead.

"That's the Boy Scouts," Drew objected.

"Just press a hand to your heart when you bow," I said to Hadji. "Now get."

"Yes, sir."

I returned to my seat, and the other three huddled around me to watch. Hadji traversed the lawn and knocked.

"Ah," said Nigel. Robbie was still in the bath, a glass of white wine in hand. Like a good butler, the Brit was setting things out. Towels, a robe, lotions and oils. He crossed for the door and opened it up.

"Your first suitor has arrived." My faux butler waved Hadji in.

The kid did his best to make a dashing entrance, cape swirling and flouncing. Hand over his heart, he bowed. "Greetings," he said in that flat, Canadian accent of his, "I am the Sultan of the South."

"Hadji?" Robbie half-frowned, half-smiled.

"At your service."

"Take your cape?" Nigel was already helping the boy to undo the troublesome clasp. Free of it, Hadji crossed to sit himself on the dry edge of the hot tub.

"I am a renowned poet in my land," Hadji said, and I noted that he was working to meet Robbie's disbelieving gaze. "Both with words and hands. If you'd like to come out and dry off, I'll show you my skill, eh?"

I winced. Oh no. He hadn't. "Did my Sultan of the South just say 'eh'?" I asked plaintively. Up till that point I thought it a dated and silly joke that Canadians said "eh." Apparently, I was wrong. There were Canadians who did say it and, alas, Hadji was one of them.

Drew, Charles and Terry had their hands over their mouths, a few helpless snorts and suddenly they were falling all over each other, laughing.

"We'll take my flying carpet to the palace, eh?" Drew chortled.

"Oh, eh, I forgot my camel!" Terry tossed in. Charles was laughing so hard he'd dropped to the floor.

This is why I work alone. "Hardy-har-har, very funny." Luckily, the gaffe hadn't set off any laughter from Nigel or Robbie, though the latter looked like he was trying to suppress a smile. Well, better that then sulking. He had risen out of the bath, and Nigel had him wrapped, toga-like, in a bath towel.

Settled on the bed, Hadji took up some oil and started very tamely with Robbie's broad feet. Nash had assured me that, delicate as Hadji seemed, he had strong, sure hands. He was also an expert at something else, something I hoped Robbie would allow.

"*A jug of wine, a loaf of bread, and thou –*" Hadji recited, "*Beside me in the wilderness...*"

The boy must have been doing something right because Robby relaxed back on the throw pillows. Nigel slipped out and headed back across the lawn. I'd warned him that he'd be doing a lot of crisscrossing tonight.

"Right," I said, "Hadji's got a few more verses to go. Bathroom break. If you guys are done laughing?"

"Eh?" Terry said and chuckled weakly.

"Oh, my stomach hurts," Drew wiped his eyes and, pushing up, offered a hand to Charles.

Along with Terry, arms about each other, they stumbled out. Nice to know this was turning into a bonding experience. Back to Robbie. Hadji had gotten Rob to roll over and, still reciting verses from Omar's *Rubaiyat*, was massaging the bartender's hairy calves. Robbie's was getting into it and Hadji was being romantic rather than submissive.

All systems go.

Nigel arrived and nabbed a sparkling water. "Nice thing you're doing, there." He gestured with the bottle at the screen. "He seems a good mate."

"One of the best," I agreed, vacating my seat. Hadji, pushing up the toga towel, was up to the thighs. Liberal amounts of oil had Robbie's reddish leg hair glinting. Best of all, he was moaning. "I'll be right back."

I took a bathroom break, splashed water on my face and did a few stretches to work the kinks out of my shoulders before heading back.

"You should tell him," I heard Drew's southern voice from the kitchen and paused on my way. He sounded impatient and angry.

"Our relationship isn't like that," Charles' said in return. His accent had thickened since he'd been hanging with Drew. The two of them sounded like they were discussing whether or not General Lee should press on to Antietam. "It is not a problem."

"I've known you your whole life, Charles. You can't shit me. There's a problem. If this isn't it, than what is it?"

"Nothing you would understand."

Shit. I slipped back into the dungeon. Had I'd missed something? I hated when things got by me. My mind cast back. Charles hadn't seemed sad or worried, our sex had been great. Then again....

Now that I thought about it, it'd been a while since he'd jumped me for a morning wrestling match. He loved to laugh and grapple and get me to overpower him. Another thing: Charles was the only one able to deflate my ego and he tended to do so whenever my vanity got the better of me. Yet except for his comment on my tux, he hadn't been doing that either. And there was his silence. Charles had one hell of a mouth and he wasn't afraid to put up a verbal fight when his hands were tied. But lately, he'd been going mute instead.

Okay. Fuck me. Something *was* wrong. And I had no time at the moment to deal with it. Nigel and Terry were staring at the screen, mouths agape.

I peered over their shoulders. Hadji had reached Robbie's hairless, freckled ass. He'd finished off his verses and was massaging it, pushing those glutes together and apart. Robbie was lying limply on the bed, humming with pleasure.

Easy, Hadji, I thought. *Easy.*

Acting abilities notwithstanding, the boy was a pro. He delved very gently into the crack with his thumbs, a shallow caress that got those thighs to part a little more. Hands stoked down the sides of that ass, under those moon curves, back up. He even worked at Robbie's lower back as he shifted himself onto the thighs.

We were all holding our breaths now. Hadji bent his head. I zoomed in the camera and we caught it. His flickering tongue.

Terry moaned almost in harmony with Robbie who shuddered. Hadji took his time, laving the sides of the crack, curving on down with it and then back up. Robbie groaned and shifted off a cock that had to be getting hard. I knew mine was stiffening up.

The boy dared to spread that ass and delve deeper.

"S-sir," Terry whispered, "May I—"

"No," I said firmly. "No jerking off." Though heaven knew, I wanted to myself.

"Jesus." A southern accent. Drew and Charles had arrived.

Hadji had his nose buried in that freckled ass now. A soft cry of pleasure from Robbie told us that the pup had just hit the spot. I could well imagine that twink tongue warmly and wetly flowing over the folds of my own tight sphincter. Robbie started to push his ass into the boy's face. Hadji should have eased off about then.

He didn't. Shit.

"Nigel," I managed. 'Get over there, sneak in and give Hadji a pinch on the ass."

"But—"

"A really hard pinch. He's carrying it too far."

Nigel ran. I barely glanced up to see the Brit's dash across the lawn. Hadji was lost, completely focused on getting his tongue into that hole. I didn't need any extreme close up to tell me that. Robbie, eyes shut, was groaning, undulating, and trying to take hold of his cock.

Nigel appeared at the door and tip-toed over. He probably could have stomped for all those two would have noticed. He glanced up at one of the cameras with a worried, reluctant expression, then reached out and pinched Hadji's ass through those thin cotton pantaloons.

The boy gasped, head jerking up. His soft lips and chin were wet with saliva. He saw Nigel and frowned with anger. Nigel, equally frustrated, pointed to the camera. Hadji's expression went from fury to dismay. As Nigel darted back out the door, the kid went back to licking just the crack, and then, with evident reluctance and longing, he moved off Robbie's thighs.

"Wh—" Robbie was still breathing heavily. "W-why are you stopping?"

"I'm sorry, sir—er, sorry," Hadji said. "I'm not allowed to go any further."

"What?" Robbie rolled over. His cock, which was short but thick, was stiff in his hand and dark red. It gleamed with precome. God, it had to be aching. Mine was and no one had been licking my ass.

Hadji wiped his lips and chin on his shoulder. "That's the rule. Only the prince you pick can... go all the way."

"Is that right?" Robbie growled. He wasn't happy, not at all. In fact he looked ready to say the safeword and put a sullen end to it all. And who could blame him? That rule had seemed a good idea at the time, but maybe it had fucked things up?

"It wouldn't be fair to the others," Hadji explained, and I was very glad for his earnestness. Robbie would have aimed a kick at my balls if I'd cut him off like that. But Hadji had those large, dark eyes, ones that clearly expressed how much he hated being unable to please. "I'm at fault. I went too far and not far enough. I don't blame you for being mad at me."

Might as well have shot an arrow through Robbie's soft heart. His outrage quieted. I imagine he still wanted to punch me in the teeth. Well, he could do that later if he liked.

"Did you... enjoy my poetry?" Hadji asked.

"Yeah," Robbie sighed. His erection was going down even as he forlornly rubbed at it. "I liked it a lot."

"I'm glad." Hadji slipped off the bed and fetched his cloak. He paused at the door to place his hand on his heart and bow. "I enjoyed it too," he added, exiting stage left.

Not bad for a first act, eh?

Hadji left the guesthouse and Nigel, who'd been pacing outside, slipped in.

"Refresh that drink, Gov?" he asked.

Robbie, seated on the bed, his frustrated cock sulking on his thigh, fairly snarled at the Brit. "You forgot to tell me about that little rule. The one that says my 'suitors' are only allowed to tease."

"I did neglect to tell you that, and I'm very sorry. But I've gotta say, you're looking at this all wrong. It's a fairytale. Each prince has got a gift and they're going to offer it to you. The best they've got and you get to pick the one that pleases you most. That little lad put his heart into showing you his gift. Why complain about what you didn't get?"

"I didn't ask for this fantasy," Robbie grumbled.

"See, now you're looking at it all wrong again. You don't ask for birthday presents, you get them because folk like you and want to show it. You've got to learn to enjoy what comes when it comes. God knows, you might not get it again. I sure don't," Nigel added ruefully. "Now, how about some more wine?"

This Englishman was a treasure and I was going to buy him a new pair of cowboy boots after this. Hadji stepped into the dungeon looking dejected and ashamed. He'd pulled off his turban so that his dark hair fell about his delicate, brown face. His head was bowed. Charles and Terry glanced my way. On their expressions I saw fear of my anger, and a request that I do something for the poor twink.

See, this is something those outside the master-slave world, like Drew, don't get. Slave types yearn to please, that's their whole deal. When they get things right, their hearts swell with pride and joy. When they fuck up, their hearts sink to the very bottom, and they can tie themselves up in psychological and emotional knots over it. What most people really don't understand is that telling your slave that his fuck-up is forgiven isn't enough. He *needs* to "pay" for the mistake in some physical way, otherwise he won't be able to let go of his guilt and blame.

Seriously. And hey, that's better than with most vanilla couples who "punish" each other for years over certain failures and disappointments. One thing most slaves can be sure of, once they've been punished for something, it's over and done with. And yeah, part of it involves pleasing the sadistic master and feeding their own masochism in the process. It's catharsis all around.

Hadji had fucked up and that meant he was going to be miserable for the rest of the night, probably for however many days until Nash returned, if I didn't take care of him right now. I took my responsibilities seriously; I'd asked for Hadji, and that meant I had to act the part of master and do my job, not just reap the benefits. Which was why I'd taken the time to ask Nash a few important questions about him.

Hadji, I'd been informed, had a daddy complex. He yearned for a stern father figure to anchor him. That was the part I'd need to play if I was going to do this right. I got up and relieved the boy of turban and cape, setting them aside.

"Terry, get ready." I said, surreptitiously snatching up a rounded paddle. I didn't want Drew to notice and he didn't, but Terry and Charles did. I saw them both shift. Between that voyeuristic rimming and what they knew was coming to Hadji they were probably feeling a little...wound up.

I grabbed Hadji by the arm and took him down to the most distant spare bedroom. It had a good, stiff-backed chair in it. I shoved the boy in, locked the door, and sat myself down.

"What'd you do wrong?"

"You told me to stop before he got too aroused," Hadji whispered. "I didn't. I got into it and forgot. I'm sorry, sir."

"You know sorry's not good enough."

"I know, sir."

"You left him mad and nearly ruined everything. Take down your pants."

Chapter 6
Three Princes

Hadji gulped, and did as he was told. He pulled them off slow, a mix of strip tease for my benefit and dread on his part. I knew he wasn't wearing underwear and I'm sure his bare skin was very sensitive to how the cloth slid over his ass before pooling around his boots. He had lithe legs with a down of black hair. The tunic hid his crotch, but not the hard-on tenting it. His breath was shallow with fear and excitement.

That's how it is with bottoms like Hadji. They yearn for pain, restraint, humiliation, even as it terrifies them. And I can promise you this, however scared he was, Hadji had likely fantasized about being in this position with me, and me doing to him what I was about to do to him. It was as much a dream as a nightmare come true.

"Come here."

He took tiny steps, not just because he had to shuffle with his pants down, but also because it was part of his ritual, to draw it out. His focus was growing tight now, entirely on me, and that paddle, wondering, no doubt, how it was going to be with me, someone so much bigger and stronger than Master Nash. I saw the sweat on his upper lip, saw his throat bob with a swallow of fear.

As he stepped close I grabbed his arm and jerked him over my lap, bending him head down. I easily captured his slender wrists and pinned them at the small of his back. His bare legs I trapped between my thighs. I could feel him shaking with fear, even as his aroused cock pressed against my knee. I used two fingers of the hand holding the paddle to slowly lift his tunic and expose that cute, brown bubble butt of his.

It was high and vulnerable, and I loved the way its exposure created goose bumps down his spine. He gasped and squirmed with shame as I rubbed the paddle over that ass and teased him by tapping it.

"Please sir, I'm sorry sir—"he whimpered.

Whack! I brought down that first smack. His body jerked and he yelped. I wondered if Nash's arm was as heavy.

Whack! Whack! Whack! The paddle struck with satisfying slaps on those orbs, mashing them, reddening them. Hadji cried out and struggled. I figured he liked that, feeling helpless in my powerful grip. He tried to kick, which had no effect at all.

Whack! Whack! Whack! I sped up the spanking. I couldn't take too long with this.

"Your butt's not going anywhere, young man," I told him. Paddling it harder. "I'm going to punish you till you can't sit down!"

I aimed my slaps up, as in ping-pong, getting him under the curve, then at one tender cheek, then the other. His erection was half-gone, from the pain. The rubbing against my leg, however, was keeping it from completely flagging.

He was sobbing now. "It won't happen again! I'll be good!"

I paused and eased away my thigh from his legs. He remained draped over my knee, trembling legs barely able to hold him up.

"Spread em," I told him.

He cried harder.

"Do it!" I snapped. Fucking twinks. Charles would have already had his legs apart, daring me to do my worst. He would also have been swearing at me, not sniffling.

Hadji opened up as much as he could given the pants about his ankles. I closed up my muscled thighs again. His brown nuts were exposed, his asshole too, if one parted those abused cheeks with the edge of the paddle, as I did. That made him shiver and moan. My cock, which had been rising up, went rock hard there in my formal trousers.

Whack! Whack! Whack!

He bucked and wept and pleaded for mercy. Finally, I put aside the paddle and rested back, feeling quite calm. I stroked his hot, sore ass, liking how my touch made him catch his breath and wiggle in pain and arousal. Unfortunately, I now had one hell of a hard-on. I checked the clock. It had seemed long for Hadji and me, but it hadn't been more than about seven minutes. Could I do this quickly?

Given how I felt, hell yes.

"It's over," I said releasing him. "Now show me how grateful you are for your punishment."

He slipped right down to his knees, his trembling hands going for my zipper. My cock popped out, stiff and pulsing with excitement. Hadji put his very wet mouth to it and I felt his tears falling on my shaft as he began to suck and bob. His lips and tongue were even softer than I'd imagined they'd be, and certainly as clever. He licked the ridges and the throbbing vein underneath, delved into my dripping slit with the tip of his tongue. That made me thrust into his hot mouth. He gagged a little then found a way to take me. Not to the root, I was too long and thick for him, but he did his best to suck and swallow.

In no time at all I felt that hardness in my balls, the jerking pulse of an orgasm. I grabbed him by the hair, cock pumping and came in his mouth. My cream spilled beyond his lips, but he swallowed as much as he could. He licked after me as I finally pulled out.

Quick, but satisfying. I pushed Hadji away as my cock went sensitive and started to shrink. His face was tear streaked, his face gooey with come and snot.

"I'm sorry I didn't do as you told me," he whispered.

I patted his head. "Apology accepted. Except for that one mistake, you did a perfect job. I'll let Master Nash know that."

"Thank you, sir." His wet eyes gleamed at that. Puppy happy now that the rolled-up newspaper was gone. I sighed. It had been fun, but I really could not understand a steady diet of such ulta-submissive bottoms.

"I have to get back," I said. "Wash up."

"Yes sir." I noted that he was rubbing at his very sore tush. He would probably spend a good amount of time admiring his reddened ass in the mirror. I wondered if Nash would make him relate the paddling, relive it, jerk off to it. Probably.

Leaving the paddle, I headed back to the dungeon. Charles stood up as I came in and Terry paused in fastening the double rows of buttons on his jacket. They kept their eyes down. Only Drew, completely in the dark, glanced up.

"Get over there," I said to Terry. He snatched up his belt and gloves and rushed out. "What's going on?"

"Nigel's moving the table and chairs," Charles responded, eyes still down. "He's been talking about how red hair isn't liked in England, and how nice it is that Americans know how to appreciate it."

"You were at the Cockpit a week or so ago," I heard from the screen. Robbie, now dressed in the white, caftan-like bathrobe we'd brought for him, was resting back on the bed. "Weren't you?"

"I was indeed." Nigel was putting aside the last chair, leaving an area of bare floor. "Not my usual scene, but I'd gone chasing after Charles."

"I take it you caught him?"

"Hence, my role here," Nigel acknowledged. "A favor owed to the Fancy Man for his generosity. Well worth it."

On the other half of the screen, the outside camera showed Terry at the door. He was putting on his belt and white gloves.

"So you're not really a British butler," Robbie went on.

"Ah, no. This," Nigel touched on his costume, "is Mason's revenge for my typecasting all Americans as cowboys. I suppose I should be grateful he didn't make me play a member of the royal family."

"Do you mind playing butler for the night?"

"Well, that depends," Nigel said gravely. "I was promised that at some point or other you'd dress up like Batman."

That got a laugh from Robbie, a big one.

"I'm going to be sorely disappointed if you don't," Nigel continued. "I've always wanted to be buggered by the caped crusader."

A knock at the door.

"Ah," said Nigel. "Looks like your next suitor has arrived."

"Send him in, Alfred."

"Very good, Master Bruce."

The door fell open and Terry marched in, then bowed smartly at the waist. Robbie gasped, and well he might have. I'd found Terry a lovely, nineteenth century military outfit: red jacket with gold buttons and epaulets complimented by dark trousers with gold stripes down either side. He looked liked he'd stepped right out of Cinderella.

"Greetings." He smiled that charming (yes, charming!), boyish smile of his. "I am the Monarch of the West."

Nigel smirked and with a wave, left them.

"Son-of-a-bitch," Robbie said, getting to his feet. He seemed to be conflicted, impressed but also bemused and uncertain.

"I clean up good," Terry remarked.

"Damn straight. Okay, Monarch of the West...I'll bite. What gift do you bring?"

Terry stepped over to the stereo with its waiting iPod and quickly found his playlist. With a press of the button, a waltz sounded through the speakers. He bowed again, and held out a gloved hand. "May I have this dance?"

Robbie's brows shot up. "You're shitting me."

In answer, Terry pulled the muscular man in. His feet began to move, so smoothly that barefoot Robbie found himself following. Terry led them about the small patch of floor. He expertly avoided knocking them into the bed or table or tub.

"Will you look at that," Nigel said, appearing at our backs. "Fred Astaire and Ginger Rogers. Heh-heh. Get it? Ginger?"

We blinked at him.

"For the hair?" he tried to explain, then sighed at American ignorance. "Never mind."

"Terry's really good," Charles said.

He was, and so was the playlist, which seamlessly melded out of a waltz into Count Basie and a quickstep. Terry was grinning now and Robbie, still stunned, was beginning to look delighted.

Damn. I was jealous. All I ever got to do with Terry was enact fraternity hazings.

I glanced at the clock. The dancing had a while to go. Time for another bathroom break.

"Pit stop guys," I said. "Charles, come with me."

I led him to the same bedroom where I'd taken Hadji and locked the door. I noticed his eyes glancing anxiously to the paddle I'd left there, wondering if he'd done something wrong.

I crossed my arms. "What's the problem?"

"Problem?" he echoed.

"I overheard, Charles. Don't try to shit me."

His face paled. "Sir, Drew was wrong. There is no problem."

"I say there is. You're keeping something from me and that's a problem. Now spill it. What did Drew think we should talk about?"

He hesitated, then finally coughed it up: "Christmas."

Okay. That wasn't what I'd expected to hear. "What about it?"

"Drew wanted to know why I was going to be spending Christmas alone. Why you weren't going to be with me, or, alternately, why I wasn't going to be with you and your family."

My turn to flush, though Charles couldn't tell. My dark skin hid my blushes quite well. "That isn't any of his concern."

"No, sir. I tried to tell him that, but he assumed that you hadn't come out to your family. I insisted that wasn't so. ...I shouldn't have gone into it, but I don't like someone making those kinds of assumptions about you."

Translation: Charles had felt compelled to stand up for me. It was difficult to fault him for that. Slave-types are intensely loyal, even when it hurts them to be so. It was one of the qualities I loved and admired about them.

"So he thinks I'm jerking you around," I concluded.

"He doesn't understand our relationship. It's not a problem."

"No," I agreed. Strangely, in spite of Charles' insistence, I was now less sure of that than ever. "But something else is. You're still holding back. You have been for a while."

He tried to meet my eyes, but he couldn't. That was admission enough.

"Do I have to beat it out of you?"

Rosy spots appeared on his cheeks. "I've been with you for three months," he said, "and I don't know where you live."

I found it very hard to swallow all of a sudden. My throat had just closed up.

"Sunday, Tuesday and Friday nights you sleep at my place, and on Saturday you go to the home of whoever you've met at the bar. The other days you're at your apartment. I don't know where that is. The one time I asked you what part of town you lived in, you said you were in the boring part." He sucked in a breath, "But that isn't the problem."

"It's not?"

"No, sir. The problem is: *no one* knows where you live. I've heard ten different people say ten different things on the subject. You live by the lake, in a penthouse, by the train tracks, in a secret room under the Cockpit bar. From what I understand, no one's ever gone home with you. Not even Robbie has seen your place."

Body language is revealing. A man crosses his arms when he gets defensive. I crossed my arms. "Why not just look me up on the internet if you want to know where I live?"

His eyes widened, appalled. I might as well have asked him why he didn't steal from me. Sometimes I forget that Charles is as old school as they come in his training. That doesn't just mean knowing the proper way to kneel before a master, it means holding to the old guard philosophy of a slave/Master relationship. Admirably direct, this philosophy, simply put was: If the Master doesn't tell you, you don't need to know.

I probably owed Charles an apology for asking that stupid question, but as the Master I never needed to apologize for anything. So I didn't.

"Okay, so you don't know where I live and neither does anyone else. Is that all?" I demanded.

"No," Charles continued on; it seemed this can of worms was now well and truly opened. "No one seems to know anything about you either. I know you have a sister, but you've never spoken her name."

"Loretta," I said flatly, though, tellingly, my throat got even tighter, as if trying to keep it secret. "We call her Lo."

"Thank you, sir." Charles was holding more rigidly to protocols than he had in weeks, like a soldier on review. "But that's not the problem." He sucked in a breath. "The problem is, I mentioned her to Robbie because I was sure he had to know about her... but he didn't. Mason, he's your best friend and he didn't know you had a sister!"

My back muscles were tense now.

"And you never mention your father—"

"That's enough." I didn't raise my voice or snarl. But I made myself clear. My father was no one's business.

Silence stretched between us. It occurred to me that I still hadn't any idea what this was all about. Charles' took it as a given that if he needed to know such things, I'd tell him. So, why did it bother him if others were in the dark as well? And why was my stomach turning over and over again with dread?

"I'd better get back. We'll finish this later." I felt cowardly, but I really did have to get back.

Charles followed me to the dungeon. The others were too engrossed with whatever was happening on the screen to notice or care, though Drew's almond eyes did give us a curious glance.

Sultry rumba music was coming from the screen. Terry, I saw, had progressed. Considerably. He was pressed up behind Robbie, hands roaming over the bartender's body. As they undulated to the music, Terry brushed at Robbie's erection, which was peeking through the robe. His hands slid up from there to find and pinch at nipples. He set his mouth to Robbie's muscled neck, nipping and nibbling before licking up to his ear. The bartender, lost in the drumbeat, swayed and rubbed up and down against Terry.

"Should I, er, interrupt them?" Nigel asked.

"I'm hoping we don't have to." What happened with Hadji ought to have been warning enough to Terry. I guess it was because as the rumba came to an end, he stopped chewing on Robbie's earlobe and, spinning the bartender around, gave him a long, tongue-twisting kiss.

"That's all I'm allowed," he whispered. Both of them were flushed, their faces spangled with sweat. "But if you decide to pick me, I promise we'll dance all night long."

Good God. I didn't think Terry had it in him. He ought to dance more. A lot more.

Robbie, dreamy rather than pissed this time, watched Terry bow himself out before sinking down on to the bed.

One hell of a second act. "Drew," I said wondering if Charles' friend could match that, "You're up."

Drew passed Terry as they crossed the lawn. "Good luck," Terry waved to him, and I gave my attention to the images being sent from the interior cameras. The door opened.

"Greetings," Drew stepped in.

Robbie, still getting his breath back, frowned with confusion.

"Who are you?" I suppose he'd anticipated knowing all three princes.

Drew bowed. I'd found him a pretty cool Samurai outfit. (Don't ask. Let's just say that's it damn hard to find a Vietnamese prince costume in this town.) He had on flowing gray silk trousers and a tunic topped with a black vest with winged shoulders. The whole enchilada was all held together by a pair of gold and purple sashes. No katanas. Swords, I'd decided would just trip up my princes. No topknot either, but I'd given him a nice, gold headband to wear.

"I am the Emperor of the East," he announced with that southern drawl, and I found myself rubbing at the pain between my eyes again. I half-expected him to ask Robbie if he wanted grits with his sushi. "And I have every intention of winning that dinner with you."

Robbie gave Drew the once over from head to foot. He seemed to like what he saw. "What are you going to do? A Noh play?"

"Something like," Drew smirked and made adjustments to the iPod. With a press of the button, the deep music of *Madame Butterfly* came wafting out.

Going to one knee, he began to sing in a sweet, clear tenor.

Between decorating the guesthouse, fitting the costumes, blocking out the action and teaching Nigel to drive, there'd been no time for a dress rehearsal. So I hadn't heard Drew sing. The pitch was on target and his Italian, as far as I could tell, impeccable. All the same, I cannot tell you how weird it was to watch this. Robbie didn't know what to make of it either if the amazed expression his freckled face was anything to go by.

"I thought I was joking about the *Twilight Zone*," Nigel murmured.

"He was classically trained," Charles pointed out. "But it's really hard to make it in opera. Especially in Atlanta."

It was, of all people, twinky Hadji, back with us again, who said it: "That's pretty queer, eh?"

"Sir?" Terry was at my shoulder. He looked anxious. "May I speak with you?"

What now? I stepped out of the dungeon with him, still hearing the strains of *Madame Butterfly*. "What?"

"Did I do well, sir?"

"You did fantastic," I said, wondering why he had gone formal with me.

"Thank you, sir," Terry had his hands conspicuously over his crotch. "Would it please you to reward me then with some discipline? I...really need it."

Translation: dancing with Robbie, arousing them both, had left Terry over stimulated. Like Hadji, he needed something to relieve it. Let's see. The gay, Vietnamese-American from Georgia was singing *Madame Butterfly*, and the dancing leatherman was asking for a fraternity hazing. This wasn't *Cinderella*, this was *Alice in Wonderland*. Totally surreal.

Slipping back into the dungeon, I snatched up another paddle. A long, flat one. No one caught me at it; they were still too stupefied by Drew's Puccini. Back down to the bedroom at the far end of the house. I locked the door and pointed to the chair.

"Assume the position, Pledge," I sighed.

"Yes sir! For the honor of Alpha Phi Theta!" As compared to Hadji, there was nothing slow or reluctant with Terry. He dropped his trousers in a business-like manner and fell to his knees. His white undershorts nicely outlined his tight ass. He bent at the waist over the chair, legs apart, butt high.

"Count it out, Pledge!" I said, gripping the paddle like a baseball bat.

Whack!

"Ah!" Terry gasped and held to the chair. "That's one, sir. Please may I have another?"

This was so bogus, I found myself thinking.

Whack! A hiss of pain.

"T-two, sir. Please may I have another?"

Here I was, a top with three boys and all I was getting out of it was a sore arm. Okay, and a quick blow job, but fuck it if I ever used bottoms for another production. I so didn't have time for this! I gave the paddle a particularly hard and angry swing.

Whack! Across the bare thighs.

"Arg! T-three s-sir! May I please h-have another."

Whack!

"F-four, sir." Terry was beginning to cry, but unlike Hadji he tried to hide it. That's what made him a leatherman. "M-may I p-please have another?"

And what was the problem with Charles?

Whack!

"That's f-five, sir. M-may I—'

"No, you may not have another. I've got to get back to directing this thing." I tossed aside the paddle.

"Yes, sir. Thank you, sir." Terry was trembling and fighting for composure. "M-may the pledge have permission—?"

"No. You don't get to shoot until Robbie makes his choice. Then, one way or another, you can jerk off. Is that understood?"

"Yes sir." For all the shakiness in his voice, he sounded calmer. Upright on his knees, he saluted me. "Alpha Phi Theta forever!"

"Alpha Phi Theta forever," I echoed, unlocking the door.

When I stepped back into the dungeon it was to find my actors butting heads around the screen. *Madame Butterfly* was still playing but Drew wasn't singing. He was swallowing Robbie's cock, or trying to.

"Blimey," Nigel said.

"How do we zoom in?" Hadji asked.

"I guess opera gives you good throat muscles," I murmured, using the track pad to get a closer look. The bartender was lying on the bed, robe bunched around his waist, moaning and running his hands over Drew's silky black hair. The singer had his nose pretty well buried in Rob's rust-colored pubic hair.

"You want me to go pinch him on the ass?" Nigel asked.

I was about to tell him that this time it had better be a kick, when Drew abruptly came up for air. He was still working Robbie's rosy mushroom head, lapping at precome, but I could see that he was also easing off.

Robbie caught his breath, as if the cool air on his dick were reviving him. "Shit," he said after a moment. "You have to stop, don't you?"

"Indeed, I must," Drew oozed southern charm. "But I'd be happy to continue if you pick me. You taste good." He planted a kiss on the tip of Robbie's still twitching cock. "Sayonara."

End of the third act. Hallelujah.

Chapter 7
The Fourth Prince

"Last potty break, children," I shouted when Drew got back. "Make sure you're in full costume for the finale and let's remember to accept Robbie's decision with grace and decorum. Drew." I set a heavy hand on one of his shoulders. "You were amazing."

"Learned it all from Charles," he winked at his old buddy. "Even the singing. Boy can hit some high notes."

My partner blushed.

"He sure can," I said, crooking a finger at him. I led Charles out and back again to that damnable bedroom. We had about ten minutes, time enough for Robbie to cool down, clear his head and make up his mind. Time enough, I hoped, to get things straight between me and my slave. Otherwise...

Otherwise I'd sweep it all under the rug. I knew in my gut I would. And nothing would ever get resolved.

"All right," I said, locking the door. "Explain it to me. Now."

"Sir, I shouldn't have said anything—"

"What part of 'not your call' don't you understand?"

His eyes dropped. He looked like he'd rather have been anywhere but in that bedroom talking with me.

"I..." He said at last and sucked in a breath. "When I..." another breath, "When I met my mentor, he gave me this ideal to go after. A master-slave relationship completely different from...from the horrific kind my plantation-owning ancestors engaged in. This magical bond... he made it sound so right, so perfect. Honorable even. I wanted it more than anything. But after spending some time in leather bars, seeing how it really was, I figured he'd fed me a fairytale and gave up on it. Then I found you."

His eyes were blinking now. "I know you don't like me to use the word, but there are so many 'Sirs' out there. You're Master. I look at you and I want to fall to my knees. Fuck, I want to grovel on my belly. You don't know how hard it is to remain standing in your presence, I feel you deserve so much more. You're so beautiful and powerful. So amazing. And I can't believe my luck. I'm still astonished that you haven't already kicked me to the curb."

His gray eyes were misty now. "Anything you want me to be, I want to be: fuck toy, partner, dog. But you hold back. If it was just from me...I'd understand. It has to be earned and I haven't earned it. But when you hold back from everyone...that means there's no hope. No one, even those you care about, are given that chance to know you. So there's no chance for me. I'm never going to good enough."

The eyes finally went down. No tears, but the lashes were damp. "That, Master, is the problem."

My folded arms slid apart and I stared down at my feet.

Shit.

And that's pretty much when I realized that in trying to avoid putting a scratch on the car, I'd driven us off a cliff. Was it too late? Or could I, by some miracle, get this car to fly?

The last thing I wanted to do was go back to Robbie and company, but the show must go on.

I got my jacket, straightened my bowtie and checked over everyone else's costume. Then, leaving Charles at the computer, I marched my flock across the lawn to the guesthouse. The crystal clear night had gone damp and cold and we all shivered a bit while Nigel knocked and poked his head in.

"Hey, Gov, ready to go on a dinner date?" He held open the door.

The inside was wonderfully warm and filled with the mingled fragrances of steamy water, burning pine and male sweat. Nigel stepped over to the iron stove and tossed in a few more pieces of chopped wood. Robbie, I was surprised to see, had changed back into his clothes. He had his hands deep in his pockets, his eyes on his still bare feet.

"You know Mason," he said, "when this started I didn't know whether I wanted to kiss you or kill you. Especially after I learned the no climax rule, you shit."

I shrugged. "That's the way fairytales work. You only get to hang with Prince Charming at the ball, not fuck him."

"Yeah, says you. You know, I never took the stories I heard about your fantasies seriously before, about how intense they were. Talk about an understatement. I sure as hell won't be forgetting this birthday."

"You're stalling, Robbie."

"Yeah." He stepped forward. My three princes straightened up and, all on their own, smiled at him. He went to Hadji first, fondly touching the kid's cheek. "Thank you, Hadji. I'm not picking you, but I'm going to tell Nash what a good time you gave me. I think you'd rather have his reward than mine."

Hadji's face grew shy and flushed at that.

A step down to Terry, who waited with shoulders back, every inch the dancing master.

"I don't suppose you want anyone else to know about this secret talent of yours?" Robbie wryly asked.

"Um, no," Terry admitted. "But I doubt it's going to stay a secret."

"Anyone gives you shit, you send them to me. Really, I've never been so surprised and flattered." Robbie gave his friend a kiss on the lips. "You can take me dancing anytime, buddy. But not tonight."

Terry nodded in acceptance.

A step to the side, and now Robbie was face-to-face with Drew. "I'm guessing from your accent that you're related to Charles?"

"An old friend of his," Drew smiled.

"You really know how to use that throat of yours, and you must be one hell of a good friend to go to this much trouble for a stranger. I'd love to let you finish me off, but...I can't. I'm sorry."

Drew shrugged philosophically. "Next time I'm in town, maybe?"

"Maybe."

"You're not picking any of the princes?" I asked.

"No. Not even," he pointed at me, "the Master of the North. Isn't that you? The fourth prince, with drama as your gift?"

"You son of a bitch," I grumbled. Actually, I'd never even considered it, but what the hell? It was a damn good idea and I'd run with anything. "That was my line! And I'm calling myself 'Regent of the North,' not 'Master.'"

He rolled his eyes. "So sorry to ruin your surprise, but I've had enough of them for the night, thanks very much. In answer to your question, no, I'm not picking anyone. I can't think of a better end to all this than a quiet dinner and good night's sleep. If that's all right with you?"

"It's your fantasy," I embraced him and planted a kiss on his freckled forehead. "Glass-slipper, you over-muscled leprechaun. All right, everyone," I said, turning to the others. "Take a bow and go change. Time to head on home."

They said good-bye to Rob and filed out. "Nigel will stick around to heat up supper and call you up a cab when you're ready to go, unless you want me to stay and keep you company?"

"No, no. Get out of that monkey suit and take Charles to bed. This thing was a three-ring circus behind the scenes, wasn't it?"

"It wasn't so bad. Did you have a good time?"

Rob sighed. "Yeah, I did. And you know what, the Cinderella philosophy worked. I forgot all about how hurt and lonely I was and just enjoyed myself. What's more... I got to feel special, the belle of the ball. When someone breaks up with you like that, you end up wondering what's wrong with you. Thanks for reminding me how desirable I am."

I ruffled his carroty hair. "Happy fucking birthday."

"Go to sleep," I told a weary looking Hadji as Charles and I tossed out trash and packed up. "We'll be here tomorrow to help you put the guesthouse back in order."

"Yes sir." The boy was padding around in jeans and white tee, looking, for the first time, like a normal young man. "And thank you," he added, rubbing at his backside as he headed off to his room.

Charles had snapped shut the laptop and was putting it away in a padded messenger bag. I'd sent Nigel back over to pull dinner out of the kitchenette fridge. It was all ready to be heated up in the convection oven: beef tenderloin with skillet potatoes and haricot verts. There was New York cheesecake for dessert, Robbie's favorite.

"I'll drive Drew back to the hotel," Terry offered, handing Charles their costumes, both on their original hangers

I eyed Terry suspiciously. His tone was overly casual. "Sure," I said, equally casual.

Drew shook my hand. "I didn't know what to make of all this at first," he admitted, "but I gotta say, it surprised the heck out of me. I had a real good time. Strange, but good. You ever need me for another fantasy, you let me know, hear? Maybe something with glory holes?"

"Count on it."

He gave Charles a hug. "Call you in the morning, brother. Or make that the afternoon." He winked.

I raised a brow at Terry. He shrugged. "You said I could get off however I liked after Robbie made his choice," he murmured. "And Drew never did get to finish, so...."

"Go." I slapped his ass, getting a gratifying wince. They left arm in arm.

I changed out of my tux into jeans and a black tee. Charles and I put on our fleece-lined coats against the cold and gathered up the costumes. We managed to haul everything out in one trip and get it into the car. Closing that back hatch made it final, like shutting down the lights of a theater. It's always odd to me when a fantasy ends. I live so much in them. Rather like coming out of the rabbit hole.

"Ready?" Charles asked, and I realized I'd been standing at the back of the Scion, gazing up at the stars.

"Actually, there's one last thing," I said, pulling the messenger bag back out. I removed the laptop and powered it up, hoping Nash's wi-fi would work out here. It did. Charles came around as the webcams inside the guesthouse displayed Robbie, seated at the table. Nigel had just set out dinner before him.

"This looks great," Robbie said.

"Comes with a free glass of red wine." Nigel worked the cork from the bottle. He filled Robbie's glass. "There you go, bon appetite and I hope you're hungry. I mean I know you're a strong, young man, but I swear there's enough in there to feed an army."

Robbie looked up from a forkful of potatoes. "Well why don't you have some?"

"I could take a portion home, yeah. Hazard pay and all."

"No, I mean, why don't you have some now? If you're hungry."

Nigel thought about that. "Don't mind if I do." He headed back into the kitchen. In a moment he had another plate out on the table. He poured himself some wine.

He held up his glass and clinked it with Robbie. "Many happy returns."

"Thank you."

"So, do you want me to phone up a cab, or are you going to spend the night here?"

"I dunno. What do you think?"

"I think you should always try new things," the Brit advised. "Do you like westerns?"

I quit the webcam and closed the laptop. It was cold and I really wanted to get home.

Charles was gawking at me. "You fucker!" he said, as I packed away the messenger bag and got in behind the wheel.

"What?" I asked as he settled into the passenger seat.

"It was Nigel all along! That's the one you planned to match up with Robbie."

Revving the motor, I put the car in reverse and rolled us down the drive and out onto the quiet, neighborhood streets. "Don't be ridiculous. I couldn't be sure who he'd pick."

"You are such a liar."

I shrugged. "It's in the fairytales. The common man, the humble one, usually wins the prize."

"So it *was* intentional!" He was frowning. "Why bother with the other guys then? Why didn't you just fix up Robbie and Nigel?"

"That wouldn't have worked." The headlights directed me windingly down the hill to the main highway. "I know Robbie pretty well. He's fatally attracted to guys who are romantic versions of me."

"Of you?"

"Guys who enjoy role-playing. They pick someone like Robbie and become his romantic ideal. They dance with him, wine and dine him. Playing that role heightens the fun for them."

"And the sex?"

"And the sex. When the initial high is over, however, and the affair is in danger of leveling out, they bail. They get to enjoy the exciting launch of the ship without ever having to suffer the arduous voyage."

"Is that how you see it?" Charles asked uneasily. "As an arduous voyage?"

"I think that depends on what kind of ship you're on. The real problem with these assholes, however, isn't the game they're playing, it's that they don't spell it out to their victims, or offer a safe word. Good guys like Robbie end up thinking the romance is for real and the break-up their fault. They didn't scrub enough floors or save enough singing mice and so the prince dumped them."

I took in a breath. Charles was notably silent.

"That's why I offered Robbie three, exotic princes," I said, "whose only aim was to romance and fuck him. Three exciting guys he knew weren't for real. To give him the subliminal message that maybe those other romantic guys weren't for real either. And to give him a comparison. Nigel isn't exciting, but he's substantial. Robbie wasn't going to see that, or desire it without the contrast."

"A voyage on a private sailboat rather than an ocean liner?" my partner ventured.

Smart boy. I took an off-ramp and headed downtown. "Yeah. Nigel's the non-prince. No art or drama, just good conversation and friendship. Of course, I couldn't know for a fact that Robbie would want him —"

"But you made sure Nigel would be the last person there." Was that southern disgust?

"I jury-rigged the situation and it went like I wanted. But there's no saying that Robbie won't be back to dating false princes in the morning." I shrugged. "If anything comes of this, it'll be Nigel's doing. He's the best birthday present I could think to give: a real bloke who will see *Robbie* as Prince Charming."

A moment of quiet as we passed down the main corridor of Westside apartment buildings. Then, "Mason, where are we going?"

Charles rarely asked that question. If I took a strange route or decided we were off for a long drive he went along for the ride. But tonight my unusual detour was making him anxious; he looked quite pale.

"Here," I said, turning the car into the drive of a brickwork apartment building. The gate at the garage pulled back and I rolled on in. I found a parking space, set the brake and turned off the motor.

"Out," I told him, opening my door. My stomach had gone tense and I didn't feel able to really talk any more.

"Yes, sir," he murmured unbuckling his seatbelt.

We left the car and headed through the garage door into the lobby. Westside apartment buildings haven't the ambience of the funky Northside lofts, nor the opulence of Eastside renovations. They're somewhere in between: mass produced during the boom for young professionals on their way up. The lobby of this one was decorated in warm browns and accented with the usual mirrors and potted plants. We passed by the mailboxes on our way to the elevators. The call button had already been pushed by a plump, silver-haired matron with a black standard poodle.

"Hello," she greeted us.

"Mrs. Lloyd. Beauty." I nodded to the dog who wagged her short, puffed tail. Charles, who normally would have been down on one knee getting to know the animal, stayed where he was. His hands were in his coat pockets, his worried eyes down.

The elevator arrived and we stepped in. Mrs. Lloyd went for floor six, I pressed nine. Beauty sat and gazed up at me. Standard poodles are hunting dogs with a knack for swimming. Among the smartest of canines, they were bred to fetch waterfowl. I think it's a damn shame that they usually only appear in shows and are shorn and clipped like topiary. It's just not dignified.

Beauty seemed resigned to it, however.

"Good-night," Mrs. Lloyd wished us as the doors opened up on the sixth floor.

"Good night," both of us wished her. She smiled as if to say, "*Such a nice pair of gay young men!*"

The doors shut and we went up three more floors. I stepped out and, feeling Charles at my shoulder, determinedly marched down to number 904. My hands were rock steady as I unlocked the door.

"Come in," I told Charles, and without waiting for him, I took off my jacket and hung it up in the closet. I assumed he'd do the same, and so I didn't say anything as I strode into the living room.

My apartment... my apartment is pretty utilitarian. There's a brick fireplace, a small balcony and a nook of a kitchen in the main living area, and then there's the bedroom and bath. Simple. Furniture-wise it's, well, barren. Outside of a bed and an old dresser in the bedroom, there's a reading lamp and an overstuffed armchair with a matching ottoman in the living room.

That's it.

No, I don't have a couch or a coffee table or rugs or sheving or a desk. I don't even have barstools for the breakfast bar. No decorations either, just a photo of me, mom and Loretta in the bedroom and this pulp-like painting of a blond jungle warrior and a black lion framed over the fireplace. I do have books. A lot of them. Stacks of them are piled up against every wall.

Charles was gazing at those books, tilting his head to read off a few of the titles: planetary sciences, South American mythology, *Gravity's Rainbow*, a book on the Boxer Revolution, *The Pickwick Papers*, a biography of Robert Oppenheimer, *The Nag Hammadí*. He righted his head and blinked at the next pile. *The Collected Works of John Milton*, plays by John Weber, scripts by Quentin Tarantino. Onto the next pile, and the next and the next. He moved just far enough to peek through the open doors and see that the sacks of books lined the bed and bathroom walls as well.

He looked like I'd sandbagged him.

Chapter 8
The Stroke of Midnight

I shifted nervously. "What are you thinking?" I finally asked.

"I'm thinking that I'm not smart enough for you," he answered.

I shrugged, embarrassed. "Can I get you something? Water? Beer?"

"I don't want anything. But here, let me get you a drink." He anxiously made for the kitchen.

"No!"

He froze. I felt bad, but I couldn't relax. My heart was pounding as if I'd just run a five-minute mile.

"Not here. Not in my house." I pushed by him, appalled at myself. Slaves liked doing things for others; it was what they were all about. And I'd just told him that he wasn't allowed.

Charles, however, didn't look hurt. He was eying me with concern. As I opened the refrigerator door I could feel him taking in the empty shelves. The only things I had in there were protein drinks, bottled water and a couple of beers. I got out a water for myself.

"Which part of you are you hiding from the other?" Charles quietly asked as I twisted off the cap and took a drink.

Fucker. "Who says you're not smart enough for me? You went to veterinary school."

"It's really hard for you, isn't it? To let anyone see who you really are. Why," he added, "are you giving me a look?"

I felt queasy, but I was determined about this. "Because I don't want to be like Nash, or those sadistic bastards who jerk Robbie around, feeding on men and tossing aside the remains. They use mystery to protect themselves and to lure in victims. I know. It's what I do to guys every Saturday night."

"What you do is different, Mason."

"Only because my fairytale ends at midnight." I met his eyes. "But what's between us isn't for a night, and I promised you something more when we got together, didn't I? So I'm... giving you a look backstage. A look at Prince Charming when he's not at the ball, not wearing the fancy clothes."

Will you still view me as your master after you've had that look? I wondered.

Charles didn't know how to respond to that. The moment hung between us. Expressions flitted across his pale face, too briefly for me to tell what he was thinking. I only knew that mind of his was branching off of what I'd said, searching a thousand different roads for something. For a way, I suppose, to handle this strange gauntlet that I'd just thrown down.

And then, to my amazement, he sat in my chair and began to untie his shoes.

"What do you think you're doing?"

"Taking off my shoes," he said blandly. "It's warm in here."

"I didn't give you permission to do that. Or to sit there." That was *my chair*!

"Mason," he said pulling off his right boot and sock, "it's the only piece of furniture you've got." He set to work on the laces of his other shoe.

He barely had it off his foot when I crossed the room and grabbed him by the hair. "Out!"

He nabbed my tee shirt. I caught his elbow and levered him up. In response he crashed into me and suddenly we were falling to the floor. We landed bruising on the bare wood and I remember thinking, inanely, that the attractiveness of those Pergo floors was less so when a body was rolling around on them.

Maybe I ought to buy a few carpets?

Charles had his forearm under my throat now, his breath hot on my face. The son-of-a-bitch is nearly as buff and heavy as I am and it was only my larger size that gave me an edge. I pressed the heel of my hand up against his chin and tumbled us. Perspiration was between us, the hard feel of male muscle, the contrast of white and black skin.

He tried to get a headlock on me. I ducked that, grabbed the collar of his tee and ended up ripping it.

"My house!" I snarled, even as his legs wrapped about my waist. I felt his powerful thighs squeeze and threw myself to the side, breaking his hold. Before he could recover, I got on him. I managed to wrestle him onto his belly and pin him. Then I captured a wrist. He tried to buck me off his ass, tried to keep his arm from being twisted up behind him, but I forced it, inch-by-inch until he cried out in pain.

He struggled, his legs kicking, his other hand pounding and trying to use the floor for leverage. I jerked up his arm again.

"Motherfucker!" he shouted.

In a fury of energy, I ripped at his torn tee-shirt until it came off in tatters.

"Other hand!" I commanded, pushing the arm up slowly this time so he hissed. He tried to keep fighting, making me work to get what I wanted. Finally, he surrendered the other arm. I got the ripped shirt about both, wrapping and knotting them together elbows to wrist and with plenty of knots in between that would get tighter if he tried to pull free. Then I pushed him onto his side. He wasn't struggling any more, just panting for breath. I admired the way the sweat gleamed on his bare chest and belly as I popped the buttons of his jeans. Back onto his face, I grabbed the waistband and jerked him up onto his knees, head to the floor. Down came his pants, exposing that white ass of his and trapping his legs.

Hadji came to mind. His trousers down, his butt mine to burn. My cock stirred with the memory as I unbuckled my belt, tore it free and doubled it up.

"No!" he shouted, and tried to straighten up. I shoved him back down with a boot to his neck.

"Naughty boys get whipped," I rumbled, and brought down my belt.

Thwack! Charles bit back a yelp. Thwack! Thwack! The belt struck his upturned ass, leaving hot red bands behind.

"F-fuck you!" he hissed. But his body tensed with fear and pain, and his arms fought against the binding.

A phrase came to mind. *Beat the sparks out of him.* I grinned and raised my arm again. The belt whistled down. Thwack! This time he cried out, and his ass jumped and wiggled to escape. Thwack! More struggling. But he knew he was trapped. His legs caught in the pants, his arms bound.

It turned him on to be that helpless. But what really turned him on was the denigrating position. Like a kid from days of old dragged to the woodshed and forced to present his ass for punishment. He got off on that, which he found humiliating, which got him off even more.

It revved me up as well. I gave all I had to smacking down that belt across his cheeks, raising welts. Thwack! Thwack! He let lose a wail. Thwack! Thwack!

His ass was completely red now, and he was fighting to hide his tears from me. It was enough, I thought, looping the belt through its buckle and over his head. I tightened it gently about his throat, leashing my whipped dog. Then I pulled off my sweat soaked shirt, rolled it and gagged his mouth to muffle his sobs.

"I have neighbors and no soundproofing," I informed him. It was arousing to think of him sucking on my perspiration. His response was incoherent, but I could guess what he was saying. My dick was thick and pushing against the buttons of my jeans. It wanted out so that it, too, could take advantage of that vulnerable ass. *Patience,* I told it, and left Charles long enough to fetch a bottle of lube from the bathroom.

Pushing him flat to the floor, I got off his trousers and sat on his thighs, pinning him. He drew in a sharp breath through his nose and jerked as I stroked his tender ass. More curses from behind the gag. He even gave me the finger with both bound hands. I laughed and continued to tease those red welts of pain, liking the way he squirmed this way and that. When I parted his cheeks, that's when he really started to fight and scream foul words into the tee. He was not playing at it either.

It was one of those things that made him so marvelous to me. He might be a slave, a bottom through and through, but he didn't let just anyone beat his ass. A man had to earn the right to do that to him. And I loved that he let me earn it.

For all his shouts and struggles, he couldn't stop me from doing what Hadji had done: spreading his cheeks wide and laving the top of the crack with my tongue, then slowly, very slowly, gliding up and down the curve. His breath through his nose quickened and he moaned behind his gag as I delved deeper, tasting sweat. I caught sight of his captured hands fisting, the wrists twisting against my knots as my tongue tormented him. The belt around his neck whipped about as he thrashed his head. No! No! Because he knew his resistance would crumble, and he'd be embarrassing himself very soon.

My trapped cock began to drool. Deeper I went into that dark, musky valley, intoxicated by taste and fragrance, until I hit my prize. Charles cried out behind the gag and his hips jumped.

I kept his ass parted and tickled his pucker with my tongue. He emitted deep, muffled groans and struggled to push up, to shove his ass at me for more. And what torment that had to be, as his cheeks were welted from the belt. He must have felt sparks of pain, even as he went after the pleasure.

Time for another sensation. I parted his ass with one hand and dribbled the lube into his crack. He gasped as the cool liquid hit. Finally, I removed the gag.

"Son-of-a-bitch," he said, but softly. He was breathing hard. I settled beside him, casually letting my finger explore that slick crack. I circled his tender hole, but I didn't enter. He wanted to hold still, but he couldn't. His ass thrust up asking even as he pushed his burning face into the floor.

I grabbed his hair and tugged, making him show me his blush. "Poor little slut," I said softly. "You want my fingers deep in your hole, don't you?" I continued to stroke and tease. "You want me to give that special spot some attention and you'll do anything to get it, won't you?"

He panted and swallowed. "Fuck you—" he managed.

I let go of his hair, grabbed the belt about his neck and gave it a jerk. "Respect!"

He swallowed again. "Sorry."

"Sorry what?" I pulled on the belt even as I pressed my thumb to his pucker, not quite entering.

"S-sorry-sorry sir," it was almost a cry.

"You know what you have to do if you want it."

Sweat trickled down from under his arms, and he squirmed. Then he swallowed. His face got redder with shame. "Please, sir—"

"Please what?"

"Fuck me, sir, please sir—"

"That's my slave," I said, but I didn't give him what he wanted. Instead I ran my finger down below to his taint, almost to his balls, then back up again to the folds of his sphincter. That always drove him nuts.

He wiggled. "Damn, you! I said it!"

I grabbed his hair again. "Yes, but you're being punished—" I said this carefully. Unlike some, I don't use the word "punish" as a code word for sex play. When I say it, I mean that I'm displeased, and the one responsible is going to be suffering something unpleasant. Which is why, even though I uttered the word lightly, I could almost feel Charles' gut drop.

"—and that means I may just tease you all night long and never give it to you. Or maybe I'll beat the sparks out of you again." I gave the welted cheeks a smack of my hand and he groaned.

I put my finger back into that warm, velveteen place, making my point. "Maybe if you show me how much you want it, I'll change my mind."

His ass had been up, but now he lowered himself completely to the floor and parted his legs, his body quivering and trembling. His pink balls were pooled there, exposed, and he knew I might well torture them. I paused to roll them in my hand making him groan and rub against the floor. His cock, like mine, had to be aching for relief. I heard him catch a breath.

That was the turning point. If I went on without giving him more, he'd assume that I really was punishing him. While I can be a mean bastard, that wasn't what I wanted. So I finally slipped my finger into his hole. He almost sobbed with relief, moaning and writhing as I explored that warm interior. I found his gland, so very sensitive, which I caressed until his hips were helplessly thrusting. Another finger in to stretch him, and now his legs were wide, almost split apart.

"Please, please—" he'd given up on trying to maintain his dignity. He'd surrendered to the humiliation, tears rolling down his red face. "I can't bear any more, sir. Please fuck your slave."

"How should I fuck him?"

"Hard and without mercy. Please, sir."

Complete capitulation. He offered it all to me and I could do what I liked. I knelt between those thighs, finally releasing my hungry, impatient dick. It was slick and ready. But there was one, delicious sensation I wanted from Charles before I let myself go. Fingers still deep within him, I grabbed his hair again and jerked up his head. The belt was still collaring him. I loved the sight of it about his neck.

"I am the only one who can do this to you," I told him, letting him feel my stiff dick on his welted ass, all the while massaging his prostate. He whimpered and bucked. "I may let others suck your dick, but they'll never do this to you, the one thing you so desperately want. They'll never fuck you. Only me. Which means that you will always have to grovel and spread your legs for me. You can fight and curse, but in the end, if you want it, you will always have to beg for it, and you will always—"

I removed my fingers and plunged my cock in, deep in to that hot, smooth, tight interior, so silken and yielding to my claim. "—have to shame yourself for me," I finished, impaling him with my cock, pinning him with my weight.

He shuddered, just as I'd hoped. Shuddered one of those bone deep, full-body shudders that reach to every nerve ending. Even my cock there inside him felt it. It made me grin, and growl and almost crow with delight. Except that I wasn't able to hold back any longer. I was thrusting and pounding at his ass, and as his trembling subsided he yelped and moaned between the pleasure and pain of it.

Getting my arms under his chest, I yanked him up, up onto his trembling knees. My muscles strained against the effort and weight, but I never stopped fucking him. I grabbed hold of his cock, slippery with precome, and pumped that too. He sank against me. I felt his sweat-damp body, felt the leather of the belt that trailed from his throat, his arms and elbows still bound there against his back. I even felt his balls swinging between those spread thighs.

"Come for me. Come now and come hard," I commanded.

He obeyed, spurting come all over my Pergo floor. The clamping of his anus on my rod sent me over the edge. I sped up, racing it seemed, and then felt it all go, as if I were soaring.

I blasted my load deep into him.

It seemed a very long time that we hung there, shivering in ecstasy. And then I came back. I had one arm still wrapped around Charles, the other clamped on his sticky, wilting cock. I felt his ribs heaving, the sweat dripping down his back, his galloping heart.

My dick slipped out of him and I rested back on my heels. He stayed where he was, shaking, waiting. I stumbled up and found some scissors to cut free the ruined tee and release his arms. Then I got the belt off his neck and felt back into my chair.

It was nice, I thought, that I had a slave to clean up the mess. Lick it clean from the floor if I commanded.

"There're washcloths in the closet by the bathroom," I told him instead. "And then start up the shower. I think...I think we could both do with a hot shower."

A short while later, naked and clean, we were settled together. I in my armchair, he on the floor by my feet, as gingerly as his bruised butt would allow. Flames danced in the hearth.

"You don't ever sit in my chair," I said. Redundant, as I knew he'd done it all on purpose. Not smart enough for me, my ass. He'd made me show him—and see for myself—that the master he worshiped was not a role I played only on stage. It existed here as well, under the costumes, behind the curtain, after the stroke of midnight. What's more, he'd changed my view of him from something that didn't belong here, in my private sanctum, to something that did. In challenging me to show him who was the master of the house, he'd gotten me to claim him as mine, like the furniture, the pictures and the books.

The change was pretty amazing. I hadn't been able to let him hang up my coat or fetch me a drink when we arrived. But not thirty minutes ago I'd ordered him to mop my Pergo floors. I'd shared my shower with him, letting him sink down on his knees to wash me in intimate places with my personal scrubber and my soap. I'd let him get the bath towels for us. I'd even had him make up a fire in the fireplace.

I felt like a real idiot.

"Can I sit on the ottoman?" Charles asked. Fucker.

"Only with my permission."

"Yes, sir," he said, resting white arms and chin on my bare knee. I ran my fingers through his still damp curls. The fire popped and flared, sending soft orange light over us.

"I was afraid," he said then, "when you brought me to this part of town...it's going to sound irrational, I know, but I was sure you were going to leave me with someone else. And I know I should be willing to accept that if you do, not try to change your mind. But I can't help it. I've barely been able to think of anything else since that scene with Nigel, when you told me you could give me to whomever you liked...."

So that's what set this all off, what had gotten him investigating me: the fear that if he didn't serve me better, I'd give him to another master. And along the way he'd discovered, to his dismay, that no one could offer him an edge, a way to make himself more valuable to me. They were all in the dark, as well.

I wondered if I ought to tell him how I'd let this all happen, how scared I'd been of taking off my mysterious armor for fear of disappointing him. Scared of scratching up the relationship. Scared because I knew it was the most undeserving relationship I'd ever been in. Charles was special. He was smart and kind, he was selfless and honest, he was funny and he had this inner strength that took my breath away.

There was no way a self-centered, egomaniac like me deserved him... but that didn't mean I'd ever willingly release him.

I squeezed his shoulder. "You're not going anywhere. In fact, you're staying the night."

"I haven't got a toothbrush."

"I've an extra toothbrush."

"All right, then." I felt him relax. "You like the *Lion King*, don't you?"

"What?"

"You never answered that question. Favorite animated film. *Lion King*. Isn't it?"

"Well...yeah. How the fuck did you know?"

He shrugged. "You're my master. Why were you reluctant to say? It's a pretty manly film so far as Disney classics go."

I snorted. "And have everyone singing 'Can You Feel the Love Tonight?' every time I walked in? No thank you!"

He laughed. "You know, the hyenas in that film maintain certain racial stereotypes—"

"No PC rants!" Fucking Afrocentric white boy. How did I manage to hitch myself to such an ultra-liberal screwball? Son-of-a-bitch made me feel like a neo-con.

Charles slipped his hand into mine and sighed contentedly. "I love you, Fancy Man."

"Don't get all queer on me," I growled, but I think he knew in that moment that I loved him, too.

If you enjoyed this story, you can sign up for a free membership at ForbiddenFiction and discuss it with other readers and the author at the *Fancy Man and the Three Princes* story page at http://forbiddenfiction.com/story/T13-1.000083.

A Fancy Man Holiday

Mason is faced with one of the biggest challenges of his life as leather-man and Master: introducing his slave and lover, Charles, to his mother. He also has an important decision to make: there is a terrible secret he's been keeping from Charles; he has till Christmas Day to decide if he'll reveal it. If he does, things might change things between them. At the same time, his friends at the Cockpit bar are having their own holiday problems. The days are counting down and Mason can't afford any mistakes or failures. But keeping control of all this may be too much... even for the Fancy Man. (M/M)

Chapter 1
The Advent Calendar

I've always viewed the holidays as the real trick-or-treat of Halloween. And no, I'm not talking about the original blackmail threat of the saying: "Give me a treat or I play a nasty trick!" I mean "trick or treat" in the either/or fashion of our modern times. Like, will the homeowner who opens the door you just knocked on praise your costume and give you candy... or will they try to scare the shit out of you?

Trick-or-treat?

Think about it: the holidays waltz in pretty much on the first of November all cheery and bright, promising us kindred fun, warm feelings, enchanting presents and souvenir memories to set on our mantelpieces. Barely have we accepted the deal when we find ourselves tangled up in those festive lights being jolted by electrical shocks. There's stress and bickering, crowds and food poisoning. Shoppers get trampled, trees go up in flames. Even Santa is in on the prank. What will we discover when we finally open those attractive gifts? Our dearest wish or crushing disappointment?

Eight weeks later we come out of it, like survivors of a polar storm, blinking against the cold, cruel light of New Year's morn and swearing never to fall for winter's yearly hoax again. Yet we always do. Including the biggest of all tricks: that everyone is welcome and there's plenty of room at the seasonal table. The irresistible nature of this fraud might explain why I picked December first to finally submit my lover, Charles, to my kinfolk for inspection. Or, more particularly, to my mother. Because, even though I knew better, I wanted to believe Momma might, just might, be a tad more open and accepting of him at this time of year.

Given the results, I'm still not sure if the joke was on me or her.

In my family, Christmas doesn't start on Black Friday. It starts on December first, Advent Day. My mother makes a special meal for her offspring—and any guest we might wish to bring. A week later will be the cookie swap party followed, ten days later, by "Gifts of the Magi day" where we set our presents under the family tree. And then, of course, there's Christmas day and New Year's Day. I swear, from my birthday (just prior to Thanksgiving) till January second, I do almost no grocery shopping. My refrigerator overflows with leftovers from the interminable family dinners, brunches and celebrations. Which was my other excuse for springing Charles on my relatives right about now. If he was at those dinners and brunches and celebrations, there'd be less leftovers to haul home.

"Mason says you're from Atlanta?"

I'd picked up Charles right after he'd completed work and we'd arrived at my mother's a little late. But we'd still gotten there ahead of my sister, which was aggravating as I'd called her and emphatically told her to be *early*. I was crossing a personal Rubicon here and could have used her at my back. But there we were, on our own in the living area of the apartment being grilled. This part of my mother's place contained a big couch and a fireplace, which this time of year maintained a pine scented blaze. There were no stockings hanging from the mantle, no tree or decorations for that matter. Not yet. That was part of the Advent celebrations. To make sure mom had help putting up wreaths, tree, stockings.

Both I and my partner had demurred on offered drinks and Momma, her dog across her lap, was now seated opposite us. You had to know her well to tell that she wasn't happy with me. I'd informed my family at Thanksgiving that I'd be bringing Charles to Advent dinner, so it wasn't that I'd surprised her. It was that his presence in her home made it difficult to pretend I wasn't gay. My mother, you see, is one of those glacial sorts: thawing toward my sexual orientation, yes, but with agonizing slowness and great resistance to being hurried. Charles was about as welcome as global warming, and I'm pretty sure she resented me "forcing" him on her.

"Just outside of it, yes ma'am," Charles answered her question, equally mild, but he was sweating. Not because he knew my mother was luring him into her inquisition dungeon—which she was—but because he was desperate to make a sterling impression and feared (rightly) that he couldn't.

"That explains the accent. But you went to college in Atlanta? Is that right?" She smiled that charming smile of hers, the one that I imagine sharks wear when they smell fresh blood. Shit. Here we go. Where was my sister?

"Yes, ma'am. Georgia State," said Charles.

"A very good school, I'm sure," my mother said in a deceptively encouraging way. Thanks to high cheekbones and a molasses brown complexion, Momma's face exudes warmth, as does her humming, alto voice. Her appearance—blue knit dress, her reading glasses dangling from a chain about her neck—was harmless and motherly. I wouldn't say this was entirely a lie, but it should be noted that I'd learned my most sadistic tricks from her.

"Mason dropped out of college to go into theater," she said pointedly and stroked the "rat's" huge ears. That's what my sister and I called my mother's dog. His real name was "Pepper," an adorable black-and-white Papillon with one hell of an attitude. Understand, I love animals, but I hated Pepper. My mom doted on the wide-eared little monster and he, in turn, stuck to her like gum on the bottom of a sneaker. His black eyes were fixed on me at the moment and, now and then, he'd growl in his throat, as if practicing.

"When he told me he was bringing a friend, I feared it was one of his theater people," Momma added as if joking. "Did you two meet at a play?"

Charles twitched and so did I. Little did Momma (or my sister for that matter) know. While I do act for a living—plays and voice-overs mainly—it is in my off-hours that I take on my most special and important roles: that of the sadist in gay male BDSM dramas. That's how I'd met Charles, when he'd begged me to be Master to his slave for one, very unusual night.

But that's another story.

Our relationship had developed quite a bit since then, and he was now my slave and sex toy full time. Literally.

"No, ma'am," said Charles. "We met at a local bar."

"In *that* part of town I suppose," Momma said with cool disapproval. Which was actually an improvement over the icy displeasure I'd gotten from her in the past. Pepper growled, a sure sign of what she was really feeling.

"Um —" Charles looked away. He wasn't sure how to respond to that.

"Yes, mother, *that* part." I smiled back at her. "Where else was I going to find a nice boy to bring home to the family?"

"College maybe? Or church?" she retorted sweetly. "Or are you a heathen like Mason, Charles?"

"He's Rastafarian," I said, which wasn't true and Momma knew it from my tone. Pepper snarled for her. "Actually, he's a regular church-goer."

She frowned at that, not quite believing me. It's funny how many devoutly religious folk view gays as akin to vampires, likely to burst into flames at the sight of a stained glass window.

"There's a church in *that* part of town?"

"Yes, ma'am, but that's not the one I attend," Charles answered. He was looking beyond uncomfortable now, undoubtedly hearing the angry under currents between me and my mother. Courageous slave that he was, he braved those waters. "I go to St. Luke and Mark's on the corner of fifteenth."

To my amazement, that struck Momma. She rocked back like he'd gotten her between the eyes. Silence hung in the air for a minute, which left me feeling very funny because I had no idea why the mention of this particular church surprised her. But then, the one thing I almost never discussed with Charles was his religion. That he was devout, I knew. He had a cross on the wall of his bedroom and said prayers on his knees every night. On Sunday he faithfully attended church services, usually before I even woke up so he could be home to make me breakfast. It was all fine by me, especially as Charles was not the proselytizing type. In fact, no matter my heretical views or very evident sins, he was absolutely sure I'd been put on this earth by his lord and savior Jesus Christ. If Charles proved himself worthy to me, he might be allowed to go to heaven. I kid you not. He honestly believed this. I'd have loved, by the way, for him to say as much to my mother, but I wanted her to think him sane.

The lull following Charles' announcement was getting awkward.

"What?" I finally asked, but before either one could respond, Pepper's big ears flew up and he shot off my mother's lap, barking. A second later the doorknob turned and, with a cool whiff of snowy air, my sister and her boyfriend walked in.

At last! As we stood, I noticed Charles wiping his hand over his forehead. It was warm in the apartment, but we'd both divested ourselves of jackets and sweaters down to our pressed shirts and so it wasn't that bad. Nerves. Poor bastard had been all nerves about this for most of the week. Now his expression was so much like the one he'd worn on our second date—when I'd tied him up and interrogated him—that I experienced a lustful thrill.

It must have shown in my eyes, as his backbone straightened and his gaze fixed on me. My sister's voice, offering excuses for being late, along with Pepper's barking, cut though that private moment.

But you want to hear about the interrogation, don't you? Maybe later.

"Pepper, stop that," my mother scolded as my sister and her boyfriend hung up their coats. I say "scolded" but there was a fond edge to her tone, the kind that said she found him an adorable rapscallion. She scooped him up, which cut down his barks and growls.

My sister, a year-and-a-half younger than me, was lean and leggy and, in three-inch, heeled boots, almost equal to me in height. With skin the color of toasted chestnuts and almond eyes like mine, she's quite the beauty. Her black hair had been done up in ringlets and, as usual, she was wearing a comfortable sweater and pencil-thin jeans. Mom was always urging her to wear skirts, so she didn't. She came to a dead stop on seeing Charles.

"Oh, hell no," she said, setting hands on her hips. "You are effing kidding me."

I knew exactly what she meant, of course, and couldn't help but grin as she drank Charles in: his curly black hair and handsome face, the way his wide shoulders and muscled toroso strained against his forest green and brown plaid shirt. I'm sure she'd have a few more "hell no's!" when he turned around and she saw how his trousers outlined his very fine ass.

Charles straightened up as she inspected him, and his hands slipped unconsciously behind his back, parade rest position.

"That is one big piece of eye candy, Mason," my sister remarked and shook her head so that her gold earrings swung.

"Lo!" my mother disapproved, but she likely thought the same and would have said as much to my sister if they'd been talking on the phone.

"I *am* gay," I pointed out, ignoring Momma.

"You really are." Lo gamely held out her hand to Charles. "Loretta."

"Charles Beaumont." He accepted her grip, his name coming out smooth as bourbon with that southern accent.

My sister's eyes went wide. "Oh, hell no," she repeated.

I'd told Charles to leave off the fact that he was the sixth of that name or Loretta would have gone on like that all night.

"You and I are going to have a talk about this, big brother," was all she said now, then, "This is Rafe," as she waved to her boyfriend who'd been hanging back.

"Rafael Olivares," Rafe put in, offering his hand to Charles almost challengingly. He was a few inches shorter than my sister, the sort of guy who'd look twinkish except that he was ropey with hard muscles. Dark-haired and golden-skinned, he wore a subdued but pricy red-knit shirt meant to display that tough body.

As he and Charles shook, he flashed me a perplexed look. In the three years he'd been with my sister, he'd never seen me with another man and he seemed to be expecting me to yell, "psych!" As if all my assertions of gayness including Charles were an elaborate joke.

"Mason," he greeted me, as the grip broke. He didn't offer me his hand and I didn't offer him mine. We just exchanged nods, as if we were a pair of gunfighters sizing each other up before a shootout.

"Well. I guess this means I can finally get dinner on the table," Momma said, dropping Pepper back into the armchair. "Pepper, stay. Mason, I need you to get down the good dishes."

"Of course," I sighed. That was always my purpose, getting things off high shelves or lifting heavy items.

"Lo, you finish off the peas while I take care of the casserole. And Rafe, open a couple of bottles of wine."

"What about me?" Charles asked.

"You're a guest. You stay here till we've got it all out on the table," she said firmly.

"But—"

"No argument."

"Momma," I tried. I wasn't liking this. Especially as Pepper had his beady little gaze fixed on Charles now. I heard the rat growl happily. *Fresh meat!* He seemed to be saying.

"No argument," Momma repeated. "You sit and relax, Charles." And then she headed for the kitchen, Rafe and Loretta in tow. Lo glanced back at me with a small frown as if she didn't like this either, but then she shrugged.

This is our mother, that gesture said. *What can you do?*

There was that, I thought. I'd brought Charles here to give him an inside look and he might as well get it full on, not softened by me. I hung back all the same.

"You doing all right?" I asked, eyes on Pepper who was giving me a doggy grin that included a lot of fang. He might well have been thanking me for bringing him such a tasty snack.

"Yeah, fine," Charles said a bit too quickly, and wiped at his forehead again. "So that's your sister, huh?"

"Yeah. Whaddaya think?"

"I think you should be glad I'm on the severe homosexual side of the Kinsey scale." He threw me one of his genuine smiles, the ones that made my heart melt. "Otherwise I'd be dating your sister."

"I guess she is pretty good looking."

"Good looking? She's gorgeous. You've got nothing on her."

There was my boy! His voice was wobbly, yet he still took the time to stick it to me.

"Mason!" came the shout from the kitchen.

"Won't be long," I promised.

The kitchen was a square affair with a large butcher block at the center; it was more intimate than crowded, even with the three of us. Lo stirred chopped herbs into the buttered peas while Momma carefully withdrew her infamous turkey casserole from the oven. She made the casserole every year for Advent dinner with frozen leftovers from Thanksgiving. Such was the tradition in our home.

I made for the corner cabinet and got down the dishes from the top shelf. They were the good dinner set: white china with gold-leaf ribbons about the edge. I did my best to be covertly quick about it. If Momma saw me rushing, she'd snap for me to slow down and even come over to direct me. I'd be stuck there forever. Did I mention that I learned all my sadistic tricks from her?

"Thanks for coming on time," I murmured sarcastically to Lo as I gave her a serving dish for the peas.

"Payback's a bitch," she murmured and smiled our mother's too-sweet smile.

For all the times I'd given Rafe a hard time, she meant. "Seriously?" I asked. Had she come late deliberately?

"Nah. But now I wish I'd thought of it."

I shook my head. Really, I love my mother and sister, but they've got this mean streak... okay, we all do. But damn.

"They're all down, Momma," I said, edging towards the door.

"The holiday pie holder," Momma said.

Fuck the holiday pie holder! I almost said. But, of course, didn't. That was in the high shelf over the oven, where all the hot air was. As I got down the decorative ceramic dish with its pine wreath design, Rafe reappeared from the laundry-cum-pantry room with two bottles of wine and set to pulling out the corks.

"And the wine glasses," Momma added as I brought over the pie dish.

Fuck! Between the hot kitchen and wondering whether Pepper was already gnawing on Charles' bones, I was the one sweating.

I'd just fetched two of the wine goblets when Pepper started barking. It was a different bark than when Lo and Rafe had arrived, more high pitched, but equally wild. He sounded like he was going crazy. Shit! Everyone exchanged looks, sure that Charles had been cornered. Even my mother wore a guilty expression, and then we were almost bumping into each other as we made for the door. I came to a stop and Loretta and Rafe knocked into me before straightening in equal amazement.

"Oh, hell no," Loretta blurted.

Charles was not, as we'd expected, standing on a chair while Pepper snapped at him—which is how we'd once found a friend of my mother's. Nor was my slave frantically trying to shake the dog free of his pants leg, as Rafe had done his first time here. Charles was, in fact, down on the rug with Pepper. Pepper had his fluffy tail up in the air, his delicate front paws before him in the classic "chase me!" pose. His big black ears were perked and there was an excited gleam in his eyes.

Charles playfully shifted, and the dog sprung to the side to block him. Back to the other side. Pepper happily danced the other way, doggy mouth seeming to laugh.

"How did your friend do that?" Rafe asked me with undisguised awe.

"I wish I knew," I admitted.

Charles was now ruffling Pepper's silky black-and-white fur.

My mother came forward, gawking.

"I don't believe it," she murmured as Pepper rolled on his back, offering his belly to Charles. That was something he only did for my mother, who now looked annoyed.

"Pepper!" she said a little too sharply. But the dog, enjoying himself too much, remained on his back, reveling in attention. It was Charles who scrambled to his feet.

"Um, sorry. I can't resist animals."

"Did I mention that Charles is a veterinarian?" I asked smugly.

"Still finishing my residency," he put in, even as Pepper sat down by his boots, tail wagging happily.

My mother pursed her lips and gave me a killer look. Her dirty little trick hadn't paid off. Yet I could see her reassessing, too.

"If you would help set the table, Charles," she said, "we'll all sit down to dinner."

Chapter 2
Oh, Christmas Tree

Of course, once we had our napkins snapped out, Momma said, as I knew she would, "Would you like to say grace, Mason?"

I tried not to grind my teeth or roll my eyes or respond with anything "smart." Momma thought it her duty to push me into the faith. In my childhood, she'd relentlessly sent me to Sunday school no matter my objections. I'd fought back by asking obnoxious questions of the teacher, disrupting the class and playing harmless pranks until I got kicked out of spiritual indoctrination.

Momma, however, was my stubborn equal and refused to give up on me. She pulled this kind of thing every chance she got. This time, however, I had a secret weapon.

"Why don't we let Charles?" I turned to my slave with a smile.

He blinked, and before my mother could object, obediently folded his hands and started in. "Lord we thank you for this bounty, on this, the first day of your most joyous season. As the innkeeper shared his stable with Mary and Joseph, may we also remember to freely share our homes and your gifts with each other. And may we do so without reservation and with all gladness. This we pray, in Jesus' name, Amen."

Rafe, Loretta and Momma were goggling again. I wasn't sure which shocked them more, that a gay man could utter such a prayer, or that I was dating him. If they'd really known the extent of it, their jaws would have hit the floor. The first minutes after that prayer were spent eating our pear and gorgonzola salads in silence.

"Well," Momma managed at last, "That was very nice, Charles, thank you. I'm happy to see my son has found a good influence."

"Oh, he's an excellent influence," I said, which got a blush from Charles.

"Does that mean you will be joining him for Christmas Eve services at St. Luke & Mark's?" my mother asked pointedly.

"Nope," I tossed back, "I've a bacchanal to go to."

"St. Luke & Mark's?" my sister cut in, passing around a basket of rolls. "Isn't that the one with the ethnic statues and murals?"

"Ethnic?" I repeated.

"All the religious figures have Afrocentric features," my sister explained. "And dark brown skin."

Why was I not surprised?

"Yes, that's right," Charles said easily. "Beautiful artwork. You should come see it."

We finished off our salads and Lo gathered the small plates, whisking them off to the kitchen. Mother set about passing the peas while Rafe, taking his cue from that, helped himself to casserole, which then went to Charles. He heaped some on his plate, but pointedly waited for me to help myself and start in before picking up his fork. He'd done the same with the salad. I may have told him to act as if we were a vanilla couple, but he'd starve before eating without some implied permission from me.

"I've heard of St. Luke & Mark's," Momma carried on the conversation. "But I've never been. A black Jesus, you say?"

"Yes. Also Magdalene, the disciples, Joseph, Mary and John the Baptist. All depicted as African," Charles said. "Which they were."

"They were Hebraic," I countered.

"Black African," Charles insisted. He said it calmly enough, but there was a gleam in his gray eyes. Bastard. "One of the oldest paintings of our lord and his followers—"

"Yeah, I know. It was created hundreds of years after Jesus died and everyone in it resembles those who would have worshiped in that church. Pretty much like every other image of Jesus in almost every other ancient church. Point is, if Jesus and family existed at all—"

"Of course they did," Momma kibitzed.

"—They likely would have had the same coloring and features as other inhabitants in that area of the world, which were closer to Indo-European than Central African."

"Nubia was part of Egypt. The inhabitants there had features like yours. And the holy family went to Egypt."

"Your holy family were Hebrews, not Egyptians."

"They could have been Ethiopian Jews, like the Queen of Sheba." Then he coolly added, "And Cleopatra."

Oh, no. He did not just say that!

"She was Greek!"

"Black."

"I take it," Loretta ventured, "that you two have had this debate before?"

I think that's when Charles and I finally realized everyone had stopped eating and was staring at us. Charles, for once, was unfazed. It was I who blushed. My dark skin didn't show it, of course, but Loretta and Momma would know.

"Yeah, we have, and I don't think it'll get resolved tonight. More peas?" I offered Charles.

"Thank you. They're fantastic, by the way," he said to my mother. "Can I get the recipe?"

"Um, yes," she said, sounding as if she'd lost her place in a conversation. I had a strong suspicion that her preconceived notions about Charles, about our relationship, had taken several hits.

"Save room for the maple-buttermilk pie," I suggested.

The maple-buttermilk pie was always served in the living area with coffee (tea for me), but only after the tree and ornaments were fetched out of the garage. Charles, having insisted, was very carefully hand washing all the precious dinner dishes while Lo and Momma set out dessert. Which meant Rafe and I were making our way to the apartment building's communal garage. There was a thin layer of snow on the ground and our footsteps crunched over it. I didn't say anything, just glanced down at the icy pavement, imagining Charles lying prone, my snow-crusted boot on the back of his neck. The frost from my ridged rubber soles would melt onto his skin, trickling down his spine so he'd shiver both with cold and terrified anticipation. His flushed cheeks would be the only thing warming him.

Mmmmm. I'd have to save that one for later, I thought.

We'd reached the parking garage, which but for the distant sound of cars motoring up and down the nearby streets was quiet as a tomb. There were metal storage cabinets at the end of each carport, big enough for a bike or some golf clubs. In my mom's locker we found a plastic bin labeled "holiday wreath" behind a familiar set of science and engineering books. Below that was another one labeled: "decorations." The tree, purchased five years ago, was in the box it'd come in, the one we'd stuffed it back into last January. I hefted that onto my shoulder and left the bins for Rafe.

Back we trudged, our breath coming out in mists before us. This time, however, Rafe made a point of keeping up with me, which wasn't easy as I take long steps.

"I'm going to ask your sister to marry me," he said, his words clear as a bell in the still air.

"Is that right?" I said back, and didn't quite manage to keep the growl from my voice. You may wonder what I had against Rafe. Logically, nothing. He earned a more than descent salary managing a credit union, treated my sister like a queen and respected my mother. But my sister was my sister. I didn't trust anyone but me to take care of her.

Rafe, on his side, seemed to have similar doubts about my intentions. I often caught him eying me like a bully he'd agreed to meet after school. I could tell, however, that he was making an effort to narrow the chasm between us.

"Has this subject been discussed?" I asked, because I did know my sister. She wasn't the sort who'd find it romantic to be blindsided with a proposal.

"It's been mentioned," he said. "Lo seemed open to it."

"Hm. And you're going to pop the question soon?"

"Yeah. I thought about Christmas Eve or day but..."

He hesitated and I knew he was thinking of my family's unique tradition for the twenty-fifth. Also about how we all brooded about it the night before.

"Best to do it when she hasn't anything else on her mind," I grudgingly suggested.

He nodded in agreement. We re-entered the warmth of the apartment to Pepper's renewed barking and I glanced over at Lo. Her life was her life like mine was mine but... a brother-in-law? I guess I'd have to learn to like him or something, especially if a niece or nephew came along.

Shit.

As the nominal man of the house it was my job to set up the tree. This one was a breeze compared to the old one of my teen and young adult years. I'd had to weave colored lights about its plastic branches and it'd taken forever. When one of those cords went blew-y, burning said branches and filling the apartment with noxious fumes, I'd taken the opportunity to buy mom a new tree. It was blue, Momma's favorite color, easy to assemble, with lights already attached.

While I worked on the tree, Rafe hung the wreath on the front door, then came back to assist Momma and Lo unwrapping the ornaments. He'd been with Loretta for three years but only this year was he being allowed to touch the ornaments. This was a signal of Momma's favor; also that she, at least, had accepted him into the family. Charles, finished with the dishes clearly wanted to help, but had to sit and watch, outsider that he was.

Pepper, however, came over and lay down at his feet, much to Momma's consternation.

The hanging of the ornaments was Momma's favorite Advent activity. It gave her and Lo a chance to reminisce over each one, like the faded angel that aunt Thea had passed on to my mother when she was a child, and the green-eyed tiger that I'd traded for one of my action figures back in elementary school. Lo's favorite was a brightly colored cowboy boot. And there were, of course, the delicate crystal ones that had belonged to great-grandma. Momma still wouldn't let anyone else handle those. Up they all went in between bites of pie and sips of coffee — and my chicory tea — turning that sapphire tree into a glittering, family scrapbook.

"Here ya go, Charles," Loretta said at one point, passing him a gold-framed picture ornament.

"Ah," he said, a boyish smile breaking across his face. He glanced my way. "So that's what you looked like with hair."

"Twenty years ago, yeah." It was the infamous photo of Lo and me as little kids, dressed in our holiday best. Meaning, in her case, a plaid red dress, and, in my case, a suit with a plaid vest. I'd complained at the time, but truth was, I'd rather liked the suit. I just hadn't liked sitting still for the picture.

"Don't see why you can't have hair again," Momma remarked. I'd known when I went for the bald look that she'd hate it and never let me forget it, and I'd been right.

Stockings were also brought out of the ornament box, along with the stocking hangers. Soon they were dangling from the mantle, red-and-green velvet that Momma had sewn together. Our names, in gold, were hand stitched across them. Next year, I imagined, there'd be one for Rafe up there as well.

Finally, with only pie crumbs left on the plates and stains in the coffee cups, we got to the tree topper. A metallic five-pointed star on a spring.

"Watch those heels," I told Loretta and went down on one knee. She still almost stabbed me with one as she climbed onto my broad shoulders, tree-topper in both hands. My mother sighed as she always did, but it was one of the few traditions I really enjoyed. Loretta and I had worked it out not long after my second growth spurt back in high school. Even though we only did this once a year, we had it down and it took me no effort to lift her, and her no effort to stay balanced as she got the star affixed.

"Will you plug in the tree, Rafe," Momma asked, even as she pushed up and headed towards her room. I brought Loretta down, and in the next moment the tree came aglow, the ornaments glinting.

I heard momma grunting as she came back, a brown-painted, rectangular box of wood in her arms.

"Here we go," she said. "All ready."

She could have sent me for it, but awkward as that thing was, the tradition was for her to bring it in. Once in the living room, however, I was allowed to take it from her and put it on the mantle, which I did. This, however, forced me to pause and look at it.

The advent calendar had been a staple of our family Christmases since I was six, yet I was always surprised anew by how rustically handsome it was. It was shaped and decorated to look like a gingerbread house complete with snow, icicles and candy canes. There were twenty-five petite drawers ("windows") set four up, six across. Each one was numbered with a little plaque that could be slipped out of its metal frame and turned around to display a seasonal picture. The twenty-fifth drawer, right under the apex of the roof, was round and had a painted wreath about it.

"This year is your turn to start, Mason," Momma proclaimed. When the advent calendar had originally been introduced, my sister and I had fought for the privilege of being first at it. Momma had stopped the bickering by establishing a rotation. The one who started one year went second the next year. My turn or not, I honestly didn't want the honors this year. I had seriously mixed feelings about this ritual, had had them for a while. Tangled-mess-with-shocks feelings that would have had the hair rising on my head if it wasn't shaven. You may wonder why. Well, that's for later.

"Right," I said. The numbers went left-to-right and up, so the first was bottom left. I pulled out the little plaque numbered with a "1" and turned it around. On the other side was a painted holly leaf with red berries. A prickly evergreen for the start of the season. That always seemed apt for our family.

I slid the plaque back into its holder. By Christmas Eve the box would look like a yuletide quilt of seasonal symbols including reindeer, bells, ice skates and a peace symbol. The holly branch displayed, I now tugged on the tiny knob, opening the drawer. Inside was a small, paper wrapped gift. I tore it open revealing five pieces of butter-pecan toffee from a fairly expensive candy store. The sort Momma bought for special occasions.

"Thanks momma," I said, offering up the pieces. Rafe didn't like candy, but he'd learned that you didn't refuse the December first advent gift—which was usually candy. That just earned you a disappointed look from Momma. Charles wasn't in danger of that; the notion of refusing anything from me or members of my family wouldn't even occur to him. You could have told him the candies were laced with cyanide and he'd still have eaten his.

From there the evening wound down. Covertly waving Charles off, I helped Mamma clear the living room of dishes and storage boxes while Lo told Charles the story of our first time doing the tree-topper trick and how close she'd come to falling off and breaking her neck.

"I suppose you want to know what I think of him?" Momma

asked as I brought the last cups and saucers into the kitchen. She was standing near the doorway, listening with half an ear to Lo and Rafe and Charles laughing.

"Not really," I replied. "But I don't think that'll stop you."

She pursed her lips at that. "I think he can't give me grandchildren."

"Oh, I don't know about that," I retorted, equally flat. "Let me borrow the turkey baster and he could have Loretta artificially inseminated within ten minutes."

"Mason!" It was a measure of her control that she hissed rather than bellowed. Also that she didn't slap me upside the head.

"Momma," I said in a very low voice and met her fierce gaze with one of my own. "You are too smart to believe, for even a second, that you can guilt me into heterosexuality. So all you're doing is expressing your resentment. I can't stop you there, but I'm not going to take it lying down."

There was a long moment of stony silence as she tried and failed to out-glare me, then I saw a twitch of a smile on her lips. More silence as we finally broke eye contact and came down into our corners like boxers who'd heard the bell.

"So what else do you think?" I asked then, as more soft laughter came from the living room.

"He's a devout Christian," she said, folding her arms exactly like me, "Who makes no bones about doing the dishes. He's polite. Stands up to you. And I've never seen anyone win over Pepper that fast."

She heaved a sigh. "If he was a she and your girlfriend, I'd have to admit, I'd love him."

Well. And wasn't that a concession?

It was shaped and decorated to look like a gingerbread house complete with snow, icicles and candy canes. There were twenty-five petite drawers ("windows") set four up, six across.

Chapter 3

The Red-Nosed Reindeer

It was still fairly early in the night when, after kisses and a quick discussion of cookie swap day, we left my mother's apartment. I decided we both needed a drink and made for the Cockpit bar, our hangout. Charles, in the passenger seat, said nothing. In fact, he kept his determined gaze on the front windshield and the dark frozen streets. But I caught his fingers tapping anxiously on his knee.

Finally, as I knew he would, he cracked. "Mason. I know you're a sadist. It's why I'm with you. But for God's sake, put me out of my misery."

"What misery?" I asked. I *am* a sadist.

"How badly did I fuck up?"

His hand, hot with perspiration, was now on my thigh, squeezing it anxiously. My dick stirred with interest. Not that it takes much to get it interested in Charles.

"How badly did you fuck up?" I echoed with an exaggerated sigh. "Charlie boy, you fucked up so badly that my mother's having second thoughts about objecting to my sexual orientation."

The pause that followed was unusually long. "I... don't understand."

"As being gay pairs me with someone as angelic as you, it's not looking so bad to her."

"No shit?"

"No shit."

"Um... wow. I guess." His hand was caressing inward. As we passed under streetlights, I caught him glancing down hungrily at my crotch.

I pretended not to notice, in part because I was driving and knew better then to engage in anything even remotely sexual while navigating iced roads. In part because we were almost to our destination anyway. The bar and its parking lot were, in fact, right up ahead, but I went for a spot on one of the side streets. A dark and quiet spot. As I cut off the ignition, Charles unbelted and turned to get out of the car. I grabbed him by his hair, jerking his head back. Instantly he froze, his whole body tensing. That sent the blood to my dick.

Charles didn't move. In his stillness was anticipation and excitement. I leaned in close, close enough for him to feel my hot, moist breath on his ear.

"Suck it."

"S-Sir." His Adam's apple bobbed with a swallow. "Yes, Sir!"

I released him. Very quickly he got himself turned around and onto his knees. I adjusted my own seat back to give him more access. His shaking hands parted my belt and took down the zipper of my black jeans. It was sweet really; he never lost his nervousness when it came to making love to me.

I wore no underwear and for a heartbeat he just gazed at my exposed cock, barely visible in the dim light. My uncut rod, though rising, was still on the soft side, wanting to be enticed into hardening. Charles drew in a breath through his nose, inhaling my fragrance, and I felt a drop of saliva strike my sensitive flesh. Then he put his arms behind his back. I usually tied him during sex, but when I didn't he kept hands away. It had to do with bondage, which Charles was very much into, but it also had to do with his odd obsession with dark skin. He didn't want to lay his sinful white hands on my sacred brown flesh.

Charles is a little strange.

Even though I was expecting it, his hot, moist tongue seemed to strike my dick unexpectedly, low near the root. I let out a grunt as he circled up, wetly anointing every inch of my staff. I could feel my cock pulsing and getting fat with the attention, and my breath quickened as each damp caress inched higher; my tip eagerly flared, but, maddeningly Charles went back down. Still, the tickle as he tongued under my foreskin was delicious, and my ass did a little dance.

My dick, thus wooed, pushed farther out, the crown sweating precum. Charles was deeply into adoring my dick now, lapping my staff like an ice cream cone, slurping up the drips of juice from the top. Every so often, his breath would warm my tight balls as he nuzzled in to lip and tongue them. Jolts went through my body, and I finally grabbed at his hair, my patience gone. He might want to savor me for hours, but he didn't get to decide how to enjoy his reward. Obedient to my demands, he opened wide and, careful with his teeth, dropped his mouth down over my straining cock.

"Yeah!" I shouted at the car ceiling as that wonderful, velvet heat enveloped me. I bucked, shoving my rod down his throat. The pull of his sucking, so heavenly, turned up the volume and the hum in my nuts became a chorale echoing through a Cathedral. A refreshing sweat broke out over my body and my ass drummed the seat. My heart thundered, matching that and the bumping of my dick into the back of Charles' throat. Even as he gagged, his tongue still tried to glide over my pulsing veins. It was like a feedback loop of buzzing and tingling. I felt sure Charles was as lost in pleasuring me as I was lost in being pleasured.

Yet, somehow, he managed to swallow me even more. By then, however, I'd lost it. My hips made a fierce and final leap, and every nerve took flight as I shot. My triumphant "Hell yes!" rang out through the car.

A long moment later I returned to earth, my cock released from

Charles' mouth to bob free. The sweat on my bare head cooled and my breath quieted. Damn, I thought, tense muscles relaxing back in the seat. God *damn*, my boy is good! I saw him wiping at the corners of his mouth where the overflow had dribbled out, licking the back of his hand. I noted with amusement that the windows were fogged. Well, that little bit of exercise had certainly eased any tension left over from dinner. I gently stuffed my damp package back into its denim wrapping and righted my seat.

"Thank you, Sir," Charles whispered. He was still on his knees, head down, but the flush in his cheeks told me he was riding on the high of satisfying me.

"You more than earned it," I said, and added, "You did good."

He knew I meant that compliment for more than just the blow-job.

A flurry of snow had hit sometime between our parking and exiting the car. It wasn't bad enough to keep any regulars from making their nightly pilgrimage to the Cockpit, but I knew it would discourage newbies and strangers. Which was fine with me as I'd had enough of being actively social and wanted to just hang with the gang.

On entering my slightly stuffy, beer-melted-snow-and-testoster-one-scented home-away-from-home, however, my hopes were partially dashed by Nash's houseguests. Every year the owner of the Cockpit flew in four or five of his old marine corp buddies to spend the holidays with him. Tonight, he'd invited these entitled out-of-towners to annex the bar. He and they were slamming balls around the pool table, roaring and shouting. Their crowing rang out in the otherwise doleful atmosphere.

Why doleful? Well, there are elements of this festive season that hit members of my tribe particularly hard. Which is why, from the second the bar's signature decorations go up, they get this trauma-tized look, as if Santa just kicked them out of the reindeer games. Not even Rat Pack Christmas songs (the only holiday music Nash allows) can alleviate the gloom. Those with kids get it the worst.

There are a handful of domestic couples at the Cockpit who've adopted or have custody. But most patrons with offspring pretended to be straight in their younger days. When the truth came out, these dads — and they're almost all dads — lost custody. They're looking forward to spending Christmas with their sons and daughters, but the holidays remind them of how little time they've had with their kids, or will have. You can tell from the way they gaze down into their hot toddies as if into crystal balls; they're seeing a future where their kid is grown up and chances to play with them are long gone.

Close behind these forlorn fathers are the orphans like whip-master Burke. The sort who never-in-their-lives pretended to be other than what they were and are without family. When they were old enough, they either ran away from their inflexible kin, or were exiled. Never quite getting over this, they've remained single.

The Cockpit serves a Christmas day brunch for those with nowhere else to go, but that doesn't save these orphans from knowing there'll be no presents under the tree for them. Nash, of course, is among the few such orphans too narcissistic to care. As long as he has a young twink to fuck and chums to party with, his holidays will always be jolly. Which also makes him oblivious to anyone else's misery. As are his friends. Anyone with even a mote of sensitivity could see this was not a night for revelry.

"Remember," I heard his distinctive bark over Sinatra's version of Drummer Boy, "Winner gets first poke at that tight ass."

Clearly they were going to take turns with Hadji, Nash's eager-to-please slave. Guffaws followed, which shouldn't have struck me as odd but for some reason did. I took all of two seconds to wonder why, then shrugged it off and returned to the beer Charles had fetched me. At my side, Burke picked forlornly through one of the bar's snack bowls for cashews.

"Hey," I said to him and peered around to the seat at his right where his muse, Katie, was usually to be found. "Where's herself?"

"With her family," he shrugged as if it didn't matter, but clearly it did. Katie was the bar's leatherfemme, a girlish lipstick lesbian. She and Burke had a strange if devoted and purely platonic relationship. But that's another story.

"For the whole month?" That was going to be hard on Burke.

"Till the twenty-sixth. She invited me to join her," he admitted, and actually blushed. "I refused. I mean, can you imagine it? Me at some uptown house, dressed up in a tie, using the wrong fork for dinner?"

He tried to laugh, but I could tell he was bothered. Really bothered.

"Katie would never make you wear a tie or use the right fork," I said confidently. Although she had altered Burke's hygiene habits (he no longer pissed in the kitchen sink), she'd never tried to alter his essential self. She loved Burke as he was, Fu-Manchu mustache included.

"How would she explain me?"

"As a good friend. Which you are."

"I'm more than that," he countered sharply. Our whip-master might not have a word for what he was in their relationship, but he was insanely jealous of it, and determined that it be recognized. "But that's the nut of it, isn't it? I don't give a shit what strangers think of us, but this is Katie's family."

"Katie would stand up to them for you."

"I know," he sighed. "I'd cause a riff between them and her. That's not the sort of Christmas I want her to have."

That sent a spark of both pain and pride through me. I sometimes forgot how gallant Burke could be.

"Is she out to her folks?"

"Oh, yeah. And they're pretty okay with it. Even urged her to bring a girlfriend with her."

"Too bad," I said. "If they weren't okay with it you could go as her fiancé. That would have them begging her to be gay instead."

He laughed then, for real, and I felt some of the tension ease out of him.

"Did you two at least exchange gifts?"

"'Course not," he scowled. "I don't give 'um, and I don't want 'um. You know that."

"Yes, Sir." I did know, but it seemed to me he ought to have something from her to open on the twenty-fifth.

Keep out of it, Fancy Man, I could almost hear Burke saying to that.

"Hey, Mason? Mason!" someone shouted, and I saw Padre Miguel waving. He was in one of the old orange booths with Owen and seemed to really want to chat.

I strode on over and gave his fist a hearty bump with my own before sliding in. Padre Miguel was the de facto leader of the bears in the parking lot. Actually, they weren't all bears or even mostly bears, but the bears stood out and Nash always called them "the bears in the parking lot." So that's what everyone called them. Really they were die-hard smokers fraternizing in the only areas where they could legally light up. During the winter months they moved to the back patio, which had a protective overhang and heat lamps.

Padre Miguel who was, yes, a licensed minster, was a bear. A round, soft, furry one. Lusciously furry all over. I won't go into how I knew this, but I'll add that his fur holds onto the cherry tobacco fragrance from his pipe making a night with him a very sensory experience.

"Hey, Padre," I said. "Happy Advent day."

"What's this, you know about Advent day?" His Cuban-American dialect, the sort that only comes from being raised in certain parts of Florida, lilted with surprise. A delighted smile flashed through his silver-shot spade beard.

"All too well," I replied then, "Owen," I nodded to the other man at the table. Unlike Miguel, who was a bottom, Owen was a fellow top and Master. An engineer in daily life, he was about ten years older than me and best known for his elaborate April Fool's jokes. Not that there was any hint, at first glance, that he even had a sense of humor. Built like a linebacker with dark beetle brows and cinnamon-stick-colored hair, he looked more like a Russian hit man. It didn't help that he almost never smiled. Just pursed his lips ironically. Rumor was that he did grin now and then, and when he did, it scared the shit out of those he had roped and bound in his bedroom.

"Mason," Owen nodded back and even at the other side of the booth I could smell the bourbon. He was wearing a brooding expression and throwing angry glances at Miguel, as if he knew he was about to be punked.

"I was just telling Owen that the bar really has to get new Christmas decorations. This is getting ridiculous," Miguel said, much too casually, and nodded to the offending embellishments.

"Good luck with that," I snorted. Our Christmas decorations date back at least five — maybe as much as seven decades. The widow of the original owner left them behind when she sold the place to Nash. He'd been using them and only them ever since. Not because his customers liked them, but because he wouldn't allow anything else.

Seriously. Every Yuletide someone tried to buy or bring in new trimmings. No go. Last year, one secret agent put a fresh topper on the tree. Nash tossed it out. I don't know if he's actually attached to these old things, or if he feels that since he paid for them (along with the bar) he needs to wring every last yuletide out of them. Maybe he likes torturing sensitive regulars, like Padre Miguel, with the sight of missing bulbs in the light strings, a "Merry Christmas" sign with only a third of its glitter, and a dingy white, plastic (and likely made of toxic chemicals) tree hung with cracked ornaments.

Saddest of all is the glowing plastic Santa in sleigh with reindeer. The colors on that antique are so faded it's hard to make out anything but Rudolf's red nose. But it's these or nothing, and the slave-type regulars, bless their enthusiastic hearts, always drag them out and festoon the bar with them as if they'll somehow make a difference. Heaven knows, none of us Master-types can be bothered with holiday cheer.

"Fucking island of misfit toys," was Owen's opinion. "Us and the ornaments. If Nash thought new shit would bring in new customers, he might buy some. But this time of year he only gets us. The same old sad sacks. Why bother to pretty things up for us? We're not going anywhere, even if the atmosphere sucks."

"Tell us what you really think why don't you?" I said, reaching for my beer — which I'd left at the bar, but, like magic, was to hand here at the booth. That's the beauty of having a slave. Wherever Charles was, whoever he was chatting with, his eyes never left me. If I moved, he swooped in, grabbed and, if need be, refilled my glass. Then he deposited it within reach. He felt particularly proud of himself when he managed to do this without me noticing.

"That's Nash's modus, right?" Owen relentlessly went on. "Squeeze out as much as he can without putting in a dime. It's the only reason he lets you hold your Sunday services, Padre. You know that, right?"

This he addressed to Miguel who, yes, held weekly Christian services at the bar as well as Christmas and Easter rites. They included a reasonably priced breakfast (sausages and pancakes, delivered from a local diner and kept hot in the happy hour chafing dishes) and were fairly well attended. Leathermen are often believers and strong ones at that.

"I know full well that Nash welcomes my Sunday flock—excuse me, 'Zoo' I believe he calls it—because he can sell them drinks," Miguel said peaceably. "He is a businessman. I don't mind rendering to Caesar, not even on Christmas day. And speaking of that," Miguel awkwardly segued. "Do you have your Santa suit, Mason?" For the secret Santa gift exchange, he meant.

"Matter of fact, I dug it out and took it to the cleaners this week. You don't have to worry about a repeat of last year's scramble."

"Pathetic," Owen cut in. "Like we're not reminded enough of what we don't have. We need to have our noses ground in it. Oh, and Padre here didn't invite you over to discuss Santa suits, Mason. In case it's not blindingly obvious, he wants you to drive me home and maybe sit on me. Because he's worried I've had too much to drink. Maybe I'm spiraling out of control. Isn't that right, Padre? Nice of you to be the bar's conscience, but I don't remember voting for that."

"I am my brother's keeper," Miguel returned with a put-upon roll of his large eyes.

"Fuck you are. You always think you know what's what when you don't know shit."

Actually, it sounded to me like Miguel knew quite a bit. Like who could, at this moment, handle Owen. Namely, another top. A physically strong one because if Owen couldn't walk straight someone like Burke wouldn't be able to keep him balanced. Someone like me would.

Thanks Padre.

"Do you want me to take you home and sit on you?" I asked Owen point blank. "Or do you want to stay and drink yourself into oblivion?"

"Don't patronize me."

"I'm not. You've already surrendered your keys." After four shots of the hard stuff our very conscientious bartenders would have asked for them. Owen had at least that much in him. I took a moment to drown the rest of my beer, then I got to my feet. "So. What's it gonna be O-man? You can call for a ride, but given the weather out there, it might be a while coming. I can drive you now. Or I can leave you with Miguel for the night."

That gave Owen pause. In fact, he pursed his lips in what might have been the beginning of an involuntary smile. *Yes,* I thought, *a night with Miguel would be quite pleasant, if, as Owen claimed, he wasn't that pie-eyed.*

"All right," he said, "To avoid that, let's go."

Charles was waiting at the iron coat rack, my jacket and Owen's over his arm; meaning he'd not only figured out we were leaving together, but which coat was Owen's. I tried not to show it, but I just loved it when he did things like that, all doggedly dutiful and attentive. It turned me on.

"Do you want me to walk home?" he asked, as he deferentially got us into those coats

"Stay here," I told him after a moment's thought. "I'll be back for you." Even though he lived close enough to hoof it I didn't feel he ought to be stomping through the snow at this hour. I could, of course, have just let him come along to drop off Owen, but I knew my fellow top was going to want to rant one-on-one, no bottoms to witness any weakness.

"Drive safe," Charles wished us.

"Yeah," I sighed, and directed my second Advent gift towards my car.

Chapter 4
All I Want for...

"Tempest in a toilet," Owen muttered as I navigated the dark streets. "I'm not suicidal. Just in a sour mood like everyone else tonight outside of fucking Nash and his fucking playmates. Half the bar in the doldrums and they're chortling away. Bugs the shit out of me. They act like they're still young and on leave. All ills are cured with a game of pool, bottles of beer and fucking a tight ass."

"Well," I said thoughtfully, "Not sure about the game of pool or the beer, but fucking a tight ass always makes me feel a bit better."

His lips twitched. "Especially if that ass's been given the right number of hard swats." A twinkle came to his brown eyes.

"I agree with all you're saying, brother," I continued on, cautiously. "But you did hit the bourbon harder than usual tonight. Come on. Miguel didn't deserve that tongue lashing, fun as it might have been for you. Something's really sticking in your craw, and it's not Nash and his fart-brained buddies."

"I hate the hypocrisy. The whole year we don't give a shit about each other, and then suddenly, we do. Food and clothing to the poor, parties and gifts. All so we can ignore and burn each other the rest of the time."

"You're Jewish. What do you care what us goyim do?"

"I care because you involve all us non-goyim in it for at least two fucking months."

"I share your disgust. But that's not what's really bothering you, is it?"

He threw me a look under his beetle brows, then glanced out the window and heaved a sigh. "Maybe this close to the end of the year,

235

I look back and reassess... things. Like my revolving door of nightly fucks. I mean, I can get guys to come home with me for an evening, but I can't seem to get them to stay. And maybe... probably that's all my doing as I've never asked for more."

"But?" I encouraged him.

"But?" He blew out an exasperated breath. "Fuck me. There's no but. I'm not after what you seem to have with Charles or what Burke has with Katie. I'm not that sort. I only think that some reliable company would be nice. To keep me from becoming one of those crazed-hoarder-internet-trolls."

"I think we can all agree that no one wants you to become one of those. You'd be too good at it."

"Damn right."

"So," I ventured, "You have any particulars for this reliable company? Looks? Habits? Likes? Dislikes?"

"I want him to stay longer than a night and not leave a mess."

"Ah. I don't know if Santa can stuff all that into your stocking."

"Yeah, I'm pretty demanding," he half laughed and sunk down lower in his seat.

Quiet descended and lengthened. We'd reached Owen's neighborhood, a nice one of small homes, most of them already bright with flickering lights on the outside and glittering, holiday trees on the inside. I pulled into the driveway of the only one that was still bare and dark.

Owen unbuckled. "Thanks for the lift," he said, pushing open the door. I might have stopped him then, told him that I got it, that I'd felt the same. But I knew he was done talking about it.

"Night," I wished him as he headed up the walk to his shadowed door.

I didn't go to sleep immediately after fucking Charles that night. With his head of soft, black hair on my shoulder and the bedroom silent save for the patter of snow on the windowpanes, I took a moment to review the events of the day: my mother and her antics, Rafe's private announcement, and Owen's rants, so on point with my own views of the holidays.

All of which got me thinking long and hard about what I wanted for Charles and myself. What kind of future was *I* after? It wasn't the first time I'd brooded on such, but I'd always felt like there was plenty of time to make up my mind about it. Now, however, there wasn't. Not since I'd decided to introduce him to my mother and sister. Now there was a deadline, something Charles needed to know on or before Christmas day *if* I wanted our relationship to go any further.

Christmas day. I brushed a possessive hand over Charles' curls, felt him sigh and snuggle in against me. Of course, I could take the coward's way out and say nothing; keep him in the dark. Which I was tempted to do, but that would be a fatal step. You have to understand: being a Master wasn't just sadistic barbarity for me. Yes, it could be like that, but at its best, the M/s relationship had a code of honor, one that went beyond safe, sane and consensual. One that involved ideals of gallantry and courage. I don't think I could have entered into it otherwise. Without such convictions, my cruel urges would have turned me into someone I hated.

For this reason, I'd vowed long ago that I'd play fair with slave types. And every day with Charles — brave, true, Charles — only strengthened my resolve. Our second date had, in fact, been as much an eye-opener as the first....

We'd hammered out a tentative relationship agreement at the Cockpit, and then gone back to his place. That's when our second date had really gotten underway. After stripping Charles down to his underwear and blindfolding him, I tied him to the bed, arms over his head, knees spread and bound to the eyebolts in either side. Likewise his ankles, so he looked like a frog laid out for dissecting.

Getting undressed myself, I'd watched his ribs rising and falling in suspense, perspiration already starting to gleam at his throat. That had thickened my cock — and his, which was trapped in his shorts.

I like my men to go commando to speed things up, but I have to say a hard cock trapped in tighty-whities is a most inviting sight. Which was why, after setting my pocket knife, a thick, long butt plug, clips, lube and an unwrapped condom on the side table, I ran my fingers over that cock, toying with it there under the fabric. Charles blushed and squirmed in response. Which made it damn hard for me to continue as planned. *Patience,* I reminded myself.

"I know you tend to curse when things get edgy," I said then, "and I like that. But I'm going to ask you to restrain yourself tonight. We're going to exchange some important information, and I want you attentive."

"Yes, Sir," he breathed back, his Adam's apple bobbing with a nervous swallow.

"Let's get started then."

Taking up two clips, I applied them to his nipples. His hiss as I pinched was delightful. Admiring his pecs, rising with the pain and all the more evident with his arms in their overhead position, I leaned in and trailed my tongue down his chest between his heaving ribs over his hard stomach. His moan as I circled round the navel and tickled him by lapping back and forth just above the waistband of his shorts had been a wonderful mix of desire and fear. I heard a breath of frustration as I skipped over his groin to lick at his inner thighs. Then his swallow and more hisses as I'd pinched tender skin on each side with more clips.

The clamps on his chest had trembled when I shoved down his waistband, letting his cock pop up fiercely stiff. Giving his balls a roll, I drew them out. They were wonderfully tight and crinkled. I saw him biting his lip and thought of what he must be feeling: helpless and spread as I pinched, toyed, and teased him. A dozen sensations pinballing through him, from the tightness of the ropes, to the aching of his turgid, desperate cock and the sting of the clamps going numb.

And behind it all: terror. Delicious terror.

As he shivered in that fear, I added clamps to the skin of his ball sacks. All this might sound, to some, rather tame, but I've found that the number of clips isn't so torturous as administering those tiny pricks and smarts leisurely, with sensual caresses in between. Real anguish, for the masochist, isn't in the actual pain, but in not knowing what's coming next.

"I'm going to interrogate you," I announced. "Every time you answer a question, I'll remove a clip. Do you understand?"

He quivered, and his cock fairly squirted out precum. "Y-yes Sir."

"When did you first have your cock sucked and who sucked it?"

Beneath the blindfold, his cheeks had reddened. It was something I'd learned on our first date: however extensive his sexual experiences, Charles was always charmingly bashful about such things. He stuttered an answer and I removed a clip from one thigh, causing him to suck in air as blood painfully returned.

"When did you first get fucked in the ass and who fucked you?"

Another answer, and the clip from the other thigh came off. Below the blindfold, his face winced. I went on to ask about his family, one question and freedom for one nipple, another and freedom for the other. His breath started to come in gasps.

Finally, I asked Charles about his obsession with race. When did it start? He trembled as he answered, knowing what was coming. I removed a clip from the ball sack and he whimpered. Next question: Why did it start? The answer to that was enlightening, and off came the remaining clip. The tingle and throb on the skin of his nuts probably didn't hurt as much as the released nipples. But they made him all the more aware of his dick, still wanting and waiting. So was mine. Charles' gasps and cries and moans had affected me like a warm wet mouth sucking me off.

I'd shifted between his legs, grabbing up lube and a condom.

"That was to tenderize you," I said, reaching under the stretched underwear and tickling between his spread buttocks. "To prepare you for four special rules. The ones I want you to learn right now. You will internalize these and make them your commandments."

"Yes Sir," he gasped, hips trying to pump.

"First rule: you may polish my boots, but you will not lick them."

That hit him. Below the blindfold his face went gray with dismay. Charles, you see, had a boot-worship fetish, and I knew by the middle of our first date that his dearest wish was to lick my boots with me in them. His head turned to the side with a very different kind of pain.

"Stop it," I told him, "it's not because you're unworthy. It's because you're not ready yet."

His head snapped back into place.

"When you're ready," I promised him. "I'll let you. Take any licks before that, and you'll be punished." I didn't say how I'd know if he took a covert lick, because that was obvious. During our first session, Charles had proved himself shockingly honest. I was altogether sure that if he ever slipped up, he'd be on his knees confessing like a penitent in church.

"Yes Sir," he croaked, and in response to that, I finally grabbed his silky cock and gave the tip a lollypop suck. His musky flavor played on my tongue, as did the beautiful shape of his throbbing red mushroom head.

"Oh, f—!" he started, remembered and clamped down his teeth over the swear word. Then tried, yet again, to buck. He was blushing furiously by now, thinking, no doubt, of how he looked, all trusted and vulnerable, red spots where the clips had been, underwear pulled down expose his arousal.

It's time, I thought then, and, taking my pocket knife, cut into the waistband at each hip, making him twitch. Ripping the shorts off, I denuded him.

"I hope that wasn't a favorite pair," I remarked, lubing up my fingers and sliding them down his exposed crack.

"Second rule," I'd said. "You will not ask me to burn or mutilate you." With my free hand I touched the calligraphed "B" scar on his hip. It had come from an actual slave brand used in the antebellum south by Charles' ancestors. "I know you asked your old master to do this to you, and he did. But I won't. You may not ask for anything like that."

I found his pucker, saw him suck in a breath of hope.

"W-what about piercings?" he boldly demanded. "Tattoos?"

I almost laughed. I'd told him he couldn't curse me out, but he was still going to show me.

"We'll see," I said, pushing two fingers into his waiting ass, slow enough to make him wiggle.

"Third rule." His body quivered as my fingers went deeper. "You can always say no."

"S-Sir?"

"You can always say no. It means you will always be honest with me about what you can and can't do."

"I—y-yes. I under-understand, Sir."

"Do you?" I stopped moving my fingers toward that sweet spot, the one he so wanted me to touch. "Of all these rules, that's the most important. Say it back to me. And you'd better mean it."

His throat bobbed, but his jaw lifted as well, as if he was trying to come to attention. "I can always say 'no.' And I'm not to do what I can't."

"No matter how much you want to please me," I added.

He didn't like that. But he licked his lips and reluctantly agreed, "I won't do what I can't, no matter how much I want to please you, Sir."

"Good boy," I said believing him, but I didn't reward him for that as he'd expected. Instead, I withdrew my touch.

He cried out and thrashed, "You—"

"Last rule, Charlie boy," I said, "You have to beg."

His jaw tightened.

"No, really," I said, and, adding a third finger, started to push into him again. "I like to hear men beg for it. And my rule is, you will never get it until you beg for it."

Hissing, he actually tried to thrash. Charles was a classically trained leatherman and leathermen, even slave-types, don't beg. A leatherman took it like a man, grunting, growling, howling, swearing. Anything short of begging. But I knew, and he knew, that he got off on humiliation. I would bet money that his cock wouldn't flag if he was shamed, it would harden. Which was good, as I got off on making him blush. It was only our second date, but I could tell that the clash between his masochistic appetites and his leatherman pride was going to be exquisite. And sure enough, Charles' hands fisted in helpless fury as I pumped my fingers into and out of his ass, and he gave me silent and stubborn refusal. *Oh, yeah. Fight me Charlie boy.* I gave the tip of his bobbing cock another suck. "Now say please—"

He couldn't swear at me, but he shook his head side to side.

"I see you need convincing." I pushed deeper into him.

Charles gasped and gasped, trying to hold out. But my fingers were just short of where he desperately wanted them. His hips moved, trying to go lower. The ropes held him back, and his frustration grew. His face got redder.

Then, "Please!" he finally barked. "Jesus, Mary and Joseph,

241

please!"

"Not abject enough. Rule number four is a bitch."

"You're a—" He swallowed that. Sweat was streaming down his body now, soaking the bed. His legs were quivering, and his ribs were expanding with every breath.

"Well?"

"P-p-please, Sir."

"Please what?"

"Touch me there..." he almost wept the words. 'Give it to me. I... beg you."

I pressed on that spongy, nut-sized spot and he jerked with a high cry. It must have felt like a spark of pleasure exploding through his groin.

I was aching for satisfaction myself by now, inside and out, so, one-handedly, I got the condom on him and slicked it with lube. Then I jerked out my fingers and shoved in the plug, making him shout. *Ass claimed*! I thought. His yell was still echoing as I rose. Next thing my ass was sliding down his rod, giving me that wonderful, aching fullness. *Dick claimed!*

I started to rock and gyrate, getting his cockhead to strike against my inner nut. A sweet wave of pleasure rolled up and down from my tailbone. Soon, sweat was trickling down my bald head. Fisting my own hard dick, I grunted and growled as I beat myself off.

"Oh, God! Oh, God!" Charles was screaming now, "C-come—?"

I reached and tore off his blindfold, wanting him to see me riding him.

"Go," I told him then.

He shouted and bucked, even as I sped up my oscillations there on his dick. Sensations fired from that connection between us, from my bouncing nuts, and from my slippery cock as I stroked it harder and harder. Under me, I felt Charles go stiff, shooting. A heartbeat later, all the muscles in my abs, glutes and legs tightened and elation burst from my prostate.

I gave a victory roar as I spurted all over his chest.

Some heartbeats later, panting and dripping, I popped off him, and rose over his heaving ribs. With my finger, I traced an "M" in the white juice spattering his stomach and chest. He swallowed hard, breath coming in gasps, gray eyes watching this ritual in fear and wonder.

Then I bent to kiss him, my tongue tangling aggressively with his, reminding him how pinned down and at my mercy he still was.

Mouth claimed.

M for Master. M for Mason. M for Mine. Mine to Question. Mine to torment. Mine to invade. Mine to pleasure. All mine.

I still ranked that as one of the best damn interrogations I'd ever done.

Now, lying next to him that December night, I felt my cock awakening at the memory of that second date. I told it to settle down. Charles had work tomorrow and selfish as I am, I didn't want him half-asleep on the job. Besides, it was good for me to remember that I'd gotten more than devilishly good sex from the interrogation. Okay. Not a lot more, but I'd said it'd been an eye-opener . My first time with Charles, I'd been obligated to inflict more pain than pleasure. The second time, however, I'd gotten to hear him yell as much in ecstasy as in agony. And I'd liked that. I'd wanted more of it. I'd also felt compelled to ritualistically claim him. Or rather, re-claim him as I'd all but carved my initials into him the first time.

Eye-opening, indeed, as it had made me realize I was even more smitten with him than I'd originally thought. I not only wanted everyone to know he was mine and mine alone, but I also wanted to be all his. His friend, partner and hero.

And, of course, being the Fancy Man, I also wanted to bring every one of his erotic daydreams to life. Granted, I probably did that each time I fucked him, but it wasn't quite the same as acting out a scene. Unfortunately, in our five months together he hadn't said a word on that subject, and it wasn't my policy to drag them out of anyone.

The most challenging problem I'd faced since connecting with Charles, however, was being open. Initially, I hadn't even shared my address, which, yes, was completely hypocritical given my demands for full disclosure from him. My intense privacy had, in fact, nearly ruined everything between us. But that's another story.

I'd been more circumspect since that crisis point, more open, which had kept our relationship strong and on track. What I might reveal on Christmas Day, however... that was going to be far more serious than a mildly obnoxious mother and her irritating little dog.

If Charles couldn't deal, he'd have to say as much. That was rule number three. And that would be that. This is what could happen if I decided to finish what I'd started and play fair to the bitter end. At the moment, I wasn't at all sure if I would. Or could. But one thing was certain: there was a deadline. I'd denied it, ignored it, and tried to hedge around it in all kinds of ways. Futile. "Trick or treat!" the Advent day calendar had snickered at me today, and presented me with that inevitable countdown.

Damn holidays.

Chapter 5
The Big Man's Suit

The season might have been upon us, and many things helter-skelter, but Charles still had to take care of cats sick from chewing on pine needles, and frostbitten doggie paws. Meanwhile, I had to record Yuletide commercials, pitching my voice down and jolly for Santa, up-and-cranky for Scrooge, and with a Yiddish dialect for Hanukkah Harry the mascot for Larry's Deli. That was the up side of this time of year. I was very much in demand. I even had, on weekends, a stint as Christmas Future at the Dickens' Fair. I would've complained about typecasting, but I'd also been promised a chance to play Christmas Present, so I was good.

None of which lessened the domestic errands I had to run. There are old school leathermen, like Nash, who believe that only the slave should do the scrubbing, cleaning, fetching, carrying and cooking. This works if the Master, like Nash, is able to financially float them both. I'm afraid, however, that fairytale bondage stories with fabulously rich Masters and their penthouse dungeons are just that: fairytales. I drive a used Scion and the only penthouse dungeon I'm going to be able to give you is an imaginary one in your own bedroom.

But I promise you, when I take a whip to your ass, you won't know the difference.

The long and short of it is that in modern M/s relationships, both parties usually have to work. And if the Master doesn't accommodate for that, all he'll end up with is a perpetually exhausted slave. Who wants that? I certainly didn't want my slave too worn out for playtime. Therefore, as Charles was at his job most hours of the day and I wasn't, I did the shopping and other household tasks.

That day, some three days post Advent, I had half-a-dozen chores including picking up my Santa suit and doing a load of laundry at Charles' place. The suit was at my trusted dry cleaners, which, unfortunately, was in the un-gentrified part of Boystown, meaning dilapidated apartments and questionable liquor stores. Sadly, it was best known for the kids who hung out on the stoops, mostly teenagers in grungy jeans and hoodies. To the untrained eye they looked dodgy but ordinary. To the police and those of us in the know, they were clearly runaways and hustlers. For not all that much they'd suck you off in a nearby alley. For a little more they'd go with you and engage in acts that were still illegal in some states. And, of course, if you were too easy a mark, they'd rob you.

The area was commonly known as "the midway" like at a carnival. Full of kids, snacks, rides and games, especially at night. As it was a few hours before dark, most of the punks were whiling away the time performing treacherous skateboard tricks on icy stairs and bumming smokes off each other. Passing them by, I had to put the brakes on my desire to rescue one or more of them, especially those with their hearts in their eyes. My gut might want to save them, but my head knew it was better to leave such missionary work to those with training and experience.

"Hey, Mister! Got a light?" I heard from some as I trudged back from the cleaners to my car, garment bag over my shoulder. A second later, a duo cut in front of me.

"Hey, man, my friend and I were wondering—" One began, then, seeing my ornery, "steer clear" expression, cut off and drew his bud away. As I watched them leave in search of another mark, however, my eyes caught sight of a kid in a woolen hat, crouched on his heels in the alley. He was rocking as if in pain. I was about to turn away when he glanced up and I froze.

No way. But as he turned his head to the side, giving me his profile, I saw that it was.

Hadji.

Hadji was a slender twink with compact muscles, beautiful, brown-sugar skin, inky hair and puppy-dog eyes. Pakistani by way of heritage, Canadian by way of birth and nationality, he was somewhere between nineteen and twenty. Last I'd heard, he was still Nash's slave and houseboy. So what the fuck was he doing here? What the fuck was he doing, huddled, forlorn and broken, in an alley?

What. The. Fuck?

Garment bag still over my shoulder, I started towards him. He'd gone back to looking at the muddy pavement, but came alert as my boots crunched on old snow. In a heartbeat he sprung into a crouch. I could tell he didn't immediately recognize me because his expression was positively fierce. Like Pepper at his meanest. Then he did a double take and realized that he actually knew the big, threatening black man looming just a few paces away.

"Master Mason!" Shock, and he instantly dropped to his knees. Had anyone else seen it, they might have found it curious because it wasn't done out of fear; nor was he offering to blow me. Rather it was like he'd forgotten his manners and was horrified with himself. Which was actually pretty much what had happened.

"I-I-I—" he stammered, giving me a chance to notice that his jeans and hoodie were damp and streaked with mud, as was his face. Sleeping in not nice places, I was guessing.

"You're coming with me," I said, checking the anger rising in me. The alley stank of shit and piss and garbage and I could see wet rats darting about. No way in fuck Haji was staying here.

"Sir," his face darkened with embarrassment "I-I really don't want—"

"I'm not asking, Hadji. Get up now. We're going." I turned then, and not even looking back, headed out of the alley.

Most leathermen are attracted to other leathermen, meaning tough guys who can really take it. Nash, however, liked his bottoms ultra-submissive. Which got him a lot of sneers and criticism in the leather community, but Nash being Nash didn't give a fuck. This actually worked in my favor as it meant that Hadji said not one word more. He just trailed after me like a newborn duckling. I felt the other boys giving us looks, but I'd made an impression and there were only a few whispered comments and snickers. At my car, I hung the suit on the hook in the back, then opened up the passenger door and pointedly looked at Haji. He meekly got in and buckled up.

As I settled into the driver's seat, I noticed he didn't smell all that good. Like dirty snow and dumpster. Pulling out, I drove for a while in silence while my passenger slumped. Now and then I glanced over at him. His bowed head underneath that woolen cap, was veiled with soft, unwashed black hair, and I thought I saw a few tears falling. He'd pulled off his gloves to warm his hands by the car heater. The way they were twisting and his hunched posture spoke volumes. He was emotionally crushed and broken, and utterly mortified to have me see him like this. Which, odd as it may sound to you, was something of a turn on. I did feel sympathy, don't get me wrong, and anger over Hadji's situation, but sadist that I am, I got a buzz from seeing him humiliated.

Want to know something even stranger? Being a masochist, Hadji was likely feeling that buzz on the other side.

"How long have you been out there?" I demanded.

"Four or five days."

"Did Nash just kick you out with nothing?"

"No, Sir." Hadji had a very soft, timid voice, which made me want to slap him, but I had to remember, he wasn't a leatherman. He was the sort of sub who needed to be meek and had served a master who got off on that. That it bugged the shit out of me was my problem, not his.

"He wouldn't do that," he went on earnestly in his flat, northern dialect, "Honestly, Sir. He gave me time to pack and an ATM card. He's been putting funds into an account for me. But I—I—"

"What?" I spun the wheel. "Spit it out."

His face crumpled and he began to cry. "I don't want his money. It's his, not mine. I can't use it. I just c-c-c-can't!"

"Okay, okay. Quiet down," I urged and gave him an awkward pat on his narrow shoulder. He responded by bending almost to his knees and sobbing. *Damn Nash*, I thought as we came to a stoplight. *Damn him and his damn, hypocritical horniness for pansy boys, who he went for because they made him feel uber-macho!* The kid should have been cursing him out, not weeping over the loss like... like a pansy boy.

"Where are your clothes and this card?" I asked as the light changed.

"In a locker," he sniffed.

"And this locker is where?"

He told me and I made another turn, heading that way.

"I had some money of my own," he explained as we drove on, "and used that. But then I ran out. And I—I thought... I thought, you see?"

"Yeah, I see. You'd better not have had sex with strangers, Hadji."

"No, Sir. Not yet. I won't lie, I tried to, but the other boys got to the marks first. *Their* customers, you know, and they don't like to share."

"They didn't hurt you, did they?"

"A little, but I got my own back. Don't worry. I handled them."

I blinked. He handled them? Nervous poodle Hadji? I remembered his initial response, crouched and looking ready to attack. He'd been rather daunting. Maybe he had handled them. And maybe I wasn't being fair calling him a pansy boy. For all his tears and meek attitude, he'd been Nash's slave. That was no easy gig.

"I'm familiar with that kind of-of lifestyle," he admitted.

My brows went up, but I actually wasn't that surprised. "Are you?"

"My family threw me out of the house when they learned I was into men."

"Harsh," I said, and felt my blood pressure notch up higher. It infuriated me when parents, finding their off-spring to be different than expected, tossed them aside like clothes stained beyond repair. How could they do that to their own kids? Good kids? I could give my own mother that much. She hadn't liked it when I came out to her, but she hadn't acted like I'd transformed into a monster. She'd still viewed me as her son.

"I worked the streets for a few months before Master Nash found me." Hadji went on, "He was visiting Ontario on a hunting trip. Stopped by Ottawa for some reason and-and picked me." His eyes welled with tears again. Luckily we'd reached the lockers. They were at a station set up for the homeless, a place where they could stash their stuff and it would be safe.

"Okay," I said parking. "Go get your things and come right back. I mean it. If you run off on me, I'll be pissed. Do you want me pissed and looking for you?"

Hadji gulped loud enough for me to hear. "No Sir."

"Be quick."

He was. Within five minutes he'd returned to the passenger seat with a military green duffle that had probably belonged to Nash. He hugged it in his arms as I zig-zagged onward. Back home, Hadji followed me up the walk, hauling his duffle while I hauled my Santa suit. I keyed open the door and Hadji, docile and resigned, trailed me into Charles' heated bungalow.

There was a little wooden sign that hung in the front window. The side facing out said "Welcome" while the side facing in said "Believe." I turned it around so "Believe" faced out. That was a signal between Charles and myself that there was an unexpected visitor inside. One who might find our habits confusing. Like, for example, Charles' habit of going to his knees to greet me. Which he would do if I didn't cue him that we had a guest. Hadji, of course, was in the know about such things, very much so, and wouldn't be shocked. But Charles and I liked to keep our private life private.

"Shower's that way," I said, pointing. "Spare towels in the linen closet next to it. Have you a clean change of clothes in that duffle?"

"Yes, Sir. What—what should I change into?" Hadji's tone was plaintive, a slave adrift and looking for direction.

"Jeans and a white tee are the uniform around here." For slaves, that was. I wore whatever I damn pleased.

"Yes, Master Mason, thank you," he said and wandered off to the bath.

I put my Santa suit away and got a load of laundry into the washer. Hadji didn't dawdle. He was out fairly quick, scrubbed from head to toe, smelling and looking much better. It appeared he did have a clean change in the duffle because his tee and jeans, even the socks on his feet looked spotless. Unlike what he'd been wearing in the alley, these fit him tightly. That was partly to display what he had, and partly because there was no belt. Master Nash would never have allowed his non-leather slave to wear leather in the form of belt or boots.

The jeans outlined Hadji's pert ass nicely. I'd had occasion to see that bubble butt exposed, even taken a paddle to it one memorable night. It made my dick tingle to think of having another go at it.

"Hungry?" I asked him, as he stood there in his stocking feet uncertain.

"Yes, Sir."

I moved my pile of books from the couch. "Sit," I told him. I'm not the cook Charles is. Heck, some days I can barely boil an egg, but I know how to grill up a cheese sandwich and open up a can of tomato soup. I was bringing these out when Charles came home.

"Mason?" he called hesitantly from the door. "I saw the sign. Who... Hadji?"

He came to a stop there in the living room, winter coat still on. He hadn't seen Hadji since October when we'd used Nash's guest-house to give Robbie the bartender a very special birthday fantasy. On hearing Charles enter, Hadji had jumped to his feet and was standing now, wet hair slicked down, hands locked behind his back. He looked like a lost kid.

"Sir," he said; that was for Charles, not me, which was exactly right. Charles was a leatherman and Hadji was not, and Nash would have beaten into him that even a leatherman slave got to be called "Sir" by one who was not.

"Hello," Charles said back and, divesting himself of his coat, smiled that warm, kind smile of his. "This is a surprise."

"More than you know," I said, setting down the warm soup, sandwich and a glass of milk. "Eat," I commanded Hadji, and waved Charles to the kitchen.

"What's going on?"

"Nash kicked Hadji out," I said. "I found him on the midway."

Charles' eyes widened. "Jesus. Nash didn't dump him there, did he?"

"No. But that's where he ended up all the same. I was waiting till you got home to get the whole story. Is it okay if he crashes here for a while?"

He rocked back. "You're asking me?"

"It's your place," I gruffly reminded him.

"I may pay the rent," he said uncomfortably, "but I think of it as our place, Sir." He threw me a look that told me he was second-guessing that now. As much time as I spent here, I did have my own apartment. Had he presumed?

"Exactly," I said, "Our. You get to have an opinion about house-guests."

"Oh. Well, I think I can deal. Unless this is going to be a long-term thing?"

"Not if I can help it. But don't ask if I know what I'm doing."

Charles grinned at that. "Of course you don't. Improvising is more fun."

I slapped his ass. "Get changed."

Chapter 6
Weather Frightful, Fire Delightful

Laundry moved into the dryer, I settled on the couch. Hadji, seated now on the floor, had inhaled his snack, leaving only crumbs and a scraped soup bowl. He finished off the milk as Charles, in his white tee and jeans, reappeared. Usually that was all Charles wore at home, but given our company, he'd added belt and boots.

"Okay," I said to Hadji, as Charles sat down beside me. "Tell us what happened."

The boy's eyes dropped. "There isn't much to tell, Master Mason. Master found his Jonny, and I had to go."

"Come again? Found his Jonny?"

"I-I'm Hadji," he said and when he got blank looks from the both of us. "From the cartoon?"

Oh. I winced and nodded even as Charles shook his head.

"Jonny Quest," I said to him. "It's an old 60's cartoon. Nash is a mega-buff. All sorts of memorabilia in his office; and he plays episodes in one room or another every time he throws a party. It's all about the adventures of this white kid, his Hindu friend—Hadji—his dog, his scientist dad, and this man of action that hangs out with them. Kinda James Bondish."

"Sounds queer," Charles gently joked and Hadji smiled faintly.

"No female characters to distract fans from the homoeroticism," I agreed, and remembered Nash and his buddies around the pool table the other night. So. The tight ass they'd been playing for hadn't been Hadji's. "You're saying Nash got himself a new boy for Christmas?"

Hadji nodded dejectedly. "He came to live with us a few weeks ago. He's my age and build. But blond and blue-eyed. Master calls him 'Jonny' and..." his voice dropped to the barest whisper, "I've never seen him so happy."

Shit. Charles reached out and, on behalf of us both, squeezed Hadji's shoulder. The kid rubbed at his eyes and drew in a breath.

"Master s-said it was n-nothing personal," he went on, "that I'd been a very good slave, but Jonny would be taking my place. M-my room. Even... even my collar." Hadji bit his quivering lower lip. "I asked—begged him to let me stay. I said I could work with Jonny and couldn't we both serve?"

I shook my head. "Nash is too 'thrifty' for that." It was one of those odd facts. Nash's frugality (let's be honest, his cheapness) had turned him into a serial monogamist, at least when it came to household slaves. He was good about paying for everything they needed, but he never wanted to pay for more than one.

"I told him I could do without," Hadji went on plaintively. "But he wouldn't listen. He told me I ought to be glad he wasn't selling me or making me leave with nothing. He said he'd even saved up money in an account for me. That's how good a Master he was. He said I'd get over it."

Tears were rolling down his cheeks. He didn't utter it, but it was there on his young, brown face. *I thought my Master loved me. I thought I'd be his forever. I did everything he wanted. I would have died for him.*

Why wasn't that enough?

Damn Nash. He could skip right to his new boy without even noticing a glitch in service. Meanwhile, Hadji bled from the gut. Poor slave had really adored that asshole.

"Hadji," I said gently, "I'm not going to tell you there's anything I can do about, well, repairing things between you and Nash. You know he's not the sort to change his mind."

"I do know that, Sir," he barely murmured it.

"But I'm not going to let you go back to the streets, either. We will find you someplace to stay. Someplace where you can..." Can what? "...find your feet."

"Yessir."

"For tonight," I added, "maybe for a few nights, you can sleep on our couch."

"I promise to be a very good houseguest, Master Mason," and to

Charles, "Sir."

"I know you will be," Charles said. "Well, I have dinner to make."

"And I have laundry," I said, which got me an odd look from Hadji.

"What can I—?" he ventured, even as Charles invited him to the kitchen to help.

We took supper in the living room, balancing bowls of Charles' pho on our knees. As a child, Charles had lived next door to a Vietnamese family and been half-adopted by them, so his cooking was very Asian-Fusion. Once a month he tossed oxtails and beef bones into a pot along with spices and ginger and brewed up gallons of delicious broth. He kept containers of this stock in the garage's deep freezer. On certain nights he'd dig out a batch, boil it up and ladle it over rice noodles and thin slices of meat. Served up with sides of bean sprouts, green onions and chili sauce, it was a warm feast for a cold winter's eve.

Hadji, who'd never had pho before, raved about it, which pleased Charles. We all took seconds and thirds. Finished at last, Charles made up a fire in the fireplace and we watched some television while I folded laundry. Hadji seemed utterly fascinated to see a Master doing such chores.

"May I do the dishes for you, Sir?" he asked when Charles started to gather up the empty bowls.

"Sure," my slave said, handing them off, and the boy happily carried them away to the kitchen.

I waited till Hadji was out of earshot, then, folding the last pair of jeans, I said casually to Charles, "I want you to go to the bedroom and listen to some music. With headphones."

He turned to me, confused. "Music?"

"Or a movie. Work on your laptop if you want. Just make sure you have the good headphones on. The ones that really block out sounds."

The color drained a little from his face then and he glanced toward the kitchen where water rushed from the faucet. There were clinks as Hadji put rinsed dishes into the washer.

"He's been through a lot," Charles ventured. Slave type that he was, he almost never questioned my judgment; but he had a soft heart. Which was why I wanted him to wear the headphones rather than listen to what I was about to do. It would only distress him and that wasn't fair.

"I will keep that in mind," I assured him.

Nodding, he left without a backward glance. I took a moment to fetch our spare pillow and some blankets from the linen closet, setting them on the couch for Hadji. Then I went to our sound-proofed garage, which not only housed the deep freezer but Charles' very fine collection of whips, ropes and other interesting items. I picked out a long, leather paddle and two bits of soft rope.

I was seated on a dining chair when Hadji came out of the kitchen wiping his hands on a towel.

"I washed the pot and stored away all the leftovers—" He came to a stop, seeing me tapping the end of the paddle against my palm. His eyes widened and his throat bobbed with a swallow. "Did I do something wrong?"

"Did you?" I asked placidly.

He licked his lips and I could see him squirming internally. There was dread in his expression, but there was arousal stirring in his jeans. He couldn't help it.

"You're angry."

"Yes, I am." My anger, in fact, was spreading cold and fast now that I was no longer resisting it. And yes, in spite of that chill feeling, I was as stimulated as Hadji over what was about to happen and sporting a boner. It felt, however, hard rather than hot.

"Tell me why I'm angry, Hadji," I said.

He flushed and his eyes ticked about, looking anywhere but at me. "Because... because of where you f-found me?"

"Go on."

"Master Mason, I couldn't have called *you*," he said desperately.

"Maybe not," I agreed, still tapping the paddle against my hand. Nash had probably hammered into Hadji that he was not fit to approach, let alone speak to a leather Master like me. If so, I could hardly blame the boy for not phoning me. "But—?"

He knew what I was after now, and winced. "But I could have called Charles. Or—or Terry."

"Or Robbie."

"He works for Master Nash," Hadji protested.

"If you were worried about there being issues between him and Nash imagine if you'd been found hurt. Robbie would have left Nash over that."

Hadji flinched, but there was still something stubborn in his posture.

"If you couldn't bring yourself to use Nash's money to stay in a hotel or someplace safer," I went on, "you could have called one of them. You have their numbers, and even if you weren't sure if it was proper, you know they'd want to help you. You do know that?"

"Yessir. But I didn't think of them because... because I never had anyone who — who cared about me before."

"I understand. But if you had been hurt, or worse, you would have left us all feeling very badly. I think you need to learn that." My voice had gotten frosty and my vexation was glacial by now. "What do you think?"

My tone was casual, but the question was critical. Hadji had, as it were, taken on the role of temporary sub to me when he'd not only obeyed my orders, but fairly well asked me for more. From all I could tell, he was adrift without a Master and desperate for someone to take on that role, even if it was only for a few nights. Much as I wanted to act that part right now, however, I wasn't going any further without his verbal consent.

"I think," he swallowed, "I think I should be taught a lesson, Master Mason."

"Take down your pants."

His hands shook as he broke open his fly and pushed his jeans down over his lean hips. He wasn't wearing anything underneath and I could see that his exposed dick had gone from excited to hiding in its sheath, furry nuts tight with fear. His thighs were trembling.

I moved a second chair beside me, set down the paddle and grabbed the rope. "Come here."

He shuffled forward, the brown of his face darkening with shame. When he got close I turned him around and tied one wrist to forearm, then the other, behind his back. He sucked in a breath. Spinning him, I noted that binding his arms had stimulated him; his dick was peeking back out and getting stiff again. I opened my legs, drew him between, and jerked him against my knee so his cock would rub over my jeans as I punished him. Latching my free leg over his knees, I shoved him down. His feet seesawed off the floor, his chest hit the other chair. His bubble butt, fine as I remembered it, became very accessible.

He gasped, bound arms twisting, pushing his teeshirt up further, trapped legs shaking in anticipation. In mortification as well, his pants being pulled down, his ass and brown nuts exposed to the brutal spanking about to descend on him. I made sure to intensify those feelings by stroking the paddle over his behind, as if warming it. Goosebumps rose on his butt and back, arms and legs. He whimpered.

"I'm going to punish you now," I said, and before he could respond, I had the paddle up and whipping down. Swack! The sound of leather hitting that flesh was like the crack of an icicle breaking off. Hadji jerked in shock and spit out a rough yelp. Again I brought it down, and again. Hadji cried out as the paddle burned and bit him.

I, myself, felt an electrical rebound, like a flash up my arm. My anger flared and sharpened and I paused to savor it. In that beat, a quiver ran up Hadji's spine and perspiration broke out across his lower back. *Yes*, I thought, and down came my fourth and fifth whacks across his tender thighs, making him jump across my knee. This time his cries were half gasps. Stripes from leather paddle remained, reddening on those little butt cheeks, and his hot body shook. He was starting to cry.

I paused again to listen. To feel the power I had over him. It felt good, but not quite right. Because he was small and thin and crying rather than cursing me. My cold fury thawed a little and I hesitated. Anger. I remembered, sending through a new cold front. He could have been hurt. Could have ended up trapped on the street like all those other young fucks. The ones who went off with strangers and all too often were found again as bodies in a ditch. The ones I couldn't save.

Irritation returned, and I tapped the paddle against his ass. He trembled and sobbed, especially when I poked at his balls. I hadn't and wouldn't strike them, but he didn't know that. I whipped him again, and again, and again, letting the sound of the paddle break against the walls. He jerked, and his legs kicked up, trying to escape the lock my other leg had on them. When that did no good, he strained his arms against his bonds and shifted his body over the chair seat. I set my hand firmly on his back to stop that. The sweat seeping through his tee drenched my palm. *No escape*, that hand promised him. And that's when I felt his speeding heart race even faster in blind panic.

"Please! Please, Sir," he howled as I beat him with three more merciless whacks. "I'm sorry! Don't punish me anymore!"

My own dick was, by now, thick and pressing against my fly. Another three slaps, hard ones that made his ass pump up. In those bounces I felt his hot little dick, still stiff, pressing through the fabric of my jeans.

And then, quite suddenly, I was done.

Hadji was blubbering by now, "Please, please, please. No more, please—"

I caught him by the shoulder and brought him up. He was quaking so badly I thought he'd crumble. I freed his arms, suddenly impatient. In my jeans my erection was raging, throbbing in a way that Hadji was not going to be able to satisfy.

"Do you see that clock there," I pointed to the one on the mantle.

"Y-y-yessir," he wept.

"You stand in the corner, pants down for twenty-five minutes. Then you'll be done and you can bed down on the couch."

"Yessir."

I left him for the bedroom. Striding in I found Charles sprawled on the mattress, laptop on his knees, headphones on. He took one look at my face, and the technology, as well as more of my books, went off the bed. He didn't say a word, he just came to his feet, undoing his belt and fairly ripping open his buttons. I had my own belt unlatched and my angry dick exposed before he'd finished. Next thing I knew his pants were down and he was flat on the bed. Spreading those white cheeks with my brown hands, I spit on his hole, then stabbed in my needy, demanding, precum-soaked dick.

He grunted at the sudden invasion and bucked up his ass. His tight tunnel felt like a bath of hot water, scalding my nuts and expanding like steam. I pushed in far as I could go, then pulled back, and made him bark and jerk again as I thrust, and thrust, and thrust. My balls were now slapping his muscled buttocks, as I'd slapped Hadji's with the paddle, and my dick was stroking and being stroked by his hot, inner walls. Sweat broke out over my body and shaved head, and I smelled our mingled male heat building. The temperature in me rose, burning away the hard frost gripping my heart. On my next thrust sparks flared up the sensitive sides of my cock, engulfing the crown.

Charles cried out and arched his back as my dick seared his prostate. I grabbed his wrists and bit into his sweaty neck in return, sucking on the salt. His pulse beat against my teeth, and I humped faster. Behind my eyes I saw flashes. Finally, a wave of fiery pleasure blazed through me and I shot into him. Charles howled, engulfed by that inferno as well. I felt him stiffen and jerk, letting go into the sheets.

A heartbeat later, he sagged, exhausted on the bed, and I, the chill gone out of me, slumped on top of him. It took me a few moments to gather myself together, to pull out and roll off him.

"Jesus, Mary and Joseph," he moaned, as soaked as I in perspiration and trembling. "You were really angry." Then he glanced back over his shoulder and threw me a shaken smile. "I'm glad you didn't do that to Hadji after beating his ass off. And you're welcome."

Chapter 7
Holiday Cookie Swap

It was holiday cookie swap day and on our way to my mother's I stopped off at Owen's. Pulling into the driveway, I set the break, but left the motor running so the heater would keep going. "Be back in a minute," I said to Charles, who was in the passenger seat, and then, to Hadji in the back, "Let's go."

Hadji had been an even better houseguest than promised. For the few days he'd been with us he'd gone out each morning to shovel the walk if needed, and de-iced the windows of my car while Charles and I stayed warm inside, eating our breakfast. A nice change. Hadji had also done dishes, swept, mopped and polished. Though, interestingly, he'd never touched my books. If there was a stack on the floor, he'd worked around them. Ditto for those on tables. Nash wasn't into books and they were clearly foreign to Hadji, as well. My reading habits, I think, were almost as mystifying to him as my doing housework and errands.

As for that first night, I had stepped out before the twenty-five minutes were up to see Hadji standing in the corner, head bowed in chastisement, tee up, pants still down, beaten ass looking red in the last flickers of the fire. Ignoring him, I'd gotten myself some water and gone to sleep with Charles. The next morning nothing had been said about it. Nothing needed to be said because stiffly moving Hadji, in both his eyes and mine, had paid for his transgression and learned his lesson.

Some outsiders don't understand that. I can't speak for other BDSM types, but in my tribe we Masters don't linger over a slave's offense, punishing him repeatedly for it. That, to us, is the definition of a bully, not a Dom. Hadji had been unsettled to learn that he'd sinned against me, but he'd known that if he took his punishment, the air would be cleared; the pain he'd feel the next morning wouldn't be a reminder of his crime, but of my forgiveness. Which was why he'd looked quite content that morning even if he'd had to sit down very gingerly.

As for where he'd be staying long-term, one answer to that came to me right away. Charles, however, had expressed reservations.

"Master Owen and Hadji? Um... I don't think they're going to like each other," he'd ventured.

"Of course they're not going to like each other," I'd responded.

That had gotten me a perplexed look from my southern gent.

"Owen has my taste in men," I'd gone on, "meaning he'll find Hadji's way too sensitive and twinkish. And Hadji goes for pragmatic, uncomplicated daddies like Nash. Owen's gonna be far too moody and intellectual for him. But Owen's in need of company, and Hadji needs someplace to stay. And he should be with a top, not a bottom."

Charles had thought about that. "Yeah, you're right. Owen will feel entitled to boss Hadji around and right now he needs that. It's just... personality-wise, they're oil and water. I can't imagine them wanting to be together for long." Then, "Not that the differences'll stop them from fucking."

I'd snorted. "One can only hope." Testosterone is testosterone and it didn't have to like someone to want to fuck them. But in this case, that'd be a good thing. In my humble opinion, both could benefit from reliable and frequent screws over the holidays. Anything to keep them from wallowing in their sorrows.

In the light of day, Owen's modest, two-story colonial revival looked like something off a Currier and Ives print: snow covered lawn, frosted roof, winter bare trees. All that was missing was a horse drawn sled. Hadji, back in his jacket and woolen hat, shifted his duffle over his shoulder as we reached the front porch.

"Master Mason," he said softly, stopping me as I reached for the knocker. "There's something I want — need to say. About... about that first night."

"Yes?"

"I'm sorry I didn't take it like a man," he blurted. "And-and it was kind of you not to yell at me about that."

Well. That sounded like a Nash maneuver. Pick for your slave a boy who easily snivels, then, when you whip him and he snivels, bellow at him for not taking it like a man. What a fuckhead.

"You may not be my kind of man, Hadji," I said, pounding the knocker, "but you are one, and you don't need to change. Just be the best you can be."

"Yessir. Thank you, Sir."

He went quiet as the stomping of boots approached. Owen fairly threw opened the door with a muttered, "You're late."

"No we're not," I said and stepped into the entrance hall.

"You can hang up your coat there," Owen said to Hadji and pointed to a hall-tree-bench from which hung his jackets and hats. "Mason, a moment," he added, striding to the doorway across from the main staircase. I trailed him into what had probably once been the "parlor." The leather armchairs, dark wood bookcases and paintings of fly fishing now made it way too masculine for that grandmotherly term.

"I don't need a keeper," he growled, arms crossing. He didn't exactly say it loud enough for Hadji to hear, but he didn't keep it low enough for him not to hear either. I sighed because it was just like Owen to have spent the night having second thoughts. Also just like him to confront me with them after I'd driven over.

"Good," I responded. "Because Hadji does."

Owen didn't like that. I was appealing to his leatherman's sense of honor. That "Master" title didn't come free among us. If you wanted it, you had to be willing to do your part and do right by the slave-types. Even twinkish ones like Hadji.

"When I called and asked," I added, "you did say, and I quote: 'Sure. Bring him over. It's not like I don't have the room.' And he is going to pay for that room." I'd convinced Hadji to think of Nash's money as a loan. He could use it, and then, when he had a job, pay it back. He'd liked this compromise, especially as it kept him from feeling like a freeloader.

"Is there some reason for getting cold feet now?" I finished up.

"Just doesn't sit right," Owen muttered. "Nash dumps him, you pick him up, and somehow this leftover becomes *my* problem?"

"Last week you said you wanted someone in the house who would stay for longer than one night and wouldn't leave a mess." I waved back. "Happy Hanukkah."

"My gift for all eight nights, huh?" A familiar twinkle came to Owen's eyes and his lips pursed in that almost smile. "All right, all right. I should know better than to try and renege on the Fancy Man." He glanced through the doorway at Hadji, who, divested of coat and hat, was standing at parade rest before the hall bench.

"Can't believe Nash kicked him out like that," Owen shook his head. "I mean, I can, but I didn't think even Nash was that much of an asshole."

"He gave him some money."

"Oh, well, that makes it all better now doesn't it?" No one could do sarcastic like Owen. Except maybe my mother. Speaking of which—

"I gotta run. But I'd like to be kept up on how he's doing, if that's okay with you?"

"You mean I gotta choice in all this?"

"Good-bye, Owen. Hadji, I'll be checking in."

"Yessir," he looked both relieved and perplexed by this promise. He undoubtedly liked that I wasn't going to abandon him, but he was also worried about meeting my lofty expectations.

I'd like to say that I had no doubts about him, but that would have been naive of me. A minimum wage job and guaranteed room and board might seem a no-brainer choice over dumpster diving, bedding down in abandoned buildings, and being brutally fucked by strangers. But that's what Hadji knew and that's where the daddy-of-his-dreams had found him the first time around. Why not go back in hopes of that happening again?

I'm not saying Hadji was naive either; but he was young and, well, human. As I made my way back to my idling Scion and Charles, I couldn't quite decide which made us—all us homo sapiens—more blind: Our earnest belief in miracles or being in love.

Held in the basement common room of my mother's apartment complex, the annual cookie swap often has the feel of a wedding or bar mitzvah because there's a color scheme and a theme. This year the colors were minty green, silver and white. The theme "snowmen." Unlike the Cockpit, decorations here were impeccable. Fun, fanciful, handcrafted and everywhere. And this didn't even include the batches of cookies.

All this industry could be chalked up to my enthusiastic mother and her equally zealous cohorts, two old and dear lady friends. They'd started up the tradition back when they were single and in high school and had kept it going without a break for over three decades. Now, of course, participants consisted of not just the original trio but one husband, five grown children, their respective spouses/dates, and one rambunctious grandchild.

This toddler was being enviously eyed by my mother. In fact, everyone was looking at the kid, remarking on her over the holiday music playing from Bluetooth speakers, until we stepped in. Then all eyes but those of the toddler locked on us.

"Mason." Momma, like her two old friends, was wearing a green dress with a handmade snowman pin. "And Charles! Everyone, this is Charles, Mason's 'friend.'"

I wondered if anyone else saw the quote marks around that word that I did.

There followed murmured hellos and too-understanding smiles/waves/nods. Then everyone pretended to go back to their conversations while continuing to glance our way.

"I'll let Mason introduce you around," Momma said to Charles. "Are those your snickerdoodles?" She acted like she was merely curious, but she was actually very curious. She was probably wondering if she was going to have to add "amazing baker" to that reluctant list of Charles' positives.

"My great-grandmother's recipe, yes."

"Well, you can deposit the bulk of your batch in that empty basket there." She pointed to a long table with a green cloth. At the center was a fanciful, winter tableau featuring a snowman family made of Styrofoam balls and pipe cleaners. To either side of this were baskets overflowing with cookies, brownies and fudge.

"Reserve two dozen for your tasting plate, there," she added, waving to a round table covered with a white cloth and sporting silver platters. Snowmen stood behind each, pipe cleaners arms holding little signs that named the cookies and their maker. "There's a holder for your recipe cards at the foot of your snowman."

"Yes, ma'am," Charles headed off to the baskets. To my surprise, Momma didn't trail after him or return to her guests. Instead she locked her arm through mine and pulled me down so that she could whisper into my ear.

"Have you heard from Loretta?"

"No. Why?"

"I called her to let her know that she shouldn't bring her ginger-molasses cookies this year as Lisa decided to bring that kind. I left a message, but she never called back. And she didn't call last night to ask if we needed help, which she said she would. And before you remind me she's forgetful, this wasn't like that. I'm used to her forgetfulness. Something's not right with that girl."

"She's probably been extra busy this year," I said, but at the back of my mind I remembered Rafe's intentions. My stomach gave a tumble. Had they eloped? "I wouldn't worry."

"Hm." Momma was unconvinced. She could always sense when something was up.

I would have fretted more about it myself, but Charles had been mobbed at the tasting table. Okay, mobbed was a little strong. My mother's two friends, Mrs. Rice and Mrs. Wu, and Mrs. Wu's two grown daughters were peppering him with questions.

"You met Mason in a pub?" Mrs. Rice, divorced, curvaceous and bronze skinned asserted.

"It wasn't actually—" Charles ventured.

"What a wonderful accent!" remarked small and ebon-dark Mrs. Wu (her husband was Chinese-American and currently hobnobbing with his son-in-laws at the refreshment table). "Where, exactly, in Atlanta are you from? I have some friends there."

"It's a suburb just outside—"

"Have your parents met Mason?" Mrs. Wu's daughter, Lisa wanted to know. Her two year old, now perched on her hip, gazed at Charles as if she was equally interested.

"They said hello to him during a video talk on Thanksgiving."

"What do they do?" Mrs. Rice wanted to know.

"My mother's in real estate — houses — and my father works in acquisitions for one of those bulk stores."

"Do you get free big screen televisions?" Dale, Mrs. Rice's ne'er-do-well son had wandered over with his latest, buxom girlfriend.

"Are there more of you at home?" Cissy Wu cooed at him. She was happily married and seven months pregnant but that didn't dim the lust in her almond eyes.

It was like an opera. Every time one singer came to an end, another entered.

"Excuse me," I cut in, "But Charles and I didn't have any lunch," I pulled him out of that cross-examination and got him over to the refreshment table, nodding to Mr. Wu and the son-in-laws as I did so.

"Thank you," Charles breathed, and grabbed up a sandwich. "That was getting a little intense."

"I could see. And it was making me jealous." I smirked. "No one gets to interrogate you but me."

As I'd hoped, he blushed.

I was reaching for a sandwich myself, about to explain to Charles who was who when my phone vibrated. Normally during such parties I keep it off, knowing all too well how my mother feels about such things. I was, however, half expecting a call from Owen telling me something had gone wildly wrong in the mere half-hour since we dropped off Hadji. Keeping my back to my mother, I got the device half out of my pocket and checked the number. I saw my sister's name. It was too late to answer, but even as I looked at the notification of her call a text came up: *Meet me outside*.

"Cover for me," I said to Charles and made like I was going to the restroom. Charles barely blinked at the command. Finishing off the sandwich, he grabbed a soda, took in a breath, and headed back to the tasting table. He made sure he was near my mother as he pointed and inquired about Mrs. Wu's artfully iced sugar cookies. As my mother turned to answer his question, I slipped out.

Cold hit me. The apartment building's common room was down a flight of stairs on the unflattering side of the building. Loretta was at the top of those stairs, bundled in a pretty blue jacket with fur trim. In her gloved hands she held a plastic container of cookies.

"Lo? What's going on?" I hurried up to her. She wouldn't look my way but I saw that her eyes were red and damp. "What's wrong?"

"I can't—I don't want to talk about it right now." Her breath puffed out like smoke with each word.

"Lo—"

"Later. I'll tell you later," she said, pushing the container on me. "Momma said not to make ginger-molasses so I went for chocolate-pecan."

"What should I tell her?" I was getting cold out there in my shirt-sleeves, but damn if I was going to leave her like this.

"That I'm sick. That a friend delivered these for me."

"She'll want to drop in on you. Make you soup and tea."

Her pretty brown face, framed within the fur of the hood, went a little gray at that. "Tell her I don't want to make her sick during the holidays. That'll stop her. Tell her I'll be okay in few days, that I'm being looked after and need rest."

I didn't like it. Not any of it. I especially disliked that she hadn't told me to say "Rafe" was looking after her. But then I already had a good idea of what might have happened.

"Okay," I said as she turned to go. "But I'm going to hold you to spilling everything. I'll be at the gym tomorrow morning, then at Charles' place the rest of the day. I gave you the address, right? It's only a few blocks from the new metro station." Loretta didn't own a car. "You can either come by, or call me and we'll meet up wherever you like. I mean it, Lo. If I don't see you tomorrow, I'll be on your doorstep by nightfall."

"Okay, I get it. I'll see you tomorrow," she promised, and I heard tears in her voice.

Shit.

Hadji and Nash broken up. Now Loretta and Rafe? Whatever prank the holidays were playing this time around, it was turning out to be a doozy.

Chapter 8

Letters to the North Pole

"I wanted to thank you," I said to Charles as I drove us home, windshield wipers going. No snow this time, but wind and some splattering of rain.

"For what?" he asked, looking up from the cakebox of mixed cookies on his lap. "I actually enjoyed the swap... once everyone stopped grilling me on our relationship."

"For the snickerdoodles."

"Pardon?"

I kept my eyes on the wet road, illuminated by my headlights. "I know how hard it is for you to feel even neutral about something passed down to you from your family. But you found a legacy you felt okay about, and shared this rarity with me and mine. Thank you."

"Oh." He sounded taken aback, amazed even. He probably hadn't seen the cookies that way, but I had.

Charles' antebellum predecessors had been slave owners, and those after the war had been equally monstrous in their treatment of African Americans. And I do mean monstrous. As a child, Charles had known none of this until his fifth-grade history teacher gave his students a roots-esque assignment to explore their ancestry. At which point, Charles' parents had 'fessed up about the plantation. They'd downplayed it, of course, and insisted that his forefathers and mothers—on both sides no less—hadn't been that bad. But sensitive little Charles, deeply disturbed by this revelation, had done his homework and quickly learned that his parents were lying. His ancestors had been "that bad."

Charles could have ended his investigations with the assignment, and he did leave off for a couple of years. He was, however, entering that age where kids have as much of a fascination for the awful and grotesque as they do for the sexual. His curiosity got the better of him, and he went back to digging into his family. He soon discovered that just about every member of his bloodline had been, frankly, horrible to those who slaved and served them. Prison-camp-commander horrible.

Of course, put in historical perspective, their behavior had been perfectly legal and even socially acceptable. But this didn't make their actions any easier for Charles to swallow. By the time he was in college, his preoccupation with his ancestors' dirty deeds had become a full-blown obsession.

Being gay and a slave-type with masochistic tendencies got thrown into the mix, and he ended up free-falling into an ever widening vortex of emotional turmoil and self-loathing. Rationally, he knew he wasn't responsible for the crimes committed by his forefathers. But he was still sure that his DNA was tainted with their sins, his blood polluted. Sometimes he even thought he might be a kind of reincarnation of those earlier Charles Beaumonts. Meaning he'd actually done all those terrible things. Either way, he was convinced that if he didn't atone in the here and now, he'd be paying forever in the afterlife.

At first, he'd tried to do that by hurting himself. Then he'd stumbled into the world of leathermen, where he'd met an older white gentleman, his first Master. This first Master had introduced Charles to the lifestyle, which gave him ways of dealing with his issues that he'd not found in religion or therapy. Most of all, it slowed his fall. But it hadn't checked it. For that he'd needed a different sort of Master.

Enter yours truly, stage left. But that's another story.

This was why I'd made it a point, just now, to thank him for the cookies, because Charles had seen them as cookies, not some haunted, family legacy. It might only have been a tiny step back from the edge, but I thought it a significant one.

"And they were damn fine snickerdoodles," I added, to lighten the mood.

He laughed as home appeared and I pulled the car into the drive. "I used to leave those cookies out for Santa, as a matter of fact."

"Aw." I cut off the engine. "That reminds me. I never asked you what you wanted for Christmas."

He laughed again. "Peace on Earth?"

"Asshole. No. Really, I want to know. What do you want or need?"

"Oh, hell, Mason, I dunno."

"Come on, Charles. There must be *something*—like when you were a kid and wrote to Santa. You did that as well as leaving out the cookies, right?"

"I surely did," he said all Southern. "Handwritten and put in an envelope to the North Pole. One year I asked for a pair of real hand-cuffs, but I only got toy ones. I made do."

"Hmmm. I'm sure."

"Did you believe in Santa?"

Longer than I did any other higher power, I thought but didn't say. "Lo and I always had serious discussions about which of the cookie recipes from the swap to bake for him."

"Aw back."

"Yeah, well, I want you to imagine you're a kid again and I'm the one who's going to be passing on your message to Santa. What do you want for Christmas? You don't have to tell me now."

He eyed me sidewise. "You're serious?"

"I surely am," I mimicked his accent.

"Well, then I do have a few wishes."

I sat back, all attention.

"First..." He sucked in a breath, "I'd like us to live together. How-ever you want, but I... I want to be there for you every day of the week, not just on the days you stay with me."

I shrugged as if that was an easy request. On the one hand, it was. I was practically living with him now and it was economically stupid for me to keep paying for my apartment. On the other hand it was my apartment. I had very strong feelings about surrendering it.

"Two," another breath fogging the window of the car. "About calling you 'Sir...' I never feel like I'm giving you all the respect you deserve. I want permission to call you 'Master,' In private, at least. And last... I'm hoping you'll reconsider your restriction on—on your boots."

I smiled. "I could have guessed that one."

"Yeah. Might I ask, Sir, when you created that rule, you said I wasn't ready...." He trailed off, but I got it. He didn't understand that and he wanted to.

"I know I joke a lot about leatherman traditions," I said, "But this one matters to me. If you're going to lick my boots, then I think you should feel that you're a leatherman honoring another leatherman. I think I should feel that way about it, too. Do you see?"

"I think so. You want me to view it as a special tradition of our tribe rather than making it yet another part of my curious obsession."

"Pretty much. I'm not saying you have to feel that way or you'll never be allowed," I added quickly, "But that's why it's been off limits. I wanted to give you time to find that point of view if you could."

"Ah." He was wearing that strange, unsettling look he sometimes had. As if I'd just said or done something that made him want to follow me to the ends of the earth.

"Anyway," I unbuckled and opened the car door. "Letter received and St. Nick will be getting back to you."

Charles got out on his side and we headed up.

"And what," he said, "Do *you* want from Santa?"

I glanced back at him and grinned. "Peace on Earth."

Charles had the next day off, which meant that we went on a morning jog to our gym and spent an extra hour there lifting weights. I certainly felt like I needed to work off the stress. And the cookies. We ran into Robbie, which was no surprise. In fact, that was why I'd switched to this place from the YMCA some years back, because I'd immediately hit it off with the Cockpit's then-new bartender and he'd said he was a part-time personal trainer here. Also that he could get me a discounted membership. As it had turned out, he was a damn good trainer and I owed most of my current, impressive musculature to him. We didn't work together much now, but he did come round to chat as Charles and I benchpressed. This morning he had a troubled look on his freckled face.

"I dunno, Mason," he said as Charles perspired under the barbell and I spotted. "I've turned a blind eye to a lot of shitty things Nash has done, but this kicking out Hadji...."

Robbie isn't a leatherman. Which is why he's the best bartender for the Cockpit. He can ignore our antics and posturing and focus on serving drinks. He is, however, a romantic and has a powerful moral code. Seeing faithful Hadji rejected so callously by Nash was almost more than he could tolerate.

"Couples break up," I said, my hands palm up and to either side of Charles' grip on the bar. I kept a light touch in case, but even though he was on his third set, Charles was still raising and lowering the weights smoothly. I tried not to let the flash of his six-pack, the outline of his body under his sweat-soaked tank distract me.

"This wasn't just a break up," Robbie refuted. "It was a dismissal."

"It was a break up," I insisted, using all my acting abilities to sound both casual and reassuring. A rift between Robbie and Nash over this wouldn't be good, and there was no point telling him that there was some merit to his outrage. "I know Nash and Hadji looked more like employer and employee from the outside, but it wasn't like that. They were a couple."

"An odd couple," Charles grunted, pumping yet another set of reps. "We Master-slave types always are."

I chuckled and silently thanked my partner for that.

"Point is," I went on, "it's really up to Hadji to decide if Nash acted well or badly. You can express your feelings to Nash, of course, and maybe it'll help him do better in the future. But going on strike over Hadji's heartbreak isn't going change what happened. Or make Hadji feel any better. Is it?"

Robbie's eyebrows, as carrot red as his hair, clashed over his freckled nose. He didn't like that, but he was having trouble arguing against it. It was lucky that he didn't know about Hadji's stint on the midway or else we wouldn't even be having this conversation. He'd have tendered his resignation. But I'd informed Charles and Hadji that they were not to mention that; all the rumor mill knew was that Nash had let Hadji go, and that the young slave had found his way to me.

"That's exactly what I told him," came an English accent and Nigel, an older, rangy, straw-haired Brit joined us. He wore sweatpants and an old tee with the gym's logo that must have belonged to Robbie as it was way too large. He and Robbie had been a pair since Robbie's birthday in October and seeing them still together and happy was a gift in itself.

"'Can't be mad because one half broke it off,'" Nigel went on reasonably and flashed his easy going grin. "I said when we heard, but he wouldn't listen." He paused, gazing down at Charles. "Blimey. Charles, you make me faint with desire when you pump your fine muscles like that."

My southern gent, finishing off with the barbell at last, grunted a laugh and wiped at his perspiring face with a towel. "Why, thank you, Mr. Nigel," he drawled knowing how much Nigel relished his dialect. "If you're fainting over little old me, then my work here is done."

We all chuckled, and Robbie, finally, relaxed.

"Speaking of which," I said to him, "Did you get a line on any work for Hadji?"

"Lots," he said. "This time of year almost every restaurant in the area needs an extra bus boy. I could take him around, introduce him to some managers?"

We all agreed that would be good. Hadji needed a job to occupy him as well as the money. And bus boy, though it might not teach him any new skills, was a good place to start.

Having showered and changed into the extra clothes we kept at the gym's lockers, Charles and I walked down the street for a big breakfast at the Hunkry Grille ("Hunk-ry." Get it?). It was one of the most popular eateries in Boystown thanks to its enormous portions. As usual, it was full to overflowing with gay men and lesbians of every stripe, and several food savvy heteros. The windows, decorated with painted, muscle-bound Santas, were framed with frost on one side and fogged from the heat on the other. Within, the maple-and-coffee atmosphere was pleasantly noisy with voices, yuletide music, and the clanking of dishes. And maybe it was the trick of the holidays working on me, but as we waited for a table, I felt rather peaceful. Like I was coming to terms with the season and starting to enjoy it. I smiled at the deliberately silly Christmas sweaters some customers had on, and joined others in making much of a tiny pet dog in an elf suit.

Once seated, Charles and I ordered up platters of eggs, hash browns and meat (sausage for me, ham for Charles) and shared a stack of pancakes, twelve-inch around and piled high. We were almost finished, the pancakes down to some syrup-soaked slivers, when my phone buzzed. *Loretta!* I thought, fishing it out of my pocket. The call, buzzing away, wasn't, however, from my sister. I didn't, in fact, recognize the number.

"Hello?"

"Mason." Rafe's voice was rough and perfunctory. "Can we talk?"

I was too stunned to answer. In the three years Rafe had been with my sister I'd never gotten a call from him. Not even to say he and Lo would be late to a family dinner. In fact, I'd been under the impression that he didn't have my number. I certainly didn't have his.

"It's important," he said into the silence, his tone half angry, half desperate.

"Um," I said, so he'd know I was still on the other end. "Now?"

"If you can. Should I drive over to your place? Wherever that is?"

"I'm out and about right now. Why don't we get together at a coffeehouse?" I gave him the name of one Charles and I frequented, and told him the cross streets.

"I'll be there in fifteen," he said, again in that combative tone, as if warning me not to fuck with him. Then he hung up.

"Something wrong?" Charles asked.

"That was Rafe. I think I'm going to be getting Loretta's story from him."

Charles looked alarmed now. He knew how ambivalent I was towards Rafe, and how protective I was of my sister. He was undoubtedly worried about what I might do and whether it would land me in jail.

"Don't sweat it," I said, pulling out my wallet to pay the bill. "I promise not to torture him unless absolutely necessary.

Chapter 9
Under the Mistletoe

Coffee's not my thing; I don't hate it, I've just never taken to it. Which was why, during our breakfast, I'd downed a glass of orange juice, two of milk and two of water rather than joining Charles in a carafe of the Hunkry Grille's black brew. I reckoned that Rafe, however, could use some good java, which is why I'd suggested this place.

I let the smell of roasted beans infuse my clothes while waiting for my herbal tea to brew. I liked this place not only because it offered tea choices rather than just coffee, but also because the design included reclaimed wood paneling, meaning barriers between the tables. Very good for private conversations.

I was pouring my tea from a tiny earthenware pot into a glass cup when Rafe stepped through the door. He caught sight of me, nodded, then took a moment to hang up his jacket and order a drink from the handsome young man with the old school tattoos. Then he came over and plopped down across from me.

"You look like shit," I said. He did. Circles under bloodshot eyes, face drawn, posture... broken.

"That's better than how I feel," he snapped back. His dark eyes were ticking about restlessly. It wasn't homophobia so much as disorientation. This wasn't Rafe's part of town and he was the sort who had to get the lay of the land before settling in. If he settled in.

Rafe's cup-a-joe arrived, black no sugar or milk. He took a tentative sip and his brows went up. "'S good," he approved as if he knew what he was talking about. Which he might. I drank my seasonal honeybush, juniper, ginger and dried pear infusion (*partridge-in-a-pear-tea* it was called), and waited.

"I suppose Loretta told you?" Rafe was back to defensive mode.

"Not yet. But when she dropped off the cookies at the swap yesterday, looking a lot like you do now, I jumped to a few conclusions. The proposal didn't go so good, did it?"

He looked down in a way that was both bashful and devastated. "I... I'm still not sure what happened. Or why. We ordered in dinner, and it was all going great. She was laughing. I thought *this is it*. So, I maneuvered her under this mistletoe I'd hung up, kissed her and then I brought out the ring."

Rafe was a romantic. Who woulda thought? "And?"

"She looked at me like I'd flashed a butcher knife. I mean her face went all scared and sick." Rafe's voice failed him. He took a moment to swallow down coffee. "I figured what it had to be. So, I told her that I understood her concerns, given her—your—father. But, she didn't have to worry. I wasn't going anywhere. I told her I wanted her to be my wife and I didn't care about anything else."

I winced. Ah. That explained a lot. "And what did she say?"

"'*I can't*.' Then she grabbed her coat. I tried to stop her, but she told me to let her go. Loudly."

I almost smiled. I can be scary when I'm upset. My sister, like my mother, can be fucking terrifying.

"'Can't.'" He repeated. "Not 'won't.' What the fuck does that mean?" He slumped in his seat. "I've been trying to talk to her, called, sent messages, even went and knocked on her door. Nothing."

"I see."

"Did you know?" he added—demanded, "When I told you I was going to ask, did you know she'd react this way?"

I shook my head. "If you were going to spring it on her from out of the blue, I could have told you what she'd do, but you said you'd talked about it. Weren't you two on the same page?"

"I thought we were." He was looking defeated now. "But I guess she didn't take those talks as seriously as I did."

"That seems evident."

He prickled at that. "Bet you're happy."

"Oh, no you don't."

"Oh no I don't what?"

"Get to use this meeting to take your upset out on me," I said, leaning back and returning some attitude. "You said you wanted to talk. I'm here. Talk."

His jaw went tight and I could almost feel him battling with his pride over this. He wanted to appeal to me, badly, but he was convinced I'd humiliate him. I watched the internal debate in his eyes and body language, enjoying it perhaps a bit too much.

"What did I do wrong?" he finally broke. "I don't want any other woman in my life or at my side. And I intend to be at her side. Like I said, no matter what. And I know — I *know* she feels the same. So what did I do wrong? And how do I fix it?"

"By taking back that line about not caring about anything else," I said, and when he scowled. "Loretta wants you to care. A lot. Because she does."

"What?"

Right. I took another sip of my cooling tea. For a moment I wondered if I ought to explain. If he wasn't sharp enough to get this, to get Loretta, maybe she was correct and they couldn't be together. On the other hand, his three intimate years with my sister, however strong, probably couldn't match my lifetime of shared experiences. It was hardly fair to expect him to see it all.

"Trust me, Loretta has thought her way up one side of this subject and down the other. But she figured out pretty quick that you can't enjoy a relationship with all those concerns hanging over it. So, like old holiday decorations, ones you don't want to put up, but can't throw out, she stuffed them onto a shelf. Out of sight, out of mind."

"My proposal brought them down off that shelf?"

"That's what I think. I mean, yes, you've talked about marriage, but Loretta probably took it as *'we'll cross that bridge when we come to it.'* Now you've called her on that. Put her down on that bridge and said *'let's go.'* That means she can no longer ignore all her concerns."

He opened the door, I thought grimly, *and they all came tumbling down on her head: the ornaments carrying memories. The tangled emotional lights. A stocking that used to hang on the mantle but doesn't any longer, and photos promising family joy and unity that didn't deliver. Couldn't deliver.*

Yeah. That would be enough to make her shout, *"I can't."*

"My sister's been witness to all the unexpected bridges our mother had to cross," I added, and tried to ignore the tightness in my throat.

"Hauling her children along with her, all because of our dad. Mom wasn't prepared for any of it. That's why Lo doesn't want to hear that you don't care. She wants to hear that you care — so much so that you've thought of every possible bridge you might have to cross and how to cross it. Especially that biggest bridge of all: having kids."

He was listening, rather intently and, I had to admit, attractively. It gave me some insight into what my sister saw in him besides his fine looks. His brow was furrowed more with worry than anger now. "Okay. I-I think I get it. I mean, I thought I'd given her worries enough weight, but it looks like I didn't."

"Not your fault," I said, admitting that as much to myself as to him. "You can't know how much weight to give something if no one tells you."

Even as I finished saying this, my phone vibrated. I held up a hand to Rafe asking for a moment and drew it half out. It was a text from Charles: *Loretta here!* Of course she was! I rolled my eyes. How nice of her to call before dropping by. Well, she was my sister, and I'd have done the same to her. Had done.

Keep her entertained, I tapped back quickly. *Don't let her leave.*

"You know," Rafe said, as I slipped my phone back into my pocket, "When I first saw your sister I thought, well, I thought 'wow,' but I also thought that I'd be the luckiest man in the world if I could be with her; then we talked and I knew for sure I'd be that lucky. Because she was wonderful and I knew that each day in her company would be amazing."

He paused, staring down into his cup like it was a magic mirror re-playing for him every second of their three years together. "I was wrong. Each day in her company has been *beyond* amazing. I love everything about her."

"Except me," I said wryly.

He shrugged. "Actually, I've always thought it right that Loretta had a big, overbearing brother. Someone to scare off unworthy admirers, y'know. Not that I'm deserving of her," he added before I could make a remark, "but I promise you, I will cherish her no matter what. And I will never stop taking care of her."

I'll certainly keep you to that promise, I thought.

"Anyway," Rafe finished up, "I thought that needed to be said.

Thanks for listening, and for being so civil about it."

I shrugged. "It was Lo who broke it off, not you. So I was a little less inclined to kill you."

He snorted and toasted me with the dregs of his coffee.

"And," I added with a breath, "I'll stick my neck out even further and say Loretta was wrong."

"Oh?" His brows went up and his black eyes met mine. "You admit she should marry me?"

Fuck you, I mentally tossed back, and drank a little tea. "It was wrong of her to say what she said, like your thoughts about marriage couldn't possibly be as deep or serious or considered as hers."

"Does that mean you'll get her to talk to me?"

"Yes. How about right now."

Ha! His stunned expression was a real treat. Maybe he'd be more fun to have as a brother-in-law than I'd thought.

"Uh—"

I pushed out from the table. "She's at Charles'. Come on. I was hoping to hitch a ride back there anyway."

Rafe parked behind my Scion and I commanded him to stay, no matter how cold it was getting. He looked put out but resigned, his jacket tight about him. Getting to the door, I noticed that the sign had been turned around. Not that Charles needed to warn me but, slave-type that he was, he'd never neglect a "rule" no matter how redundant and unnecessary. If an uninvited guest was waiting for me, the sign got turned around. As I quietly stepped into the fragrance of woodsmoke, I heard my sister's voice from the living room.

"Most of the time it's pretty quiet. A lot of paperwork. But when there's a fire or flooding, it's like those moments in a war room. I turn into a general sending out orders, getting the ball rolling."

She was talking about her job. I'm still not sure how it had happened, but Loretta had ended up working for an emergency management agency.

"Do you like that?" Charles asked. "Getting the ball rolling?"

"Oh, yes. And I'm really good at it, just like Momma. A blizzard hits, half the city loses power, snow caves in roofs, or traps people, and I just turn on. I seem to know exactly what's needed and in what order. Shelter, supplies, heat. Bam, bam, bam! I make the calls and things start happening."

I stepped in to find Charles on the couch and Lo in the plush armchair, the one that offered a good view of the fire. There was a pot of coffee and a plate of the holiday cookies between them. Charles was grinning, and his eyes danced as he caught sight of me. "You're a lot like your brother," he said. "He's the same when putting on a play. Seems to know exactly what's needed and how it should all go... and woe to anyone who doesn't listen."

Cheeky, I thought, and imagined how a good paddling of his ass ought to go. I could make that play happen. Maybe tonight.

Loretta, legs looking extra long in skinny jeans, leg warmers and above-the-knee boots, glanced up from the book she was flipping through (my stellar astrophysics text). She still looked drawn and stressed, but her eyes were no longer red.

"Hey," she breathed, as I leaned over the chair to kiss her.

"Hey back. See you found your way."

"Easily. This is a great place, by the way, and so close to the restaurants and shops. Why aren't you living here again?"

"Because it's furnished," I joked. My apartment, which Loretta had visited a few times, was essentially bare but for a bed and a chair.

"Hm. That does make it harder to pile up your books on the floor, though I see you've been trying." She waved to one of my stacks in the corner. "Oh, and sorry about yesterday. I was in a bad place."

"You still are from the look of it."

She let out a sigh. "I suppose you're wondering what happened?"

"I know what happened. Rafe proposed and you said 'I can't.'" I steeled my resolve. What I was about to do wasn't going to improve sibling relationships, but I knew my sister. Better to push her into action than give her time to think. "He called me wanting to talk. We talked. He really thinks you two should discuss it and I think he's right. Which is why I brought him over. He's waiting outside."

Her jaw had fully dropped by now and I could see our family temper flaring. Good! Mad was better than woeful.

"You *what?*" She pushed to her feet. "What the—? How *dare* you? Damn it, Mason, you had no right!"

"Nope. None at all. But I did it anyway. Too bad for you."

She hit me in the shoulder. It was a hard hit and if it'd been in a delicate place it might have hurt. "Ouch," I said anyway.

"You fucker!" Her shout bounced off the rafters. "You unmitigated, interfering asshole!"

"Are you going to tell me I don't understand?" I challenged, which got me a very scary look. For a moment she was the spitting image of our mother, and not in a good way. Then she turned around, giving me her back and fumed.

Charles was standing, his face pale and worried. I jerked my head for him to leave us.

"I'll put on the headphones," he murmured, crossing out.

Lo sucked in a breath. "Rafe doesn't understand," she growled, a gauntlet of sorts tossed down at my feet. "That's what matters."

"You're right. He doesn't. Which is why cutting him off like that wasn't fair. Look, Lo, I get it. He proposed and all you'd ever experienced of our parents' marriage, every single thought you'd ever had about it, flashed before your eyes like some kind of unfolding car crash. And you imagined it happening to you and Rafe. Am I right?"

"You know you are," she growled back.

Taking a chance, I pushed at her shoulder, getting her to reluctantly turn around. "I totally empathize with your visceral first response to that. I would have said 'I can't!' too. I also get that the minute you were forced to say that aloud, you also had to face that it was over between you and Rafe."

Her furious eyes welled. "Yes," she said. "Rafe's not going to go back to what we had after proposing. He'll keep wanting to marry me. And yeah, all that shit avalanched down on me at once. Can you blame me from going into an emotional fetal position?"

"Not in the least."

"Made me mad, too," she admitted. "That he'd upended everything like that. Furious. I didn't want to explain things in that state. And that made me even madder: that he didn't get it."

"I'm sure. Because he's usually pretty in sync with you and usually does get it. But this was a big deal for him—"

"Obviously," she threw me a "duh" look.

"He wasn't totally blind to how you'd take it, but he wasn't totally prepared either. And then you gave him that answer and he had his own visceral response. But now he's thinking again, and you really should talk to him."

"About what? That something as wonderful as a proposal, as special as his offering that to me, sent me screaming into the night? It's fucked up, Mason. He had a ring you know. Flashed it at me. I didn't see facets of color and some unbreakable promise in that diamond. I saw things shattering apart."

That was my sister. She and I might not be so similar on first meeting, but get us talking and we were like that double cherry Shakespeare mentions. Sharing the same stem.

"Yeah," I gave her a little shake. "But Lo, have you thought that maybe you're wrong?"

"Wrong meaning what happened to dad and mom couldn't happen to me and Rafe?" Her lips tightened. "I can't give into wishes and maybes, Mason."

"I'm not telling you to. I'm saying you're wrong to assume you can decide what's best for Rafe. If you don't want a husband, or don't want him, that's one thing. But you wouldn't love him if he was stupid. So, evidence that I've seen to the contrary—"

She snorted and threw me a dirty look.

"—I'm guessing he's pretty smart. Don't demean that. Give him the intel he needs and let him decide for himself if he can deal. Unless you want to explain all this to Momma?"

"Ouch! Fuck you, Mason. That's dirty. Clever," she added with admiration. "But underhanded."

"Thank you. That mean you're willing to talk to him? You should make up your mind about it before he runs down his car keeping the heat going."

It was clear she'd rather face a firing squad, but she nodded. I walked her to the entrance where I helped her on with her fur-trimmed jacket and handed over her purse. As I opened the door and she caught sight of Rafe's red car, she put her hand on my arm.

"You know I wouldn't let anyone but you talk me into this," she grumbled.

"I should hope not."

"And since we're on the topic, and fair is fair, let me say: I absolutely love Charles and you'd better not let him go. I'm serious. I don't care how gay he is, if you do something all wrong headed and lose him, I'll snatch him up. Make him mine."

"That's not going to happen, trust me. I don't let go of anything I've claimed. Of course, there's not much I can do if Charles comes to his senses."

"True." She kissed my cheek and strode out and down the porch stairs for Rafe's car. "Tell him that when he does, I'll be waiting."

Chapter 10
Wassailing

Charles' tight, muscled ass was up, all bright red from the wooden paddle I'd used on it, just the way I liked it. He was kneeling on the bed, his ankles bound to a spreader bar. His wrists were, too, right between, so that he couldn't straighten up. A kowtowing position with his balls dangling and swinging between his quivering thighs. His cock was erect, as hot in color as his butt with need. But he wasn't getting any relief yet. In fact, the paddling had only been the appetizer of tonight's play. Now we were onto the entree. Pouring oil into my hands, I stroked down his crack, down to his little pink sphincter, past it to his taint, and back up again.

"Damn you!" he hissed, twitching with helpless yearning. A confirmed bottom in every sense of the word, Charles was enslaved to his prostate and always desperate to have something stimulating it. Anytime I came near his ass he got a gut churning need to be penetrated. I was naked myself, and my own cock was at attention. I moved a little to the side, so he could see me, and gave myself a stroke.

"You fucking son-of-a-bitch." he growled. He wanted my dick in him. Badly.

I kept one hand on his ass, switching between tormenting his crack and brushing over those sensitized cheeks. He wiggled as much as he was able. He also glared back at me, and at my handsome rod which I was lovingly fist fucking. Sweat had been glistening on the muscles of his back, and now it was beginning to trickle down. Best of all was the shiver. I love to see men shiver. And it's even better if they shiver with anticipation. As Charles was doing now.

"Bastard! Bastard!" he choked, even as his ass tried to thrust back at me, tried to get me to impale him with my fingers or cock rather than making him helplessly moan and gasp, wait and watch.

"Want something?" I purred, gliding my thumb down first one side of the velvet smooth skin of his crack then the other, then, once again, passing over that hungry hole, making him whimper. Shifting down, I pressed his taint and, leaning in, tickled his hole with my tongue, tasting sweat, musk and almond oil.

He shivered again and groaned.

I went on lapping at that cluster of nerves, making him struggle and strain in his bonds. In my mind, I could imagine how it must feel for him, the bindings about his wrists pulling, yet holding him tight, knowing he was vulnerable in every way to whatever I wanted to do to him. There had to be one hell of a knot in his stomach, a buzz in his balls, and his dick was probably pulsing like his racing heart.

My own dick was throbbing hard, come to that. It wanted me to enter that ass and start thrusting. *When he cracks*, I told it.

Charles was making strangled sounds now and I knew his face, pressed into the mattress was hot with shame. Even as I was imagining what he was seeing and feeling, so he was imagining me. Gazing at his beaten ass, his bowed, submissive, humiliated, gift-wrapped position. Having my way with him and him unable to fight or escape.

God, I so wanted to fuck him. *Hurry up and crack, Charles!*

"No!" he barked, as if hearing me, and tried to thrash away. I punished him for that by licking the back of his balls, and reaching between his legs to rub his pre-come slick cock.

"No... no!" He had to feel the pressure building and feared he might come without permission, which to Charles would be nigh unforgivable. Yet to avoid that he'd have to humiliate himself, and he both wanted to do that, and yet couldn't bear it. Have I mentioned how much I adored my conflicted, complex slave? Including how much he made me work for what I wanted. Almost as much as I make him work for it.

"Please," he finally whispered. At last! Entree finished. Now we could get to the sweet stuff.

I went from licking his balls to sucking at them. One, the other, they were tight and salty with sweat, and wonderful little treats in my mouth. I also squeezed a beaten ass cheek with one hand and continued to rub my thumb over his leaking cockhead with the other. The mix of intense pain-pleasure-need caused him to jerk and choke.

"Please, Sir," he almost sobbed the word. "Please fuck me, Sir."

Now, I thought, letting his balls out of my mouth and dropping the one hand down from ass cheek to his hole. I pressed a finger to it. He squirmed.

"Please, please, sir. I'm your slave. Use me please." His ass rocked towards me, submissive as you could wish.

Now! My straining cock demanded, and all thoughts vanished as I went up onto my knees and drove my slick rod into that tight, hot heat. He cried out as my length first penetrated, then stoked over his gland, and then I was beating him with my body like I had with the paddle. He yelled and cried out as our balls slapped and sweat fairly sprayed off our bodies.

"Let me come," he begged. "Please!"

"Go!" I shouted, even as I fired and stiffened. He spurted not a moment later onto the large towel protecting the sheets. As we both shuddered to an end, huffing and shrinking, I grinned. Damned right I can direct a play, I thought.

"God, Mason," Charles said to me a little later after we'd rinsed off and snuggled in, all naked under the blankets. My southern gent still seemed to be panting with exhaustion. "I was in good shape before I met you, but I swear, all these horny romps have me ready for the Olympics."

"Hm. Which sport, that's the question."

He quietly laughed and eased in contentment against me. That's yet another of those things vanillas don't get about us BDSM types. It doesn't make sense to them to come out of being bound and punished feeling good. Yet you ask masochists how they feel afterwards and, whether or not sex was involved, they'll almost always say "relaxed!" Those powerful sensations: pain, lack of control, fear even, lets them release all they couldn't let go of otherwise and, if done right, leaves them tranquil.

Controlling and inflicting pain left me feeling the same. Which is why, I think, we sadists can say we understand masochists even if we're their diametric opposites. Either way, it was wonderfully peaceful to lie with Charles, all worn out under downy quilts while listening to the wind outside. The only thing that didn't satisfy me was that he wasn't pressed in close enough. I wanted us entangled.

"Get in around me," I told him.

"Sorry," he said, throwing a leg over me and wrapping his arms about my chest.

I got an arm about his ribs in turn, enjoying the feel of smooth hard muscle against smooth hard muscle, warm skin against bare warm skin. I even closed the gap between our crotches so that our satiated cocks were nestled together. Ah, yes. That felt right. Wonderful. "Nothing to be sorry about," I breathed out happily. "Unless you were doing that 'I'm not worthy' thing?"

"I was, kinda," he admitted. Meaning he'd wanted to hug and hold me, but didn't feel, in his lowly slaveness, that he had the right. "But that's me and my neurosis, both of which you knew and accepted when you claimed my sorry ass."

"Your lily-white southern ass," I corrected, and felt him chuckle.

"Not so lily white at the moment, " he murmured and wiggled a little, aroused, and blushing, I'm sure, by the memory of what I'd done to him. Then, "Remember when you thanked me the other day?"

"What about it?"

"I wanted to thank you, too. For introducing me to your family and their friends."

I had to laugh. "You're thanking me for being a sadist?"

He nudged my chin with his nose. "I don't know what you mean. Your mother has been lovely and your sister's a delight. Neither the dinner nor the cookie swap was torture."

"Come on, Charles, it's hard enough for a man to meet his boyfriend's relations. For a slave to meet his Master's nearest and dearest? I'd amp the discomfort level up to eleven. I've been putting you through the psychological ringer with all these holiday events. Don't tell me otherwise. I've seen you sweating."

"I've been nervous, yes, but not because anyone's been unbearable. What's had me sweating—and is probably going to keep me sweating—is that I don't want to reflect badly on you."

"You mean like Dale's date?"

I could almost feel him wince. "She was a very nice young lady," he demurred.

"For a bimbo."

"Mason!" he chided. "Don't be sexist. Though, I will agree that she didn't make me think all that well of Dale."

"Actually, she was an improvement over the last date he brought to one of Momma's parties."

"Ouch. Well, I certainly don't want make that kind of impression. I'd hate to have you regretting that you showed me off to your nearest and dearest."

"You can cast aside that worry, Charles." I kissed him, and felt his heart pound steady against mine. "You're making a sterling impression. In fact, you're making me look like a genius for picking you."

"Really?" I could hear his sleepy smile in the darkening room. "Then I guess we'd better not tell anyone that I was the one who picked you."

Bastard.

I tried, that week, to keep from calling up Loretta or Rafe, figuring I'd done all the interfering I'd been invited to do and would learn the results soon enough. I did get an email from my sister telling me she and Rafe were discussing the matter. So. There was that.

I also had to resist calling or sending any kind of message to Owen or Hadji. How could they work out their new housemate situation with someone watching over their shoulders? On my visit to the Pit on Wednesday night, however, I got updates on several fronts. First was from Robbie who was happy to report that Hadji was gainfully employed at a small but well liked cafe. He'd been at his new job for a few days and was, evidently, proving as competent as expected at clearing tables, washing dishes, handling spills and other such work.

"The manager's ecstatic about how well he scrubbed down the kitchen," Robbie told me as he pulled an ale for me and set it on the bar. "His only issue is that Hadji won't do anything unless he's told to do it. And exactly how to do it. Also, when he makes mistakes, he agonizes over them. The manager keeps telling him to trust himself and relax, but he won't."

Everyone listening — tops and bottoms alike — rolled their eyes and laughed.

"That'd work if he was one of us," Al, a dark-haired stork of a bottom, threw in, and his fellow bottoms — Carl, Terry and Charles — all nodded. "But it's counter-intuitive to a puppy like Hadji."

"Tell the manager," I said, "to let Hadji know this is a practice period. He gets a pass on all mistakes. That'll ease his nerves. It might even get him to show a little initiative."

"I wouldn't hold my breath on that," said Terry.

"I'll text him," Robbie said.

Soon after that I ended up at the pool table, playing a few games. My long reach and steady eye made me relatively good at it, but I was up against Gina. Gina was an olive skinned leatherdyke, head puckishly-half-shaved, who had hands steady as a surgeon's. To add to this, I was hampered by a nearby tray table on which Robbie had set a big bowl of steaming wassail. Every year he made some kind of holiday punch, his gift to the regulars. Last year it'd been glogg, and the year before that a flaming German brew called punschgühbowle. This year it was wassail, and quite a show piece it was with baked apples bobbing about on top. Everyone was dipping out cupfuls for themselves and trying not to bump into us pool players, even as we tried not to bump into them or knock our cues into the wassail. Gina, who was fairly petite, was having an easier time doing this than me.

In between taking her shots, Gina gave me the dirt on Nash. She worked in tech repair and he'd recently called her in to set up some new, digital devices for his house; so she knew the latest.

"He and his marine buddies have a full calendar," she said tapping a ball into one of the pockets. "Skiing trips, hunting. All sorts of shit. I think they're trying to impress the new boy. Who I met."

Several nearby conversations went quiet and cups of wassail came down from lips. Gina glancing up from chalking her cue, saw curious eyes and shrugged. "Kid's real pretty. Has this innocent, blond, boy-band aura, so Nash and his buddies can fantasize that they're defiling him." She rolled her eyes. "Innocent, yeah. He's about as naïve as a Taiwanese street hooker."

"Nash know that?" someone asked.

"Of course. But the man and his bros are still gaga. They'd fuck that kid all night long if they were still as young as they pretend to be. They take him with them everywhere and, like, dote on him. Never seen a slave so spoilt."

Which didn't bode well for Hadji getting his place back. If he wanted it back, which he probably did. Poor fucker. Later on that night, an hour or so after I'd lost badly to Gina, Owen got dealt out of his card game and came over to stand by me at the bar, a cup in hand.

"Wassail, huh?" he said, staring into the drink. "That's just apple cider, right?"

"With one hell of a kick, or so I was told." I hadn't had any myself. I wasn't quite in the mood. "Word is Robbie dumped in a bottle of apple brandy and another of maple whiskey."

"Wanted us sad fuckers to cheer up and start wassailing, huh?" He lifted the cup in toast to me and took a hearty gulp. Then after smacking his lips and nodding as if it would do, said, "Hadji's been good as gold." He made it sound like a complaint.

"That a problem?" I asked.

"It is. He's too quiet, too clean, and too obedient. You know what I mean."

"Owen, my reputation as a match-maker aside, I'm not trying to hook you and him up. Hadji's your housemate, not your slave. I mean, yeah, he's still a slave-type, and like one of the boys here, at your beck and call. But he's not expecting anything more to happen between the two of you."

"More has happened," he admitted. "But that's not news."

"Nope. Mazel tov. Was it satisfying?"

He shrugged. "I think we both got what we needed. But not what we really wanted. Maybe that's the real problem. We don't want this. We just need it."

"The holidays are like that sometimes," I said. "Like when you were a kid and your mother bought you underwear rather than the expensive toy you'd been hoping you'd get."

He eyed me sidewise. "My mom always gave me toys. Not always the ones I wanted, but nice ones all the same. What kind of mom did you have that she'd pull such a nasty trick?"

"One who taught me how to be a sadist."

"Getting a boy to eagerly open a Christmas gift expecting a toy," he mused, "only to be stunned and humiliated by packages of underwear. That is seriously fucked up." He raised his wassail in a toast to my mother. "Give her my compliments. She raised you right."

To deal with disappointments and be realistic, I thought. Maybe Owen had a point.

"I'd like to stop by sometime and check up on Hadji," I ventured.

"You can do that right now if you like. I'm giving him a ride home. He was suppose to walk on over here and meet me out in the lot."

"Out in the lot?" I frowned. Temperatures were due to hit record lows.

"His idea, not mine. I suggested he come in, but he refused."

Had he? I made for the door. Charles got there before me. I sometimes wondered if he thought we were racing to see who could nab my jacket first.

"Hang out in here for a minute," I told him. "Hadji's in the lot and I want to have a quick word with him."

He raised his brows.

"Only talk," I said, giving him a kiss that included biting his lower lip. Yes, only talk this time with Hadji, though I liked the idea of pushing down a man's trousers out there in the cold and dark, having my way with him up against the car. All that heat between us while surrounded by all that wintery briskness, like a steaming cup of peppermint chocolate. Which I'd have preferred to wassail.

Yum. Maybe with Charles. *Later*, I thought stepping outside.

Chapter 11

Parties, Parades, and Panfish

Sure enough, Hadji was in the parking lot. He had on his knit hat and a too-big jacket that had probably been Owen's, and was moving about in front of Owen's car, keeping himself warm.

"Owen said you'd be waiting out here. What the hell?" I demanded; the air was frigid. Not down to where eyelashes stuck together, but enough to make me glad of the woolen extras under my sweater and jeans. And to not want to stay out here long. "You'll freeze."

He turned my way and, to my surprise, offered me a smile rather than his usual, doggy cringe. "No, sir. I'm Canadian. And I've got clothes on." This last was in reference to Nash's favorite uniform for his boys: a leather jockstrap. Hadji joking about that made me pause and give him a second look.

"A shame about the clothes," I lobbed back. "But really, why don't you come inside?"

"Master said I wasn't allowed... I mean," he stumbled. "Master Nash. Staying away from the bar was one of his rules. I know it shouldn't matter now, but it does. I feel wrong just being out here in the lot. I couldn't possibly go inside."

I nodded my understanding and blew out a puff of air. "Okay. So. How are you doing otherwise? Everything alright?"

His eyes dropped. "Not really, Sir. I'm sure Master Owen told you. Please don't be too angry with me. I swear, I follow all his commands to the letter, but he's never happy with me. He just frowns and grunts. I don't know what I'm doing wrong."

I forced down a smile. "I'm not angry and you're doing fine. Owen frowns and grunts because he's a grumpy cerebral Master, not because you've done anything wrong."

"Cerebral?" he asked blankly.

"In his head. The opposite of Master Nash who's a man of action and doesn't spend a lot of time thinking about things. Master Owen likes to think. A lot. And usually, what you're seeing and hearing from him has to do with those thoughts, not you or anything you've done."

"He's very smart isn't he?" Hadji sounded daunted. "Like you."

That made me shiver. Yes, indeed. I was smart in that way. Too much for comfort sometimes. "He is very smart. Also very moody."

"Well, how can I know if I'm doing things right, then?"

"If he rants about how you did something wrong, then you probably did it wrong. All the rest of the time you can assume you've done good and he's upset about something else."

"Oh," he accepted, but he didn't look convinced. In fact, he seemed even more troubled.

"I get the feeling that's not the only thing on your mind," I ventured.

"It feels so strange!" he blurted. "This morning, at breakfast, Master Owen told me to sit and eat with him at the table. He said it irritated him when I stood to the side, refilling his coffee. I did what he wanted, but it didn't seem right. Which is really wrong. Whatever Master wants, I should be happy to do. I always felt that way with Master... Master Nash, but I don't with Master Owen."

"That's because he's not *your* Master, Hadji. You know that, and he knows that. He's *a* Master. You may feel the need to do what he says, and be pleased if you please him. But there's no reason to be ashamed if serving him or any other top doesn't feel the same to you as Nash."

His head dropped then, spilling hair in front of his face. "I miss it. All the things I used to do for Master. Fetching him his rooibos tea, sitting at his feet when we watched movies. I miss it all so much."

I let out a breath, a puff on the freezing air. "I know. That feeling's not going to go away anytime fast. But try to keep doing these new things, however strange. You may be surprised at how soon they start to feel like normal. Speaking of which, how's work? You've never actually held a regular job, have you?"

294

"No, Sir. But it's a lot like dealing with one of Master Nash's parties — clearing the tables, cleaning up spills. Only not as messy. I think I'm getting the hang of it. And I am glad that Robbie warned me about being hit on. Men keep asking if they can call or text me or meet me after work for coffee and it's hard to remember that I don't have to, um, service them like I did Master Nash's guests."

That's what two years of being Nash's special pet would do to a slave, I thought.

"I'm very proud of you, Hadji. And if it's alright, I'll check in with you again next week."

"Yes, Sir, I'd like that. Thank you, Sir."

With that, I hurried back inside to let Owen know Hadji was waiting. Canadian or not, it was too cold for him to be hanging out there.

"See if you can't get him to wait on the back porch next time," I advised Owen, "with the heat lamps."

"Good idea," he said, and joined Charles and I as we left.

As for that idea I had about going at it against the car... I decided to save it for a less polar night. Instead, I went for very toasty sex in front of the fire.

The season was in full force by now, keeping me too busy to be on guard for tricks. "Come in and know me better, man," I boomed at Scrooge as "Christmas Present" during my on-stage stints at the Dickens Fair. That role was a whole lot more fun than the silent and forbidding Christmas Future. But it was C.F that everyone wanted to photograph. I got stopped for selfies more times than I could count when I wandered about the fair all black robed, face hidden within a cowl.

There were holiday movies to see, and the local street walk to take in. Also the "parade" put on by the Cockpit's dykes-on-bikes, which they used to collect toys for the kids at a local women's shelter. They and anyone who wanted to join them decorated up motorcycles and trucks with lights and banners and garlands. Then they chugged around Boystown saluting cheering pedestrians. The largest of our dykes (our 'Ursula' as the bears called her), came last as beardless, gender-neutral, biker-Santa. Charles and I hooted and whistled as she roared by.

In addition to all this, we had parties to attend. Charles shyly asked me if I'd accompany him to his modest, animal clinic's to-do. The lovely ladies he worked with had nothing but praise for him and told me of all the patients crushing on him, both two-legged and four.

More selfies.

I drank my fill of eggnog and buttered rum. Made small talk, and replenished the cookie jar with the sweets everyone seemed intent on giving us. All this occurred during the week after my talk with Rafe and Loretta. And no, I didn't hear from either during that whole time. I did get reports from Robbie about Hadji, who, after work, now hung out on the bar's heated back porch waiting for Owen. But I didn't hear from Nash's ex-slave directly till the afternoon before Momma's Magi-Day supper. He called asking if Charles and I were free to come over for dinner (!). Curious and amazed by the invite, we arrived with two six packs of good ale and a gifted gingerbread cake.

Hadji opened the door, which gave me a moment of déja vu to when he'd always raced to open Nash's door for visitors. Unlike those times, he was decently dressed in a standard white tee, jeans and sneakers. He was also willing to shyly smile and welcome us in, rather than jumping back as if we'd slap him aside if he didn't move quick enough.

"What's for dinner?" I asked as he took our coats. Delicious fragrances drifted our way: butter, wine and onion.

"Fresh caught walleye," Hadji said, "We went ice fishing this morning."

"We?" I followed him past the stairs and back toward a sizzling sound. Owen's kitchen was done up in yellow wallpaper featuring fish and nets. The man himself was cooking away at a black, antique stove. He had on a moth-eaten sweater over his gray tee and was switching between a huge, cast-iron skillet and a smaller saucepan.

"Hey," he said waving a spatula that he then used to transfer crisped fillets from skillet to platter.

"Master Owen took me along," Hadji answered my one-word question while pulling back a chair for me at the table. It was set with dishes patterned with sailing ships.

He had? I exchanged a look with Charles. He shrugged and shook his napkin across his lap.

"How'd he do?" I asked Owen as Hadji brought over a bowl of roasted root vegetables and another of smashed potatoes.

"Great!" Owen said with real enthusiasm. "The panfish were biting. But it was Hadji hooked the prize: a five-pounder."

The lad, putting down an oven-warmed loaf of sourdough, shrugged like this was nothing. "I did a lot of ice fishing as a kid. And Master Owen's got great gear. That really helps."

"After stuffing the freezer we still had a lot," Owen went on, "so I thought you two might want to help us eat it."

He set that lot on the table, and the fragrance of the *beurre blanc* sauce spooned over those filets had my mouth watering. Who knew Owen could cook? Or that Hadji could fish? We dove in, Hadji and Owen regaling us with tales from their chilly adventure as we feasted. An hour later, sated with good food, good drink and good talk, I allowed myself a smug, mental pat-on-the-back for doing right by these two.

Then someone started pounding on the front door, loudly and insistently.

"What the hell." Owen tossed down his napkin. And to Hadji, "No, I'll get it. Probably some kind of delivery. I'm expecting a few things."

"There's herbal tea, Master Mason," Hadji said in the lull, "and coffee, Sir?" He added looking to Charles.

"Sure," I said for us, "And I hope you like gingerbread cake? We've brought some for dessert."

"I love it," he said, rising. He was just reaching to clear the plates when we heard Owen's step returning, and his voice murmuring to someone else. Someone with equally heavy footfalls. Then,

"Hadji?" Owen sounded irritated, but not at Hadji. He entered the kitchen followed by Nash.

Trick or treat.

Shit, I thought, as Nash strode forward in that way of his, as if he

owned the place. He had on big snow boots, briar pants, a red flannel shirt and a hunting vest, all of which accented his still powerful body. I wouldn't have been surprised to see a shotgun under his arm. He'd doffed his trapper's hat, which he held in one hand, exposing his wavy, salt-and-pepper hair. He looked the epitome of the "Daddy-Master" that slave types like Hadji craved.

And, in fact, Hadji had jumped back on seeing him, almost knocking over a chair, while Charles automatically rose in respect. I stayed seated as was my right. I even sliced myself some bread and leisurely buttered it.

"Sorry to interrupt dinner," Nash said, not meaning it. "I heard Hadji was staying here. Nice of you to take him in, Owen."

"He's a good tenant," Owen said and crossed his arms.

"Master!" Hadji gulped and stared wide-eyed with disbelief, his breath coming quick enough that his ribs could be seen under his tee. Then, as if he realized Nash was really there, and not some fever dream, he collapsed to his knees and bowed to the floor.

Nash, in response, tilted his head as if critiquing the abasement. Then he snapped his fingers. Hadji went flat onto his belly, hands to head in total surrender. *Forgive me, Great Master, for not groveling enough before.* His pose said. *Step on me, walk on me. I live only for you to use me!*

"Up," Nash commanded, apparently satisfied, and the young man rose to stand at parade rest. "Looks like Owen's been keeping you fed."

"I had to use some of the money from the card," Hadji blurted with a panicked look. "To pay Master Owen for food and rent. But I've a job now and I'll replace it."

Nash seemed surprised by that. Even a little troubled. "S'your money, boy. I said as much when I gave it to you and I don't go back on my word. No need to repay." He was eying his ex-slave now as if seeing him in a whole new light. Then, being Nash, he dismissed those reflections as pointless.

"Well, I'll make this brief and not overstay my welcome." He might not be a naturally polite fuck, but Nash knew how to behave in another's house. Especially when he'd dropped by uninvited. "Long and short, things didn't work out with the new boy and I want you back."

FUCK! For some reason this upset me. Really upset me. But I wasn't sure why. It'd been what? Four weeks tops, since Nash had severed his contract with Hadji. Why shouldn't the leatherman be allowed to change his mind? And there was no doubt that Hadji wanted this. The slave might well celebrate it as a Christmas miracle. I should've been happy for him. But I wasn't. I was righteously annoyed. Owen, in fact, looked more resigned than I, like he'd been expecting this all along. Maybe that's what irked me. That I ought to have guessed this would happen and hadn't.

Or maybe I was taking it too personally. I was the one who'd set Hadji on a new path. Now Nash was snatching him back to the old one, and Hadji probably wouldn't feel one iota of regret about it. Totally ridiculous and very unfair to view Hadji as a pawn in some game between Nash and myself, but fuck it. I still felt like I'd lost some sort of important contest. Or had I? Strangely, Hadji wasn't falling forward to embrace Nash's knees in a paroxysm of gratitude. He was still breathing hard, but his hands, there behind his back, were fisting and opening as if he was trying to work through something.

"Hadji?" Nash frowned. "Go get your things. Chop-chop," and to us, "Me and the buds are spending Christmas at the Montana ranch. They're waiting at the airport."

But Hadji didn't move. "Master Nash," he said softly and after licking his lips several times. "Master... Master Nash, I—I can't."

I straightened, as did Owen and Charles. I wondered if Nash had heard that little switch there, from "Master" to "Master Nash?"

"What?" Nash scowled and looked like he thought this a bad joke. "What the fuck do you mean you can't? Like hell you can't! I won't say it again. Go get your things."

"I can't. Please listen," he half begged, half, to my amazement, demanded. And hard as it must have been for him, his eyes came up. "You are—were my Master and you had every right to tell me to go. It didn't matter when or why. But the reason that I had to go—"

"Oh, good God! You're on your own for a few weeks and you start spouting queer shit? Relationships end, boy. That's life. You should thank your fucking stars that I want you back. But if you don't come now, I might change my mind. I'm already going to punish your ass purple for this."

Haji's face flushed dark at that tantalizing promise, shame and desire in his dilated eyes. Nash certainly knew how to bring his puppy to heel and I thought sure Hadji would race off to pack.

"Master Nash," he said instead and with astonishing courage. "You were the one told me that a slave ought'n stay with a Master he can't please."

"I don't believe this!"

"I'm not the one you want," Hadji cut in. "You want Jonny, whoever he may be. Not Hadji. You've always only wanted Jonny."

"Yeah, so? I told you that day one."

"Being told, Master Nash, is different than knowing."

My brows shot up and I looked to Owen who appeared equally stupefied. Where was this coming from? Hadji hadn't, to my knowledge, been any more of a deeper thinker than Nash. Yet he'd clearly been going over this, and his views on what he'd do if Nash ever wanted him back had radically changed from the day he'd sobbed over his loss in my car.

Maybe it was simply a result of being away from Daddy? Masters can help their slaves grow and develop. Or they can keep them stunted. However brief, Hadji's time interacting with the world, free of Nash, may have been enough for an important and long overdue growth spurt.

"I saw how happy you were when you found Jonny," Hadji went on, quite earnestly, and as if he and Nash were the only ones in that kitchen. "And I was glad for you even if — if it hurt."

"Fuck me," Nash groaned again.

"I hate being without you. A lot. But, I want you to find him, and if I'm there taking care of you, you might not go looking."

"So you're saying you want me to be happy, and as I was only happy with Jonny —" Nash, brow furrowed, had to take a moment to work it out himself, "You're making sure I go out hunting for another one rather than settling for you?"

Hadji nodded, looking as wretched as he probably felt.

Hands on his hips, Nash considered that. And considered it more, as if he was trying to find a way around it. At last, he let out a disgusted breath. "That's damn noble of you. Fucking stupid, but almost leatherman worthy."

No almost about it, I thought fiercely. It was one of the most overlooked aspects of Master-slave relationships. Slaves were the courageous ones. Their bravery and self-sacrifice never ceased to amaze me. Hadji had certainly left me and Owen as stunned as Nash.

Hadji blinked, astonished himself by Nash's words. "Thank you, Master Nash."

"And if that's what you think," Nash went on with a shrug. "Your loss. Guess I'll have to do without. Or, fuck it, maybe I'll head through the midway. I'm sure there's some boy there eager to service five randy old men in exchange for a free flight to Montana. Owen? Walk me to the door, will ya?"

He flashed me a toothy grin, then turned on his heel and strode out. No one said anything as we listened to the two men murmuring. Then the front door shut.

"Please, sirs, if you'll excuse me," Hadji said very quickly. He looked grey and sweaty of a sudden. He didn't wait for our permission, but darted to the nearby powder room, where he was very evidently sick.

"Should I?" Charles asked.

"Leave him be," I said.

Owen appeared a moment later, a decidedly odd expression on his face. He was holding his cellphone, looking at its face as if he couldn't make sense of what was on it.

"What?" I asked.

"Nash just asked me how much I was charging Hadji for room and board. Said he wanted to pay for next month. He made the transfer and left. But I just looked at it." He held up the phone. "He's paid for the next four months."

"I guess," I said after a moment digesting that. "I guess the Grinch's heart grew a little."

Chapter 12
Gifts of the Magi

Charles and I helped Owen wash the dishes, then went home leaving the gingerbread cake. We talked about what had happened on the way.

"That was one of the bravest things I've ever seen," I said at one point.

"For Hadji, you mean," Charles ventured, his eyes on the wipers pushing snow this way and that over the windshield.

"Well that's it, isn't it? If we soldier our way beyond our personal limits, even though it scares us sick, then we're being heroic. Hadji went beyond his, all to do what he thought was right."

"I dunno," Charles demurred. "Seemed to me he did what his personal limits demanded. As a slave, how could he do other than offer his very best service to his Master? Come to that, how could he do less for the man he loved so much?"

We were paused at a light, which gave me a chance to see something of Charles' face in the dark car. His expression, what I could make out of it, was thoughtful and troubled. "Nash was the one who had the courage," he asserted as the light changed.

"Being selfish is brave?" I scorned.

"There was more to it than that," Charles protested. "It couldn't have been easy for him to admit, in front of you and Master Owen, that things hadn't worked out and he wanted Hadji back. But he did it anyway. Being able to make tough decisions like that, with no rules or code to guide you... I don't know how you Doms do that. I mean, things don't always work out for me, but at least I can take comfort in sticking to protocols. You Master-types are in free fall, changing direction without a compass or guide. When I had to live that way, I was always stressed and petrified. You're the brave ones."

"You're giving us too much credit. What's hard and scary for you is easy for us. And isn't that the definition of courage? That what you're doing has to be hard and scary? Nash didn't lose his dinner over his decision, Hadji did. So, Hadji's the brave one."

"Oh, well, if you're going to define yourself to victory," Charles chuckled.

I lightly elbowed him. It proved my point, though, didn't it? We decision-making Doms got to define ourselves to victory. Subs didn't; the one choice they consistently made was to be vulnerable, trusting another to take them to the edge and no further. That, in my book, took a great deal more courage.

I spent the next afternoon wrapping up gifts and hauling them down to the car then, just like on Advent Day, I picked up Charles from the animal clinic and drove us to my mother's. I was almost as tense about Magi day as I'd been about December first. What was I going to say to Loretta, I wondered during the drive, if she and Rafe had decided to break up? Charles, noticing my tension, stayed quiet through the ride.

Loretta, as it turned out, had gotten to Momma's before us. She was alone, but she didn't seem sad or upset as she hugged and kissed us both, then helped us to bring in our gifts. Pepper tried to do his usual: barking and taking bites at our ankles as if he'd win a prize if he made us fall and spill the presents.

"Pepper," Charles said mildly, and just like that the rat was at his heel, tail wagging.

"Oh, hell no!" Loretta said to that. We got everything under the tree even as Momma stepped out of the kitchen to give us orders like a drill sergeant. The right food was transferred to the right serving dishes, and as I was setting them on the table, I noted five places. Sure enough, not ten minutes later, Rafe arrived, gifts in arms. As he did his usual dance to avoid Pepper's bouncing, barking nips, I noted that he didn't look too bad, either. A bit harried like someone who'd rushed over from work, but far better than when I'd seen him last.

I had no idea what he and Lo had decided, but, clearly, they were still together.

Dinner tonight consisted of chestnut soup followed by Momma's signature, port-glazed duck breasts with raisin and almond pilaf (Momma's nod to the Middle East Magi), and green beans. The conversation did not include historical arguments. Instead it bounced between a variety of topics, with Loretta and Rafe taking part as if they hadn't been through a heart-breaking argument some twelve days back.

We retired to the living area where, once again, Pepper decided to settle at Charles' boots rather than on his usual cushion in the corner. Charles reached down to rub the rat's belly and Pepper made happy whimpering sounds while kicking out a leg. I think at this point, Loretta and Rafe were ready to keep Charles in the family if only to deal with Pepper. Momma, though friendly and polite, still looked torn. I would have said she wasn't ready to give up her long war on my sexual orientation and, by extension, her religious view of it as "sinful." But I think her lingering objections to Charles had more to do with Pepper. Momma liked that her little rat was a terror, but with a word, my boy could transform him into a pussycat. And the dog fawned over him. Momma didn't know how to feel about that.

Charles had asked to bring dessert, and Momma—again in an amazing show of acceptance—had agreed. His pear and cranberry crisp was served in the living room with coffee and my chicory tea while we admired the presents. I had to admit, I got a certain, childish delight seeing those inviting boxes piled up under the blue tree.

"Mason, how it is you always have the best wrapped gifts?" Loretta groused. "It's not fair what you can do with ribbon. All those elaborate patterns. How did you get so good tying things up?"

Charles swallowed wrong and ended up coughing. Rafe slapped him on the back.

"Boy Scouts, remember?" I said in answer to Lo's question, and smiled innocently.

"I think it's about time for the Advent calendar," Momma said looking to where it sat on the mantle. The sixteen "windows" between December first and tonight had been turned around by her, their little painted designs of bells, a nutcracker, a poinsettia and such revealed. "Loretta, it's your turn."

My sister popped up off the couch, she pulled out the number

"18" plaque and turned it around to display a picture of a beribboned gift. Then she opened the little drawer and fished inside.

"Let see," she said, sitting down, a little drawstring bag in her hand. Momma frowned, which should have cued me, but Lo already had the bag open and was shaking it. Into the palm of her hand fell a diamond ring.

"What the—" Momma gasped, even as Loretta grinned "gotcha!" and Rafe plucked up the ring and slipped it onto her finger.

"OH MY LORD!" Momma grabbed Loretta's hand to peer at the diamond. And then she wrapped her arms around her daughter. "Ohmylord, ohmylord!" she kept saying, and pulled her-soon-to-be-son-in-law into the embrace.

I gave them a moment before rising and hugging my sister tight. "Good on you," I whispered.

"It was a long talk," she whispered back. "Thanks."

I shook hands with Rafe and muttered a "welcome to the family." Charles congratulated them both and Momma, well, she wiped her eyes. Loretta, looking shy, fetched the mini-gift cards she's switched for the ring and handed them out. Rafe, well, he put his arm around her, lifted his chin and looked me in the eye. There was no mistaking that message. *She's mine to protect now*, it said. I nodded back, acknowledging and agreeing.

Which I guess meant we were both going to be calling each other: "brother."

The following Sunday was the Cockpit's gift exchange and my annual gig as Saint Nicholas or "Master Claus" as everyone unimaginatively called me. As Charles' rotation had him working that day, I went on my own, red-and-white suit beside me. It was one of the few parties I looked forward to as I liked digging into the black bag, pulling forth a present, and calling out the name attached. The recipient was required to open it right then for all to see. Given that outrageous sex toys were the norm, this resulted in a lot of hoots and laughs.

My job, as the literal and figurative M.C. of this event, was to remark on the recipients good or bad behavior over the past year and give them some pointed instruction on how to use the new toy — more hoots and laughs — after which their gift-giver would come forward to be thanked. Sometimes with a hug. Often with a threat to use the toy on them. It was the sort of good fun and relief we all needed at this point, with Christmas barreling down on us like a runaway sleigh.

It was mid-afternoon and as I stepped into the bar I instantly noticed the difference. First, instead of the usual chili smell from the happy hour table, there was the spicy fragrance of tamales, thanks to Padre Miguel and his congregation. There was also a countertop kettle of tortilla soup, and a huge plate of loaded nachos. For a wonder, however, the food was being ignored. There was a reason for this — the second difference. It had everyone gawking and pointing, me included as I made my way up to Miguel.

"What the — ?" The old decorations... they were still there, but they'd been brought back to life! Every bulb was working on those strings of fat, primary-hued lights. In fact, they were bright enough that I could actually see parts of Cockpit normally hidden in shadow. The silver tree was full and lush, not shaggy and broken. And it gleamed like new. Ditto for the ornaments. Those vintage glass and foil pieces, the star topper included, might have arrived from Wool-Worth's this morning.

Best of all was the Santa flying down from the ceiling. He and his reindeer were no longer missing their colors; back again was the red in his coat, the brown and white fur of those proud caribou. There were the blues, pinks, greens and yellows of the presents in the bag and, best of all, Rudolf's nose wasn't the only part that lit up. From back to front, the sled glowed.

"Amazing, huh?" Padre Miguel was beaming.

"Did you do this?"

"Nope. This is how we found it when the bar opened up today. Shocked us all."

"Fuck me," I said. "I'm going to have to leave out cookies and a bottle of scotch on Christmas Eve, because the big man is fuckin' real."

"You and me both. You know, I really hated those antiques, but now that I see them like this, as they were originally, I love 'em. I mean, they're kitschy — "

"That's one word for them."

" — But they go with the bar. If the Pit were in a better part of town, we'd be stylishly retro."

"Good thing we're not then."

"Maybe Nash wasn't being cheap," Miguel went on thoughtfully. "Or, not *just* cheap. Maybe he knew that for all their faults, these were the right holiday decorations for this place. Maybe that's why he refused to throw them out."

"Maybe." It was the Padre's job, as a minister, to be charitable. Even so, I thought he might be onto something. If it had been simple cheapness, Nash wouldn't have objected to someone else bringing in new ones. But he had. Maybe in his eyes the decorations had always looked like this.

"Well," Miguel said. "I'd best get your area cleared for the gift giving."

He made for the tree, and that's when my eye caught sight of the one man not looking at the restored decorations. Seated in a booth, he was eating tamales and watching with amusement as everyone else talked about the miraculous transformation. I strode up to him.

"How?" I demanded.

Owen tried to look innocent. Which, being Owen the mischievous, was utterly impossible. "I don't know what you mean."

"Yes you do. If this was April first, I'd say it was one of your best jokes yet. How did you do it? How did you even come up with it?"

"Well, I've been thinking about it since Miguel's bitch fest that night you took me home. On the one hand, you've got Nash who fucking loves these stupid decorations and won't throw 'em out for no one. On the other hand, you've everyone else, who hates them and would happily burn 'em if they could. How do you make both sides happy? Quite a puzzle. I like puzzles." He flashed a grin, the most wicked I'd ever seen and I finally understood what bottoms meant when they said that when Owen really smiled, he was friggin' scary.

"Answer: you dump 'em *and* you keep 'em." His eyes twinkled. "I scoured the internet for replicas and replacements. The lights were easy as that old style is still made. The ornaments and topper were harder. And I almost gave up on the Santa. But then I found him. A box of this was what I was waiting for that night Nash showed up.

Good joke, huh?"

"Inspired."

"Wasn't too expensive either. I talked Robbie into opening early for us. Then he, Hadji and I did some holiday magic. Oh, and FYI, the originals have been destroyed. So if Nash tosses these out he won't have any. But I don't think that'll happen. Know why?"

"Why?"

"Nash is out of town till the second week of January."

"So?"

"So, Robbie's going to take down the decorations that first week and pack 'em up. Nash won't know anything's changed till next year. He'll open up the boxes and find all his seemingly old decorations reborn. Won't that be a hoot?"

Oh, I wanted to be there when he opened them. Please, Santa, I wanted to see that trick played on Nash for next Christmas.

Mystery solved, I headed into the men's restroom to complete my change into "Master Claus." The suit wasn't the usual worn by mall Santas; instead of baggy red pants, I had tight, revealing ones and the coat stayed mostly open. After wiggling into the former, lacing up my black combat boots over them and slipping on the jacket, I headed out. I got whistles as I adjusted the big black belt so that the "v" of rabbit fur trim framed my bare chest.

"Oh, Santa baby!" Gina purred.

And Nigel, there with Robbie, ventured. "Mason, mate, I've a new fantasy of you sneaking into my bedroom to fill my stocking."

That got a laugh and several other jokes having to do with reindeer, packages and chimneys.

Miguel and crew weren't quite ready, but the bar's patrons were already gathering around the tree. Which meant it was time to fetch the gifts from the back porch. It was bracingly cold out, also misty and fragrant with pipe, cigar and cigarette smoke. Several bears turned as I appeared.

"Is it time?" they asked.

"Almost," I said, darting under a heat lamp. They set to knocking ash out of their pipes and snuffing their cigarettes in ashtrays.

"Master Mason," I heard, and there was Hadji, bundled in hat and jacket, seated on one of the picnic tables. He was right next to the sack of gifts in fact.

"Hey," I said as the last of the bears funneled into the bar. "I hear you had something to do with the bar's transformation?"

A smile flickered across his sad face and his dark eyes actually sparkled. "I'm sworn to secrecy. I like your outfit," he added, with interest. "It's very... fetching."

"And cold," I laughed, wrapping my arms about myself. "You know, there's something I've been wanting to ask: Hadji can't be your real name. Do you want us to keep calling you that?"

He was both surprised and shaken by the question. After a moment, he shook his head. "I'm not ready to give up anything Master Nash left me. I'll keep it until... until..." His words petered out. Until Nash took it back? Until another Master re-named him? He looked perplexed. "Master Mason... did I make a terrible mistake?"

Shit. What does one say to that? *I don't know*, was the first answer to come to mind. God complex aside, I can't tell the future. But I didn't think that'd help. So, "I don't think so."

"These past weeks, without Master Nash... it's like a part of myself was missing," he went on. "Then, the other night, when I saw him I was-was whole again. Now I'm not again and I'm so scared that I'll always be this way, and that I ruined everything. Not just for me, but for him. Who will take care of him now? Who will make sure everything is as he likes it?"

"He is a Master, Hadji. Those things are for him to work out. Not you."

"I... yes. But the worries won't leave me. Nor the feeling that I made a horrible mistake."

"*Buyer's remorse* it's sometimes called. When we pay out a lot for something, and then wonder if we wasted our money. But I don't think you did that." A cold breeze cut around the tables, piercing right through the cheap and thin material of my costume. *What I suffered for my art*, I thought wryly and leaned in closer to the lamp and its radiant heat. "Nash has to find the right boy to be the best Master. And you need someone who sees you as his ideal, not a consolation prize. Otherwise, you can't be at your best. And that doesn't serve anyone, does it?"

"That's what I thought. Now I'm not so sure."

"I know. But when you meet your real Master, the one who sees you as his perfect slave, you will be."

Miguel poked his head out. "It's time!" he said, and I heard chants from within: "San-ta! San-ta!"

"Coming." I swung the bag over my shoulder.

"Is that how you see Mr. Charles?" Hadji asked then. "As your perfect slave?"

"Perfect slave, partner, friend, lover. But don't you tell him, that. He's got a swelled head as is."

He laughed, and it sounded genuine.

Chapter 13
Midnight Services

Christmas itself arrived at long last, with, of course, a chaser of Christmas Eve. By this point I felt like our quaint Advent calendar ought to contain little lists of obligations in each box instead of candies. It seemed like I'd been through twenty-four days of non-stop duties. Which, actually, made Christmas Eve very strange; after all that build up, I had not a thing to do that night.

Momma didn't require my presence. Her tradition was to get all gussied up in her best black dress and hat and join Mrs. Wu and Mrs. Rice at a late night supper put on by the senior church ladies. It was attended almost exclusively by said ladies, who enjoyed a lovely crown roast supper with a towering croquembouche for dessert. Afterwards, lit tapers were handed out and the women, warbling carols, promenaded to services.

As for Loretta, she was with Rafe and his family, her soon-to-be-in-laws. They'd be enjoying a far more modest meal, then off to their church. Meanwhile, on the far side of town, Charles and members of his congregation were serving up Christmas dinners to the homeless before attending ceremonies.

And the Cockpit was closed. Not because Nash wanted it to be closed on Christmas Eve, but because the bartenders had negotiated—strongly negotiated—to have both Thanksgiving Day and Christmas Eve off. So. heathen that I was, I had nowhere to go and nothing to do except brood on tomorrow and what I'd finally decided to do. *What a time for there to be no one around to keep my mind off that*, I thought. Then again...

"Hello?" Owen answered the phone brusquely, so I figured he

was in a good mood.

"Hey. Doing anything tonight?"

He snorted. "Not a damn thing. My eight crazy nights are over."

"Wanna play some gin rummy?"

"Sure. I'll order Chinese."

About half-an-hour later, I arrived at Owen's. He opened the door as I left my car and stepped out to gaze up at the night sky.

"Nice evening," he remarked, as I strode down his walk.

"Beautiful," I agreed. It really was. Clear and filled with stars, not too cold. Between the snow blanketed rooftops and festive lights, Owen's neighborhood was almost magical. And so wonderfully quiet.

"Where's Hadji?" I asked, entering the warm house and shrugging off my jacket.

"Church. Did you know he was Presbyterian?"

"I seem to recall him saying that once, yes."

"He walked off to the nearest Presbyterian," Owen led me into the sitting room where he'd set out cartons of just-delivered food and a deck of cards. "Said he knew it was queer, but he liked to listen to the choir."

"Huh," I said to that, and settled in for some pan-fried dumplings — with plenty of hot sauce — Chen pi chicken and Szechwan shredded beef. Also Chinese beer. It turned out to be an amazingly pleasant evening. *Maybe*, I found myself thinking as Owen dealt the cards, *I should convert to Judaism*. This was the first Christmas tradition that had ever felt exactly right to me.

"Did ya hear the real story about Nash's new boy?" Owen asked, cards fanned in one hand, chopsticks nabbing another dumpling out of the carton.

"No. I barely got to talk to anyone while I was playing Master Claus, and I haven't been to the Pit since."

"The break up wasn't mutual. Word is Jonny ran off with the credit cards."

"Whoa. All of them? From Nash and his buddies?"

"Yep. They'd come back into town from their Colorado ski trip and Nash and his cronies were all sated with sex and liquor, dead asleep. Jonny decided it was time to bail and, after cleaning out their wallets, did."

"Wow. Well, that's always that risk when you get street fare."

"Mm." He set two low cards face-up on the deadwood pile and snatched up a fresh pair from the deck. "Nash made one hell of a mistake."

"Dumping Hadji, you mean?" I switched out a very low card for one of Owen's higher rank discards, then pinched up a mouthful of beef.

"Damn skippy."

"Nash must have realized that, or he wouldn't've have wanted Hadji back."

Owen snorted. "Nash realize he made a mistake? No way." He went for my throw-away and set down another of his own. "All he saw was that his precious hunting party was missing a boy to fuck. That's why he came looking for Hadji. He doesn't realize he blew it, and probably never will."

"Narcissistic is a Master's middle name," I reflected.

"Bullshit. It's about that yin/yang partnership. If it wasn't, we wouldn't take on slaves at all. There's plenty of ways to get our jollies without having to think about the needs of a sub."

"There is that." The new card I'd gotten from the deck was a good one, and as the points of my remaining deadwood cards counted under ten, I decided to knock. I set my final, eliminated card face down and fanned out what I had.

Owen grunted and did the same. Son-of-a-bitch if he wasn't the winner by a little. He smirked, took up the cards, shuffled and dealt us each a new hand.

"Nash didn't even realize what he had in Hadji." He went on then. "He's going to be hard pressed to find a slave like that again. Especially one that loves him in addition to all the rest."

"Being loved doesn't matter to Nash. Just being feared and respected."

Owen rolled his eyes at that.

"You seem to have changed your tune on Hadji." I took down some beer.

He shrugged, discarded some cards, then finished off the last of the chicken before picking up new ones. "I wised up to what you were telling me and looked at him as my renter rather than my probable slave. Once I did that, I saw that we weren't so incompatible. I need my space when I'm working. Hadji gives me that. And he needs to be told what to do, kept busy so he feels useful, and I can certainly give him that."

"And you both like to ice fish."

"Yep. Unexpected bonus, his being a fisherman. And I'll tell you what else, I think Hadji's more of leatherman than he thinks."

"Standing up to Nash like that you mean?" I re-arranged the cards I'd just fetched up from the deadwood pile. Almost there. "That's what I thought, too."

"Gutsy. I'd betcha Hadji hid his real spine from Nash because that wasn't what Nash wanted." Owen took his turn discarding and picking up, then drowned a dumpling in hot sauce before popping it into his mouth. "He certainly knows how to take a whipping."

"He does at that. Damn fine ass for a twink."

"Yep. But I do wish he wouldn't break down into sobs so quickly."

"You'll firm him up." I hoped for luck as I took a card from the deck. Shoot. Not yet.

Owen nodded and slipped the card I'd just rejected into his hand. "A little training and we'll make a man of him. And won't that fuck with Nash?" he flashed his scary smile at me, then slapped down his discard. "Gin."

The Cockpit Bar's Christmas Breakfast was going strong when Charles and I arrived the next day, and I had to say everyone and everything looked more festive surrounded by the bright new/old decorations.

It was warm inside with bodies, noisy as it hadn't been since late November, and the holiday music playing was anything other than Rat-Pack. I'm pretty sure we were all grateful for that. In fact, it felt like all the issues, problems, hiccups and crushing depression that had been on the horizon at the start of the month had happened (or not) and were now receding from view. The only hurdle left was New Year's Eve. Easy by comparison. I was the exception to that, of course. My biggest hurdle would be happening this afternoon. Well, that would be over, one way or another, by day's end.

I'd deliberately timed our arrival so that we'd completely missed morning services, which meant we had to wait in line for the food. That was all right. It gave me a chance to exchange holiday hugs and greetings with the regulars I counted as my second family. Also to hand out gifts, which, this time, Charles was hauling around in a cloth grocery sack.

I was greeted with cheer by the three, bottom musketeers: Al and Terry and Carl, also by Gina who was there with her girlfriend. I gave them their presents, and they handed back their own for me and Charles. Which had Charles blushing because, as much of a regular as he'd become in these last five months, he hadn't realized that so many viewed him as a good friend and brother, too.

We reached the happy-hour table decked out with chafing dishes, but took only modest helpings of eggs and skirt steak knowing that we'd be having lunch with my family in a couple of hours. I directed us to a booth already crowded with Robbie, Nigel and Burke and forced them to make room. Jordan, the Pit's jet-haired bi-bartender, making extra cash by working this morning, brought over orange juice.

"Don't you two look nice," Nigel complimented. Charles and I had exchanged our jeans for regular trousers and our tees for sweaters over long-sleeved shirts. Very suburban gay, I thought.

"We've another to-do after this," I said.

"And what did you get from Father Christmas this morning?"

I shook my head. "We're holding off on that till later. But I do have a few things for you two." I rifled through the grocery sack and handed them over.

"You are a right mate for remembering me," Nigel said sincerely.

Robbie handed back packages for us. Burke, ignoring it all, concentrated on his breakfast. Until, that is, I set a large-ish, elegantly wrapped box before him.

He scowled at it and, after taking a gulp of coffee and licking at his mustache, growled. "No gifts. You know I don't like 'em."

"It's not from me," I said. "I'm only the delivery boy."

"I know what I'd like you to deliver to me," Nigel quipped, and Robbie fondly nudged him.

Burke, seeing that he wasn't going to get out of this, tore at the pretty paper and bow, then flipped off the lid. With an annoyed curl of his lip, he pawed through the layer of tissue paper under that. Then his mouth dropped open.

"There are five kinds of really good leather in there," I said as he looked at the tanned hides. "Kangaroo included."

"Is that good?" Nigel whispered to Robbie.

"Yes," he whispered as loudly back. "It's one of the best for making whips."

Burke saw the little card then and opened it. And then he was un-manfully swallowing and blinking back tears. "My Angel remembered me," he said, meaning Katie.

"I got it a few days ago with orders to give it to you no matter what," I told him. "Merry Christmas, you mustachioed motherfucker."

Everyone at the table echoed that sentiment, and admired the skins with him. *Bless Katie*, I thought. She'd given Burke a taste, perhaps his first, of what it was like to have a gift waiting under the tree on Christmas morning.

We finished up, handed out whatever gifts we had left, and made our way out. Padre Miguel was at the door, wearing a pastor's collar over his gray tee and motorcycle jacket. He gave us cherrywood-tobacco-scented embraces.

"Have I told you how sexy you look in a collar?" I purred, swatting his plump ass.

"God be with you, too, Mason."

I was weaving my Scion through a sepia landscape of the snowy woodlands some twenty miles out of town when Charles said, very quietly from the passenger seat, "Excuse me, Sir, but might I know if this next event is going to be one of those unpleasant surprises?"

I twitched and gave him a quick glance. He didn't look worried, but he did look like he was actively working to remain calm and prepared.

"There's been something troubling you about Christmas Day," he explained. "You've been tense about it since your birthday. Now here it is, and we're going to a gathering with your family that isn't at your mother's, and that you haven't discussed with me. Also, your hands look like they're about to crack the steering wheel."

Shit. *There goes my best-actor-in-a-leading-role award.* In truth I felt bad. Which wasn't typical for a sadist like me, but it wasn't right to spring this on Charles last minute and I'd known that. That I'd waited till now, kept him wondering, wasn't some kind of Dom game, it was just cowardice.

"We're going to visit my father," I said. There. It was out in the open. "And I didn't mean to deliberately hide that from you, it's just that we—Momma, Loretta and I—don't talk about Daddy. Not to anyone who doesn't know him."

"Okay," Charles said. He'd turned in his seat, all attention.

"He's in a mental health facility. He's been there for almost ten years."

Silence. Then, "Mason, I'm so sorry."

I lifted a hand, waving that off. "Momma, Lo and I drop in on him, each on our own," I visited him once a month, in fact. "And all together on holidays. Like Easter and, well, Christmas. Momma calls to see if he's having a good or bad day so we know what to expect, but no matter what, we share a family meal with him on those days. Today we'll also open our presents with him."

"That must make you feel very odd about Christmas," Charles said.

"It is what it is." I took in a breath. "He was one of those sharpest-in-the-box sorts. An engineer. Kinda like Owen: cerebral, but on the lighter side. Much lighter. He's a voracious reader. Soaks up information like a sponge."

"Like you," Charles murmured.

Too right, I thought. "For thirty-five years he was totally fine and in good health." I paused, turning the wheel to take us up a hill towards a very nice, stone and glass structure. The extensive lawns were under blankets of blazing white snow. Against them, the trees looked like modern art exhibits of bare twigs and branches.

"Then, when I was twelve, he started talking to himself. Murmurs at first, then strange words. His gaze sometimes went flat, as if he'd

317

stepped into another reality. I mean, we were used to him getting lost in a book or in his head, but this was different. Like he couldn't see us even if he wanted to. We excused it. We shouldn't have, but we didn't know what was wrong. There wasn't any history of schizophrenia in his family, you see."

"Shit," Charles breathed.

I got us to the top of the hill and directed the car towards the parking spaces. I saw Rafe's car, meaning he, Loretta and Momma were aleady here. I was the late one this time. I found a spot, set the brake and cut the ignition. Through the front windshield the windows of the place reflected back the rolling white hills of the winter world behind us. How many Christmases had I looked at these great glass panes and that scenery in them?

"One day," I said, continuing the story, "Pop's job called to say that he was writing up nonsense, and gave him time off. Then he slipped the leash."

I paused, and decided I didn't want to describe that bleak day when my father had locked himself in his office and started breaking things. Or how, after calling the police to knock open the door, we'd found him huddled in the center of the room surrounded by splintered furniture and ripped up books scratching the messages he was hearing into his brown arm with a gold letter opener. It'd been December first. Advent day. And it had put an end, forever, to us kids looking forward to turning around that first number on the wooden box.

Unbuckling, I threw open the door. Charles hastily followed. The walk had been shoveled but it was still wet and a bit slippery under our boots. Our breath puffed out as we made for the front door. Inside, we crossed a fine, mostly empty lobby. I waved to the woman manning the desk there. She waved back, and I led the way to the elevators. There was more to tell, but I couldn't go on for the moment.

"A lot of things make sense now," Charles ventured as we waited for the elevator. "Especially the mental health questions you asked me at our first meeting."

The doors opened and we stepped in.

"Is that why you accepted when I asked for help?" he wondered aloud. "Because you couldn't save him and you need to save someone?"

I shrugged. Charles is way too astute sometimes. The elevator deposited us on our floor.

"When this sort of thing happens to someone you care for," I said, walking us through yet another lobby, "you feel like you're in limbo. The man you loved isn't dead, but you're still mourning for what you've lost. And you don't know if you can hope that he'll be resurrected. You don't know if you dare."

Charles nodded as I stopped at the visitor's window. The gent there greeted me by name and wished me Merry Christmas. Then he had us sign in. He handed us visitor badges to wear and buzzed open the door. Beyond was very like a hotel, a nice one, with individual bedrooms and several shared areas: entertainment room, gym, library. All these were decorated for the season with simple paper ornaments and garlands. The patients within were wearing their best, waiting for visitors. They were of all ages from college to senior citizen, and though some had that flat look I hated, and some were muttering to themselves, most were aware and friendly. Other families had arrived, and several of the patients were opening gifts.

In the dining area, at the corner table by the window with a grand view of the woods, was my mother. She was pulling ham sandwiches from a picnic tote while Loretta poured butternut squash soup from a thermos into paper cups. My father, who was talking to Rafe, caught sight of us and stood. In my childhood he'd seemed a great tall tree, but I'd matched his height in my teens and now he was the shorter one. Gray hair frosted either side of his bald head, giving him a professorial air. Likewise the lines of time and thought etched into his walnut brown face. An arrowhead nose he'd passed on down to me separated dark eyes under thick brows. Today, there was intelligence and humor in them.

He smiled. It wasn't the beaming grin he'd had in his prime, the one that had drawn everyone into his orbit, but it was earnest and real. I released a breath. It was going to be a good day.

Chapter 14

Noel

The conversation over lunch went pretty much as I imagined it would. After introducing Charles, who very stiffly and nervously shook hands with my father, we hunkered down to eat and Momma, as she always did, told Daddy all the gossip from the cookie swap.

"That right?" he responded now and then, enjoying his sandwich.

When Momma was done, Daddy nodded, as if impressed by all the news, then turned to Loretta.

"So, a May wedding, huh?"

That was all that was needed. Momma and Loretta launched into plans.

Throughout all this, Charles kept quiet. I think he was too amazed that I actually had a father to join in. Rafe, who had met Pops for the first time last Christmas, was more at ease. But I'm sure he still regarded his fiancée's father as an unknown quantity. Which, like an unstable particle, he was. So Rafe didn't say much either. As for me, I joined in where it mattered, telling Daddy all about the Dickens Fair and my radio commercials, and the possibility that I might be playing the title role in Henry V sometime in March. But I could almost feel my father absorbing what wasn't being said as well as what was being said. Calculating and working out equations.

I waited.

"So, where is it?" he asked, at last.

"Trunk of Rafe's car," Loretta said.

Daddy pushed up. "Come on, Mason. Why don't you and Charles help me?"

"Keys?" I held out my hand to Rafe. We headed off, and I knew that by the time we got back Momma and Loretta would have dessert and gifts out on the table.

Back at the locked door, my father nodded to the attendant at the desk and got us buzzed out.

"Loretta tells me you got Pepper to roll over," Daddy finally spoke directly to Charles as we reached the elevators.

"It... wasn't that hard, sir," Charles demurred.

My father laughed."Don't sell yourself short, son. That rat's menaced almost everyone who's ever visited my wife and is canine-non-grata at two clinics and at least three groomers. I'll bet you anything you like that you'll be Pepper's new doggy doctor very soon."

The elevator arrived and we stepped on. Silence followed for a heartbeat as we watched the numbers tick down.

"You're wondering why I'm living here when I'm so lucid, aren't you Charles?" Daddy said then.

Charles' gray eyes flickered, but after months with me, he wasn't easy to rattle. "I presume, sir, that you are on medications that manage your condition very well. But that they aren't always reliable."

"Got it in one," My father smiled and gave him a sly look as we exited into the downstairs' lobby. "Exactly right. If I have a bad day and relapse, I'd rather be here than putting that extra burden on my wife or offspring. You picked a sharp one, Mason. I knew you would when you finally got around to it."

Daddy led the way out of the building into the cold, which he didn't seem to feel though he was wearing only a flannel shirt. He went straight to Rafe's car, which my father had seen just once, but remembered.

"I take it," Charles murmured in my ear, "that your father hasn't any objections to your orientation?"

"When I came out to him, his first words were, 'Son, tell me something I don't know,'" I murmured back. How big a thing could such proclivities be, I mused to myself, if you were dealing, on a daily basis, with the question of what was and wasn't real?

I keyed open the trunk and there was the damned Advent calendar.

"Made this myself when Mason and Lo were little," my father told Charles in a tone that said he concurred with my feelings about it. "My wife maintains the tradition, to the point of bringing it here so I can see the finale. I've asked her to stop, but then I realized she needed it, so..."

"S'all right, Pops," I said, lifting it out and into my arms. "It makes her happy."

"It's like a holiday stalker," he demurred. "Every Christmas you poor kids get haunted by it. Speaking of which, you do know that Loretta's going to want me to walk her down the aisle. When she gets to thinking of that, I mean."

I took in a breath of the crisp air and made a conscious effort not to stumble. Yes, Loretta would, and I wouldn't want to be in my father's shoes when she met his eyes, heart-on-sleeve and asked. Shit.

"It's not going to happen," he said, moving us back toward the building, our footsteps sounding on the damp asphalt.

"Of course not," I said, fighting off disappointment.

He shook his head, getting us back inside where it was warm, and then paused us there in the empty lobby. I adjusted the bulky Advent calendar and Charles at my back, tried to play invisible.

"You can't have Banquo's ghost plaguing a wedding feast," Daddy said in that too reasonable tone of his. "All I'd do is take attention away from Loretta, and have her and everyone else worrying what might happen. Who needs that on their special day?"

"You don't have to offer evidence to me. I'm not going to fucking argue with you." I'd done enough of that in the past, begging him to come to my plays, to my high school graduation. I'd learned my lesson. He was determined to keep himself out of the picture.

He got that wry look again, and to my slave's dismay, I'm sure, turned to explain it to him.

"My life is a sort of hop-scotch game. I see my daughter one lucid day as a child, the next as a young lady. And the next with an engagement ring on her finger. It makes the question of whether we're living in a holographic universe other than metaphysical to me." He grinned, loving that joke. "I'm in one reality, then another, and when I surface back to the original, things have changed. Which further erodes certainty. My wife, bless her heart, tries to ameliorate this by showing up wearing her old dresses, her hair done up exactly the same. But I think we all know it's a wasted effort. And I'm making you uncomfortable, Charles, aren't I? Well, that's what I am. The uncomfortable pea under the family mattress."

He released Charles then, and my slave exhaled. I might have said he was relieved, but his gaze was firmly locked on my father with a kind of wonder. Almost, I'd have said, as if he regretted being set free.

"And that's another reason," Daddy said to me, "why I can't walk Loretta down the aisle, even though you think I should. You'd look at the wedding photos, see me in 'em, and always be reminded of how much I'd missed of your lives. Weddings pictures should remind you of glorious moments and the hopeful futures. Not the problematic past."

Damn. I still loved listening to my pops talk. Even when I didn't like what he was telling me. Even when I wanted to yell and berate him for being wrong. Which he wasn't. And was.

"You'll walk her to the altar," he told me.

"I can't take your place," I said tightly.

"'Course not," he retorted, a little harshly, then more steadily. "But you can take *your* place. You've been there and I haven't. End of argument."

He'd given me similar orders in the past, just as heavy if not heavier. To take care of my momma, to watch over my sister, to be my best self. And like an eager sub, I'd tried my hardest to obey. To please him. Because I never knew when I might come to see him and find that flat look in his eyes and be told that, this time, he wasn't coming out of it. On that day I'd know that whatever conversation we'd had last was the last. Which was why I never wanted to fail my father.

"What will you say to Loretta?" I asked back at the elevators.

"The truth. Favorable as the odds are that I'd be okay, it would devastate me to relapse on or before the day. Or, worse, get weird during the celebrations. For her sake and mine, I'd best not chance it." He paused, then added. "I'll also tell her that wherever I am, I am always with her. Doesn't everyone feel better when they hear that?"

My father's a bit of a skeptic, but unlike Owen, he's never bitter. He's a compassionate man. At least, he tries very hard to be.

There was coconut cake and thermoses of coffee and tea waiting for us when we got back. Also all the gifts that had been under the tree, Christmas stockings included. Momma pretended that we hadn't kept them waiting. Loretta and Rafe, however, gave us a knowing look. Pops had asked them to join him last year in fetching the calendar, and I'd noted that they'd taken a lot longer than needed to bring it back. Also that Rafe had looked a little shellshocked afterwards, which Charles did now.

Loretta hadn't ever mentioned what Daddy had discussed with them during that little errand, but I had an idea now. Other fathers grilled perspective suitors. Mine just opened himself up and let them see exactly what they were getting into. If they kept coming back after that, then they were worthy of his children.

I placed the Advent calendar at one end of the table, and we set to having dessert and opening presents. There were enough gifts for everyone, including treats in the stockings—candy and tangerines, which we shared around. Charles was effusive in his thanks for Momma's gift of new oven mitts ("To make more of those snickerdoodles of yours"). When all that was left were crumpled papers and piles of ribbon, Momma waved to the wooden box.

All but the circular window at the top, marked "25," had been turned around. As I'd started off the countdown, I got to turn that one. On the other side was the Christmas star. As I clicked it into place, Loretta reached up and, as was the tradition, we both pulled open that last, largest drawer.

Inside were six, tiny, plastic bags, each one containing a silver charm. Hearts with a dove cut out at their centers."To remind you all of the love and peace we feel during this season of our Lord's birth," Momma said, utterly sincere.

I did my very best not to roll my eyes. Everyone else expressed their appreciation of the charms.

"It's the thought that counts," Charles whispered in my ear.

I suppose he was right. It was always the *wish* to feel such things at this time of year that mattered.

The ride home wasn't exactly relaxed. More like Charles and I were a bit wrung out and preoccupied with a lot of thoughts. As we left the woodlands and got back on the road to town, however, I finally asked him: "Are you smitten with my father?"

He threw me a guilty look. "Shit, Mason, a little, yeah. He's like a cross between my old Master and you."

I chuckled, but Charles remained uncomfortable. "You know, when Loretta came over all upset about Rafe, I thought, I mean..."

"You thought my father bailed on my mother or something to that effect, leaving Lo with a complex about marriage."

His face went deep red and he actually shrunk into himself. Which, of course, turned me on.

"I did worse than assume, I profiled," he said, as if confessing a crime. "Jesus. Sir, I know how very bad that was —"

"Balderdash. It was perfectly logical."

He blinked. "Balderdash."

"I like that word and I feel like saying it. Left over from the Dickens fair. *Balderdash*. Single mother, dad out of the picture and not spoken about, daughter gets proposed to and freaks... you'd have reached the same conclusion no matter what race she was. Don't beat yourself up about it. That's an order."

"Yes, Sir. But if that wasn't the issue, why was Loretta so upset?"

I winced and felt my gut knot. Here it was. "A ten-percent chance that she might end up like her father, that's what upset her. That's the risk she and I have of developing the same mental illness. Having seen what our devoted mother went through, what she still goes through for our father..." I shrugged. "Why would you do that to someone you love? My father didn't know and couldn't spare our mother. But we can."

"Which is why Loretta said she couldn't," Charles said very softly.

Clouds came in as we neared home. They and the sinking winter sun darkened the afternoon. Snow, a very light flurry this time, powdered the near empty streets and sidewalks. I brought us into the drive and we hustled, gifts in our arms, back into the house.

"Sir?" Charles queried after we'd set our booty out on the living room table. I was staring at the empty fireplace and I must have zoned for a moment, because I think this was his third time saying that.

"Get changed into your usual," I told him. "I'm going to make up the fire. And then... I'm going to give you your Christmas present."

He frowned at me, disturbed by my tone perhaps, but "Yes, Sir."

The fire was licking to life as I settled onto the couch, a narrow, relatively small box tied with a gold bow at my side. I'd had it stashed away in my car since before my birthday and had brought it in surreptitiously with the other gifts. I tried not to look at it or think of what I was going to do.

"Sir?" Charles was standing in front of me, back in his uniform of jeans and white tee, ready, I was sure, for any crazy idea I might have in mind. Huh. Bet he wasn't ready for this.

"I haven't forgotten about your letter to Santa," I said, and when he shook his head confused, I reminded him. "What you wanted for Christmas. Your three wishes."

"Oh," he said and his eyes dropped to his bare feet. He wasn't going to ask or beg or hope, his posture told me. He was going to accept.

"I'll get to those later. They're contingent on this." I handed him the box, then rested back and tried to look relaxed rather than like I was mentally biting my fingernails.

He must have sensed my mood, as he pulled at the ribbon with trepidation rather than interest, and his hands fumbled as he shook open the box. He looked, blinked and then sunk to his knees there before me. Inside were two collars. One was a silver chain, similar to a dog's choke chain but with enough small differences to pass as a necklace. This he could wear to work and out in the world. No one would give it a second thought, but he and I would know it was my chain around his neck.

The other was more classic: a band of soft black leather with a buckle at the back and a ring pierced through at the front for hooking on a leash.

"That's for wearing to the Cockpit and at home," I told him as he lifted it out and ran his fingers over it gently and lovingly. He glanced up at me, eyes welling, and then he kissed it as if it were a holy relic.

"Really?" he asked at last.

"Really. Rent with the option to buy you said." I kept my posture casual, my voice lazy, as if I didn't care. Inside my heart was pounding. He could say no. *And he should say no*, part of me thought, *if he had a drop of sense.*

Charles licked his lips. "That was bullshit. I figured there was no way you'd let me be your slave even temporarily unless I made it seem like it was only for fun. A test drive around the block, nothing more. My hope was that once we were together I could... maybe change your mind."

"Seems your plan worked," I said, drawing in a deep breath. Here goes. "And better than you imagined. I don't want to just collar you, Charlie boy. I want to marry you. Would you be interested in that?"

Chapter 15

Peppermint Hot Chocolate

Charles' gray eyes got huge and I think he forgot to breathe. "Marry?"

"Yeah. You know that thing that only heteros used to do? But now it's fashionable for us queers?"

"Marry." He carefully set aside the box, as if the collars were fragile and he didn't want to break them.

"It's pretty simple. We get this license and meet up at your weird-ass church and all our friends watch as we exchange vows and some holy man pronounces us spouses for life."

"No," he said and my heart faltered. "No. No. You can't!"

What? Loretta had said 'I can't' to Rafe, Hadji had said 'I can't' to Nash, and now Charles had decided that I ought to be saying 'I can't' to him? *What the fuck?*

"Can't? Can't what? Propose marriage? I just did."

"No!" he jumped from his knees to his feet. With all his strong muscles, he could do that, and my, didn't he look sexy when he did. "You can't marry something like *me*!"

"Some*thing* like you? Have you been reading Nation of Islam stories again? You do know that white folks are not Frankenstein monsters created by a mad black scientist. Though, if you were I'd probably be into that."

He threw up his hands, made several attempts to say something, then finally looked at me with a kind of desperate pain. *I can't make myself any clearer*, his eyes said. "Okay, I get it," I responded. "I'm the Raja and you're the untouchable, yes?"

That caused him to flinch. Yeah, it didn't sound so right when the simile was all about darker folk being discriminated against by lighter folk. Tough.

"Yes," he admitted, "and that means you're not supposed to love me—not like this if at all."

"But you love me."

"Of course! How could I not? And I don't mean just because you're my Master. I knew I was going to be hopelessly in love with you from that first evening when I approached you—got in your face, and instead of kicking my ass as I deserved, you took me up and showed me such mercy, such kindness—"

"Kindness?" I echoed, and I wasn't sure whether to be insulted or not. "There are scars on your ass I put there that night."

His gaze locked with mine at that, and I swear it smoldered. "Yes," he breathed, and I read his thoughts very clearly in his eyes: *if you would ever care to honor my unworthy flesh with more, Sir...*

And didn't that make my nuts tighten up. For a heartbeat we both lost the thread of the conversation, then his expression went a bit strange and his breathing grew shallow.

"Are you having one of those moments, Charles?"

"Fuck." He swallowed. "Yeah. I really want to grovel at your feet right now."

"Not allowed unless *you* intend to propose."

That jerked him back from the edge. His jaw tightened. "You are such a dick."

"Is that why we can't marry?"

"*No.* For God's sake!" He looked about ready to tear out his curls. "I'm serious, Mason. I'm not *the one.*" He gave that last part an odd emphasis, and this time his expression was eerily familiar. As if... as if I'd ruined his fantasy.

I lifted a brow at that. *No way*, I thought. "Okay, I'll bite. Who is *the one?*"

"Someone worthy. Someone brilliant and strong and amazing. Someone not..." he vaguely waved down at himself.

"Not with your family history, not with your skin color, not with your accent and not a slave-type?" He had me now. I didn't know if I was more fascinated or flummoxed. "That's your penultimate fantasy? Me finding some bold young black stud to wed while you remain

329

slave to us both? And for my edification and jollies, does this include you being the creamy filling in the Oreo?"

This time I got a wince. Charles was so ridiculous sensitive to racial epithets he wouldn't even eat those cookies, let alone say their name.

"Not the filling, and fuck you back," he said, making me grin. "But yes. That's what I imagined — dreamed would happen. I've even prayed for it the times I've seen you troubled. That your one, true, spouse-for-life, who you very much deserve, will finally appear. And that when he does, if I'm very lucky, and have proved myself to you, you'll let me stay on. And I'll have a home with the two of you. Be able to watch you be happy."

I remembered seeing Charles once looking at me like I'd sandbagged him. At that moment I was experiencing the same. I am the Fancy Man and bringing fantasies to life is my thing. But this.... Fantasies I'd heard, in the hundreds, but none had ever left me so thunderstruck.

"Holy Moses. You really are a fucking masochist." It was like I hadn't really understood that, on an atomic level, till now.

"Yes, God damn it! And that's not my only fantasy, if you want to know. It's just the best one. I know you've been wondering why, in all these months, I've never proposed a scene like every other bottom who's ever wanted the Fancy Man. It's because if you were to bring my fantasies to life, you'd land me in the hospital. A milder one has you beating the shit out of me with your fists and a baseball bat while telling me what a fucking piece of dirt I am. That's what they're like."

He was breathing hard now, flushed and miserable. I wasn't surprised by this confession, nor even, as he might imagine, disgusted. Such nightmarish flights were a part of him, like his curly hair and gray eyes. No, they didn't bother or disturb me. But I was irked. If he'd been haunted by such thoughts, he ought to have said. Why hadn't he — ?

Oh. I winced. Shit. *Rule two.* Fuck me. Rule number two nixed requests for the rough stuff. Charles had clearly assumed that sharing these fantasies would be seen as breaking that rule, and so kept quiet. Meanwhile, I'd assumed he wasn't ready to share, and so hadn't inquired. Fuck me again. I'd inadvertently created a don't-ask-don't-tell law. Okay. I was going to have to do something about that. It couldn't be good for him to keep such notions under wraps.

"Well," I said at last, "that explains why you haven't ever asked me to make real one of your fondest sexual hopes. As for the best one where I marry someone else and you remain our slave... I'm afraid you're out of luck there. I've got my own fantasy and it doesn't jive with yours. The question is, am I going to get mine? Will you marry me?"

"I-I—" Was he going to faint? "Mason—"

"Yes or no, Charles. And remember the third rule. You *can* say no. You can say no because you don't want to chance the future you'll have if I come down with my father's illness—"

"What? That was never—do you actually think I'd ever give that a second thought?"

"You'd better. I won't marry you unless you do."

His turn to be flabbergasted. "Fuck you!"

"Just what a man wants to hear when he proposes," I mused, even as Charles started to pace in anger, arms waving about.

"Good, sweet, loving Jesus! Is that why you took me with you today? So I would think about what might happen to you?"

"Yep. I wanted to make sure yours was an informed decision. And let me point out here, that my ending up like my dad is a very real possibility. You go on a lot about what you might have inherited from all those past Beaumonts. Well. Back atcha."

He glared at me. "That's below the belt. And for the record, nothing is going to drive me from your side but you. And if you aren't in your right mind, then not even that!"

"Fine. In that case, you can also say 'no' if you don't want to be married to me, or if you don't love me. But you can't say 'no' to me because it ruins some fantasy version of my life you think I ought to have. As the Dom, I get to direct all fantasies. My own included. As the sub, you have to trust that I know best."

He continued to pace, looking a bit frantic now. So I pushed up and stretched.

"I've dropped a lot on you," I said, "Probably time to give you some space. I'll head to the coffee shop for a little. Let you focus on whether or not you can do this."

"Damn it, Mason, how would I know? This isn't a question I'd ever imagined being asked. How am I supposed to know if I can be a-a..." He couldn't even spit out the word. "And to you? And I can't help it if it feels wrong to me for all the wrong reasons. And there's your fucking rule three which says I have to say 'no' even if I want to please you, so I can't even factor making you happy into my answer. You fucking sadist!"

"Much as I'd like to take credit for this mental torture, I hadn't any idea it'd go this way."

"But it has and my mental torture is still getting you off," he grumbled, "isn't it?"

Not so much, Charles, I thought, *I am on pins and needles myself wondering what you'll decide. So who's the sadist now?* I snatched up my jacket, which I'd set by the gifts on the table and shrugged it on before he could help me. Then I turned to him, and, touching him very gently on the shoulder, met his eyes.

"Calm down and think about it. I'll be back in an hour or two. Oh, and FYI, this isn't a package deal. If you can't marry me, I'll still put the collar on you. You don't have to worry that refusing the one loses you the other."

"Well, and isn't that's a fucking relief," he muttered not quite sarcastically.

"Charles?"

"What?"

I kissed him light and quick. "I love you."

With that, I left.

The coffee place where I'd met with Rafe was open Christmas day, so that's where I went. I'd noticed last time that they had a peppermint hot chocolate special and as I still hadn't gotten around to that drink; it's what I ordered. There were a moderate number of patrons, but it was quiet and friendly. The right place to sit and wonder if I'd fucked everything up.

I knew that Charles still wanted to be my slave. I also knew that

I didn't want to lose him. But now that I'd proposed I felt, like Rafe, that I was at a bridge which had to be crossed. In spite of what I'd told Charles, I wasn't sure I could go back to our old dynamic if he refused me.

Which was a revelation to me. It was as if our months together had uncovered a hidden yearning I'd never known I possessed. Now that I saw it, I couldn't deny it. And it hadn't only been Charles who'd brought that yearning to the surface. There'd been Leo, the humble, elderly painter who, after decades of bowing to everyone else, had courageously dared to be himself, and in doing so, had found love at last. Also Burke and Katie, who'd defied all opinions and fiercely created their own, unique union. And Robbie and Nigel, who hadn't expected to find true love, but had.

They'd all bravely faced and crossed their bridges. Including, most recently — and most unexpectedly — Hadji. He'd left the Master he loved so much because he loved him so much. That little slave's example had forced me to finally acknowledge that Master though I was, an M/s relationship wasn't going to be enough for me. I wanted more. I wanted what my parents had had before my father's illness — and still had in spite of it: a partnership of support and delight. It was why I was the Fancy Man, because satisfying my own desires had never been enough. I wanted to satisfy the desires of another as well. I could no more refute this than I could my sexual orientation, no matter how un-leatherman it might seem.

I'd finished my peppermint cocoa by now, which had been small and rich, and was wondering if I wanted another when a fresh cup of it appeared before me. Startled, I looked up to find Charles dropping into the cushions on the other side of the table.

"I took a cab," he said impatiently. "I thought about it and I didn't want to wait for you. I need to tell you what I've decided now."

"All right," I said carefully.

"Here's the thing." He was gazing down, his fingers laced together as if in prayer. Whatever he was going to say, it wasn't going to be easy for him. Nor, I suspected, for me. "I keep running into these 'can't do it' feelings. I know I ought to trust you, blindly and forever, but my fucked up psychology says it's not right that I should be anything so important, so exalted as your... as your..."

"'Husband' is the word."

"Yeah, that's the word and I can't bring myself to say it, not in reference to my—my lowly self. So, according to holy rule number three, I should tell you 'no.' And if you'd asked me yesterday, I would have. But today, I can't. No matter what my fucked up psychology believes."

Did that mean he was saying "yes"? "Is this something religious? You can't say 'no' to me on Christmas Day?"

"No, it's something medical. That ten percent chance of you ending up like your dad. You waved that in my face to make me rethink everything, to consider what I might be getting into if I married you. Well, I did, but not like you expected."

"Oh?"

He tapped the table with an index finger and his gray eyes met mine. "Marriage gives me the legal right to take care of you no matter what. Right now, if you were hospitalized I wouldn't be allowed to do anything. I couldn't carry out your wishes, or tend to you. But if I'm married to you then I can. For life. That trumps everything."

I rolled that around in my head for a moment. "So, you have to be my spouse to be the best slave you can be?"

"Something like that." He said it with a little chagrin, and plenty of apprehension, as if he saw that bridge, too. The one that had to be crossed one way or another. "It also goes the other way. If I'm married to you then my family won't be able to take me away if I get sick, or decide what ought to be done for me. It's all up to you, and that really matters to me. You are the only soul on this Earth I want making decisions for me, Sir."

"That very reasonable and rational," I sipped at my second cup of peppermint chocolate, wetting my dry tongue. "But I have to know, all this aside, do you *want* to marry me?"

"Of course I do!" he fairly shouted, then seeing the looks, dropped his voice. "Jesus, Mary and Joseph, Mason. If my fucked up psychology would let me believe I was at all worthy of you, I'd've gone all queer and thrown myself into your arms when you asked. I'd have screamed 'Yes!' at the top of my lungs. My God. How can you even think I wouldn't want something like that?"

"Ah." A big knot in my chest unraveled and I laughed with relief.

"I guess I should be grateful you decided to confuse me instead."

"Yeah, well." His cheeks flushed and his eyes dropped. "It was only fair given how much you'd confused me."

I took a hearty gulp of my drink, enjoying a final taste of rich dark chocolate and sharp mint. "Shall we go home and seal the deal?" I asked, setting the cup down and starting to rise.

"I'd like to, but before we do, I—h—have one request... require-ment." He was shifting uncomfortably. It suddenly felt like that hour before our second date, when we'd sat together and negotiated the terms of our relationship. I settled back and waited.

"If I'm going to be your spouse for life," Charles said, "I want a coda added to rule three."

"My. We are being brave. And this addition would be?"

"I have to tell you when I think you're doing something that might be bad for us. And you have to listen."

I know what you're thinking: *what a modest request.* No big deal, right? A vanilla couple, like Robbie and Nigel would certainly think so. In fact, they'd probably be surprised that Charles had to ask for it at all. But in our dynamic I decided what was good for us. Charles' only task was to focus on me. To suggest such a codicil to one of *my* rules was rather like asking God to amend one of His commandments. Relationship heresy. I was amazed that he'd even thought about do-ing it. That he'd actually done it left me speechless. And very close to not-good-angry.

"It's only for when I have to think like—like a h-husband," he rushed on into the silence. "That's the difference between a slave and spouse, right? The slave isn't supposed to think of the relationship—he doesn't have to. But the spouse has to. You can't ask me to take vows to you, before God, that I'll uphold the wellbeing of our mar-riage, without giving me a way to do that."

His eyes came up at last, and his chin. Funny. When we think of courage, we usually imagine firefighters in the middle of a burning building or soldiers in a war. But really, it's on the smallest scales were bravery most matters. Like my Momma who'd done all she could to maintain family unity when her husband's illness threatened to shatter it. It would have been so much easier for her to have given up on Pops, but she'd flat out refused to do that. I saw that same kind of refusal in Charles right now. He'd bow, shake and submit to my anger over his insolence, but he would not crack. This addendum was non-negotiable. Either I agreed to it, or we didn't marry.

Wow. I really didn't deserve this wonderful asshole. But fuck if I wasn't going to keep him. Forever.

"You're right," I said. "There is that contradiction if we marry between your position as slave and your position as spouse. This coda resolves it. And it's damn smart. Okay. Request granted. Dreaded rule number three will now require you to tell me when I might be screwing up our marriage."

"Thank you, Sir," he said, and his gaze flickered aside uneasily. I might have agreed it was a good and right idea, but that didn't mean I was going to forgive him for suggesting it. Today, however, was Christmas, and I was in a gift-giving mood. And then it hit me that we were going to go through with this and I felt a powerful mix of elation and disbelief, like I'd just gotten the most incredible surprise of my life.

"I guess this means we're engaged."

Chapter 16

Epiphany

Sex with Charles is always hot, but there was an added something that first time I saw him wearing nothing but my collar. Especially when I hooked my finger through the ring.

Collaring in our tribe can be a big deal and is sometimes done like a wedding before witnesses and with a party. But Charles and I both preferred something far more intimate. The first thing I did was to order him to shower and cleanse himself, figuring a ritual bath was in order. While he did this, I put out rope and other items, and dressed myself in jeans and black tank, complete with boots and belt.

Fresh from the bath, black curls damp, his white skin ruddy, Charles knelt before me. Naked slave to clothed Master. Stepping around behind him, I lowered the collar. He trembled as I slowly buckled that strip of soft, black leather about his powerful throat. Its simplicity complimented him as much I'd hoped when I picked it out. And it made him look damn sexy. Then I leaned in and bit his neck above and below it, causing him to gasp. I went on to run my hands down the sides of his throat, over the collar to his bare shoulders down to his biceps and the chain tattoo on his right upper arm. He shivered.

"What are you feeling?" I asked.

"Owned," he breathed. "Owned at last. And by you, Sir. I can hardly believe it."

I stepped around and took hold of that ring at the front. "Master. From now on, at home or in the appropriate venue, you call me 'Master.'"

I tugged him up and over to where I'd set up two chairs next to the dining table. Getting him kneeling, one leg on each chair, I bent him flat on the tabletop. This was a position I'd seen on the internet and always wanted to try. What better time than this, to consummate Charles' collaring? Rope went under and, as if the table were a big gift, up to either side so that the ends could be bound around Charles' wrists. Left wrist to the right, right to the left. This crossed his arms behind his back, forming a kind of bow on the gift. The chairs, already set wide apart, gave me access to all those delectable, vulnerable parts. All I needed to finish it off was to wrap more rope about his muscular thighs and tie them to the chair backs.

He wasn't completely immobile, but he was held steady and helpless. My dick thickened with interest. Where to start was a no brainer. I slipped under the table, loving the fact that he couldn't see me, couldn't know what I'd do. His crotch, cock and balls, had been recently shaved clean by yours truly. I eagerly set to licking that smooth, sensitive groin area and his breath caught.

"Oh, Jesus," I heard him whisper with a mix of desire and dread. That made my cock twitch. I circled round the root of his dick, avoiding it as it rose and hardened, its tip already weeping precum. Closer, closer, over his clean skin. Finally, I dropped down to tongue his tight sack, sucking on first one ball than the other.

He grunted with pleasure and rocked a bit, enjoying, no doubt, that warm pull and how it created excitement in his nuts, like bubbles in a drink fizzing. Finished there, I took hold of his hot dick and mouthed his flared, cherry tip.

"Fuck," he hissed. And the heavy snake in my hand twitched and burbled up more of its juice. I licked up those drops, swirling about his satiny rod as if following the stripe on candy cane. Then I warmed the veins I'd missed. Over my head Charles writhed and groaned. His roped thighs started to tremble, and his hips thrust. He didn't get his cock sucked often. I liked to keep it starved so that when I did give it attention, it drooled and throbbed and every touch of my mouth was heavenly torment.

I returned to his knob, exploring his very sensitive slit with the tip of my tongue. He grunted and thrust so hard the table shook and the chairs wobbled. But he didn't get what he was after, which was his dick into my mouth. Chuckling, I moved out from under the table.

"No," he cried, wanting more. "Don't stop."

"Time for a different angle," I said. "But first...."

I placed myself where he could see me and broke open belt and jeans to display my hard cock. Charles was still bucking, his dick trying to find me and my mouth. The sight of my staff, which he wanted to suck in turn, and could not, doubled the agony.

"Fuck you," he panted, "Fuck." His hands were twisting in the ropes, his muscled body sweating and squirming over the tabletop. I stepped around. His ass was at just the right height for penetration, but though I was hard and ready, it wasn't time for that. I bent and licked at his taint, pressing it with my tongue, then moving up very slowly to tease his crack, which smelled of soap from where he'd washed.

"Oh no, oh no," he gulped, because much as he wanted what I was about to do, he knew I would torture him with it as much as pleasure him. I laughed and licked up one side of those spread cheeks, the other, coming close but always avoiding his pucker. As he'd thrust his cock at me, he now bucked back his ass. I easily avoided it.

Lightly, I set a hand on the base his spine and caressed him, raising goosebumps. "What's the first rule?" I asked, almost casually.

"What? Oh," he huffed. "Bastard!"

I licked the sides of his crack again, tickling down to his taint, then back up, stopping just short of that wonderful cluster he so badly wanted rimmed. He whimpered.

"First rule?"

"I may polish your boots, Sir—"

I slapped his ass hard, making him yelp. One big, red hand print appeared on his white buttocks. "You said it wrong. Try again."

"Sir, I may polish your boots but—"

Slap! A red hand appeared on his other cheek. "Still wrong. Again."

He growled obscenities, then he stilled and I knew he'd understood. Also that he was pissed at himself as well as at me. "I may polish your boots, *Master*—"

I restored my tongue to his ass, and rimmed him till he was shouting and flailing against his bonds. When I pulled away this time he almost broke into tears of frustration.

"Go on," I said, grabbing a bottle that was near to hand and lubing up my fingers. "You may polish my boots but?"

"B-but," he gasped, and gasped before he was enough in control to go on. "But not lick them until you think I'm ready. If I do, I'll be punished."

I pushed a finger into his hole and he sucked in a breath. As I leisurely drew it out and in again, his muscular shoulders rolled and his bound arms pulled. How that had to feel, his wrists crossed and tied to the table. His legs spread, tied open and shaking under him, his hard and hungry dick bobbing and still weeping with need. All while hot, buzzing pleasure played games in his ass.

Games only his Master could bring to that desired climax.

Helpless, helpless, he must be thinking, his gut dropping. The idea of it sent sparks through my nuts.

"Second rule."

"I-I-I will not ask to be burned or mutilated."

"Good."

"B-b-but maybe pierced," he threw in.

I laughed and added a second finger and pumped in and out, rubbing those soft sides. He squirmed and moaned.

"Third rule?"

Charles was dripping sweat and huffing. But he still managed to growl, "Your fucking third rule is that I can fucking say no, and I have to if I can't fucking do something even if it fucking pleases the fuck out of you, you fucker!"

God, I loved this man!

"And?"

"And, once we're spouses for life, if I see you fucking up the marriage, I have to tell you and you have to listen."

I added a third finger, stretching him and going in deep to give him what he almost wanted, a touch to his prostate. He let out a cry, and began to buck and thrust and writhe in earnest. It was a good thing the table and chairs were very sturdy, otherwise he'd have toppled them with his wild jerks.

"Oh, Jesus!"

My cock was more than ready by now. It was stiff, my balls high with power and need. It wanted to pummel that ass and to shoot fast and hard and deep.

"Last rule."

"Fuck you!"

No, I'll be fucking you, I thought, milking my slick cock. *Come on, Charlie, you know you want it.*

"Last rule." My three fingers were still inside him, pressing, rubbing, tormenting that delicate place. His dick was spilling its juice all over the floor, and his hips were gyrating.

"You... damn it... I-I-have to beg."

"Again."

"I have to beg, Master. And I will—I-I will. Please, fuck me. Please, Master."

I would have held off for more, but I was raring to go and didn't want to wait a second longer. Popping out my fingers I dove into that eager, waiting heat. I shoved so hard I would have knocked him off the table if he hadn't been tied to it. The chairs rocked, my belt flapped about, and he shouted. And so did I. And then I was beating his ass with my cock, my nuts hitting his, my belt buckle tapping at the fading hand print I'd left on his butt. Both of us were grunting and sweating as the friction built.

"Come," I told him as pleasure sizzled through my groin and my nuts. A second later, I shot into him, yelling my triumph. His dick, all but trapped under the table, let loose as well. I felt him jerking against me as he came, then the world spun away as if I was soaring like a comet into space.

I came on down, stiff arms to either side of him, puffing over his still bound and exhausted body.

"Sweet Jesus," he murmured.

"Oh, yeah," I said in return. "Merry fucking Christmas."

If December twenty-fifth included sex like this, I thought, then maybe I could get to like it again.

The sixth of January found me at the Cockpit for happy hour chili and beer. It was a good day for it, icy and gray. Inside the bar was back to normal, holiday lights and decorations gone till next year. The patrons, as well, were looking like their old selves. Many of them were back from spending the holidays with family and were showing off photos of their kids or gifts they'd gotten like new belts, motorcycle helmets, boots, and utility knives.

I, myself, had just come from my mother's where I'd packed away all of her yuletide paraphernalia. We could have done it on New Year's morning, when family and friends showed up for Hoppin' John and cornbread. But Momma always insists on waiting till January sixth, AKA Epiphany. Which means that decorations which took three or four people to put up are taken down by me and her. Read that as mostly me.

To be fair, she always has the ornaments rewrapped and nesting in their box by the time I arrive. The stockings, too. That leaves me the removal of the topper, folding up the tree and getting the wreath back in its container. Of course, while I'm doing all this, Pepper runs about barking as if I'm robbing Momma, which doesn't help. With all returned to the storage unit, there's only the Advent calendar to haul away and fit back into her closet.

"When Rafe and Loretta have my grandchildren," Momma remarked that afternoon as I maneuvered through that closet with the box, trying not to trip on her shoes or knock down her dresses. "They'll be the ones to count down the calendar."

I almost said that it couldn't happen soon enough, but Momma would have slapped me upside the head. And it wouldn't have been true. I didn't hate Christmas, nor that wooden creation my father had designed and hammered together and then, with his wife, painted so fancifully. In fact, even in those first few years after my father's breakdown, I'd still looked forward to the Advent calendar, as had Loretta. We knew that countdown would lead us not only to presents, but to the best gift of all: a visit with our father.

As I settled the thing at the back of the closet, and with a hiss, pulled a splinter out of my finger, it occurred to me that I still felt that way. The problem was that childhood excitement had been tempered by that trick-or-treat element. The one that had seeped in steadily, but irrevocably with each passing Christmas. Would December twenty-fifth bring us our father, or that flat-eyed stranger? Not knowing which we'd get, not being able to control it, had added an element of dread to the anticipation.

I came out and Momma insisted that I take home some coffee cake she'd baked (two-thirds of it, at it turned out) before walking me to the door. She was right, I thought then, and kissed her goodbye. The calendar needed to be enjoyed by children again, innocents who would see it only as a countdown to Christmas, no emotional strings attached.

"See you for Loretta's engagement party!" Momma shouted as I got into my car. Right. And I'd thought the partying over. I hadn't mentioned my engagement, of course. I was holding off till we were closer to Lo's day of days. Charles had shyly asked for a wedding in July, the month we'd met, and I'd agreed so long as it was a small and casual affair. Let Loretta have the bells and champagne. We were friggin' leathermen. Beer and barbecue in the park for us, thank you.

I took the coffee cake to the Cockpit and set it out on the Happy Hour table knowing that it'd be descended on and consumed within seconds. Then I settled with a bowl of chili at the bar.

"What's what, Fancy Man?" Owen sat down beside me with his own bowl and a handful of stale crackers. I'd seen him here for New Year's Eve, but hadn't talked to him since our gin rummy game.

"I mean," he added, "What's what besides your collaring your slave? I swear, the bottoms against the wall haven't talked about anything else since Boxing Day."

"Oh? I hadn't noticed," I remarked innocently. A lie, of course. For all his natural modesty, Charles had been standing proud, neck high every time we'd dropped in. Initially, in fact, he'd been mobbed by his fellow bottoms who'd alternately cheered him and slugged him on the shoulders, congratulating him. Katie, back from visiting her parents, had squealed and kissed him. All of which had caused his face to burn with pleasure.

"Yeah, right," Owen said now. "Well, felicitations. It's about fucking time and I'm very happy for you both."

"Thank you. And how about yourself? Any prospects on the horizon?"

"Actually, and this isn't yet for public consumption, I might have found someone longer-term than usual. Not that I know for sure, mind you, as we haven't had many playdates, but... maybe."

"What? Who? Anyone I know?"

"Miguel."

I rocked back almost off the barstool. "The Padre? No way. You're fucking with me."

"No joke," he said with a sly half-smile. "Hadji's been hanging out with the bears while he waits for his nightly ride home with me."

"He doing okay?"

"At his job, yes. Emotionally..." He shrugged. "Better. Thanks in part to the bears who've taken him under their paws. He's acting more leather and I can't wait to see how Nash reacts to that."

I shrugged. "Nash will have to swallow it. The bears won't cotton to anyone telling them who can stay in their den."

"True that. Anyway, couple of days before New Year's, Hadji asked if he could invite someone over for dinner. I reminded him that it was his house, too, and he could do what he liked. Next thing I knew, the good Padre was in my kitchen cooking up frozen walleye. Seems he's been counseling Hadji, as a friend I mean. We got to talking, one thing lead to another, as they say and, well...."

"A devil like you and a man of god like him," I shook my head. "I don't care what you say, it's your best joke yet."

"S'not like he's taken a vow of celibacy," Owen pointed out. "Far from it actually."

"Oh, I know, believe me," I smirked.

Owen raised a brow, then nodded as if we were in some special brotherhood. "Man's furry ass can take a belting, too," he mused, a compliment. "And fuck does he smell good."

"Hmmmm," I agreed. "One hell of a New Year's resolution, giving someone like Miguel a try. Good on you." I meant it. Owen tended to shy from relationships with men like the Padre because they required him to be more open and vulnerable. That he'd even considered this was a brave move on his part.

He shrugged and scooped up the last of his chili with his last cracker. "Kinda funny, isn't it? How we finish off all this holiday-nostalgic-hoopla with New Year's promises of change? Then again, it is human nature to wallow in an imaginary past while looking forward to an imaginary future. We can't ever seem to be happy with the now, can we?"

"Maybe that's why no one wants to take a selfie with Christmas Present," I reflected. "Only Christmas Future."

I drank another beer with him, then headed on home. I was hauling the last box of books from my place up the walk when Charles threw open the door, letting out the delicious aroma of Pho. There were new bookcases here and there—Charles' Christmas gift to me—turning the little bungalow into something of a library. We ate dinner in the living room, bowls balanced on our knees, watching a movie.

When it was over, and the dishes in the washer, I looked down at Charles, seated on the floor at my feet. Muscular, handsome, curly black hair, beautiful gray eyes.

"My apartment's empty," I said. "So I guess I'm moved in." I said.

"Guess you are," he agreed.

"That leaves only one more thing on your wish list to Santa, doesn't it?"

He frowned and thought back. Then his mouth dropped open and he shifted onto his knees. "No shit?"

"No shit. Strip. I want a good view of your naked body while you do this."

He got his clothes off in record time while I settled myself in a chair, my feet flat on the floor.

"How would you like me to proceed, Master?" he asked, standing before me at parade rest, the fire flickering behind him. He was as bare and beautiful as a Greek statue, wearing, of course, only his black collar. My collar.

"Hm. Would I be right in guessing that you've been having fantasies of doing this since you first laid eyes on me? That maybe you've been imagining each and every step you'd take given the chance?"

He ducked his head and smirked in answer. Of course he had.

"That's how I want you to proceed. Just like you envisioned."

"Yes, Master. Thank you." He shut his eyes then, and took in a shivering breath. Trying to remember it all, I imagine, so as not to leave out a single thing. Then he gracefully sunk to his knees and started by bowing down till he was pressing his forehead to my boots. It was as elegant and submissive an abasement as I'd ever seen, displaying every stunning line of his back muscles and spine. After a moment savoring that profound deference, he lifted his head, stretched out his collared neck, and took his first long, loving lick of my boot.

I settled in to watch as he worked his tongue over my shoe leather, right boot first, between the laces, up either side of the heels. Then he moved to the left. Watching him aroused me. It also moved me, this intimate moment between us. He was demonstrating all his submission, all his slavish devotion, without an ounce of fear or a hint of his issues. All that was in it was his love. All his love.

And I, at my most masterful at that moment, was showing him all mine in letting him do this.

He went at it for about an hour, drawing the action out for as long as he could; finally, he gave a last lick to the toe of my left boot and settled back on his knees to bow to the floor, like a dancer completing a ballet, or a holy man a sacred rite. And it occurred to me then that though I hadn't directed it, I'd finally done it. I had brought one of Charles' fantasies to life. Which, I realized, had been one of my biggest fantasies.

"Who do you belong to?" I found myself asking him in that profound, almost stunned silence.

"You Master," he breathed and trembled with, I knew, deep emotions.

"Who do you submit to?"

"*You*, Master."

"Who will you abase yourself for?"

He leaned forward and pressed his forehead against my shoes once more. "You, *Master*."

Reaching down, I ran my fingers through his soft, black curls, my heart welling over with pride and love and so many other feelings I couldn't name. *I'm looking forward to next Christmas*, I found myself musing, and then with some amazement, double-checked that.

Really?

Yes. Really. To next Christmas... and to all the holidays and seasons in between.

Well, fuck me. I laughed inside, and drew Charles up and into my arms. *Then let the countdown begin! I am so ready for it.*

If you enjoyed this story, you can sign up for a free membership at
ForbiddenFiction and discuss it with other readers
and the author at the *Fancy Man Holiday* story page at
http://forbiddenfiction.com/story/T13-1.000254.

About the Author

Julian Keys (also known as Thirteen) is an award winning erotica writer currently being published by both ForbiddenFiction and Beautiful Trouble Publishing. In addition to the gay bdsm *Fancy Man* series, Julian's work also includes romantic, heterosexual novellas like *Valentine Prayers* and *Pretty as a Picture*. Along with editor's choice, year's best and special contest awards, Julian won the Blue Moon award for best M&M 2009.

Works by Julian Keys

Fancy Man Series

Leather Wishes: The Adventures of the Fancy Man

or get them individually:

Fancy Man and the Black Lion's Mark
Fancy Man and the Southern Gentleman
Fancy Man and the Lipstick Lesbian
Fancy Man and the Three Princes
A Fancy Man Holiday

Other Works

Executive Benefits
An Act of Charity
A Many-Colored Lantern
Savory & Sweet
Exchange of Heart
Down to the Bone
A Special Occasion

About the Publisher

ForbiddenFiction.com is a publisher devoted to writing that breaks the boundaries of original erotic fiction. Our stories combine intense sexuality with quality writing. Stories at ForbiddenFiction.com not only arouse readers through sensations, but also engage them emotionally and mentally through storytelling as well-crafted as the sex is hot.

ForbiddenFiction.com is also designed to be a social reading environment. You'll have fun even if just reading the latest post each day, yet you will have the chance for so much more. Readers and authors can be part of ongoing discussions of specific works and individual authors as well as more general topics.

Sign up for a FREE Membership today at ForbiddenFiction.com.